THE
TRAITOR'S
KINGDOM

ERIN BEATY

{Imprint}
MAKE YOUR MARK

NEW YORK

SQUARE
FISH

An imprint of Macmillan Publishing Group, LLC
120 Broadway, New York, NY 10271
fiercereads.com

Our books may be purchased in bulk for promotional, educational,
or business use. Please contact your local bookseller or the Macmillan
Corporate and Premium Sales Department at (800) 221-7945 ext. 5442
or by email at MacmillanSpecialMarkets@macmillan.com.

Library of Congress Control Number: 2018955949

ISBN 978-1-250-25097-1 (paperback) / ISBN 978-1-250-14234-4 (ebook)

[Imprint]
MAKE YOUR MARK

@ImprintReads
Originally published in the United States by Imprint
First Square Fish edition, 2020
Book designed by Natalie C. Sousa
Imprint logo designed by Amanda Spielman
Square Fish logo designed by Filomena Tuosto
Map by Maxime Passe

10 9 8 7 6 5 4 3 2 1

I HOPE   ENJOY   AND IT BRINGS YOU   TO THOSE YOU LOVE,
        YOU   THIS BOOK,   CLOSE
BUT IF   DESPISE   MAY IT   SHARPLY ON YOUR FINGERS.

To Mom, who showed my sister and me that being intelligent should be a source of pride. And Dad, who showed us that real men want to be around women who can think.

1

FOR SOMEONE WHO hated fighting, Clare was getting pretty good at it. Sage now had to break a sweat to defeat her friend, which was impressive today, given how cold it was. The massive stone walls of Vinova, Demora's outpost fortress, offered shelter from the winter winds that swept across the eastern plain but did little to hold in warmth. Repelling invasion and resisting siege had been first in the builders' minds. Now that the southern nation of Casmun was opening diplomatic talks, it was the location that mattered for Sage's position as ambassador. Self-defense was important for life in general, however, and so Sage insisted her best friend and companion train in combat.

Clare's face contorted into a scowl of concentration as she gripped a lightweight sword in one gloved hand. Her eyes narrowed over the shield on her left arm, but that wasn't what Sage was watching.

Beneath her knee-length skirt, Clare's boots shifted in the dirt, and Sage unconsciously leaned to the right, bracing her own feet on the frozen ground, still waiting for the movement that would give her friend away. Rare was even the most seasoned warrior who could attack without some warning in body language. At not quite seventeen, Clare was nearly two years younger than Sage, and she'd begun her training only a few months ago.

It was a sharp, slight movement a split second before Clare lunged that gave her away, but it was enough. Sage met her on the left and blocked the swing with her shield before catching Clare's sword with her own, lifting the blade up, around, and back down. The motion drew them up against each other as their hilts locked. This time Sage left herself open to a countermove.

"What are you forgetting?" she asked, bearing down until the tip of Clare's sword touched the ground.

In response, Clare pivoted and rammed her shield into Sage's exposed side.

Your shield is also a weapon.

Sage grinned as she fell back, but her friend didn't smile as she jerked her head to toss her thick braid over her shoulder. Her brown eyes flashed in silent challenge, and her slight frame trembled with something other than cold. "You don't have to keep telling me," Clare spat.

She was angry now. Which meant things were about to get interesting.

Rage was useful in a fight—Sage knew that firsthand. It heightened the senses and brought strength and endurance, but she'd also experienced the recklessness that easily took over. Clare's lack of control could force Sage to react in a way that might hurt one or both of them.

"Anytime now," taunted Clare, her words muffled behind the shield.

Sage moved several careful steps to the right, forcing Clare to adjust her stance and give herself more time to think. *What would Alex do?*

The thought of him brought an involuntary smile to her lips. Last year Sage had lashed out in anger while sparring with Alex, and he'd disarmed her and smacked her rear end with the flat of his blade in a single move. Alex wouldn't escalate this. He would stay methodical, meeting her at her level, never forcing her back too much but never conceding ground, either.

Clare was waiting for her to make a move. Sage shifted to walk to the left side, twisting her curved sword in a lazy arc, briefly reflecting a ray of sunlight that had escaped the blanket of clouds above.

Her friend didn't take the bait. She was in control right now, but it wouldn't take much to tip that balance.

Sage began running through a series of basic arcs, slices, and parries, stripping her movements of the personal style she'd developed over the last year and a half. She imagined herself as the clock in the chapel tower—gears and pendulums and arms rotating but anchored firmly from the center and therefore restricted and predictable. The only sound was their heavy breathing and the steady clash of metal on metal.

With only the slightest twitch in warning, Clare broke from the rhythm, countering a parry with a slash across Sage's leg close enough to catch the fabric of her breeches. Clare's eyes widened in shock, but Sage didn't acknowledge it, refusing to leave enough time for fear to get ahold of either of them. Their sparring dropped all feel of formality and rote practice. Even if neither truly wanted to hurt the other, it suddenly felt *real*, and they danced around each other with intense concentration and vague smiles.

Sage pressed Clare hard, slowly draining the reservoir of rage. Her friend managed to hold her temper in check, and there were no damaging hits to either side other than a few earsplitting shrieks as swords grazed across shields.

After nearly twenty minutes, the fire was spent. Sage rested on a bale of hay outside the horse paddock, fiddling with the hole in her breeches. The cold had begun to make itself known again, starting with her nose. Next to her, Clare's breath frosted in the air between them as she slowly came back down from the exertion. Every few seconds she cast a guilty look at Sage's leg, but Sage studiously ignored her concern. She didn't think the skin was cut, though it was hard to tell with gloves on. Either way, her friend shouldn't feel bad about it.

"I think your clothes give you an advantage," Sage said casually. "It's harder to see what your upper legs are doing. Makes you less predictable."

"Finally, something I have over you," Clare said, pulling her skirt down as far as it would go. The hose she wore underneath was thick enough to hide the shape of her legs, but she was still self-conscious. There was no bitterness in her voice, though, only weariness, which was good.

Sage shivered and ran a hand over her head, pressing down the hair that had escaped the short horsetail in the back. She could tell by her shadow that she looked like a half-drowned cat. Clare's mahogany braid was flawless, as usual. "We still have time for a bit of *tashaivar*," Sage said, glancing at the angle of the sun.

Just then the chapel bell tolled, its pulses echoing off the bare stone of the fortress and its surrounding walls, declaring three hours past noon. Clare hopped up, energy restored. "No, we don't."

Sage groaned inwardly, but a deal was a deal—Clare submitted to Sage's combat training and Sage took lessons from her friend in diplomacy. Besides, a hot bath was what she needed now. Cold had seeped into her toes, and the dampness under the Casmuni-styled clothing she wore for sparring chilled her skin. The loose breeches and jacket were meant for desert wear and dispersed body heat quickly. Though her teeth had begun to chatter, Sage volunteered to put Clare's weapons away so her friend could clean up first.

Clare was done by the time Sage entered the dressing room connecting their suites. When they'd taken up residence at Vinova several months ago, Sage had worried at the cruelty of putting her friend in rooms meant for the wife of the ambassador stationed at the border stronghold. After all, Clare was supposed to marry the son of the previous ambassador, Lord Gramwell, who was expected to be an emissary in his own right someday. She'd spent nine months living with her betrothed's family, preparing for the role.

It would never happen now.

A Kimisar arrow may have killed Lieutenant Lucas Gramwell, but Sage could never forget that he'd taken it in protection of her. Clare didn't blame her, except perhaps in her worst moments, which—thankfully— were becoming more rare. And it wasn't as though Sage had come through the battle unscathed. She and Clare spent many nights sleeping in the same bed, comforting each other through nightmares. Now they occurred maybe once a week, and more often it was Sage who woke screaming and thrashing.

In waking hours, Clare's episodes of anger usually sparked over something trivial and then simmered below the surface until they burst forth in the middle of training, over dinner, or during a diplomacy lesson. It was a reaction Sage herself had experienced after her own father's death six years ago, so she didn't judge her friend harshly. Time was the only thing that could truly heal either of their wounds.

Sage loosened the laces of her jacket with her right hand as she dipped her left into the bathwater. Just right. She shed the rest of her sweaty clothes and hopped in. Clare rolled her eyes as water splashed onto the polished wood floor, but Sage barely noticed as she ducked under the surface and pulled her short, sand-colored hair free of its leather tie. The left side of her body tingled with a sensation stronger than an itch, but she ignored it and lifted her head out of the water, reaching for the bottle of hair tonic.

"We're almost out of this," said Sage, pulling at the cork with her teeth to avoid taking her left arm out of the water. The scents of orange and jasmine wafted from the open bottle.

"Let me get that." Clare finished tying the bodice of her simple gray dress and moved to help Sage get the last of the hair tonic out. Rather than just dab it on Sage's wet hair, she began to lather it, too. She often did such things, finding quiet ways to make up for losing her temper. Sage didn't think the silent apologies were necessary, but they made her friend feel better.

"When did you last hear from Major Quinn?" Clare asked casually, as if she didn't know. Bringing up Sage's betrothed was another way of smoothing roughness between them.

At the mention of Alex's name, heat crept into Sage's cheeks, and she tried to reply just as casually, "Two days ago."

"How is the training coming along?"

Alex commanded the Norsari, Demora's elite fighters. Last spring the army unit was reestablished twenty years after having been disbanded. As it turned out, the initial company had been ready just in time to face a Kimisar force coming through the southern nation of Casmun. Now the Norsari were being expanded to a full battalion. The increase had been planned from the beginning, but now it was a necessity. Kimisara's king, Ragat, had been killed at the Battle of Black Glass, and no one in Demora knew what the combination of warm spring weather and a new ruler would bring. Whatever it was, the Norsari would be at the front lines. As would Alex. Sage tried not to think of the added distance and danger as she gently rubbed a washcloth over the pink-and-white scars on her leg. "They'll be finishing up their seventh week now."

Clare used a small pitcher to rinse Sage's hair. "Will he be able to visit?"

Sage shook her head and wiped suds from her eyes. "He can't afford to be away that long." The training camp was over a hundred and fifty miles to the west. At best, it was four days of hard travel to Vinova and another four back, and the winter weather didn't help. "Maybe when they've finished in another six weeks."

Yet she knew he wouldn't. Alex couldn't justify such a trip in the face of his responsibilities, especially considering they weren't married—and he was restricted from marrying until age twenty-four. Sage frowned thoughtfully and counted the days from midwinter in her head. Then she smiled.

His birthday was tomorrow. They had only a year left to wait.

2

AN HOUR LATER it was Sage's turn to scowl. How could eating be so complicated?

"Today you have an earl from Reyan on your left, a lower Casmuni prince on your right, and I am a Demoran countess," said Clare from her seat across the table, which was spread with more dishes, utensils, plates, and goblets than Sage could keep track of. "The earl only speaks his own language. I speak Reyan and Demoran, and the prince speaks Kimisar and Casmuni. Whom do you address first and in what language?"

Diplomacy gave Sage headaches and even a few nightmares. At least Kimisar weren't in the mix. The best Demora could ever hope for with them was an uneasy truce and constant denials that any of the raids in Tasmet were from their country. Reyan was a longtime ally, but the relationship with Casmun was still new. The nations' royal families wanted it to succeed, but the common people on both sides were slower to change after generations of hostility. The process was delicate, especially after last summer's events.

"Have I shared water with the prince before?" Sage asked. Casmuni didn't think it polite to fully address or use names with a person they hadn't been formally introduced to.

"Yes, but it was years ago, and you aren't sure if he remembers."

Dammit, her friend was crafty. But ambassadorship could be that complicated, and not being prepared could cause disaster on a national scale. Sage never felt more in over her head than she did during these lessons. She suddenly grinned. "I'll leave you to chat with him while I address the messenger who just walked in."

Clare turned around to see Master Finch approaching with a scroll bound by a violet ribbon. "That looks unusual," she said.

Sage untied the ribbon and unrolled the parchment, then spent several minutes silently studying the words. Clare kicked her under the table. "It can't take that long to read," she scolded.

A slow smile had spread across Sage's cheeks. "I think we should change the prince on my right to a princess." She flipped the page around to show Clare it was written in Casmuni. "Lani is coming to visit."

"When?" Her friend seized the official-looking parchment, drawing her brows down as she scanned it, reading slower than Sage had. "Sooner than this summer?"

"Tomorrow."

The lesson forgotten, Clare jumped to her feet. "Spirit above, we've got to get ready!"

"Can't we at least finish eating?" Sage gazed longingly at the covered dishes and their still-empty plates. Time in the tilting yards always made her hungry. Sometimes the promise of food was the only thing that made etiquette lessons bearable.

"Are you kidding?" Clare was halfway to the door, casting a look over her shoulder that indicated that if Sage didn't come along, she would drag her. "We won't have time to sleep tonight."

With a sigh, Sage pushed her chair away from the table and followed her friend, but not before grabbing a bread roll. Or three.

Sage had once seen a Norsari company march into battle on a moment's notice. That was the only thing she could compare the activity around the Vinova Fortress to over the next hours. Clare took charge of the kitchens and household matters, having food and rooms prepared.

Alaniah Limistraleddai would be the first Casmuni to set foot in Demora in over two hundred years, and she wasn't an ordinary emissary;

she was the king's sister and the highest-ranking *chessa*—princess—in the nation. "How many in her retinue?" Clare asked again.

"Twelve," Sage answered without looking at the note. "Plus sixty soldiers." That wasn't very many, considering Lani's status.

"She could've given us more warning," Clare grumbled, counting chickens plucked and laid out.

"*An ambassador is always ready to receive,*" Sage recited with a grin.

Clare grimaced. "Thank the Spirit that Papa began cleaning things up when he and I were here last summer. We'd be much worse off now if he hadn't." She referred to her fiancé's father, a retired diplomat who had been recalled to act as ambassador at the Vinova Fortress near the southern border, when Demora had been preparing to reopen relations with Casmun. That was interrupted by the Kimisar staging an attack, and Sage had fled into Casmun with the king's youngest son, accidentally becoming the first Demoran they'd spoken to in generations. Lord Gramwell led the effort to retrieve the prince, escalating to the Battle of Black Glass, in which the Demorans and Casmuni fought the Kimisar and won. His only son didn't return from the fight, and once the dust had settled and the prince was returned home, the grief-stricken ambassador asked for permanent retirement.

Sage was appointed to replace Lord Gramwell and kept Clare with her, both for companionship and to keep her friend from having to return to her father now that her betrothed was dead. On paper, Sage was the most qualified person in the realm for the position. She'd learned the Casmuni language and established a good relationship with their royal family, but she was still an eighteen-year-old commoner with no formal training, and she wondered if she would be replaced at some point. Not that King Raymond had ever indicated she might be.

In the meantime, she subjected herself to Clare's lessons. Between her friend's knowledge and what she'd learned about Casmun's people and customs, Sage hoped to be worthy of the job.

Their first test arrived in a matter of hours.

3

THE NEXT AFTERNOON, Sage and Clare stood atop the highest watchtower, wrapped in furs, watching the Casmuni party approach. Most of Sage's traveling experience was with military units, and the size of Princess Lani's caravan unsettled her. "Why would she need all those horses and wagons?" she murmured.

"Gifts," said Clare tersely. "This is more than a friendly visit, Sage, and diplomacy dictates we reciprocate with something of equal value."

Sage felt herself blanch. "We don't have anything here yet." Demoran resources were strained due to the conflict with the Kimisar in Tasmet. Grain and ore shipments from the west side of the Catrix Mountains had been reduced to a trickle, and the northern ports tended to shut down in the winter. "Doesn't she know she's several months early?"

"I'm sure she does." Clare shook her head. "I don't know what she expects of us."

"We might be able to do much with warm blankets and hot water." Sage pointed to a bundled figure on a white horse. Were she not out front and wearing a curved golden sword, Lani would've been unrecognizable. "She looks cold."

Fortunately, firewood was plentiful in this area. There was so much dead brush and so many fallen trees in the woods nearby that none had needed to be felled yet. Sage ordered the fires in the bedchambers to be stoked higher, and more kindling delivered to the barracks. "And double the amount of hot water on hand," she called to the steward as she followed Clare down to meet their guests.

They waited atop the steps to the main keep as the entire retinue filed into the main courtyard. Lani and her inner circle continued through the second gate. As the princess far outranked Sage and Clare, they came down to meet her as she dismounted. They curtsied together, but before either could get a word out, Lani strode past them and up the stairs into the stone building without invitation.

"Yes, yes," she said in her own language. "Get me warm, and then we will talk."

Sage and Clare scrambled to keep up with the princess, who headed straight for the hearth at the end of the receiving hall. Three attendants followed, picking up the clothing their mistress had begun to shed. A thick headscarf came first, freeing her ebony braid, followed by gloves and an outer jacket. Though finely woven, the sturdy clothes the princess wore were similar to what Sage used for sparring in the yards. Casmuni women usually wore long skirts like Demorans, but they were much more practical about changing into breeches when riding or practicing *tashai-var*, their form of close combat. Not oblivious to her servants' discomfort, Lani gestured for them to join her in the circle of warmth. They all sighed a little.

"I am sorry to be rude," the princess said in Casmuni, stretching her hands toward the flames. Her bronze skin had rosy splotches where it had been exposed to the wind. "But I have not stopped shaking from cold since we crossed the river. It will take months to get used to." Lani sighed, her greenish-brown eyes resigned. "But midwinter has just passed, so it will get warmer, yes?"

"Um . . ." Sage glanced to Clare, who appeared to have caught that Lani intended to stay a long time. "The days may be lengthening, My Princess, but the coldness has only begun for Demora." Lani's mouth dropped open in horror, and Sage rushed to reassure her. "But we rarely have snow here."

"What is *snow*?" asked Lani, repeating the Demoran word with interest. "Will we have it in Tennegol?"

Most of Casmun was desert or rain forest, and Sage struggled to explain it. "It is when the rain gets so cold it becomes like wool and sits on the ground."

One of the servants dropped the clothes she held and began crying. Another tried to comfort her. Lani glanced at the girl before addressing Sage. "Feshamay comes from a city to the far south. Even Osthiza has been cold to her at times. Do not worry," she told her attendant. "This *snow* cannot be higher than your toes."

Sage exchanged glances with Clare. This would be an interesting visit.

"You wish to travel all the way to Tennegol?" Sage asked, pulling the conversation back to the princess's apparent intention to visit the Demoran capital. She herself hadn't been there in almost a year. When Sage and Alex were returning from Casmun four months ago, royal couriers had met them on the road with the request that she turn back to Vinova and take the post of ambassador. Alex had also been promoted and continued to Tennegol for fresh Norsari recruits, to bring the number up to a full battalion. Between missing Alex and being so isolated, Sage felt a little homesick, and she'd be happy to serve as Lani's interpreter and guide. Clare looked excited, too, though she must already be tallying all the messages to send and supplies to be gathered.

"Of course I must go there," said Lani. "You have two princesses, and I must choose the one who will best suit Casmun."

This was going to be a *very* interesting visit.

4

THE REASON FOR Lani's surprise arrival was now clear: the extra thirtysome desert-bred horses and the heavily laden wagons the princess arrived with were negotiation tools. King Raymond would be more open to discussing the marriage of one of his daughters to a Casmuni prince after receiving such generous gifts.

Sage decided their conversation would be best continued in private. Outside Clare, the residents of Vinova Fortress understood only rudimentary Casmuni phrases, but it was better to be safe. After assurance from Lani that she intended to pause here for a few days, Sage left Clare to take the princess to her chambers and the hot bath that waited there and went to check on accommodations for the rest of the Casmuni.

In the main courtyard, wagons were being unloaded and horses were being led straight to the stables. Lani's escort all carried weapons, implying the extra cartloads of newly forged swords, spears, and knives were intended as gifts—a positive sign, as Casmuni made it a point to give weapons only to those they trusted most. Sage would have to make King Raymond aware of the underlying message.

She returned to the inner walls and the guest quarters. Lani was already setting up her rooms to her liking, having the maids unpack clothing and hang bright tapestries over the bare walls. Feshamay sniffled as she sorted a trunk of fabrics.

"I told her to make something warm to wear with the cloth of her choice," Lani explained as she sipped a cup of hot tea by the fire. "It was all supposed to be for your princess, that we could make her Casmuni dresses right away, but there is more than enough."

"Yes, about that," said Sage, taking a seat in the chair across from Lani, shifting to keep her left side away from the heat. She couldn't tell what her friend was wearing under the blankets draped over her lap and shoulders, but her long black hair tumbled free around her to dry from her bath.

"I thank you for all of this," Lani said, raising her cup. "It is just what I needed."

"I am well thanked," Sage replied. "What was it you were saying—"

"I have a new scabbard for you," Lani interrupted. "Reza made it. There wasn't time for her to finish it before you left, which is why the one Banneth gave you with your new sword was plain."

The original *harish* gifted to Sage had been lost in combat, buried under the mound of melted stone that gave the Battle of Black Glass its name. Reza was the Casmuni king's ten-year-old daughter. "I will gladly accept," she replied, then took advantage of Lani pausing to sip her tea to blurt out, "Why are you here, Lani?"

The princess wrinkled her brow. "To learn about Demora, of course. To open trade and begin our friendship officially. I told you I would come."

"Yes, but we did not expect your arrival for several months."

"That was before we learned about King Ragat," said Lani.

Sage had only recently received the official news of the Kimisar king's death. It had been suspected last summer, but within Kimisara itself the truth had been obscured for a long time. Confirmation through spy networks had taken months, then it took several more weeks for the information to reach her at the outpost. She and Alex had discussed some of the implications in their last letters, but all they could do was speculate.

"After Sinda's treason last summer," Lani continued, flinching a little, "our people are worried for the future, especially as our relationship with Demora is not officially defined. I am here to define it." She smiled mischievously. "And to plan your wedding. You need my help for it to be a proper affair."

Sage shifted uncomfortably, thinking her friend must have misunderstood how long she and Alex still had to wait. "That's not for another year."

And then only if they could find a way to see each other. Her heart squeezed a little. What had seemed a short time ago yesterday once again felt like forever.

"I can stay that long."

Sage breathed a sigh of relief. "So when you talked of choosing a princess..."

"She can go to Osthiza ahead of me," said Lani carelessly. "Then the Casmuni people can see we are now allies. Kimisara will see it, too."

Sage had tutored both of King Raymond's daughters, the older of whom was now only fourteen. The thought of one of her former charges being forced to marry so young made her queasy. "I don't think our king will be ready for this kind of agreement."

"Which is why I need your help," said Lani.

"I was only an apprentice to a marriage maker," Sage objected. "And I was ill-suited for the job. I did it for less than a year."

Lani gaped at her. "Banneth doesn't want to *marry* her, Saizsch. She is only a child, yes?"

It had been the Casmuni king's son Sage was thinking of. "But Hasseth—"

"Is twelve years." Lani's cup clattered back onto its saucer. "By the Spirit, Saizsch, you of all people should know my brother would never do *that*!"

Of course he wouldn't. At fifteen, a newly crowned and frightened Banneth had been forced to marry a girl who hated him. Sage slumped against the back of her chair. "Well, what else am I to think when you talk of dressing a Demoran princess in your clothes and taking her away to Osthiza?"

"Oh, well." Lani looked a little guilty. "We only wish her to live among us for a few years. If she were to develop affection for Hasseth over that time, we would be most pleased."

Sage narrowed her eyes. "I imagine you will encourage that."

"We will do everything to make her happy," Lani countered calmly. "But we will never force her." She arched one perfectly shaped eyebrow as

15

she sipped her tea again. "For all you know, we may not find her queen material. Perhaps it is your country who will reach for what it cannot have."

"Perhaps," said Sage, mirroring the princess's expression, then grinning when Lani did.

One of the maids offered Sage a cup of Casmuni tea, then refilled her mistress's. Sage warmed her fingers on the porcelain and sighed. "I missed this brew," she said. Rose and jasmine. It felt auspicious. "I think the princess who would suit this idea best would be Rose. That is also our name for your *risha* flower."

"And you think your *Risha* will transplant well?" asked Lani. "She likes to visit new places?"

Sage snorted into her cup. Rose had actually traveled very little in her life and once confessed to Sage how maddening it was to be so sheltered when she longed for a storybook adventure. The Demoran princess would probably pack her trunks that night. "She will be open to the idea," was all Sage said.

Queen Orianna, on the other hand . . .

"I am glad you are now on my side, Saizsch," said Lani smugly.

"I am on the side of Demora," Sage retorted. "And Rose."

Lani shrugged. "And I am here to ensure they are all the same."

They went back to their tea, an idea forming in Sage's head. Clare joined them a few minutes later, taking a brief respite from the preparations she'd already started for the journey. "I've drafted the message telling Their Majesties to expect us," Clare told Sage, accepting a cup of tea. "After you've looked it over, I'll finalize and send it. The sooner the better."

"How long will it take to get to Tennegol?" asked Lani.

A courier changing horses frequently took two weeks to make the distance between Vinova and the Demoran capital, but a large, diplomatic caravan took at least twice as long, especially in winter weather. "About thirty days," Sage answered. "But I was thinking . . ." She glanced sideways at Clare.

"Yes?" said Lani, raising her eyebrows when Sage didn't finish her sentence.

"Perhaps you would enjoy stopping at the Norsari camp on the way,"

Sage said innocently. "Your soldiers might be interested to see some of their training. They could spend a few days showing each other fighting techniques. As a show of goodwill."

"Hmmm." The princess gazed at the hearth thoughtfully. "Is Lieutenant Casseck still serving with them?"

"Captain Casseck now," said Sage. "Yes."

"*Kap-tan*," Lani repeated slowly. "This is a promotion of rank?"

"Yes."

Lani's already flushed cheeks darkened a little as she buried her nose in her teacup. "I think I should like to congratulate him in person."

5

HE WAS TRYING to write her a letter.

Alex sat on the cot in his tent, a board across his knee and a quill in his ungloved hand. The weather was turning into full-on winter, though it was milder here in the south, and he wore an extra layer of brown clothing. It was a new uniform he'd designed for the Norsari, with better camouflage qualities than the black traditionally worn by cavalry, and Alex still reflexively brushed the sleeves when they caught his eye, thinking they were dusty.

He flexed his cold fingers and frowned at the parchment waiting for his words. Sweet Spirit, he missed her.

Ideally this would be something to replace the lost letter. Alex had sent it to Sage over a year ago and found it among her things after the Kimisar raid had forced her to flee into Casmun. He'd carried it with him as he followed her, but when he'd been captured and tossed into prison for a few days, they'd burned all his clothes to prevent vermin. While the pages had been full of phrases and descriptions that made Alex blush to remember now, she'd obviously treasured it.

He still felt those things about her, perhaps even more strongly than he had last year. The problem was how, at the moment, those feelings were overlaid with aggravation. Everything he thought of writing was tainted by the emotion.

His frustration wasn't over his responsibilities. Commanding the Norsari was a dream assignment—not to mention he was now the youngest major in Demora's history. Nor was it because his uncle the king had appointed Sage ambassador to Casmun. There was no one better for the job. They were both in the best possible places considering the state of the world.

The world, then. The world was what kept them apart. That and a stupid army regulation.

In reality, lifting the age restriction on army officers being married wouldn't change their situation much. Norsari assignments were riskier and more secretive than those of the regular army, and fighting with the Kimisar in Tasmet was expected to escalate when spring arrived. Sage would still be a foreign emissary with responsibilities of her own.

But at least when they were together, they could *be* together.

They had less than a year now, though. Some days were easier to bear than others. On Chapel Days, routines were relaxed, but that only gave him more time to miss her. When he'd felt the clouds gathering in his mood that morning, he'd removed himself from the company of even his best friend and second-in-command, Captain Casseck. Nobody needed to see their commander pouting like a child.

Alex clenched his fist and pounded on the writing board hard enough that it flipped off his lap, dumping the inkpot across the page and onto the ground. He quickly scooped the glass container up and kicked loose dirt over the puddle, cursing the ruined letter. Not that he'd gotten down more than a few words. Last time he'd been pouring his heart out. Somehow trying made it more difficult.

"Permission to enter, sir?" came a familiar voice from outside the tent.

Alex didn't feel like being formal. "Yeah, come in, Cass."

Captain Casseck ducked inside with a cold breeze. Outside the sun was nearly at its peak, shining harshly from the cloudless sky. His friend stood straight, looking down on Alex for a few seconds, like he was assessing him. His blond hair brushed the ceiling of the tent. "You sick?" he finally said.

The hint of amusement Alex heard annoyed him. Cass could always read him like a book, sensing Alex's attraction to Sage back on the night he'd first met her—and been irritated as hell by her. "Just wanted to be alone for a bit."

"That's why I came to talk." Cass grabbed the collapsible chair to swing it around, then sat on it backward, facing Alex. He folded his arms, focusing serious blue eyes on him. "It's been more than ten weeks since you've taken time for yourself. You need a break."

Norsari training was intense, and Alex knew men needed time to unwind, so they additionally rotated through having a full day off. Most went to one of the two nearest villages, hiking or riding up the Kaz River or out to the Jovan Road. Due to secrecy, such amusements had been forbidden last year. Now the Norsari re-formation was to be known, and word of the summer's battle in Casmun would soon spread to all corners of Demora.

It would also make Alex's name even better known. As if he didn't already have enough pressure to succeed.

Alex flipped the stained parchment over and began writing to hide the knot that suddenly tightened in his stomach. "I've hardly done anything today."

"Not good enough. You need to get out of here," said Cass. When Alex didn't answer, his friend tried a different angle. "It would be good for the men to see you trust me to handle things while you're gone."

"You mean good for you."

"That, too."

Alex scowled. His friend was right, though—even if a commander was well liked, there was something about having him gone that changed the mood in an army camp, made it relax where no one realized it was tight. "All right. Next Chapel Day."

"Today," said Cass firmly.

"Are you giving orders now?"

"Since you're leaving me in charge, yes."

"Fine," Alex sighed. Having resigned himself to the idea, the weight on his shoulders had already begun to lift. "I'll go . . . somewhere."

"Excellent." Cass stood with a grin.

There was too much triumph in his friend's tone. Alex's suspicion was suddenly aroused. A courier was due today, but he could hear more activity outside than that arrival would've produced. He narrowed his eyes at his friend. "What the hell is going on?"

Casseck only saluted and turned to duck back outside. "You have a visitor, by the way," he called over his shoulder.

Visitor?

A hand caught the tent flap before it closed, and in strode a small figure dressed in Casmuni riding clothes. Alex jumped to his feet just in time to catch Sage as she pitched herself into his arms.

Sweet Spirit, he was dreaming.

Her freckled cheeks were flushed and her nose cold as it brushed against his, and then their lips met, and he knew it was real because not even his dreams were this good. It had been so long since he'd seen her—nearly six months—that it was almost like the first time they'd kissed. Tentative at first, and then eager. Then desperate. Alex lifted Sage up and against his body, then moved to pull her legs around his hips so he could sit down with her in his lap.

He forgot they were both wearing swords. His straight, heavy Demoran blade jabbed against the cot and tipped it down, causing the other side to go up, catching on the curved Casmuni *harish* she carried on her hip. For a few seconds he struggled to keep his balance, but it was no use. Alex fell back, trying to protect her from being hurt as he did, landing awkwardly on the hilt of his sword and hearing the crack of splitting wood as the leg of the cot snapped. "Ow," he said.

They looked at each other, blushing, before laughing. Sweet Spirit, he'd missed that sound.

Sage grinned and pushed stray shoulder-length hairs away from her face as she untangled herself from his legs and the canvas of the broken cot. "I guess you missed me as much as I missed you."

"More," he said, and Sage rolled her eyes, but he pulled her close again before she could say anything. After kissing every inch of her exposed skin—she was heavily dressed and there wasn't much, so he covered everything twice—Alex finally got around to asking why she was there.

"Princess Lani," she said a little breathlessly. "We're on our way to Tennegol with her. Thought we'd stop here since it was on the way. Promote goodwill, all that."

"Good thinking," he said absently as he started his third pass. How could he have forgotten how wonderful she smelled? Even after days of riding, the scent of floral soap clung to her hair and clothes, but it wasn't just that. Somehow he always felt like he was breathing sunshine in her presence. Tasting it, too.

Casseck's voice interrupted them from outside the tent. "Major, I have all reports and readiness," he said formally. "I relieve you, sir."

Sage glanced over her shoulder at the captain's silhouette against the canvas wall. "What does that mean?" she asked quietly.

"I stand relieved," Alex called back, and Casseck's shadow disappeared. He turned to Sage, feeling almost giddy. "It means he wants me to leave. I promised him I'd take the day off."

For a second she looked overjoyed, but then guilt took over. "Oh, no." Sage shook her head. "I don't want to disrupt anything."

Spirit bless her for trying, but it was too late for that. "It's all right," he assured her. "I need a break, and . . ." Alex cleared his throat. He had an idea, but Sage would be reluctant if she thought it was taking him away from his duties. "I could use your help with something."

A spark of interest lit her face as he knew it would, and Alex leaned close to whisper in Sage's ear. When he sat back, her gray eyes were wide. "Really?" she asked.

He nodded sheepishly.

She bit her lip, even as it turned up at the corners in eagerness. "I don't know how much I can do in just a few hours."

Alex shrugged. "Anything will be better than nothing."

"Isn't it a little cold for that, though?"

"I have a place in mind."

6

SAGE RAN TO get what she needed, then changed clothes in Alex's tent while he went in search of food and other supplies. He'd said it would take at least an hour to get where they were going, so they had to hurry if they wanted to be back by dark. They headed north, Alex not even waiting until they were out of sight of the camp before taking her hand.

Cold mountain air from the west chilled them at first, but their brisk pace kept them warm after the first quarter mile. Sage asked Alex all about his training, reveling in his happiness and pride in what he was doing. The Norsari were down to the last three weeks of their time here, and he enthusiastically described his plan to divide the soldiers into elite squads and platoons with specific skills such as archery or knife fighting. Competition was already fierce for those spots. No man would be in a special unit without a high level of achievement in every other category, however.

When that topic was spent, Alex asked about her time at Vinova. Sage described Clare's lessons in diplomacy and deportment, and he laughed. "I'd forgotten how much of that was drilled into me at a young age," he said. "I hated it, too."

"I don't *hate* it," she said. "It just makes me feel inadequate."

He leaned down to kiss her ear. "Never, Sage."

"Hmmph." She nudged him away with her shoulder, then stopped as she recognized where they were. "Is this it?" she asked. "That lake we found last year?"

"Yup." It wasn't overly large, but Alex said the size and number of fish the Norsari had caught meant the lake was fairly deep. A light fog drifted across the surface, indicating the water was warmer than the air. Sage walked to the edge and dipped her fingers in.

"It's warmer than I expected," she admitted. "But still too cold. We won't last ten minutes."

He tugged her elbow. "This way."

They walked around the south shore. Last year they'd paused at the lake only long enough to get a drink before returning to camp. Now, as the steam became thicker, Sage detected a whiff of sulfur in the air. "It's fed by a hot spring?" she asked.

Alex grinned and nodded, leading her over the narrow stream whose heat she felt through the soles of her boots, and stopped on a pebbled beach upwind from the drifting steam, which now had a strong, acrid scent. Here the lake water had a yellowish tint, and the ground was noticeably warmer.

He wrinkled his nose. "Sorry about the smell."

Sage shook her head and smiled. "I think the trade-off will be worth it."

Alex began collecting wood for a fire to keep them warm when they got out of the water. She watched him coax the flames to life, taking in the small differences in his appearance from when they'd parted almost five months ago. His black hair had been sheared off in the Casmuni prison, but now it was nearly as shaggy as it had been when they'd first met. He'd grown out his beard again, too. Shaving every day had become impractical, he'd written, apologizing, but this closely trimmed, Sage considered it the best of both worlds—dashing and mature in appearance, yet not too rough on her face. Or maybe she'd just gotten used to it. Once he'd built the fire up to his liking, he looked at her. "Ready?"

Sage nodded and turned away to hide her flushed cheeks, wondering why it hadn't fully occurred to her how much she'd be stripping down in front of him. Being embarrassed was silly, though. He'd taken care of her wounds last summer; it wasn't like he didn't already know what she looked like undressed. For that matter, she, too, knew exactly how he looked without all his clothes. Well, almost all of them.

Focus, she told herself sternly. *Alex needs your help.*

With her back resolutely to him, Sage peeled off her layers until all that remained was the boyish linen underbreeches she'd always preferred, much to her aunt's dismay, and a long, sleeveless Casmuni silk shirt. The air on her exposed legs made her feel unbalanced as one burned with cold while the other merely had gooseflesh. Leaving her clothes in a messy pile, she stepped quickly past a shirtless Alex and into the water, going deep enough to cover her shoulders before she dared to turn around. Not quite bath warm, but almost as pleasant, though the farther she went from shore, the cooler it got. Alex followed, wearing only undershorts.

Seeing him like this would *never* get old.

To cover the fact that she was staring, Sage gestured to Alex's left shoulder. "New tattoo?"

Alex paused in water up to his waist and twisted to show her the sharp, angled head of a bird and the wings, which stretched a few inches around to his chest and back. The shape arched over the ones she already knew, designating cavalry and other army units he'd been a part of. "Norsar," he explained.

The swift and deadly raptor the Norsari had been named for. There was little detail in the design on his skin, just a dark silhouette. Much like the last thing a norsar's prey ever saw—if anything—before they were snatched into oblivion.

Sage shivered, and not from cold. "All right," she said, turning away and pushing out into water deep enough to go over her head. "The most important thing to remember is to stay relaxed. If you get too tense, it's harder to stay afloat." She glanced back.

Alex was gone.

Her heartbeat pounded in her ears as Sage spun around, calling his name, squinting down into the murky water, but she couldn't see past the sun's glare on the surface. He'd followed her too far, right over the ledge of stone where the bottom dropped away. Terror clawed at Sage's throat. Spirit above, was she strong enough to drag him to the surface? Would he panic and pull her down with him?

A hand on her lower leg made her scream, but it didn't yank her under. Instead it followed her body upward, and Alex broke the surface in front of her, tipping his head back to keep his hair out of his eyes, which were bright with merriment. It took Sage several seconds to comprehend that he was treading water effortlessly.

"You ass!" she shouted, shoving him away and then splashing him for good measure. "You already know how to swim!"

"Of course I know how to swim." Alex laughed and wiped water from his eyes. "But I knew you wouldn't be able to resist teaching me if you thought I couldn't."

Sage scowled. "You're still an ass." But she let him pull her closer.

"As long as I'm your ass." Alex wrapped his arms around her and kicked to take them back into shallower, warmer water. When they got to where he could stand, he lifted her legs around his waist, like he'd tried to so disastrously earlier.

She hooked her feet together behind his back and settled against him, vibrantly aware of every place they touched. "I should punish you for that," she whispered against his mouth.

"How do you know I wouldn't enjoy it?" he asked, the coarse hair of his beard brushing her lips. His hands traced her thighs up and to the small of her back.

Now her heart was pounding for an entirely different reason.

He moved to close the minuscule gap between them, but Sage leaned away. "I noticed you aren't afraid that everyone knows we're out here together."

"And I noticed what you aren't wearing under this shirt." He slipped his hands beneath the silk and up her back, drawing her against him.

"Alex."

He stopped, waiting. Sage looked down and away, tracing his right bicep with her fingers. The muscle beneath the scarred and inked brown skin was solid as iron. There was a slight difference in texture where it was tattooed in soft shades of green and violet, rather than the stark red, blue, and black on the left side. Soldiers didn't risk their sword arms, which made the sage leaves and flowers on the right all the more meaningful. She was his strength. She was what he risked everything for. "Have you changed your mind, then?" she whispered.

"About bedding you?" Alex brought one hand around and pushed her chin up to face him. "Or rather, *not* bedding you until we're married?"

Sage took a trembling breath as she met his smoldering, almost coalblack eyes. "Yes."

"No."

"Then you can't keep doing this," she said, shaking her head to hide the disappointment on her face. "You can't keep bringing us to the brink of control. One day you'll cross the line. And you'll hate yourself for it." *More than you should*, she added silently.

Alex sighed and put his head on her shoulder. "You're right," he said, then kissed her collarbone. "I'm sorry." He slipped his other hand out from her shirt.

"Why do you have to be so damn honorable?" Sage asked, sliding her fingers up to the back of his neck, threading them in his wet hair.

He lifted his head to meet her eyes again. "For you," he answered seriously. "Otherwise, what's the point?"

HONORABLE DECLARATIONS ASIDE, Sage let Alex keep her in the water longer than she should have, then spent even longer nestled against him by the fire. They shared the food he'd brought and sipped Casmuni tea and talked about the places they wanted to show each other someday. Alex promised to take her to the eastern hills where his grandparents lived, and Sage told him about the vast fields of grain in Crescera, bordered by wide stretches of woods she could navigate blindfolded. In those precious hours there was no war, no thoughts of months apart both now and later. But all too soon their time was gone.

They returned to the Norsari camp as the mountain peaks were swallowing the last streams of sunlight. Under Sage's breeches and shirtsleeve, the tight pink skin itched and chafed as she walked. The sulfurous water had dried it out, and she'd have to rub it down with the oils that kept it supple and encouraged healing. Alex had wanted to see her scars again. She could barely stand to let him, but he insisted.

"It's so ugly," she whispered, holding back tears as he ran calloused fingers down her left leg. She hated how his touch felt different there, like it was farther away in some places but on the bone itself in others.

Alex bent down to kiss a spot above her knee. "Sage, I remember it at its worst. I thank the Spirit every day that you were strong enough to survive this. Most aren't."

Perspective. She was alive. Others weren't. Even through the haze of agony, she'd smelled the charred flesh of hundreds of corpses. Men she'd killed by unleashing the weapon that then burned her. For a time she wished it had taken her, too, because of what she'd done. It was that memory as much as the fire itself that haunted her dreams.

Alex's bearing had been slowly changing as they walked back, and as the camp perimeter came into view, Sage watched him pause and fully resume the mantle of command like an invisible cloak. She loved it in some ways—it meant there was a side of him that was only for her. Yet it also meant there were times and places she couldn't exist in his life. "What happens when you're finished here?" she asked softly.

"We go to Tennegol and present ourselves to the king. Do a few demonstrations, mostly for the council, to assure them I've done a good job training the Norsari." He squeezed her hand and glanced down with a wink. "And when I'm not busy with that, I'll be mussing up your hair in dark corners."

It was a running joke between them, as he'd made a mess of her hair the first time they'd kissed. And the second, for that matter. She burst into a giddy smile. "You'll be there at the same time? Why didn't you say so before?"

He shrugged, grinning. "Didn't occur to me until now. I think I was overwhelmed by your arrival."

It was almost too good to be true. "Now I'm gladder than ever that Lani came, otherwise I wouldn't be there." Sage paused. "Then what?"

"Tasmet and the border with Kimisara," he replied, sighing as the reality of their situation intruded. "We haven't heard anything for months, but who knows what kind of chaos King Ragat's death will bring? The Kimisar may be more desperate than ever, and new rulers often think they have to prove themselves. We have to be ready for anything."

It wasn't like Alex to shy away from a fight, yet he didn't appear eager for once. She laced her fingers with his. "You sound worried."

"Not like you think, probably," Alex said. "It's just . . ." He drifted off, the invisible cloak pulling tighter around him.

She understood. The pressure to succeed. The need to prove he had this job because he deserved it and not because his father was the commanding general. Not to mention the stakes were higher than ever before. Sage felt sure that no one who'd actually served with Alex could doubt him, but thousands knew him only by name.

"You are your father's son," she said. She'd met General Quinn once, and it was undeniable how alike they were—not only in looks but in bearing and drive. In the way they cared for those they commanded. "But you've earned everything you have. Everyone here knows it."

He shook his head. "Outside the Norsari it's different. Many don't believe I deserve this command."

"And some never will." She tugged at his arm to make him face her. "Alex, you can't let that rob you of what you've accomplished."

"It's all for you, you realize?" he said solemnly. "Everything I do, everything I have, is yours."

Sage rolled her eyes though his words warmed her deep inside. "Then what motivated you for the first twenty years?"

Alex shrugged one shoulder. "I don't know. Prestige. Rank. Fixing things that were broken or wrong. Protecting the realm." He hesitated and glanced away. "Revenge."

She knew what he referred to. He'd almost left the army after his first skirmish, physically sickened that he'd taken a life, but then a friend had been killed. From then on, there was always one more death to avenge, one more wrong to right, until he no longer kept count of the bodies.

And then it was Alex's own brother who was slain.

"You're not a monster," she whispered.

He shook his head. "You have no idea how much I want to pay them back for what happened to you. For Charlie." Alex closed his eyes and took a deep breath. "I worry it will cloud my judgment."

"You're better than that."

"I'm not sure I am."

"You must be," she said firmly, reaching up to turn his face down to hers. "This cycle of violence won't stop until people like us say, *Enough*."

"Both sides have to say it, Sage."

She stood on her toes for one last kiss. "Someone has to say it first."

The way he kissed her back told Sage she'd reassured him, and it gave her a measure of comfort to counter her own deep uneasiness. Because when it came to being a monster, that word was reserved for those who killed hundreds with a single act of rage and anguish.

People like her.

8

SAGE KNEW THEY'D been spotted by sentries because Casseck walked out to them with one of the teenaged squires, looking apologetic. "The courier from Tennegol arrived an hour ago," he said. "Everything is waiting for you in the command tent."

Alex returned the captain's salute without any sign of weariness or frustration. "Very well. I'll head straight there." His other hand released Sage's as they both unshouldered their packs for the squire to take.

"Mistress Fowler's dispatches are there, too, as he had them." Casseck dropped his hand. "I told the mess to bring your supper there. The rest of the officers will be dining in the Casmuni princess's tent. I told Her Highness it would be better to have you there, but she insisted." He shrugged helplessly. "She said she wanted to honor my elevation. At least I think that's what she said. I hope she understands I was only in charge for a few hours."

Alex's eyes darted to Sage, but she blinked innocently. "That's fine, Captain," he said. "You never had a proper recognition of your promotion. Enjoy yourself." He put his hand on the small of Sage's back and guided her in the direction of the command tent. Once out of earshot, Alex said, "I'm not sure we should encourage Princess Lani's interest in him."

Sage snorted. "You try telling her no."

The table under the main tent was almost overflowing with documents, and half of them were Sage's. She groaned. "This is going to take all night."

"Tell you what," said Alex. "Let's sort into two piles: things that matter to both of us, and everything else. We'll only worry about the first tonight."

He was right—there was no need to rush to handle everything now. Tennegol was already going to hear back from her sooner than they expected. Sage joined Alex at the table, sitting across and a bit to the side from him, and opened the message on top, which bore an official seal. The single sentence within took her breath away.

The presence of Ambassador Sage Fowler and Lady Clare Holloway is requested in Tennegol by His Majesty at the earliest possible date.

It did not say why.

Alex was watching her. "What's wrong?"

Sage tore open the next message. "Clare and I have been called to the capital immediately. I don't know the reason, though."

The next letter was a personal one from Princess Rose. Sage tossed it aside for later.

Another note, this one from Aunt Braelaura. Later.

A letter from her cousin Hannah, who was now thirteen. She got straight to asking if she could be in Sage's wedding, with a heavy hint that she'd be willing to stay at court for the next couple of years. Sage was more interested in little Aster's note scrawled at the bottom of the parchment, but still, later. She dropped it on the table and picked up the next.

Personal letter from Crescera's high matchmaker, Darnessa Rodelle. Sage paused only long enough to note that her former employer had a new apprentice and desired any information Sage had on the shifting political landscape, as it would affect future matches. That would require a long response, and anything Sage would write now could change when Lani threw Casmun into the royal mix.

The last correspondence was from the queen herself, saying she'd be happy to celebrate Sage's marriage when she arrived in Tennegol. Didn't anyone in this country think about things *other* than weddings? Sage grimaced and looked up. "What do you have?" she asked Alex.

"Standard yearly list of changes to army regulations," Alex muttered as he tossed several pages onto a stack of opened messages. "Only regular replies and reports so far. The official order to return to Tennegol is here, but that was expected."

"You're called back early?" Sage brightened at the thought of traveling to the capital together.

He shook his head as he set another parchment aside. "Just on completion of training. It does say come *immediately*, but that doesn't necessarily mean anything. This looks important, though." Alex picked up a triply sealed letter and showed it to Sage. One of the wax disks had the impression of a quill crossed with a sword. An intelligence report.

Sage watched as Alex broke the seal and read the letter, her impatience growing as he inhaled sharply but said nothing. "What's happened?" she demanded when she could wait no longer.

"Kimisara officially has a new king," he said. "Ragat's son Mesden has ascended to the throne."

Sage dug through her memory. "But Ragat's previous wives died childless, and the last he married maybe twelve years ago. This Mesden must be only a child."

"He's six." Alex frowned at the page in his hand. "Not old enough to rule." He shook his head. "Which means a struggle over who gets to hold the reins of power."

"Then won't the fighting be within?" Sage took the parchment from him and scanned it. "And there's an official regent already—Mesden's mother, Queen Zoraya. It's settled."

"Sage," said Alex quietly. "Do you know what happened to Ragat's first two queens?"

"Only rumors," she said. "In Crescera people said both were executed because they couldn't provide an heir." She frowned. "Terrible as that is, it's not like Demoran kings didn't do similar things in the past." *D'Amiran family kings*, she added silently.

"And this Zoraya lasted several childless years."

"So?"

"So she's a survivor," said Alex. "Not only that, but she was cunning enough to wrest control from probably a dozen men who would kill for her position. Powerful men who probably won't take defeat well."

"And you think they aren't done fighting for what she has?" Sage offered the parchment back. "Are you afraid someone like that can't last?"

Alex shook his head as he refolded the dispatch. "I'd be more afraid of someone who actually can."

9

CAPTAIN MALKIM HUZAR stood one step behind and to the side of the smaller throne on the dais, his face carefully blank. In this situation, like most others, he was to be invisible, part of the decorative wall hangings. The young king fidgeted on his velvet cushion, but the movements of the last half hour had changed a bit.

Mesden needed to urinate.

In the larger throne next to the boy, Queen Regent Zoraya ignored her son as she listened to Brazapil Donala droning on and on, but Huzar knew she was aware of his discomfort. While most mothers were mindful of their children, Zoraya took it to a new level. As the boy was all that had stood between her and being disposed of in the last seven years, it was understandable, yet she also loved him fiercely. Perhaps because for many years she'd had no one else to love—a desolation Huzar knew only too well himself.

The glint of light off the queen's tightly pinned hair flashed in the corner of Huzar's vision. He wondered if any in the kingdom knew how long it was when unbound, that it almost reached her feet in blue-black waves.

He knew.

Mesden, unable to catch his mother's eye, stole a glance at Huzar.

That was dangerous.

Zoraya kept the young king mostly away from Huzar, afraid her closeness to the captain might become public knowledge in an offhand childish statement, but the boy couldn't be completely ignorant of how much time they spent together. Nor could anyone else, for that matter.

Huzar pretended not to notice Mesden, focusing on the increasing frustration he heard in the queen's tone as she argued with the man in front of her. She'd kept her temper in check all afternoon, but now her voice had a knife's edge, cutting through the space between her and Donala, the wealthiest member of her council. Rather than the layers of nobility of Demora, Kimisara had only the rank of brazapil between peasants and royalty. Anyone could claim the title as long as the parcel of land they owned was large enough to be called a brasa. The system allowed landowners almost complete autonomy, reminiscent of the country's loosely unified nomadic history, but it tended to make them outspoken. With the weight of over a dozen brasa in his pockets, Hanric Donala was the boldest of all.

He'd also been the council's choice for regent, yet Zoraya had prevailed, thanks in great part to information Huzar provided. She'd seized the moment, interrupting the ministers just before their official vote, carrying the royal declaration with her name at the top and Mesden's childish scrawl at the bottom. As the brazapilla themselves had drafted the document, they couldn't dispute its legality.

Nor did they even try, with Huzar's sword to back her up.

"Yes, I know the glorious plans my husband had for our nation," the queen snapped, her patience finally spent. "But perhaps you've forgotten his lack of achievement."

Huzar tensed and the entire room of courtiers gasped audibly at her insult to King Ragat's memory. Zoraya stood, sweeping her silver threaded gown around her. Silver was the color of mourning in Kimisara, used to remind anyone in a widow's presence not to tarnish the name of her departed husband. No one knew how to react to a woman doing that herself.

"I will not pretend my son has inherited a position of strength, nor will I refuse to acknowledge whose fault it is," she said. The room was silent, save for the soft snores of the hound dozing at the foot of Mesden's carved chair. "Demora surely knows this as well, and we will appear weaker still if we deny the truth."

Beside Donala, a weaselish man who gobbled up every scrap the more powerful brazapil threw his way, ventured to speak. "Kimisara is not weak, My Royal Lady—"

Zoraya cut him off. "Our people are starving, Brazapil Nostin. Three years ago we were decimated by a blight that killed most of our harvests and reduced our stores to nothing. The next year, wildfires destroyed half our forests and grassland, leaving no game to hunt. Then we made an alliance with that Demoran traitor, Morrow D'Amiran, and he turned on us. Tell me, was that the best time to plan the largest invasion in a hundred years?"

Huzar had been there when Ragat tried to invade Demora through Casmun. It had been a disaster, though mostly due to a Casmuni weapon of fire, which melted the valley—and the men in it—into a solid wall of black glass.

The queen paused and looked around, her reddening cheeks seeming to draw color from every blanched face watching her. "No. It was not. Anyone who believes so is a fool, and I am no fool."

"Then, with respect," said Nostin, his tone dripping with condescension, "I must remind My Royal Lady the Demorans cannot be trusted. This plan to talk with them will not end well."

Huzar almost laughed out loud. After several battles against one of Demora's most capable soldiers—a man his own age named Quinn—and losing every encounter, Huzar would gladly face him again before turning his back on the snakes in this room.

"Maybe so." Zoraya took three steps toward Nostin and Donala, head high. "But I consider us fortunate that they've even agreed to meet with us."

Donala bowed. "Then we will make all effort on your behalf."

"And I will be there to ensure you do."

At that, Huzar's impassive face slipped, and his eyes darted to the queen. She'd not said anything to him about attending the talks herself.

Zoraya's blue eyes swept the room again, meeting Huzar's for the briefest of seconds. "I have written the Demoran king to say I will be there."

"Surely that is not necessary—"

"I believe it is," she interrupted. "My presence will show the Demorans how serious we are." She narrowed her sapphire gaze on the sputtering pair before her. "For we *are* serious. We can never regain our strength without a time of peace."

The queen pivoted back to address the young king, who was astute enough to realize how tense the situation was and had stopped wriggling for the last few minutes. "Come, my son," she said. "We have finished our work for today."

Mesden hopped down from the throne. The dog at his feet was instantly awake and alert, trotting after his young master. When the two reached her side, she took her son's hand and strode down the steps of the dais. The crowd parted silently for her, which she barely acknowledged. When she reached the double doors of the throne room, she stopped and turned back to face the sea of councilmen and courtiers. To everyone else, she appeared to be shaking with rage, but Huzar recognized it as fear, and his stomach turned over in anxiety.

"And I will say this only once, *Brazapil*," she said, emphasizing the title like it was a crude word. "I am regent, yes, but I am also queen. Ragat's death does not take that away. You will remember to address me as such. Or you will be made to remember."

With that, she exited the room. Huzar counted slowly to ten from his place on the dais, then left to follow.

"Was that wise, My Queen?" Huzar asked softly as he closed the door behind him.

She didn't answer him from where she stood gazing out of a window at the bustling courtyard. A voice from below called up a blessing to her, and she smiled a little and lifted her ringed hand in response.

Huzar approached but stayed out of sight of the window. Zoraya was five years older than him, but the twelve years she'd been married to Ragat had aged her appearance beyond that. Not that it made her any less beautiful. "I must be strong for Mesden," she said without looking away from the activity below.

"Yes, but you are making powerful enemies," Huzar said.

Zoraya shook her head. "The real power lies with the people. They are tired of the demands of the brazapilla. If I am the first to ever make their lives better, we will see who has their loyalty."

It was difficult to tell whether that was out of genuine concern for the people or for her own welfare. She'd come from humble origins, which made the former easy to imagine. Huzar sometimes tried to picture her as the careless girl she must have been, before the king plucked her out of an obscure village and made her his wife, the third queen he'd had. The first two had not met pleasant ends. Zoraya possessed a talent for survival that her predecessors had not.

"Do you know why he chose me?" the queen said quietly, as though hearing Huzar's thoughts. "My parents had ten children, and I was the only girl." She turned to face him, her cheeks still flushed from the confrontation in the throne room. "Because of that, I was believed to be fertile, and that sons were more likely. My role was clear from the beginning." Her chin lifted. "But it also made me a queen. If I lose that, I will lose everything, starting with that which is most important."

Mesden.

"Where is the king?" Huzar asked. Though he kept his distance, he rather liked the boy.

"I told him to relieve himself and then go outside and expend some energy. The nursemaid is with him." Zoraya took a step toward Huzar and put her hands on the front of his jacket, tracing the white four-pointed star of Kimisara embroidered in the leather. "We are alone."

Those last words had become a signal between them, but Huzar wasn't ready to let his guard down. He placed his hands over hers, which were smooth and fragile in his own. "You didn't tell me you intended to go to the negotiations," he said.

The queen tilted her face to meet his gaze. As always, the brilliant blue of her eyes was startling. "How could I do otherwise? You and I both know the brazapilla cannot be trusted to be honest with me, or to work toward my goals."

"That's why I was supposed to go with them."

"Yes, but you have no authority. You would only be able to tell me what happened after the fact."

"It's not safe," Huzar insisted.

Zoraya smiled coyly and tugged the lapel of his jacket. "But my most faithful bodyguard will be there."

He frowned. She overestimated his skills.

The queen lowered her gaze to their now intertwined fingers. Her long black lashes fluttered on her cheeks. "Perhaps I also felt I would miss you," she murmured.

Huzar had come to know two different women in Zoraya over the last six months. One of cunning manipulation and another of sweet vulnerability. The question was which of those he was seeing now.

Also which had pulled him into the bedroom the first time.

"Malkim," she whispered, leaning into him. "I can't do this without you."

In the end, it didn't matter. He loved them both.

10

HER SCREAMING WAS a sound Alex would never be able to forget; he still heard it in his dreams.

Alex jerked awake. It was muffled by distance and the walls of canvas between them, but the sound was unmistakable: Sage was screaming.

He threw his blanket aside and jumped off the broken cot. Grabbing his boots and sword belt, he tore outside and ran in the direction of the Casmuni camp, where Sage was staying. Heads peeked out of other tents as he sprinted past, but he didn't acknowledge them. The noise stopped suddenly as Alex skidded to a halt outside Princess Lani's tent, gasping for air.

Several Casmuni guards appeared out of the shadows, spears leveled at him. Two more stepped outside the tent, sheathing their curved blades. When they saw him, they issued a few orders to the men surrounding Alex, who lowered their weapons and backed away.

Everything was silent.

Had he imagined it?

A glance around told him he couldn't have. At least a dozen Norsari had also come running, weapons in hand. And there wasn't silence, either; there was quiet sobbing.

Sage.

Still carrying his boots and sword, Alex strode barefoot to the heavy tapestry that served as a door to the royal tent. The guards stepped to block his path, and Alex made to shove them aside. "Get out of my way!" he snarled.

Whether or not they understood him, neither obeyed, putting their hands on Alex's shoulders to stop him. Alex twisted around, forcing them to counter. He growled. "I said—"

"*Chet!*" came a woman's voice. "*Hasta vos nel.*" *Do not restrain him.* The Casmuni princess stood at the curtain, holding it open for him.

Alex shook the men off without looking at them and strode inside. It was dark, but the glow from the iron stove was enough for him to see by. Lani stood before him, her black hair in a single braid down her back as she tugged a wool blanket around her. "You heard her?" she asked in Casmuni.

"I hear her now," Alex replied, though it was difficult over the echo of his pounding heart. "What happened?"

He took a step in the direction of the sobbing, but Lani put a hand on his chest. "Please, be calm."

"But—"

"She is well cared for, Maizshur," Lani said firmly, lisping the same consonants in his rank as she struggled with in Sage's name.

The sobs took on a retching quality. Another voice, soothing and feminine, came from behind a partitioned area. Alex slowly realized Sage must have had a nightmare, and Lady Clare was comforting her. "You have seen this before?" he asked.

Lani shook her head, then seemed to think better of her answer. "Once, in Osthiza, in the time she believed you were dead. She carried much guilt then." She glanced over her shoulder as the choking noises stopped. "Clare told me this happens at times, but it is the first I have seen on this journey."

Alex's Casmuni vocabulary wasn't very large, and he had to pick through the words he knew to make a coherent sentence. "In her sleep she is on fire," he said.

"*Da.*" Lani nodded once.

"Clare helps her through this?"

Lani nodded again. "I think she likes that Saizsch has this pain." Alex's mouth dropped open in horror, and she sighed. "That is not the best way to say it. Her love died, and Saizsch was wounded. In this way they share suffering from the battle. You understand?"

Despite the awkward wording, Alex did. "I'll stay until I can see her," he said.

"She's asleep." Clare was pulling the partition closed behind her as she stepped out. "I'm sorry you heard that, Major."

"I think everyone for five miles heard her, Lady Clare."

Clare sighed as she came closer. After thanking Lani in Casmuni, she focused back on Alex, and the princess returned to her own sleeping area. "It doesn't happen as often as it used to."

"But it does happen." Alex stepped around Clare and went to the partition. With the hand still holding his boots, he pushed the curtain aside. Sage lay on the thick carpets in a tangle of blankets, curled up on her right side. Her hair and clothes were dark with sweat, her breathing shallow and regular. An empty chamber pot sat near her head.

"She's getting better, I promise," Clare whispered. "She didn't actually vomit this time."

Such a casual statement that spoke of many times the nightmares were worse. Alex stepped back, dropping his boots and sword belt to put his face in his hands. "I let her go up there," he gasped.

The tide of the battle had suddenly turned when Kimisar came at them from two directions, and Sage had asked to help the soldiers struggling with the Casmuni waterfire. Alex had agreed, sending Lieutenant Gramwell as protection. When the hillside collapsed, pouring the weapon's fury onto the invading ranks of Kimisar, she had fallen with it. He choked back a sob. "I thought it would be safer away from the fighting. It's my fault."

"No, Major," Clare whispered. She reached up and drew him into her shoulder. "You can't blame yourself for that, not when she saved us all."

Alex pulled away, shaking his head. "And how can you forgive me when you know I sent Luke after her?"

Clare's pale face almost glowed in the dim light. "He was where he needed to be for Demora." She paused. "And I know either one of you would give anything to bring him back. That's how I can forgive."

44

All Alex could think of at that moment was revenge for Luke and Sage. Spirit damn this endless conflict. How many more friends would he lose in the coming years? How many men would Demora end up sacrificing for what was only ever a few months of peace? How many years would Sage be tormented by nightmares?

This cycle of violence won't stop until people like us say, Enough.

Sage bore scars and dreamed of fire and could forgive.

Clare had lost her future and could forgive.

During the battle, the Kimisar Captain Malkim Huzar, surrounded by his dead and dying countrymen, had given Alex the cloak off his back to carry Sage away, even knowing she was responsible for the destruction around them. He could forgive.

Alex wasn't sure he was ready.

11

ALEX HELPED SAGE mount a white Casmuni stallion. The desert breeds were smaller than Demoran warhorses, and this one was the size of his own mare. Sage didn't need assistance, he just wanted to touch her as much as possible. He kept a hand on her lower leg. "Where's Shadow?" he asked.

The horse he'd had since childhood had been having trouble bearing the weight of a fully armed soldier, so he'd given her care over to Sage. She smiled apologetically. "The cold weather's been hard on her, and I thought the journey might be a little much. She's happy, though. Enjoying retirement. The cook's daughter has been spoiling her rotten."

Alex ran his free hand over the stallion's muzzle. "I assume Lani loaned you this one."

"He's mine, a gift from Banneth." Sage blushed a little, and Alex wondered if the horse was actually meant to be a wedding present. "He sent several more for King Raymond."

Alex handed up the reins, debating whether to mention the other night. Clare was adamant that Sage didn't want him to know, and yesterday she'd acted as though nothing had happened, laughing and joking as she practiced the Casmuni fighting art, *tashaivar*, with Lani and Clare. He decided these last moments weren't the time to bring it up, either. His right hand still rested on her leg. When he finally let go, she'd be gone. "I'll be in Tennegol shortly after you," he said. "Then we'll have lots of time."

The smile she returned didn't quite reach her eyes. "We always say that, and yet it never happens."

"This time it will."

They'd spent last night discussing the implications of Kimisara's new king and regent with Lani, Clare, and his officers. Not even the Casmuni princess was optimistic.

Sage nodded absently. "How many days now?"

"Three hundred forty-eight," he replied without hesitation.

"If we're on the same side of the mountains then." Sage smiled sadly.

"I'll move them out of the way if I have to," Alex promised.

She chuckled, but it only lasted a single breath. A few yards away, Lani's mount stamped its hooves impatiently. The princess tilted her head in the direction of the path back to the road. "Time to go," Sage said.

Alex nodded. "I'll see you soon," he said. "I love you."

"I love you, too," she whispered before tugging the reins to one side. The horse turned around, and Alex's hand slipped away. When she reached Lani and Clare, together they led the way up the trail to the Jovan Road. Alex watched the group until all had left the camp, then turned back to his tent with a sigh. Today the Norsari were focusing on knife fighting and throwing, competing to find the best among them for a special platoon, but the other officers would have to handle it. He had all the less important correspondence to catch up on.

That was what no one told you about command. All the administration work meant less time actually soldiering. He'd observed his father enough to expect some of it, but he also felt like it was a test: sift out the important parts and delegate the rest. He was terrible at delegating. Casseck had chastised him more than once for not passing tasks on to him or others.

He stared at the stack of parchments on his desk. They were already sorted into critical and noncritical, and sometime last night Sage had further organized them by topic—supply, army-wide general messages, current events summarized by each province's ruling duke, annual reports on road conditions. Each perfectly fit his officers' collateral duties: Hatfield, Casseck, Tanner, and Nadira. It was like she knew. Maybe Cass had put her up to it.

Alex turned and walked out of the tent, calling out to the first squire he saw.

The fourteen-year-old came running. "Yes, Major?" he gasped, his voice cracking out of nervousness as much as because of his age.

Alex pointed behind him with his thumb. "Inform all the officers they each have a stack of dispatches to attend to on my desk. I want a summary from each by tonight."

The teenager saluted and ran off, and Alex headed for the training grounds, loosening the dagger at his belt as he went. He was a soldier first and foremost. Everything else could wait.

Despite missing Sage, Alex was in a good mood that evening as he leisurely read the personal correspondence he normally set aside until official dispatches were taken care of. All the officers but Cass had made their reports on the contents of their stack, and none had taken more than ten minutes. In total, they'd each spent only an hour of their time and saved four or five of his own. Next time he wouldn't hesitate to divide the task up.

Alex finished another letter and set it aside. Mother was over the moon about his sister Serena's new baby, but she sounded eager to visit him when he arrived in Tennegol in a few weeks. He was the only son she had left, now that Charlie was gone.

The last parchment was a brief note from Colonel Traysden, the minister of intelligence, which was slightly unusual in that it was personal. Alex would've expected it to pertain to the Norsari, as the spymaster had also been the commander when they were disbanded over twenty years ago, but instead it was about Sage.

Once again I congratulate you on your promotion, Major. We will let you be the one to share the news with Mistress Fowler.

It was straightforward on the surface, but Alex had been promoted five months ago, and Sage had been there when he received the notification. Colonel Traysden was getting on in years—he was older than Alex's father, the commanding general of the western army—but his mind was sharp as a razor. Knowing Traysden would never have made such a mistake, Alex scanned the words over and over, searching for a pattern or a code embedded within. Nothing.

He was still frowning at the letter when Casseck walked in, carrying the dispatches he'd been assigned. Alex glanced up. "Report."

Cass handed him a page. "Here's a list of the pertinent changes in army regulations from the past year."

Alex dropped Traysden's note and perused Casseck's, which was also short. Hardly anything in that package had applied to the Norsari. "Very well." He looked up at his friend again. "Thanks," he said, referring to both the summary and helping him delegate it.

The captain nodded but didn't turn away. His lips pinched with the same suppressed smile he'd worn when Sage had arrived. "There was one other change you might be interested in." Cass pulled a set of pages from under his left arm and dropped them in front of Alex. "Article Twenty-Nine."

Alex knew that particular regulation by heart. He'd tried to find a way around it, but the simple language had made it impossible. Casseck grinned as Alex snatched the parchment up to read it himself.

And suddenly Colonel Traysden's letter made perfect sense.

12

THE CASMUNI RETINUE traveled slowly, a consequence of its size and the cold weather, which included snow in the second week. Sage had wondered how Lani's shivering attendant Feshamay would handle waking up to her first snowfall. She was surprised when the girl turned to Sage and whispered that it was the most beautiful thing she'd ever seen. Feshamay never complained about the cold again—as long as snow was present.

Three weeks out from the Norsari camp, the road left the trees and opened into the valley. Sage eagerly searched the northeast slopes of the lower mountains for the first signs of the capital city. As Tennegol came into view, she pointed it out to Lani, who rode next to her, bundled as heavily as ever. The princess squinted at the snow-covered roofs and domes in stark contrast to the evergreen trees outside the city walls. Casmun's own capital of Osthiza was built in terraces over a small mountain of stone, so Sage thought the sight would impress her friend. Instead, Lani pursed her lips. "I cannot decide whether your city appears to be tumbling down from the palace above or climbing up to it." She cocked her head to the side. "Or perhaps it was built in the valley and then pulled up like a blanket to keep the mountain warm."

Sage chuckled and nudged her horse forward. She'd named the young stallion Snow, as his color warranted. "As if this country needs more of it," Lani had said. Now the princess looked back over the bare lower plains dotted with skeletal trees. "I think I prefer Casmuni deserts to Demoran ones."

"It's not a desert," Sage said. "In spring and summer the entire valley is green. Most of our fruit is grown here."

"Your *snow* cannot hide from me that everything now is dead or dying," retorted Lani. "If it comforts you not to call that a desert, I will humor you."

A royal procession exited the city gates and came to meet them. Sage recognized the copper tints of Prince Nicholas's hair before she could see his face. Beside him, a rider with golden curls bounced along, who at first glance appeared to be the queen, until Sage saw it was Rose. The princess had changed quite a bit in the last eleven months. Now fourteen, it was very easy to see the woman she would soon become. Lani's long-term plan of uniting Casmun with Demora by marriage suddenly seemed plausible, and Sage wasn't sure how she felt about it.

Nicholas looked proud to have been chosen to lead the delegation, but it was the right kind of pride—a sort of gratitude rather than arrogance. He rode up to them and bowed from his saddle. Rose stayed back a little, but lowered her head in greeting

"It is lovely to see My Princess again," said Nicholas in Casmuni. "I and my sister"—he gestured behind him and Rose nodded again—"welcome you to Tennegol."

"It is well to see you, Nikkolaz," Lani said, though her attention was fixed on Rose, whose cheeks were flushed from cold and excitement. "Your sister is even lovelier than Saizsch has told me."

When Nicholas translated, Rose's smile faltered as she appeared to grasp the implications of the foreign princess's interest in her. Her blue-green eyes darted to Sage on Lani's right, and Sage smiled reassuringly.

"You must thank Palachessa for her kind words," Rose said haltingly. "I look forward to sharing water with her."

Very good. She referred to Lani properly as My Princess and knew not to speak to her directly until they'd been formally introduced. Lani looked pleased when Nicholas again translated. She twisted in the saddle to speak to her maids. "Who has the water? We can do this now."

Sage put her arm out to stop Lani from reaching back. "My Princess, I expect our king and queen wish to share water and give names to you all at once with proper ceremony."

"Oh, yes, that will be better." Lani turned back to Nicholas. "You may take us to the palace now."

The prince hurriedly directed the greeting party to reverse. As Sage, Clare, and Lani made their way to the front with Nicholas and Rose, Lani glanced over at Sage with an arched eyebrow. "Your *Risha* is not the child you described to me."

"She has changed much since I last saw her," said Sage. "But she is still a child."

Lani smirked and looked forward again. "If I know anything about girls her age, she does not think she is."

13

AFTER THE FORMAL sharing of water with the royal family in the throne room, Princess Lani wasted no time in asking to meet with the king's council. As all the lords and ministers were present for her reception—and probably expected the request—the meeting was arranged for the very next morning. Sage and Clare met Lani after breakfast to accompany her.

"Last night, your *Rosa-chessa* expressed an interest in learning *tashaivar*, Saizsch," said Lani, attaching the Casmuni royal title to the princess's name as was their custom. "I think her father agreed to it to please me, rather than her."

King Raymond hadn't been very open to letting his daughters train with weapons, though in her letters, Rose confessed Nicholas had been giving her private lessons. Sage tallied another reason she believed Rose would embrace Lani's plan to have her live in Banneth's court.

Sage and Clare dropped back to enter the council chamber two steps behind the princess. Everyone in the room rose to their feet and bowed. Sage searched for the only council member she'd met, the minister of intelligence, Colonel Traysden, but he wasn't present. One face she did know was Ash Carter, who stood by his father the king. Sage frowned. The illegitimate prince hadn't been included in last night's reception. It wasn't fair for him to be depended upon so much but kept out of sight, even if he generally preferred to be overlooked.

"Where are *Orianna-sandra* and *Rosa-chessa*?" Lani demanded in accented Demoran. "Is something happened that they are late?"

"Ah," said Sage, trying to recover from the fact that Lani had spoken Demoran, something she'd never heard her do beyond a few words. Apparently she'd been practicing. Sage wondered how much of her translating last night had been unnecessary. "You requested to meet with the king's council, My Princess," she explained.

Lani's greenish-brown eyes swept the room as she frowned in bewilderment. "For talk of a future in Casmun for *Rosa-chessa*, yes. Where is she and her mother?"

Sage knew Lani only appeared clueless when she wanted to. The princess hadn't expected to see Orianna or Rose there, which was why she knew the Demoran words to ask about their absence. Lani wanted the men in the room to explain why they felt it right to discuss and arrange Rose's future without her or her mother present.

To his credit, the king looked ashamed, a blush rising from the fringe of hair over his ears. "I believe there was some misunderstanding as to how deeply we were to discuss such a matter. If Palachessa will excuse us for a few minutes, I will send for them. Mistress Sage, Lady Clare, will you please escort our guest to the gardens? We will send for you when my wife and daughter are on their way."

His answer was complicated enough that Sage had to translate, and Lani nodded magnanimously. "Yes, I will walk until then." She turned and swept out, but once in the passage, the princess dropped her innocent confusion and rolled her eyes at Sage and Clare. "Councils in Demora are the same as in Casmun," she said, switching back to her own language. "Little consideration for those most affected."

"Surely with Darit on Casmun's council now there is more thought," said Sage, referring to the desert warrior who had saved her and Nicholas and was one of Banneth's most trusted friends. He was the interim finance minister when they left, but Lani had mentioned he had since been installed as minister of war. "If My Princess would take a seat, there would be even more."

Lani shrugged. "Perhaps someday I will." After a few turns they entered the palace garden, which was lovely even in the winter months, thanks to a hot spring directed to run through it. As they stepped outside, Lani turned her face to the bright azure sky and sighed a little. "I have much missed the sun. This is the first day without clouds since we left your Norsari."

The three of them strolled between trees and the fountains that steamed a little in the chilly air. Color rose in Sage's cheeks as she remembered the spring Alex had taken her to and how different she wished it could've been. That silly army regulation shouldn't even apply to him; it was meant to guarantee commitment to being an officer, not just joining for the prestige of a commission and a better marriage. Alex had made captain at twenty, three years ahead of the average, and now he was a major. The only thing that threatened his loyalty to the army was that it kept him from being with her.

"I have a question," said Lani, interrupting Sage's brooding. "Why are you called *Miztrez* and not *Lady* like Clare? Is that the title for emissary?"

Sage shook her head. "For that we say *Ambassador*. *Mistress* is the address for a common woman."

Lani frowned. "If *Ambassador* is your true title, why is it not used here?" When Sage shrugged, the princess stopped and stamped her foot. "You have been letting these men call you by the most common address, when you have more regard from my country than all of them put together?"

"She has a point, Sage," Clare said.

Sage shrugged again. "I'm the ambassador. Calling me 'Mistress' does not change that."

"I assure you it does," said Lani. "That is what titles are for, to remind others of the respect you are owed. You cannot perform your duties if that is forgotten."

A flush crept up Sage's neck. "It's difficult for me to demand such a thing. You were born a chessa and taught from the cradle to expect it. I was born a nothing."

"So was Darit. Now he is minister of war, second only to the king in Casmun. You, too, are no longer nothing."

"I thought My Princess was second." Sage arched an eyebrow. "It sounds like you are also reluctant to assert your place."

Lani's scarlet lips twisted up in a smile as she took Sage's and Clare's arms and continued on the path. "Then it is well we are here to remind each other."

The three of them had reached the far end and turned around when a messenger approached and bowed low. "If Her Highness would return to the council chambers, the queen and princess will meet her outside the doors."

Sage translated and Lani nodded cheerfully. They headed for the main passage, where Ash Carter waited with Orianna and her eldest daughter. As the group came together, Rose released her half brother's arm and hugged Sage. "Thank you for insisting we be included."

"Thank *Alaniah-chessa*," said Sage. "Your happiness in all of this is most important to her."

Lani waved off the gratitude of both the queen and princess. "I have half a mind to make those men wait for us a little longer, but my toes are aching with cold. Shall we?"

14

SAGE WAS PREPARING for bed when she heard a knock on the door of her suite. Since Lani's insistence at the morning's council meeting that Sage be addressed by her title of ambassador, she was feeling much less self-conscious about the grand rooms she'd been given. As the princess said, they were as much to show other people her valuable role as anything else. She'd even consented to letting the maids help her undress, though their shock at seeing her burns was a little uncomfortable. They'd been dismissed for the night, however, so Sage pulled a dressing robe around her and answered the door herself.

A page gave her a handwritten note from the queen, asking if Sage could come to her chambers to discuss a personal matter. Sage hadn't had a private moment to speak to Orianna since arriving yesterday, and she was more than happy to go. In re-dressing herself, Sage chose a gown the queen had given her shortly before she'd left last year. She'd never had a chance to properly thank Her Majesty, let alone wear it.

The queen herself opened the door, wearing a welcoming smile. Her plain dressing gown and the blond hair twisted into a simple knot at the back of her head was as informal as Sage had ever seen.

"Thank you for coming, Sage. I wanted a few minutes with you before the king returns." Orianna directed her to a seat by the fire. "You look lovely in that color, my dear. I'm glad to finally see you're able to wear it."

"Thank you, Your Majesty. This is my favorite Demoran dress. Your taste is exquisite."

The queen sat across from her. "I noticed you said Demoran dresses. Princess Alaniah's clothes are causing quite a fashion uproar. We'll be seeing similar dresses on ladies at court within a week."

"The *chessa* will be more than flattered, I'm sure." Sage started to fold her hands in her lap, but the queen reached across the space between them and took the left one.

"I'm told you were gravely injured in the battle last summer," Orianna whispered, rubbing her thumb over the shiny and mottled skin exposed at her wrist. Sage only nodded. "You have suffered much for Demora," the queen said sadly, squeezing and then releasing Sage's fingers. "It is not something I will ever forget."

Sage flushed and tugged her sleeve lower. "I'm only a loyal subject," she said.

"Which you proved again today in council. I'm most gratified Rose and I were included."

"That was Lan—Alaniah," Sage said. She wouldn't take credit for what she hadn't done. "I'm ashamed to say I was ready to begin without you."

"Sometimes it takes an outsider to see where things are wrong." The queen sat back and studied Sage with solemn blue-green eyes. "Now I need you to tell me what you did not say this morning."

"Your Majesty?" She hadn't lied or misrepresented anything. Nor had Lani—the princess had been simple and frank in presenting her idea, though Sage had softened some of it in translation.

"I need you to tell me if you approve of Princess Alaniah's invitation. Do you believe everything she says? Will my daughter be respected and cared for?"

Sage thought carefully before answering, as the queen's trust in her was frightening. "The Casmuni king is earnest in his intentions. He wants to solidify friendship between our nations and thinks this will show his people that. It's a wonderful opportunity for Rose to learn and also represent Demora. I know she can do it well."

Orianna twisted her hands. "Is there a Casmuni prince close to her age?"

Lani hadn't mentioned Hasseth, but the queen was no fool. "Banneth's son is twelve," said Sage. "I think they'd be most pleased if a match came of it, but I swear to you that they will not force such an arrangement." She thought over every conversation she'd had with Lani in the past month. "Whether that happens or not, I believe a secondary purpose of having Rose there is to teach Banneth's daughter Reza about Demora. Perhaps someday she will be considered a match for Prince Nicholas. That would be many years away, but the groundwork might as well be laid now."

Sage paused again, thinking of some of Her Majesty's frustrations in her position. "The earlier Rose becomes involved in matters of state, the more knowledge she will gain, and the less she will be put aside in decisions later. I know you would wish that."

The queen nodded as she gazed into the fire. "I knew this day would come," she said softly. "It is quite a burden to carry and give birth to a child who can never be truly yours." Orianna shook her head as she blinked back tears. "Rose is eager to go. Why would she want to leave me?"

Sage searched for a delicate way of saying that Rose had been so restricted by her upbringing that stretching her wings was not only desirable, but necessary. "She has no fear because she doesn't understand the difficulties that lie ahead, but that's a lesson we all must learn in some way. King Banneth is a good and honest man. She will be safe and cared for, I promise."

Orianna managed a smile. "Thank you," she whispered.

"I'm glad I could set Your Majesty's mind at ease." Sage sat back, exhaling heavily. "Are there any other matters you wished to discuss?"

The queen's mannerism suddenly changed, a mischievous smile tugging at the corners of her mouth. "Now that you mention it, I heard you visited Major Quinn on the way here."

"I assure you the goodwill between the Norsari and the Casmuni guards was more than worth the delay in our journey," Sage said quickly, hoping her face didn't flush too much.

Orianna's smile widened and her eyes twinkled. "Is there any news you want to share?"

"Um." Sage blinked in confusion. "No, Your Majesty. We were only there for two days."

The queen watched her for a several seconds, as though she thought Sage was hiding something. Then she shrugged, momentarily disappointed, before smiling again. "I think I should invite Lady Quinn and her daughters to visit while the major is here."

Alex's mother had welcomed Sage with open arms, and his sisters were a clever, cheerful bunch, but Sage was rather jealous of what little time she had with Alex. It pained her to agree that was a lovely idea. They talked of small matters for the next few minutes, and Sage stifled more than one yawn, thinking longingly of the soft bed waiting for her. Fortunately, the door opened and King Raymond strode in, Ash Carter right behind him. Sage and the queen rose to their feet and curtsied. Finally she'd be dismissed.

"Ah, Ambassador," the king said cheerfully. "I'm sorry to have called you this late, but I imagine you're eager to know why I summoned you to Tennegol."

Suddenly sleep was the last thing on Sage's mind. In all the fuss over Lani, it had been frustrating to have the reason for her own urgent summons seemingly forgotten by everyone. "I am ready to serve as His Majesty requires," she answered.

Raymond gestured for Sage and his wife to sit, and Ash dragged two more comfortable chairs close to the fire. "Before we begin, Ambassador," said Ash. "I understand you visited Major Quinn on the way here. May I offer—"

"I've already been assured my nephew is in good health," the queen interrupted. "And Norsari training is progressing admirably." The second sentence was directed at her husband.

Both Ash and the king stared at Orianna, then exchanged glances with each other. Sage shifted uncomfortably. It was bad enough that the royal family knew about her and Alex, but to openly talk about their opportunities for private time together was downright embarrassing.

"Well then," said the king, turning his bright hazel eyes to Sage. "First, I'd like to thank you for the work you did today in council and last night at the reception." He smiled a little. "Princess Alaniah is quite a force of nature. Am I correct in assuming you did not translate everything she said with complete accuracy?"

Sage cringed. "Some phrases do not sound right when directly translated, Majesty. I promise no true meanings were lost."

The king chuckled. "You are becoming quite the diplomat." Before she could respond, he waved his hand to indicate she should not. "Which is why you are here. You know King Ragat of Kimisara died last summer?"

"Yes, sire, but little else." Alex was the one who would deal with the result. Were they trying to tell her she wouldn't see him for years? "Much will change with the new ruler."

King Raymond nodded as he studied her, but it was Ash who spoke. "Kimisara has said it wants to negotiate an end to the current conflict."

Sage's mouth dropped open. She wasn't sure what she'd expected, but it wasn't that. Years—generations—of fighting did not simply end. "Ca-can we trust they're serious?" she stammered.

"We have reason to believe so, or at least some of them are," said Ash. He was the right hand of Demora's spymaster. He would know. "Before we even considered it, however, we laid down a strict set of terms for a truce. They've kept to them for the last two months, and so we've agreed to meet with them on the spring equinox."

The king nodded soberly. "If these negotiations are successful, they could be the first step toward a lasting peace."

Sage felt a thrill to her core as she imagined it. Peace.

She and Alex could have a real life together. Separated often by duty, yes, but Alex's parents had managed it for almost twenty-five years, even raising a large family. Sage was so lost in imagining the future that she nearly missed the king's next words.

"Your presence is requested at these talks. Ambassador."

There was an emphasis on her title. Sage jumped a little as she came back into the present. "I am . . ." She struggled to envision the role she'd play. "I am to report on all this to Casmun?"

King Raymond shook his head, his eyes never leaving hers. "Along with the crown prince, I wish you to be my personal representative."

15

SAGE'S MOUTH DROPPED open in shock. She was technically an ambassador, but to Casmun, a nation she knew better than any other Demoran. That appointment was logical. This was unthinkable.

"Your Majesty, I'm not qualified—"

"You are. You speak their language, and you have intimate knowledge of recent events between our nations. You also have the perspective of Casmuni interests."

"Sire, they will never take an eighteen-year-old girl seriously!" Panic made her nearly shout.

"You'll be nineteen by the time these talks finish," said Ash with a teasing light in his black eyes. Sage threw a scowl at him before she could stop herself.

The king only smiled and pulled a folded parchment from his blue velvet coat. "Queen Regent Zoraya herself will be attending."

"Then she must expect you to attend, Your Majesty," Sage insisted.

"Perhaps, but I only have this note from her." He offered her the page. "It may be a ruse, to lure me from Tennegol."

Ash leaned forward, his dark eyes now serious. "Reports indicate Queen Zoraya is exerting her strength, but she has vulnerabilities. Prince Robert will be the primary negotiator and have royal authority, but we believe she will best respond to another woman."

Sage's eyes drifted to Orianna, who'd been silent. "Then why not Her Majesty? They're both queens and mothers; surely there's a bond there."

An uncomfortable silence stretched out between them all until Sage realized why. "I'm expendable," she whispered.

The king shook his head. "Not expendable, merely less of an appealing target should things go wrong."

In the last couple years, Kimisar had made two attempts to take royal captives for ransom in shielding their retreats. Sage had been involved in thwarting both. Sending Robert was already risking enough. She'd walked into dangerous situations like this before, though not with quite so much foreknowledge. Nor with as much scarring.

You can turn it down, Alex had said when she was appointed ambassador. *You've already given so much.*

He'd known she wouldn't, though. Sage flexed her arm unconsciously, feeling the tight skin pull across her elbow. Others would suffer if the war continued. Clare's scars were internal, but they wouldn't stop her from duty any more than the burns would stop Sage. With her friend by her side—because there was no possibility of going without Clare—maybe they could reach this queen in ways others couldn't.

Alex wouldn't be happy about this. Sage pictured him ranting against his uncle the king for putting her in danger. It also meant leaving him behind, as he would often leave her, for the good of Demora, but if he could make that sacrifice, Sage could do no less.

She took a deep breath to steady her words. "I will endeavor to serve Demora as I am called to."

Everyone smiled and relaxed a little. They'd known how much they were asking.

"When do I leave?" Sage asked. Queen Zoraya's note said the talks would be at the Arrowhead Crossroad in Tasmet. The equinox was six weeks away, but the journey would take nearly a month.

"As soon as possible," said Ash. "But you might as well wait for the Norsari to get here." He grinned. "After all, they're the ones we're assigning as your protection."

It wasn't thoughts of the peace talks that kept Sage awake into the wee hours of the morning, nor was it imagining a mission with Alex—it was how the queen, the king, and Ash had all expected her to have some kind of news. Alex had postponed dealing with most of his messages in favor of spending time with her. Would that reflect badly on him if they realized it? Or had she missed something in her own messages?

Sage threw aside the bedclothes and went to her desk, where she searched through all the parchments she'd received in the last few weeks. Many were regular reports, such as the annual summary of changes and additions to laws of the land made in the past year. Alex had gotten one, too. Her hand froze in the act of setting the page down.

One thing he'd received was a similar compilation of army policies and statutes.

The silly smiles. Hints of congratulations. Inviting Alex's family to visit.

There was only one regulation that affected her. While it didn't seem possible, there was no other explanation she could come up with.

Sage shoved back from the desk and yanked on her boots. Rather than change again, she wrapped a thick dressing robe over her nightgown. No one else would be roaming the passages at this hour. She let herself out of her room and headed straight for the library.

The heavy double doors were locked, but instead of waking the master of books, Sage pulled a long metal pin from her pocket. Lock picking had been a Norsari lesson she'd attended last spring. She doubted anyone had expected those skills to be put to use in the palace, however.

Tumblers fell into place, and she turned the knob quietly and eased the door open. As a royal ambassador, she had the right to access the library at any hour she chose, but it would probably be less awkward if no one discovered her entering without a key. Sage slipped inside, deeply inhaling the familiar scent of parchment, leather bindings, and dust. Light from the half-moon streamed in from the windows of the dome overhead, allowing her to find a lantern quickly. She lit the wick with a slight tremor—fire contained in hearths and lamps were tolerable from a safe distance, but sparks and flame at her fingertips were the stuff of nightmares—and closed the glass over it before beginning her search.

The military section was a familiar one. Her gaze drifted across the spines of books on warfare and tactics. Rather than search for the most recent full edition of rules, Sage opted for a ledger that documented army-wide messages. She flipped to the most recently dated pages until she found what she wanted: the summary of changes made in the year 510—the ones Alex would've received. Her finger drifted down the lines of script until she came to Article Twenty-Nine: Regulations Concerning Married Soldiers.

Subsection Fifteen:

Previous: No commissioned officer shall be united in marriage until the age of twenty-four.

Current: No commissioned officer shall be united in marriage until the age of twenty-four or the attainment of the rank of major, whichever comes first.

Sweet Spirit.

16

USING A SWIFT-TRAVELING tactic he learned from the Casmuni army, Alex brought the Norsari into the capital two days earlier than expected, hoping to impress the king and the royal council. He led the soldiers onto the palace parade grounds, struggling to keep his eyes from wandering to the observation platform above. Whether or not she knew about the change to Article Twenty-Nine, Sage would be up there, bouncing on the soles of her feet as her gray eyes glowed with excitement—an excitement he'd felt, too, until cold reality shattered it.

But he still had to be worthy of that pride.

The men came to a halt and pivoted as one to face the king and assembled ministers. Alex raised his hand in salute.

"Norsari Battalion One, reporting for orders in service of His Majesty," he called in a voice that echoed over the enclosed grounds. The king smiled and returned the salute. Colonel Traysden wasn't there, which was a surprise, but Ash Carter stood at his side. Word was that Ash had finally accepted an officer's commission and moved away from regular army operations, spending a great deal of time with the master of intelligence.

"Very well done, Major," said King Raymond. Alex dropped his hand when he did.

There was no way he could avoid seeing her now. Sage stood to the king's left, wearing a heavy cloak over what had to be that green dress she'd worn in Casmun. The one that took his breath away. Her cheeks were flushed, and though Alex couldn't have described what about her smile made him conclude it, he had no doubt that she'd heard the news.

Damn.

Focused on him, she didn't appear to notice the patronizing smirks the noblemen around her wore. One of the ministers leaned closer to the king, speaking loud enough for Alex to hear.

"Such an *outstanding* display by your nephew, Your Majesty."

His gut clenched. It was already starting.

"How *accomplished* he is for his age." Sarcasm dripped from the adjective, letting everyone know the speaker's true opinion. The agricultural minister had a son in the army who was several years older than Alex. He'd only made captain last fall.

Alex dropped his gaze as others chimed in, competing to point out his connections, what made him special.

"The very image of his father, wouldn't you agree?"

"The Quinn legacy is secure now."

Alex ground his teeth as he stared straight ahead. Somehow he'd hoped the Norsari arrival would put those doubts to rest, that people would remember they'd won an impossible battle last summer and made new allies, but none of that mattered. He was nothing but a privileged child riding the wagon of his father's success. Someone the rules didn't apply to.

Or worse, had rules changed for him.

He pivoted around and gave the command for dismissal. As the Norsari headed toward the barracks for a much-deserved evening of rest and relaxation, Alex glanced up again. Sage was frowning at the cluster of noblemen. The king caught his eye and gestured for him to come up to meet them. By the time Alex climbed up the stairs to the platform, Sage had disappeared, he knew, to let him focus on duties.

It was hours before Alex made it to the barracks himself. Due to his rank and position, he had his own room this time, one with proper furniture. A note lay on the table, but he ignored it and picked up the bags the squire had brought in and set them on the bed. Slowly and deliberately, Alex unpacked a few things and placed them where he could use them over the next week. As he set aside clothing to be washed and mended, his eyes darted to the folded parchment. If he read it, he had to deal with it.

Yet he hungered for anything of hers so much that it wasn't long before he picked it up. The precise script was short and direct.

You know where I'll be.

Alex closed his eyes and exhaled through his nose. How long had she been up there in the garden, eyes shining, trembling all over, waiting for him to bring her the news they'd wanted to hear for almost two years?

Casseck knocked on the door before leaning into the room. "Didn't expect you to still be here," he said.

With a sigh, Alex dropped the parchment back onto the table. "I'm about to leave."

His friend eyed him with concern. "Better to tell her sooner rather than later."

Alex pivoted to face him. "This is the right decision, isn't it?"

Cass shook his head. "Oh, no. I didn't get involved in your last fight, and I sure as hell am not doing it now."

"I know how you stepped in before, Ethelreldregon." Alex narrowed his eyes as he emphasized his friend's given name like it was a weapon. "Both at the beginning and the end."

Casseck winced. He detested his first name, but Alex had intercepted much of the hazing it had attracted in their childhood and that gave him unspoken permission to use it—sparingly. "She might actually understand. It's not as if you're changing what the situation was always supposed to be."

Alex snorted. "How much money are you willing to back that idea up with?" When Cass didn't answer, Alex turned back to the table. "That's what I thought." He picked up the note and tore off a section of the parchment that wasn't written on. As Casseck watched, Alex carefully scrawled three sentences on the piece before signing it and folding it in half and handing it to his friend. "Do me a favor and take this to her room. Leave it where she'll find it when she comes back."

Cass hesitated, then nodded and took the note. "Good luck."

The garden was warmer than outside the castle walls, but the trees had still shed their leaves for the season. He could see Sage's outline through the bare branches of the weeping willow. As he approached, she stood from where she sat on a blanket, but waited until he came into the shelter of the tree before stepping closer.

No matter what came after, he could enjoy this moment. Alex nudged her cloak aside and wrapped his arms around Sage's waist and lifted her up as she threw her arms over his shoulders and kissed him. For several seconds he savored the taste of her mouth and the feel of her warm body against his. His determination wavered. How could he want anyone—anything—more than he wanted her?

Sage pulled her face back and bit her lip, smiling shyly. Alex brushed his nose along the length of hers. "I hope you haven't been waiting long."

"Not too long," she said softly. She tightened her arms around his neck and sank against his chest. They fit together so well it made him ache. "Oh, Alex, no one can stop talking about the Norsari. Even those who doubted you were up to the task were blown away. I'm so proud."

Even those who doubted.

Alex slowly lowered her to her feet. "We need to talk."

Sage nodded and sat back down on the blanket she'd spread out, pulling him with her. He settled as close as he could and held her hands. They were small compared to his own. Calloused, but not as much. Paler. More scarred. He turned her left hand over and gently ran a thumb over the healed burns. She shivered.

"Sage . . ." He hesitated, hoping she'd say something so he could gauge the best way to proceed, but she didn't want to ruin this moment for him. "I think you've actually heard my news," he said finally.

"What news?" she asked, blinking innocently.

"You can't fool me, Sage. Who spilled it?"

Her face fell. "No one. I just . . ."

"Figured it out," he finished. Of course she had. Well, at least now he didn't have to go choke someone for making this more difficult.

"I still want you to tell me," she said, squeezing his hand.

"Does anyone else know? Did you make any preparations?"

"Of course not." Sage shook her head, then looked a little guilty. "Well, I told Clare. I thought the news would be a little hard for her at first, which it was, but after a few days she was able to be happy for us. She promised not to tell anyone yet."

A slight relief. Alex stared down at their hands, as if the right words were inked into the skin there.

"I don't need anything special," Sage said. "I'd rather just have you and me and our closest friends. The queen said your mother and sisters will be here soon. We can wait for them."

Mother surely knew about Article Twenty-Nine. Father never kept anything from her. She'd probably heard before the council did.

Alex didn't care for a big wedding, either. He'd nearly jumped on his horse and chased Sage down the night he'd become aware of the change, ready to take vows at the first chapel they could find—until he realized what else it meant.

"Have you heard where we're going next?" she asked, distracting him from the memory. Her gray eyes sparkled in the dim starlight.

Alex nodded silently. Uncle Raymond had already told him his first mission would be to attend talks with Kimisara. Sage was to represent Demora alongside the crown prince, and the Norsari presence would provide security while making it clear the last treaty between their nations had been nullified. Under the agreements over twenty years ago, the elite unit had been disbanded as a condition of peace.

That peace had not been kept, and so the Norsari were back.

It would also be the first time the regular army would see them in action. All eyes would be on them. On him.

And while Alex was glad to be the one charged with Sage's safety, it complicated matters even more.

She was still waiting for him to speak, an expectant smile on her face. Alex took a deep breath. "Sage, we can't get married now."

Sage furrowed her brow, confused but not angry. Yet. "But I thought the regulation said—"

He put his fingers to her lips to stop her. "Let me be more specific."

More honest. It was what she deserved.

"I don't *want* to get married."

The words hung heavily in the air between them, both the truth and a lie at the same time.

17

HE DIDN'T WANT to marry her?

Alex's fingers were still on her lips, and his eyes were pleading, but Sage didn't understand.

"Please, let me explain," he begged, though she hadn't said anything. She hadn't been able to find the words.

"I found out the night after you left. I wanted to come to you as soon as I heard. But then . . ."

A sudden tightness in her chest made Sage struggle to take even shallow breaths. He'd been as happy about the news as she had. So why–?

"You changed your mind?" Sage said, hearing her own voice as from the bottom of a well. "You don't want to marry me anymore?"

His other hand came up to frame her face. "No, Sage, I do," he said earnestly. "I just don't want to marry you *now*."

When Sage was eight, she and Father had come across a small lake with a high overhang of rock. They watched boys older and younger than her leap off the ledge into the water, screaming in joyful terror on the long way down. She'd pleaded with her father to let her go up there. *Are you sure?* he'd asked a dozen times, and she begged over and over until he relented. But then he'd taken her to the top of the shelf, and she'd peered over the edge and discovered she wasn't nearly as ready as she'd thought she was. In the past months, she'd worried that when the day finally came, marrying Alex would make her feel the same way. *It's much bigger than I realized.*

But it wasn't her who felt that way. It was him.

Sage leaned away, dizzy. "Let me guess," she said dully. "This isn't about me."

Alex nodded, apparently not catching her reference to their argument last year, which had been about going with the Norsari to the training camp. Then, he'd worried that in a dangerous situation, he'd choose her over his responsibilities to his men. But this time his duty would be to *her*.

She sat back, feeling herself collapse from within, as though everything inside her had been ripped out.

"Don't you see, Sage?" His tone became pleading. "The regulation change will only ever apply to me. This was done specifically for us."

"And you don't think we deserve it?" She twisted away, disbelief receding enough for anger to claw its way into her heart. "You don't think we deserve some kind of reward for what we've sacrificed, for what we've achieved?"

"Not everyone will see it that way!" Alex said. "They'll see the general's son being given special treatment *again*. The king's nephew getting a whole law changed just for him. You heard them today. None of them believe I deserve this promotion. Do you think they're saying anything different in the regular army?"

Sage's cheeks raged with heat. She'd heard the sarcasm and veiled insults, but none of that mattered to her. "You'll change their minds when they see what the Norsari can do," she insisted, desperately trying to hold back tears.

Alex shook his head sadly. "Not without going into battle, I won't, and I can't expect men to fight with me if they don't respect me." His voice dropped to a whisper. "I'm teetering on the edge of spectacular failure, Sage. I can't afford anything that looks unfair. It'll only be used against me by those who don't want or expect me to succeed."

But he'd *earned* everything. He'd already succeeded where others would have failed. Couldn't he believe that?

Couldn't he believe her?

Apparently not.

The thought pounded in her mind, driving a stake deeper into her heart with every echo. Sage yanked her hand away and pushed to her feet so suddenly Alex nearly fell over backward. "I need to go."

He was beside her in an instant, straightening her cloak. "I'll walk you to your room."

"No, thank you," she said coldly.

His hands stopped. "Are you sure?" He searched her face, eyes fraught with worry.

"I just need to be alone right now." She couldn't even bear to look at him.

Alex swallowed and nodded. "All right."

"Good night, Alex." She turned to walk away, but he grabbed her arm and pulled her gently to him. After a moment of hesitation, he turned her chin up and kissed her softly. She barely felt his lips, but she tasted the apology he couldn't put into words.

He continued holding her face, lowering his forehead to hers for a few seconds before finally releasing her. "Good night, Sage."

She left without another word, without looking back. The path to her rooms was short, but Sage wasn't sure how much longer she could hold herself together. This morning she'd been so happy, thinking the world was hers.

And though she'd told the king and queen she'd go to the peace talks, she hadn't really felt sure she could handle it until Ash said the Norsari would be going. She could do anything with Alex by her side. Maybe Their Majesties knew that, too.

Except he didn't want to be by her side right now.

Where did that leave her?

Sage let herself into her room and bolted the door. Thinking she'd be out late with Alex, she'd dismissed her maids for the evening, and there was no one to help her undress. As she tugged awkwardly at the laces in the back, Sage remembered thinking earlier that maybe Alex would be willing to help her get ready for bed. And then . . .

The dress came loose enough for her to shift around, and Sage twisted out of the sleeves and bodice, trying not to think of the hungry expression on Alex's face the first time he'd seen her in it. She hurled the gown across the room, unable to see where it landed through the tears now streaming down her face. She didn't bother with nightclothes, just crawled into the big feather bed still wearing the silk underdress. As Sage folded the coverlet back, a scrap of folded parchment on her pillow caught her eye. She opened it without thinking. There were only three lines inside.

I love you now more than ever. Please believe facing you tonight was the most difficult thing I've had to do. All I have, all that I am, is yours forever.

Love,

Alex

Sage crumpled the note and threw it at the fireplace.

18

AT LEAST SHE hadn't told anyone, Sage reminded herself as she lay in bed the next morning, willing herself to get up. She wouldn't have to endure questions and looks of pity from anyone except Clare and the king and queen. Maybe Alex's mother and sisters. She liked them all, but Sage wasn't sure whose side they would be on, or which would be worse—pity for her or agreement with Alex.

A soft rapping on the door made her groan. Dealing with cheerful maids wouldn't help her mood, but a hot bath might. She couldn't have one without the other. By the fifth series of knocks, they were loud enough that she couldn't claim to have slept through them. "Coming," Sage called, rolling out of bed. She tugged on a dressing gown and went to the door, rubbing her face and hoping it wasn't obvious she'd been crying.

Clare stood outside, looking guilty. Next to her was Lani, which explained the vigorous knocking. Both studied Sage anxiously. "Who told you?" Sage asked in Casmuni so anyone who overheard wouldn't understand.

"Captain Casseck," said Clare, wringing her hands. "He asked me to leave a note from the major on your pillow, and of course I had to ask why."

Lani scowled. "I am still angry you did not tell me of this change of rules. Perhaps if you had, I could have arranged so much for your wedding that he could not have done this."

"The major is under a great deal of strain," said Clare. "He must not be thinking clearly." Lani rolled her eyes.

"I don't want to talk about it," said Sage, turning away from the door but leaving it open so her friends could enter. The pair followed her inside and took seats as she did by the hearth, which had burned out in the night. Sage stared at the floor. Alex's note hadn't made it all the way to the fireplace and lay in a crumpled wad at her feet.

"Clare tells me you are going to speak with the Kimisar," said Lani. Sage nodded and nudged the parchment with her toe, wanting to be rid of it but unable to make herself push it into the ashes. "I have decided to speak with your Raymond King about the wisdom of me also attending. They are your nation's talks so I would not wish to intrude, but I believe Banneth would want me to go."

Clare gave Lani a light kick, and the princess glanced at her before continuing. "Of course, I will only pursue this if you believe it is a good idea, Saizsch." She paused. "This is your mission, and I will respect that."

Sage couldn't help but smile. Lani's enthusiasm was just what she would need to get through the next few weeks. "Thank you, My Princess," she said. "I would be most pleased to have you along."

"I am well thanked," said Lani cheerfully. "Do not worry, Saizsch. We will make Ah'lecks regret this. He will change his mind before we depart."

"Oh, Sweet Spirit, no!" moaned Sage. She put her face in her hands. "Lani, please promise me you will stay out of this."

Lani crossed her arms and slouched in her cushioned chair. "I am only trying to help."

"I know," said Sage with a sigh. "And for that I am grateful." She lowered her hands to look at her friend, whose scarlet lips pouted beneath her fierce green eyes. Even before breakfast Lani wore face paint. "I just wish to keep things simple."

"Good luck with that." But the princess smiled a little. "I will obey your wish, but know I am prepared to make things complicated anytime you change your thoughts."

Clare bent down to pick up the note. Sage didn't object as her friend opened and smoothed the parchment over her knee to read Alex's words. "What are your plans now?" Clare asked.

"I don't know," Sage said. "We were supposed to spend all his spare moments together, but that's pretty much ruined."

"Because I was thinking," said Clare. "What if we left early?"

Sage glanced up in surprise. Leave for Arrowhead without Alex?

"If we want to go into these talks prepared, my sister, Sophia, would be the best person to talk to," Clare continued. "She has firsthand knowledge of everything that's happened and understands the concerns of the local people."

Sophia was only a little bit older than Clare, and they'd been close growing up, though they hadn't seen each other since Sophia had married Count Rewel D'Amiran. Her husband had been the younger brother of the duke who'd allied with the Kimisar and started this whole mess two years ago, when Sage had been working as the matchmaker's apprentice. After everything went wrong and Duke Morrow D'Amiran was killed at Tegann, Rewel fled from Jovan and deep into Tasmet, taking Sophia, who was carrying his child. A few months later she gave birth to a girl, and the count abandoned her and the baby to General Quinn's advancing forces. No one had heard from him since, but it was assumed he'd thrown himself on the mercy of the Kimisar.

The whole situation angered Sage like no other, not only because poor Sophia had been given to an abusive husband, but because it was the D'Amirans' scheme that had ended with the battle at Tegann and the death of Alex's brother Charlie. She'd been glad to hear from King Raymond that one of her priorities in these talks was to get Rewel D'Amiran back so he could stand trial.

In the meantime, Sophia and her daughter, Aurelia, resided at Jovan Fortress under a state of quasi-arrest, though no one held her culpable for her husband's actions. As young Aurelia was technically the heir to the province, the king hoped to use her and her mother to stabilize Tasmet once Rewel D'Amiran had been brought to justice.

Sage had already been leaning toward going through Jovan for Clare's sake, but the distance was greater than going through Tegann. In waiting for the Norsari to finish their demonstrations to the council, their caravan wouldn't have enough time to stop at Jovan longer than overnight. If, however, they left ahead of the Norsari, Clare could spend more time with her sister.

Lani looked interested. "If this is south, will the weather be warmer?"

"Much," said Clare, though Sage knew she was exaggerating a little. Most of the better weather would be due to the coming spring.

"Then I am for this," said Lani.

"What about you, ambassador?" asked Clare. The hope on her friend's face shone a ray of light into Sage's pit of misery and self-pity.

Clare had stood by her through everything and put aside her pain to be glad for Sage when they'd thought she'd be marrying Alex now. The idea of making Clare happy raised her own spirits. And it was a good idea. Not only would the countess be a wealth of information, there were few who had more to lose in these talks than she. King Raymond's assurances that she would be taken care of aside, Sophia deserved someone to represent her at the table.

Not to mention Sage had no real reason to stay here now.

Her smile was hard-won but genuine as she said, "I think the sooner we leave, the longer we can visit."

19

ONCE THEY HAD His Majesty's approval, Sage, Clare, and Lani threw themselves into preparations for leaving as soon as possible. It was Lani's idea to arrange only what they would need to get there, then have the rest of the ambassador's retinue and supplies follow on the date originally planned, enabling them to leave sooner. His Majesty then suggested the Norsari travel as though Tennegol's representatives were with them, effectively acting as a decoy as they headed into a possibly dangerous situation. To outsiders, it would appear only a small party was traveling through Jovan. One of Lani's maids and about two-thirds of the Casmuni soldiers would stay in the capital, continuing to learn more about Demora and preparing Rose for her journey.

The distraction of planning was welcome, as was Clare's excitement. Most of Alex's time was taken up with demonstrations and meetings with the king and his council, but he didn't try to visit Sage that day, either because of his duties or because he was avoiding her. Instead, she received a note in the evening, saying he'd heard she was leaving and asking if they could talk. Sage sent the folded page back with her two-word response written at the bottom. *Not tonight.*

Sage wasn't sure she could handle seeing him. His rejection was still as raw and painful as her burns had been in the first weeks, a comparison that only reminded her of how lovingly he had cared for her then. Arranging their departure took two full days, however, and she expected him to seek her out the second day. Lani dressed her that morning, then painted her face and styled her hair—at least as much as Sage would endure—so when she crossed paths with Alex, Sage would look her best.

"He's not going to change his mind," Sage insisted as Lani arranged her sandy locks into a braid that hugged her head like a crown. "No matter how pretty I look."

Lani shrugged as she pushed a jeweled pin into place. "Perhaps not, but you can make him wish he had."

It was pointless, however. She never saw him that day.

After last-minute checklists that night, Sage was trying to think of excuses not to leave Lani's suite, but thanks to Clare's excellent management skills, everything was ready. There was nothing left to do but go to bed, even if sleep wasn't likely.

"The major will come to see us off tomorrow morning, I'm sure," Clare said as they walked back to their rooms together.

"I almost hope he won't," said Sage.

They stopped outside Sage's door. "Do you want me to stay with you tonight?" Clare offered. "I'm all packed, but I can bring my last-minute things to your room."

It was tempting, but Sage knew they'd spend whole the night talking. Just because she wouldn't be able to sleep didn't mean Clare had to suffer, too. "No, I'll be fine," she said. "Get some rest. The journey is long."

Clare squeezed her hand and turned to her own room across the passage. "Good night, then."

"Good night." Sage closed the door but left it unbolted for the maids to enter in the morning. A low hearth fire scattered light across the room, and a shadow she knew by heart sat in a chair next to the fireplace. Her stomach fluttered in anxiety and—truth be told—elation, but Sage refused to acknowledge it or him. Alex's dark brown eyes followed her as she crossed the room to her dressing table and began pulling pins from her hair.

"You didn't even tell me yourself that you were leaving," he said as the twists came down around her ears, the free strands barely brushing her shoulders.

"I knew you would hear about it," Sage replied, her fingers trembling as they hunted for stray pins.

Alex stood and came closer. "How am I supposed to protect you if you go off like this?"

"The Norsari are to guard the talks," she answered, still not looking at him. "We'll meet you there. Until then, Lani's entourage will be more than sufficient."

He stopped close enough that she could feel the heat of his body, but he made no move to touch her. "Is this really because you want to be away from me?"

Sage dropped a handful of pins on the table. "It's because Clare wants to visit her sister, and I have no reason to stay here." She turned to face him. "Correct me if I'm wrong on that last part."

"No," he whispered. "I don't have the right to ask you to stay."

For him it was always about what was right. She both loved and hated that. "Please give my apologies to your mother for not staying to receive her."

"I will."

"And your sisters. I'd promised Brenna she could practice languages with me."

"I will."

"And Amelia—"

"Sage." Alex reached up to her cheek. "I don't want to talk about my family right now. I want to talk about us."

She resisted the urge to lean into his touch. "I don't think there's anything to discuss."

"Maybe not." The firelight reflected in his eyes, adding a warmth she couldn't help but feel. "I saw you several times today, though I didn't think you wanted to see me. You looked so beautiful." His fingers traced her jaw, and he smiled tentatively. "It was like falling in love with you all over again."

"And yet not enough to change your mind."

His hand froze, and he narrowed his eyes. "You think that's what this is about? That it's a matter of not loving you *enough*?"

She knew that wasn't true. Alex had crossed a desert to find her and endured days of interrogation to keep her safe. If anything, he loved her too much. Sage shook her head to deny that, but Alex misunderstood. Something she couldn't define dropped away from his face, and suddenly his lips met hers with a hunger she'd never felt before. His arms went around her and crushed her against him.

Sage's feet left the floor and a second later her back was against the wall and his hands were everywhere—her hair, her hips, her waist, her breasts. She couldn't breathe or see or touch the ground, but it didn't matter because he was her air. He was her sky, her earth. She kissed him back with everything she had, understanding instinctively that this was what he'd always been holding back. This was what he'd always wanted.

The hilt of Alex's sword dug into her ribs, and she pushed it aside and followed his belt to the buckle in front. She tugged at the free end until the catch released and there was a heavy thunk that echoed through the room as his sword and dagger hit the wooden floor. Her own belt slid down over her hips to join it. She felt loose, weightless. Probably because she was now being carried.

The soft mattress hit her back, and he was over her, kissing every inch of her exposed skin and loosening the laces of her bodice. Sage's own fingers tugged at his jacket until he rose up to yank it over his head rather than remove it properly. His linen undershirt came half off, and she sat up and threw it aside, then laid one hand over his heart, feeling its pulse, rapid and strong, and looked up at him.

Spirit above, he was so beautiful it took her breath away.

All I have, all that I am, is yours forever.

Alex hesitated, his mahogany eyes searching hers, the muscles of his chest and arms tensed. Sage slid her hand up to his neck and lay back down, pulling him with her. His kisses became more urgent as he gently drew her loose dress off her shoulders and lower. Once her arms were free of the sleeves she buried her hands in his hair while he pushed the fabric over her hips. When the dress was gone his hand worked its way back up her leg and under her thin silk chemise.

It was like fire, like rain, like lightning where he touched. Her own fingers explored his chest and back. They had slept in the same bed before, nestled together, touching each other as much as they dared, but they'd never gone this far. It all felt natural. Perfect. Every fiber in Sage's being cried out that nothing they both wanted so badly could be wrong.

And yet something wasn't right.

"Alex," she whispered.

He rose up to bring his lips to hers. "Sage," he said against her mouth before kissing her deeply and desperately. The heat of his skin was intoxicating.

When I say over and over that I want you to be mine, it is only because I am already completely yours.

Alex had insisted on waiting, saying it was what *she* deserved, no matter how much they wanted it. Now he was willing to admit defeat. To do what he felt was wrong. To fail.

All to prove something she already knew.

"Alex," she said again.

He lifted his head to meet her gaze. She thought his eyes would burn right through her as she put a hand on his chest, holding him away. "I love you," he whispered, but he must have seen something in her expression because his voice trembled.

"And I you." Sage shook her head. "But you don't want this."

"I do."

"So do I. But not enough to make you hate yourself." Her eyes filled with tears. "Because you will, and I can't do that to you. I *won't* do that to you."

For a long moment he held perfectly still before rising up and turning to sit on the edge of the bed, resting his head in his hands. She listened to him breathe slowly for a dozen heartbeats, the sound echoing through the otherwise-silent room. Then Alex stooped down to the floor to grab his shirt. He threw it over his head and moved to find the rest of his clothes, keeping his back to her.

Sage sat up and reached for her robe. She stood, wrapping it around her as she watched Alex dress, though he wouldn't meet her eyes. The restraint was back. She could see it in every movement, every breath he took, but now she realized it had always been there.

His leather sword belt creaked as it settled around his waist. Alex dropped his hands and stared at the floor. "I'm sorry."

"Don't be," she whispered. Not after seeing how far he was willing to go for her sake.

He exhaled and looked up, eyes pleading. "You do know why I can't marry you, right? Please say you understand."

There was a chasm of difference between knowing and understanding. Sage had never heard him so desperate for her reassurance, which was why she was able to pull the dressing gown tight over the hole in her chest and whisper, "Yes. I hate it, but I understand."

Alex watched her for a long, silent moment, as though trying to assess whether she truly meant it; then he took three steps to close the gap between them. He put his hands on both sides of her face so she couldn't turn away. "I love you, Sage Fowler," he said. "Of everything I've said and done, *that* is truth."

Those had been the words he used the night she'd learned how he'd lied to her about who he was—not a common soldier following orders, but the captain manipulating her with them—and she'd slapped him with all her might. It was almost like he was begging her to do it again, to find the rage and use it to rise above the despair, but she couldn't. There wasn't anything left in her but sorrow.

When she didn't answer, Alex leaned down, resting his forehead on hers, and whispered, "Please tell me you know that."

Sage closed her eyes in a vain attempt to hold the tears back. "I know."

And she did. It was the only thing that made this bearable.

Almost.

Alex kissed her one last time, putting every word he couldn't say into it, but the wall was there.

The wall was there, and it wouldn't come down again.

20

THE ACHE IN Sage's chest of the past two weeks was much eased by the expression on Clare's face when they exited the Jovan Pass and came into sight of the castle where Sophia lived. Spring weather had scattered the valley with wide patches of yellow-green grass and white mountain flowers, making the granite walls stand out from the rocky landscape. It looked as welcoming as a fortress could—and much larger and more comfortable than the one guarding the Tegann Pass to the north. Sage wasn't sure why Duke Morrow D'Amiran had chosen to live there, even with its more strategic location.

They were barely inside the second gate of Fortress Jovan when Clare dismounted and ran into her sister's arms. Both women cried freely as they embraced on the steps leading into the main keep. In the four years since being separated by Sophia's marriage to Rewel D'Amiran—a match arranged by her ambitious father rather than a matchmaker—the pair had suffered much. Lani, who'd been informed of the abuse Sophia had endured, studied the young countess with interest. "She carries herself well," the princess declared. "Better than others I have seen."

"I imagine you would, too, once you were free of such an arrangement," said Sage.

"She is not free yet."

Sage swung her leg over Snow's back. "As the mother of a D'Amiran child, she'll never truly be free."

Lani looked horrified. "Surely the girl will not bear the treason of her father?"

"No, absolutely not," said Sage. "But others may seek to use both of them for their own gain. There are still some who consider the D'Amiran family as the rightful rulers."

"Demora is a volatile place," Lani said.

Without thinking, Sage snapped back. "Says the princess of a nation whose king was nearly assassinated by one of his own ministers." Then she blushed. Lani's lover had been the mastermind of the plot and been summarily executed. "I'm sorry to remind you, Palachessa," Sage said, using the title she called Lani by less and less frequently.

"I suppose that is a fair assessment," Lani replied, though the smile she wore as Sophia and Clare approached was a little strained.

The countess was a taller and curvier version of her younger sister, with hair a few shades lighter and brown eyes with hints of gold. Between their ethereal loveliness and Lani's brash and colorful beauty, Sage felt like a mouse among peacocks. Or, she thought—catching a glimpse of the flyaway strands of her short hair—maybe a hedgehog was a better analogy.

Sophia ignored the awkward curtsy Sage tried to make with her knee-length riding tunic and addressed Lani. "I welcome you and thank you for coming. I have missed Clare so, and it is lonely out here while I await justice to arrive." Her accent was aristocratic, emphasizing the lack of contractions, but the tone was soft and grateful.

Embarrassed that she'd somehow expected the countess to acknowledge her before the princess, Sage introduced Lani formally. "My Honorable Lady, this is Princess Alaniah of Casmun."

Sophia looked briefly baffled when her royal guest drank from her waterskin and then offered it to her, but she went with it and sipped daintily. Lani took the skin back and recorked it with a flourish. "Now you may call me Lani," she said grandly in Demoran, which she'd been working to speak well in. "For you are beloved of my friend and therefore beloved to me."

"I am honored, Your Highness," said Sophia. She took Lani's arm in her own and looped the other through Clare's. "Allow me to show you to your rooms so you may clean up and rest from your journey."

Together they started for the main entrance of the keep, Sage trailing behind. When they reached the wide double doors, the countess turned back to address her. "Will you see to the arrangement of housing your party, Mistress Sage?"

"I . . ." Sage felt mildly insulted, but then she remembered Sophia was excited to see Clare and had a princess to host. It was natural for Sage to take care of the mundane details, especially given the language barrier between the fortress's guards and the Casmuni escort. She chastised herself for briefly considering that beneath her. The position of ambassador was going to her head. "I would be most glad to, Your Ladyship."

Yet it turned out there was little for her to do. The Casmuni with them had mastered enough of the local language that everything was half accomplished already. Sage arranged what she could, then returned to the keep. No one was waiting to show her to her room, but she wandered the passages until she saw familiar baggage going into a doorway. She followed it in to find Clare pulling dresses from her a trunk to be hung up to allow the wrinkles to settle out.

"Everything with your entourage is settled, my lady," Sage said with a mock bow.

Clare glanced up with a frown. "No need to be rude. It wasn't like Sophia asked you to muck the stables."

Sage stood straight, ears warm with embarrassment. She hadn't meant to sound so sarcastic, but being ignored had hurt more than she wanted to admit.

"Sophia was rude first," said Lani, entering the room. She arched an eyebrow at Sage. "It was not something a guest of status should expect to perform."

Clare's frown deepened, but Sage waved her hand dismissively before her friend could say anything. "It needed to be done, and I handled it. We're here so Clare can visit Sophia." Sage walked around to help Clare shake out her dress. "How is your sister doing, then?"

Her friend relaxed a little, but her brow furrowed. "Sophia's changed. She's unsure of herself, fearful."

"I did not see that," said Lani.

Clare shook her head. "You didn't know her before. She used to be so spirited. Nothing ever made her back down from what she wanted."

Lani flopped onto a long chair near the hearth. "There is little else to want. She has a lovely castle and lands to rule as well as a daughter to raise. Someday she will marry again and her husband will be better, though that is not saying much."

"She'll never have what she really wanted," Clare said with a sad smile. "When we were young she used to crow that she would marry Prince Robert, and I would be her lady-in-waiting until she matched me with some less important count or earl."

"Little girls always wish to marry princes, not realizing they are men like any other." Lani rolled her eyes. "Many times they are worse."

Clare sighed. "All that ended when she married Rewel. I remember her wedding–his cruelty must have begun early because her smile was fake from that first day." She turned her eyes to Sage, pleading. "I'm sure she didn't mean to slight you. Don't be too hard on her."

"Of course not," Sage assured her. She avoided Lani's critical gaze, knowing the princess was displeased that Sage had let Sophia roll over her, but it still was difficult to think of herself as important.

If Sage had trouble demanding proper respect from someone as kind and timid as Sophia, however, it didn't bode well for the coming negotiations.

21

THERE WAS, OF course, no easy way to correct their hostess. When Countess Sophia addressed her as *Mistress* at dinner that night, Sage didn't object, even when Lani pinched her under the table and scowled. The second time, Sage cleared her throat as soon as she saw the princess's hand reaching for her leg again.

Sophia stopped midsentence, the briefest shadow of annoyance crossing her face. "Yes?"

"It's just that, ah," Sage mumbled, then spoke louder at the feel of Lani's fingers on her pant leg. "I would ask you use my proper title. Please."

The countess looked at Clare. "What does she mean?"

Clare pressed her lips together before answering. "Sage is an ambassador, Sophia. You really should call her that. Not..." She drifted off, uncomfortable.

"I see." Sophia glanced back to Sage. "I did not realize you both were appointed."

Sage would've been happy to leave it at that, but Clare objected, cheeks splotchy with embarrassment. "She's the *only* ambassador. I'm her companion."

"An invaluable companion," Sage quickly asserted.

The countess's eyebrow shot up. "It appears I misunderstood this arrangement. You must admit it is unusual, considering Clare's rank."

Sage would have wriggled with discomfort if Lani's painted fingernails weren't still poised to dig into her leg. "Everything about this situation is unusual, I think."

Sophia dipped her head slightly. "Please accept my most profuse apologies, Ambassador," she said stiffly.

"It's an easy mistake to have made," replied Sage. She was eager to move on, and when conversation turned to what had happened during the Concordium escort, Sage was glad for once to talk about it.

"I know very little of what happened," said the countess. Her daughter had been brought to her halfway through the meal, and the toddler snuggled in her lap while Sophia stroked her hair. "My husband was secretive, hiding his guests from me, never explaining why shipments of weapons and food came and went."

"The supplies were for the army the count and Duke Morrow D'Amiran were raising," explained Sage. "Much was provided by the dowries of several nobles in Tasmet—marriages all done quietly and without matchmakers. My employer, Mistress Rodelle, noticed them, but we didn't realize it was part of a greater trend until the plan was almost complete."

"You realized," murmured Clare.

"Only because I was keeping the books for her," said Sage. "When all the information was in one place, it was obvious."

Sophia watched her without blinking. "What made you decide to apprentice for the matchmaker? Was it in hopes of getting a better match than your name would otherwise earn?"

Lani scowled at that, but Sage wasn't insulted. "Many people thought so," she admitted. "But the truth is my interview went very poorly, and Mistress Rodelle didn't think she could find anyone to marry me."

"Poorly?" Sophia tilted her chin down just like Clare did when she was confused. "Forgive me, but you do not strike me as one who could not remember all the proper responses."

Sage's face grew hot with the memory of how easily the matchmaker had baited her into throwing a tantrum. "I have a temper," she said simply, and Lani snorted. "But she thought I could be useful," Sage continued. "I could either go back to my uncle's home, or I could work for her and maybe one day be free. It was the best choice I had at the time."

Mistress Rodelle's words from that morning suddenly stood out to her: *One of the simplest ways to get the result you want is to create a false choice.*

At the time, Sage had thought she was referring to her tactic in getting men to choose the wife she wanted them to have by using Sage as a less appealing alternative, but it was now clear Darnessa had used the same manipulation in getting her to take the apprenticeship. Sage had believed she had nowhere else to go, and her uncle had worried she'd be on his hands forever otherwise. The matchmaker hadn't only wanted Sage's assistance, however. She'd always intended to help her find her way—with or without a match.

Sage suddenly missed Darnessa with a fierce ache. She would know what to make of this mess between her and Alex. The woman had understood both of them better than they understood themselves. It seemed impossible that the matchmaker could have made a mistake in pushing them together, but there had been several events since then she couldn't have foreseen.

"And now you are engaged to marry the king's nephew," said Sophia in awe.

"Only his nephew by His Majesty's first marriage," Sage said, experiencing the same discomfort Alex had with the unearned respect. The fact that his aunt had been King Raymond's first wife elevated him in the eyes of everyone else, though she'd died before he could know her. "He's a soldier, nothing more."

"And the commanding general's son. That's not nothing."

Sage frowned. Sophia didn't know anything about Alex, but she was immediately drawn to respect the things he had no control over. "He's Alex. That's what matters."

The countess kissed her daughter on the crown of her head and laid her cheek against the chestnut curls. "We all become who we were born to be, Ambassador."

"My father always said birth was a curse no one realizes they have the power to break," replied Sage.

"Odd he should say that, considering the name he gave you." Sophia caught the horrified glance Clare shot at her and straightened. "I mean no disrespect," she said quickly. "I just find it curious he would saddle you with the assumptions people would always make based on your name."

With the exception of Rose, which was used only for a princess, botanical names were usually reserved for illegitimate children. Sage's parents had been married, but the name carried special meaning to them, and Father had always prided himself in flouting convention. She shrugged. "Perhaps he wanted me to understand why making assumptions is wrong." Clare's look shifted to Sage, and she realized she'd stepped in it as well.

"Do you wish to know what my father told me?" asked Lani. She waited until everyone focused on her. "Always eat dessert. Is it coming soon?"

As Sophia signaled to the steward to clear their dishes, Lani caught Sage's eye and winked. Sage grinned back, gladder than ever the princess had come along. Clare only frowned.

22

SAGE'S INTERACTIONS WITH Sophia thawed a little over the next few days, but she still had trouble gaining any information that might be useful at the peace talks. The countess appeared content to let others make decisions for her, and General Quinn didn't keep her informed of his actions in Tasmet, which surprised Sage. She would have to have Alex speak to his father about that. Actually, she should do it, as diplomacy was her job.

Then again, it seemed out of character for the general to leave someone in Sophia's position in the dark, given how much he shared with his own wife. Maybe the information was too sensitive or uncertain to share, a thought that only made Sage more apprehensive about what she was heading into. Even with Prince Robert and several others present, King Raymond had put a great deal of trust in her. What if the Kimisar queen saw through Sage's reason for being there and refused to speak to her at all? What if the whole thing was a trap?

In the meantime, Clare delighted in her niece and lavished attention on the little girl, and it was encouraging to see her friend's joy. It raised another worry in Sage's mind, however. Back in Tennegol the idea of the negotiations and their consequences had seemed important but still distant. Watching Clare and her sister with Aurelia made the idea of failing even more terrible. Though they were relatively safe and happy now, the future of the countess and her daughter hung in the balance.

Perhaps that was the real reason for Sophia's coolness toward her.

Since that first evening, the countess had dodged most of Sage's attempts to flatter her and gain her confidence. She remained out of reach, like a tantalizing piece of fruit on a high limb.

On their last day, Sage sat on the watchtower at dawn, having been unable to sleep, letting herself feel lonely and miserable without Alex, remembering a morning much like this one where they'd stumbled across each other at Tegann. It was the day he'd kissed her—first out of necessity, in pretending to be a couple hiding in a closet when their eavesdropping was about to be discovered, then because he'd wanted to.

When they were together again at Arrowhead, Sage suspected Alex would hold her at arm's length, at least when others were around. That would be for her professional image as much as his. How he would act in private was questionable, especially after that awful night.

The soft whisper of fabric across the wooden floor behind her made Sage look over her shoulder. Sophia stood there, clutching a trailing brocade cloak of dark blue, almost like a royal train, around her. "Am I disturbing you, Ambassador?" she asked softly.

"No, Your Ladyship," Sage said, dropping the foot she'd propped against the wall. *Not a very ladylike position*, as Darnessa would have scolded. Similar internal admonitions had plagued Sage all week in Sophia's refined presence.

"I hate that," Sophia said with sudden venom. "Being called 'Your Ladyship' when I should be called 'Your Grace.'"

It took Sage a few seconds to understand what the countess was talking about. Technically, with the death of Morrow D'Amiran, her husband, Rewel, had inherited the title of duke, which made her the Duchess of Tasmet. The distinction of the higher address seemed a little silly to Sage, but it was probably one of the few things Sophia had to hold on to as she waited for justice to fall on the husband who'd abandoned her and betrayed Demora. "If you wish, I will call you that, Your Grace," Sage offered.

Sophia looked a little smug—or maybe just content; it was hard to tell. "I wanted to ask you a question and a favor."

"Anything I can answer and do, Your Grace."

"What does the king intend to do with my daughter?"

"Um." Sage hesitated, mentally berating herself for the clumsy syllable. "I'm not sure he has any kind of plan yet, Your Grace." Every time she used the obeisant address, Sophia looked distinctly pleased. If only Sage had known how much that title could have gained, maybe the countess—duchess—would've been friendlier from the start.

"When Rewel dies or is executed, Aurelia becomes heir to Tasmet, does she not?" The gold flecks in Sophia's eyes hardened.

That was something Sage couldn't guarantee. "As far as I know," she replied.

"Will the king send someone to take guardianship? To marry me?"

The questions were likely rooted in how much Sophia thought Sage knew about matchmaking, but those instincts told Sage the answer was probably yes, especially if these talks failed and the province came under threat again. Jovan Fortress would be more strategically important than ever, as it stood at the gateway to eastern Demora. If Sage succeeded, however, and brought a measure of peace to the region, it was possible for Sophia to avoid such an arrangement. "There's a chance he won't think it necessary, Your Grace, if you show you can manage the province yourself."

Sophia frowned doubtfully. She tugged the heavy cloak tighter around her and exhaled slowly through her nose, the air misting around her face and briefly obscuring her eyes. "Perhaps I could, if it weren't for those still loyal to my husband's family."

She referred to the vassals who'd rebelled two years ago. Many had been imprisoned, but a good number pleaded ignorance to the duke's plan. In fact, it was only the lower, less powerful nobles Duke D'Amiran made sign a document committing them to his cause. His strongest allies were still out there, but there wasn't enough solid evidence to arrest them yet. "If they're loyal, though, how can that trouble you?" Sage asked.

"They have minimal allegiance to me," said Sophia. "It is Aurelia they want. Whoever controls her controls the province."

There wasn't much to control. The population was generally sparse and the land difficult to farm. Men had fought and died over less, however, Sage supposed. "Who's giving you the most trouble, Your Grace?" she asked.

Sophia looked down and away. "Baron Underwood. Lord Fashell."

Sage knew them both. Lord Fashell had provided the duke with most of his material stores, but who could legally blame a man for supplying what his overlord requested? As for Baron Underwood, his home sat at the intersection of the Northern and Tegann Roads, an important trade hub. His allegiance to Morrow D'Amiran was known, but again, nothing he'd done was overtly treasonous.

As one of the highest-ranking nobles of Tasmet, Baron Underwood would also be at the talks with Kimisara. If Sophia was saying his loyalty was now to Rewel's cause, every move he made would be suspect.

"What do they do?" Sage asked.

"Send spies mostly," said Sophia. "Constant messengers who overstay their welcome. Offers to provide protection. Then they send troops to patrol the area without my asking, and expect me to provide for them."

Alarming. "Do you think they aim to take Aurelia from you, Your Grace?"

Sophia bit her lip. "Do you think they would try such a thing?" Her voice was a little panicky.

Sage wanted to say no, but that wouldn't be honest. "I don't know, Your Grace. Have you written to General Quinn of your concerns? There are fewer soldiers here than I would've expected. Maybe he could send more."

"He is more concerned with the talks at Arrowhead, convinced the threat is from the Kimisar."

Sage considered carefully. Appealing to the king could only make the duchess appear weak, possibly making His Majesty believe she needed a guardian. Sophia would lose all autonomy. Sage could speak to the general, but she had little military expertise so her claims might be as dismissed as Sophia's. She brightened suddenly. "It's still some time away, but Ash Carter will be coming through here at the end of the month on his way to check on the talks. You can tell him your concerns, and he can investigate. I'm sure General Quinn will listen to him."

Sophia frowned. "The bastard prince is reliable?"

"He's highly respected in both the army and the council," Sage said, wincing. His origin wasn't his fault—and by most standards, it was understandable that the grief-stricken king had found comfort with someone after the death of his first wife. But Sophia's disgust was also understandable, as her husband was known to have had several mistresses. No children from those liaisons, fortunately.

The duchess nodded, though the words were a little sour as she said, "I will follow your advice."

Sage smiled. This was progress. "I'm most grateful I could offer it, Your Grace. Was there also a favor you wished to ask?"

"It is for Clare."

"Then likely cheerfully done, Your Grace."

A flash of what might have been jealousy lit Sophia's eyes, but it quickly vanished. "You are taking my sister into danger," she said. "From what she tells me, this is not the first time, either."

"I would never compel her," Sage insisted. "If she wishes to remain here with you, I'll respect that." A hollow formed in Sage's chest at the thought. How would she do this without her best friend?

"She will not stay, though I asked." Sophia's words were clipped, tense. "Her attachment to you is too strong."

"I think it's devotion to duty as much as anything, Your Grace," Sage said, trying to keep relief and triumph out of her voice. "And she was trained for this. I'm grateful to have her instruction."

"Then you must promise me you will do your utmost to protect her. Other than Aurelia, she is all I have." Sophia looked straight at her.

Sage had already done that for years, from that first night Clare had broken down crying on the way to the Concordium. She put her hand over her heart. "I swear it, Your Grace. I will give my own life for hers if necessary. You may hold me to that."

Sophia nodded, her eyes as hard and bright as brass. "I will."

23

WHEN HE RODE into the army's main camp at last, Alex was relieved to see he'd arrived ahead of Sage. He directed everything to be set up for her and left Casseck in charge while he reported to the commanding general, his father.

Alex walked into the sea of army tents with his head high, trying to exude the confidence he didn't feel. Eyes followed him every step of the way. Several glances he met were hostile, but most soldiers feigned disinterest until he passed. Then the quiet jeers started.

"There goes Uncle Raymond's pet."

Alex kept his eyes forward. That was essentially what the council members had said, but the disdainful words from someone he'd likely served beside cut deeper. He continued on as though he hadn't heard, hoping the closely trimmed whiskers on his face were enough to cover the clenched jaw beneath. The tension grew with each step as he waited for the next insult, but there was only silence now. It was almost a relief when he crossed paths with the recently promoted Major Larsen, who was high enough in rank to say what he thought to Alex's face.

"Well, well, if it isn't the General's Little Acorn," said Larsen with a smirk, extending his hand to imply that he was only teasing Alex good-naturedly.

Acorn was a reference to the silver oak leaves Alex wore on his collar, the signet of his rank. Most of his peers were only making captain. He gritted his teeth and shook the cavalry officer's hand, and Larsen held on longer than courtesy dictated, keeping Alex from moving on.

"Haven't seen you in over a year, Young Quinn." Larsen's voice boomed over the quiet. "Finally ready to get back to work?"

Most soldiers only knew Alex been gone on a training assignment, unaware that in that time he'd traversed hundreds of miles of desert and buried a dozen men under his command, including a close friend. They may have heard of the Battle of Black Glass, but Alex couldn't blame anyone for believing the scope of it had been massively exaggerated—the idea of melting an entire valley was ludicrous to those who weren't there to see it. Snapping back at Larsen would only give the insults weight and tell everyone how to get under his skin. Instead, he met the other major's crushing pressure on his hand, baring his teeth in what no one would call a smile. "Absolutely. Palace food is too rich."

Judging from his confused expression, Larsen didn't expect Alex to agree with him, but Alex wasn't in the mood to play this game. He tightened his grip until Larsen winced. Alex's smile became more genuine as he turned Larsen's hand over and released it, immediately slapping a piece of metal in the major's palm. "For being the first to welcome the Norsari back," he said.

Norsari. The word echoed around the small circle that had gathered around them. It would be all over camp by sunset.

Larsen raised the coin to look at it, shifting to hold it by its edges. Like the various professional guilds, each army battalion had its own. While on leave, soldiers who met could challenge each other to produce their coins. Whoever didn't have his handy—or had the most tarnished one— usually had to buy everyone a round at the pub. Typically they were made from silver or brass, but there was no shine to the one in Larsen's hand, only the dull gray relief of a bird of prey like the one tattooed on Alex's shoulder. The reverse side was blank.

"That's flinting steel," said Alex, nodding to it. "I wanted something that would also be useful."

Major Larsen stared at the medallion. "You've been busy."

"A bit." Alex shrugged modestly. "You should join us for morning exercises," he said. "Anyone who can keep pace with us is welcome to apply for a transfer." He took a step back, starting to enjoy the shock on Larsen's face, but less was more right now. "If you'll excuse me, I have to report." He turned his back on the cavalry officer and strode away, forcing a few gawkers to scramble out of his path.

People would still talk, but this way he'd taken some control. If Alex was lucky, awe of the Norsari return would spread faster than disdain for his promotion.

A pair of sentries outside General Quinn's tent came to attention as he approached, indicating he should go on in. Alex returned their salute and continued inside, keeping his hand up to render it to his father, who sat a table covered with maps and dispatches. Next to him was Colonel Traysden, the minister of intelligence, who'd been absent from Tennegol, and behind him hovered the general's staff officer, Murray, who now wore the insignia of lieutenant colonel—another promotion that reemphasized to Alex how long he'd been away.

The general saluted from his seat. "Ah, it's good to see you again, Major." He looked genuinely pleased.

Alex dropped his hand when General Quinn did. "It's good to be back, sir," he said.

His father stood and walked around the table to meet him. "None of that for a minute," he said. The general held out his hand, which Alex reflexively took, only to be pulled into an embrace. "I've missed you, son."

It was more than the contrast between this and Major Larsen's greeting that caught Alex off guard. He couldn't remember the last time his father had hugged him, and it certainly wasn't in front of his officers. Then again, they hadn't seen each other since Alex's secretive orders to report to Tennegol a year and a half ago. He stole a glance at Traysden and Murray, who didn't appear embarrassed to witness his father's display of affection. Awkwardly, he squeezed back. "And I you, Father."

General Quinn's eyes were a little misty as he turned back to the table, stroking his iron-gray beard, which was a shade lighter than Alex remembered. "The ambassador will be here in two days," his father said.

"Some of the Kimisar have already arrived, but they've been coming in small, individual parties, forcing us to split up to escort them across the border. It's been frustrating."

"I tend to think it indicates there is little union between the brazapilla rather than a desire to inconvenience us," said Traysden, referring to Kimisar noblemen. He scratched the shaved stubble on his head. "But neither reason is encouraging for these talks."

"Not that I was terribly optimistic," said the general, settling himself back onto his chair. "Before we discuss official matters, is there any family news?"

"Oh, yes." Alex dug into his jacket for the packet of personal letters. Father had always corresponded regularly with all six of his daughters, trying as best he could to stay involved in their lives over the distance. Alex offered the tied bundle to him. "Mother wants your permission to let at least one of the girls attend Princess Rose when she goes to Casmun this summer. I don't know the details, really."

The general snorted a little. "Casmuni didn't waste any time, did they?" He took the stack and used his dagger to slice the twine that bound them, immediately breaking the seal on the thickest letter. That he would read personal messages in front of others was surprising, but there was something decidedly human about the eagerness to hear from his wife. She used to stay with him in the field for weeks at a time, young Alex and his sisters in tow, often leaving with another baby on the way. In the last few years she'd visited less frequently, due to both increased danger in the region and to focus on preparing her daughters for being matched, and, thanks to Serena, now she had a grandchild, too.

A gold coin slid out of the letter and into his father's hand. For a moment the general stared at it; then he looked up at Alex. "You didn't marry her."

Colonel Traysden frowned from his side, steel eyes narrowed.

"I, uh, no. I didn't," said Alex.

"You were made aware of the change to Article Twenty-Nine, were you not?" his father asked.

Alex nodded. "Yes, I was. I just thought it more prudent to wait."

The general's mouth twitched. "How so?"

"I realized the change would only apply to me, and likely only ever me. I didn't want to be seen as an exception to the long-established rules."

His father's eyes crinkled in amusement. "I see." He glanced at Colonel Traysden. "Pay up, Kristor."

Colonel Traysden grimaced and dug into a pocket, then flipped a gold coin at the general. "I'll be damned, Penn. You knew him."

"Of course I know him." General Quinn stacked the coin on the table with the one from Mother's letter. "He's my son."

They'd made bets on whether Alex would have married Sage. Apparently his mother and the minister of intelligence had believed Alex would take advantage of the change, but his father hadn't. A flush crept up Alex's neck. If the general had felt it was pointless, though, why did he bother authorizing the change to Article Twenty-Nine?

"Well, that complicates things a little," grumbled Traysden.

"Not really," said Alex's father. "She's already coming to the talks, and his duty puts him close to her."

"What?" blurted out Alex.

His father focused on him again. "The plan was to utilize your closeness to Ambassador Fowler to facilitate the passage of information. She could act as both observer and courier, reporting to the king on matters that are too sensitive to put into dispatches."

"And I ruined that by not marrying her?"

Traysden shook his head. "The general is right. We submitted the change in rules before we knew the king would send her in an official capacity. It's no longer necessary for you to be the reason she's here."

"Even with such a visible position as she now has," General Quinn said, "you'd be surprised how little scrutiny a woman gets, especially when standing next to the man everyone expects to be a threat."

Alex felt dizzy. "Did Mother know that was your intention in modifying the regulation? To essentially make her daughter-in-law an intelligence agent?" Maybe that was why she hadn't tried to change his mind when she heard about Alex's refusal.

"Lady Quinn?" Colonel Traysden smiled ironically. "Who do you think has been filling that role for the last twenty years?"

Alex stared at the two of them. A hundred slightly odd childhood memories suddenly made sense. Not only that, but Mother had personally brought Alex's brother Charlie to the army camp to begin his page training almost three years ago. It was at that time that General Quinn grew distrustful of D'Amiran family activity, enough that he assigned Alex to the Concordium escort the following spring with the secondary purpose of spying on the duke as they passed through Tegann. Father had never named his source, but now it was obvious who had raised the alarm.

Mother.

24

THE JOURNEY FROM Jovan to Arrowhead had been eye-opening to say the least. Having traveled the Tegann Road with Darnessa and the Concordium brides, Sage had thought she knew what Tasmet was like, which wasn't that different from Crescera. The main contrast had been homes that were more defensible than those in the sleepy farming province she grew up in, but customs and living conditions were generally the same.

Southern Tasmet was shockingly different.

For over fifty years, Kimisara's kings—up to and including the recently dead Ragat—had encouraged their people to stage attacks into the territory they still considered theirs. As a result, the local population lived in fear, cowering behind fortifications. In almost two generations, few additional fields had been cleared for crops, and no new mills or foundries of any size built. Prosperity only made people a target, both for raiders and the D'Amiran family's confiscatory taxes. Everywhere Sage, Clare, and Lani went, commoners and nobles alike begged to know what these talks meant. Rumors about Demora's weakness—which had a basis in fact—had led many to believe King Raymond had decided Tasmet wasn't worth holding on to. Many spoke of fleeing through the Jovan Pass and into the Tenne Valley, which Sage knew could be disastrous in Demora's current state of limited resources. The entire country was strained to the breaking point.

It was all well and good accepting this job back in Tennegol, where the confidence of the royal family and the promise of glory pushed her doubts aside. Now, faced with the reality of what hung the balance, Sage realized she was in way over her head.

Every mile they traveled stretched her nerves tighter. By the time the Casmuni caravan was met by sentries outside Arrowhead, Sage felt as fragile as a leaf clinging to life in the last blustery days of fall. The only thing that kept her hanging on was Clare and Lani's faith in her.

Then she recognized Alex riding to meet them, and it was like a cold wind stripping her brittle form from the branch at last. He was coming to stand by her side, but not in the way that mattered most. Not in the way she needed him.

Lani and Clare watched her warily as Alex approached. The morning after that awful night, he'd still come to see her off, and both friends had witnessed their awkward good-bye, not understanding what had happened that made everything worse. They hadn't pressed her for details, either, for which Sage was grateful.

Alex pulled up his brown mare and bowed from where he sat. "Palachessa, Ambassador, my lady. Welcome to the Western Army's main camp," he said formally. "Everything is ready to receive you." He raised his head and focused directly on Sage, seeking to meet her eyes.

Sage looked away.

Lani tugged her scarf away from her neck. "Are the Kimisar arrived, Maizshur?" she asked in accented Demoran.

"Some, Palachessa," he answered. "The rest should be here tomorrow. We've already set up your accommodations on the northeast side of the camp. The Kimisar will be to the west." As much as the Demorans and Kimisar hated each other, the animosity was even worse between Kimisar and Casmuni. Apparently the general thought it best to separate them.

"How was your journey?" Alex asked as he turned his horse around to lead them back. Sage looked forward again, but not at him.

"Long and cold," Lani said, nudging her stallion ahead. "I am ready for a hot drink." She glanced deliberately around at the bleak landscape of boulders and scrub bushes with the occasional stubborn tree. "Is this the land you have been fighting to keep? It does not look worth much."

Alex didn't respond to the princess's baiting, and they rode in silence until Casseck met them at the camp perimeter. Lani sat up straighter and smiled, distracting Sage for a moment as she detected a bit of uncertainty and bewilderment in the princess's mannerism. Cass's apparent obliviousness to her overtures probably wasn't something she was used to.

"Ambassador?"

Sage reflexively glanced at Alex, then found she couldn't look away. His jaw and the skin around his eyes were tight, but as her gaze locked with his, there was an instant softening of his expression, telling Sage his tension had little to do with her. Part of her yearned to do what she could to make it better, until she remembered her comfort was the last thing he wanted, especially here.

He tilted his head toward the center of the camp. "If you and Lady Clare will follow me, I'll take you to your tent."

Breaking her focus from Alex, Sage turned to find Clare, but her friend shook her head and said she'd help Lani settle in first. She smiled encouragingly as she turned her mount away. "Don't wait up for me."

There was nothing to do but follow Alex, which Sage did numbly. He led her to an enormous tent with several Norsari guards posted outside. Sage dismounted before anyone could attempt to help her and handed the reins to the waiting page. Her saddlebags were quickly grabbed by Alex, who gestured for her to enter the tent first. She marched past him, then stopped suddenly inside the shelter, her mouth dropping open.

A ring of comfortable settees and couches were positioned around an iron stove in the enormous open space at the center. Rugs with colorful, ornate designs covered the ground completely, though several errant blades of grass had managed to sprout up between a few, reaching in vain for the sunlight they missed. A large table occupied the far side of the tent, set with carved wooden chairs. Two rooms on either end were partitioned by heavy tapestries tied back to reveal separate sleeping areas. One was twice as spacious and furnished as the other. Vases of flowers, glowing lamps, and colorful tapestries were spread throughout the space. It was much more than she would've arranged for herself.

Lani said trappings like this were more for others to see how high-ranking a person was, but this declared Sage was on equal footing with the crown prince. Maybe even higher as far as accommodations went, since he was also a soldier, and less likely to want these comforts in his tent. Sage shuddered, squeezing her eyes shut against the sudden burning of tears.

All the conditions she'd observed on the way here—burned-out farmhouses, towns where no one trusted one another, entire generations who'd only known fear—came rushing into her mind. The future of thousands of citizens, the lives of the soldiers around her—Alex's included—depended on these talks.

Depended on her.

She stood shaking, eyes closed, until Alex came in behind her. Sage felt the gentle pressure of his hand on her lower back. "Are you all right?" he asked softly.

Sage wrenched away, spinning to face him and backing away. "No, I am not *all right*," she snapped.

He stayed in place, holding on to her bag, the one full of books and documents she'd been studying but that were useless because she was the wrong person for this role. She was going to fail and people were going to suffer because of it. People were going to die.

Killing people was what she was good at, after all.

Alex shook his head. "Sage, I still want to marry you. It's just . . . complicated right now."

That wasn't why she was upset, but it was something she could tether her emotions onto here and now, something she could fight, even if it felt wrong to blame him. "And that's what I've always been, haven't I?" she said bitterly. "A *complication*." The word stuck in her throat. He'd called her that back at Tegann, trying to explain why he'd hidden his true identity for so long.

Alex winced. "The best complication. One I never regretted." His mouth hardened a little. "And as you might recall, I offered to give all this up for you." He gestured to the rank on his collar. "You refused to let me."

The air whooshed from her lungs as she realized he was right. She hadn't wanted to take away the future he'd worked so hard for, and this was the consequence of that decision: she would always have to share him with the army, which meant there were times when no matter how much she needed Alex, duty had to come first.

Sage's shoulders slumped as the flare of anger dissipated, allowing the weight of her purpose here to crush her again. She looked down at her boots.

Alex crossed the space between them in two strides, dropping the bag and putting his hands on her shoulders. "Sage," he whispered. "Nothing has changed. Not really."

He was wrong. Everything had changed. He wasn't the same person who asked her to marry him under the willow tree almost two years ago. She wasn't the same person, either.

Maybe that was the real problem.

Alex tipped her chin up. "I love you. Can't that be enough for now?"

"I don't know," she said dully.

His eyes were full of sympathy. Pity. "I think you need some rest."

Somehow she suspected he knew she wasn't just tired, but she nodded and didn't resist as Alex led her to the larger partitioned area. "Thank you for letting me take care of you," he said.

Was that what he was afraid of? That she would resist letting him do his job and make him look foolish? She stopped by the low, wide bed and faced him. "I'll do nothing to interfere with your orders," she said. "You know that."

He shook his head. "That's not what I meant." His hand came up to stroke her cheek. "Sage, there's nothing more important to me than you. I wonder if you'll ever let me treat you like you are."

Sage backed away, just out of reach. "Interesting statement, considering—" She broke off and looked down. Again it had been automatic to blame Alex, but fighting with him was a poor substitute for fighting by his side. "I don't want to get into this right now," she mumbled.

Alex nodded and lowered his hand. "I have many duties, but you're my primary one. Please don't hesitate to let me know if you need anything." She understood he was saying if she went to anyone else, it would reflect poorly on him. Alex leaned down to kiss her forehead. "I love you," he whispered.

Then he was gone, drawing the curtains closed behind him.

Sage stayed in place for several seconds before unbuckling her sword belt and tossing it on the bed. There was only one dagger hooked to it, the one Alex had given her back at Tegann, the one that bore his initials. The other knife he'd given her last year—identical except for the letters *SF*— she pulled from her boot and tossed beside it. She should have taken off her dusty riding clothes, but she was too tired to go searching through her trunks. Her one concession to keeping the bed clean was to lie down on top of the coverlet rather than between the sheets. Just before she closed her eyes, a piney scent with a floral hint drew her attention to the small vase on the table a few feet away.

Delicate purple flowers raised their heads over thick oval leaves.

Sage.

It didn't bloom this time of year, and the nearest village or manor that would've had a garden hothouse was ten miles away. Tears spilled out of her eyes and back into her hair.

There's nothing more important to me than you.

An apology.

I wonder if you'll ever let me treat you like you are.

A plea.

I love you.

A promise.

He meant all those things, but the restraint was there. The wall was still in place.

Worse, Sage now realized she'd built one against him, too.

25

CAPTAIN HUZAR FELT naked without a sword or daggers, but no weapons were allowed within the negotiation tent or the clear area surrounding it. He probably could have snuck one past his escort, a silent and grizzled lieutenant named Tanner, but getting caught would have him removed from the talks at a minimum. His queen was already risking too much by attending; there was no possibility he would leave her without his protection.

With talks opening tomorrow morning, Huzar had asked to inspect the meeting place. The Demoran ambassador had gotten there a few minutes before him, however, and he had to wait his turn. He didn't mind too much, as it meant catching a glimpse of who would be across the table. It was difficult to resist pacing, though.

The hanging canvas that served as a door was drawn aside, and Huzar dropped his crossed arms in surprise. A small, pale figure stepped out, wearing a finely woven tunic long enough to reach her knees over light breeches. While she carried no weapons, a Casmuni-style sword belt sat on her waist. Her sleeves draped long over her hands, so he couldn't see any burns or scars, but Huzar knew the young woman instantly.

She'd survived.

His path had crossed hers several times in the past two years. The first at been outside Tegann, the day after he'd ordered his men to abandon Duke D'Amiran. She'd climbed a tree and killed his black-tailed hawk with an expertly aimed stone from a sling, cutting off his last means of communication with the soldiers he'd sent back to Kimisara. Months later she'd helped the young Demoran prince escape Huzar's attempt to take the boy hostage, defeating three of his men as they pursued the pair. Then in the southern pass, he'd watched her unleash the terrible Casmuni fire weapon, only to be swept into its wrath. He'd followed her down into the canyon, but Quinn had gotten there first. When he went seeking Quinn the next day, it had been as much to learn about her fate as it was to ask for the return of the Kimisar prisoners. At the time, no one was sure she would live.

But it was her now, very much alive, striding away from the meeting tent. Barely two steps behind her was Quinn, dressed in shades of brown and green like his escort, rather than the black cavalry uniform Huzar had seen him in before. The Norsari had adopted a more camouflaged uniform, which was appropriate to their purpose of stealth. And death.

Quinn glanced in their direction, a flash of recognition on his face as he met Huzar's eyes. While the Demoran didn't break his stride, one hand did come up, ready to nudge the young woman in a safer direction if necessary, but she continued moving away. Huzar almost smiled. That was exactly how he would have reacted if guarding Zoraya.

Lieutenant Tanner spoke for the first time. "That was her," he said, nodding at the woman as she vanished into the Demoran camp. "Along with Prince Robert, Ambassador Sage Fowler will be negotiating with your queen."

Sage Fowler. Huzar finally knew her name.

There was a lack of noble title, though he would've been surprised to learn she was born to privilege. Huzar had also spent enough time in Demora to know only a bastard or peasant would bear such a name. Perhaps this was a test, to see if the Kimisar would consider her appointment an insult. Maybe it *was* an insult, but he doubted it.

So why her?

Huzar had seen Zoraya struggle to stay informed as the council ministers went around and over her, dismissing her as a mere woman. From the outside, it was easy to assume that Sage Fowler was meant to occupy or entertain the Kimisar queen while the real talks took place among the men. But if that was truly the intention, a noble-born lady would be a more logical choice.

The Demoran king had to know what this Sage Fowler has done in service of her nation. She'd been a player at Tegann, saved the life of his son, and single-handedly stopped an invasion. It would be a waste for a person of such value to be used purely as a distraction.

Through all these thoughts, Huzar kept his face blank. Once the ambassador was out of sight, Lieutenant Tanner indicated Huzar could continue to the tent himself. The inside was as he expected—no places for weapons to be hidden, the furniture and decorations sparse but comfortable. Maps were hung in prominent places, with ink, quills, and blank parchment by every seat at the long table. Huzar nodded after he finished his inspection and allowed his escort to take him back to his own camp.

In her tent, the queen sat in a high-backed chair at the apex of a V-shaped table. The design frustrated the ministers, who were unable to confer with those across from them without speaking loudly enough for Zoraya to hear. Brazapil Donala, as usual, had claimed a seat on the queen's right, facing the minister of war, General Oshan, also as usual. The two watched each other like mountain wildcats—deceptively lazy, but ready to pounce. Huzar went straight up the open area in the middle and bowed low. "I have seen the meeting place and am satisfied My Queen will approve," he reported.

"Very good, Captain," said Zoraya, and he stood straight. "What are your other impressions?"

He hesitated, not wishing to imply another woman at the table would be a matter of concern, but not wanting the queen to be taken by surprise. "I have also seen the ambassador sent to negotiate alongside the crown prince."

"I'm told she is much younger than My Queen," said Oshan from her left. Everyone was a child to the balding general, but Sage Fowler was young enough to be his granddaughter. "Less than twenty years in age."

"She?" Zoraya raised her eyebrows. "Is this true?"

Huzar nodded once. "I cannot speak for her exact age, but that appears to be accurate." The queen frowned.

"They say she's not of noble birth," said Brazapil Nostin, his thin mouth pinched in disgust. He stroked the chain of office around his neck with fingers whose nails had been chewed down to the quick. Huzar considered him near useless, as did most others, except perhaps Donala, who kept him close as a lackey.

When Huzar didn't deny the brazapil's statement, Zoraya's frown deepened, a crease forming in the middle of her brow. Nostin continued, "You can see by this the Demorans are not taking us seriously, sending a common girl to the table."

"She may be of common birth," Huzar felt compelled to say. "Yet she is anything but common."

Donala leaned forward, interest sparking in his blue-gray eyes. "You know this woman."

"I do." A glance at the queen told Huzar she was intrigued. "She is not to be underestimated."

Huzar told them everything he knew about Sage Fowler, how she'd been wounded in the Battle of Black Glass, and how scarred she must be. His audience remained tight-lipped, asking few questions, but the curious light in Zoraya's eyes steadily brightened. By the end of his tale, Huzar could tell how eager his queen was to meet the Demoran woman herself.

That was Sage Fowler's purpose: not to distract the queen regent, but to disarm her personally, emotionally.

It may have been an effort to make these talks succeed. Or it might be an attempt to take advantage of Zoraya, though Huzar doubted that would work. Even if the queen and the ambassador did make a personal connection, he knew what both women were capable of, especially when their survival was at stake.

He left the queen's bed in the early-morning hours, bending low to kiss her cheek before slipping out of the curtains that divided her sleeping area from the rest of the tent. It was imprudent for them to continue their liaisons here, but when Zoraya had asked him to stay last night, her blue eyes pleading, he couldn't refuse. He could never tell her no.

Huzar set his weapons belt on the V-shaped table quietly, then cinched and buckled his jacket down in the dark. When he reached for his sword, he heard a shout in the distance, followed by several others in unison. Quickly he pulled the belt around his waist and exited the tent through a loose flap not visible to the guards posted out front. The frosted grass crunched under his boots as he followed the sound he'd heard.

Kimisar were forbidden to enter the Demoran camp without an escort, but the noise was coming from the south, and Huzar was able to skirt around the edge until he found the source. A cleared area was being used for exercises. He recognized the majority of the soldiers as part of the Norsari Battalion—Lieutenant Tanner was walking among a platoon at the far end. A number of regular soldiers stood off to the side, observing. Some of them frowned as additional men joined the columns, but the Norsari welcomed them, though most had trouble keeping up.

"Are you lost, Captain?"

Huzar turned to find Quinn himself standing beside him, his cheeks flushed with exertion. This close, Huzar could now see Quinn's rank—he'd been promoted. "No," he answered neutrally. "Only curious what I was hearing."

Quinn nodded, his sharp, almost-black eyes taking in Huzar's uniform. "I remember you from Black Glass," he said. "Though your appearance tells me much has changed since then."

Huzar tugged his maroon cloak around one shoulder to straighten it over his spotless jacket, the white four-pointed star bright in contrast. The last time they'd met, Huzar hadn't eaten a full meal or bathed in weeks, and wore the same clothing the whole of that time. "I am now in close service of the queen."

Quinn folded his arms across his chest. "I imagine your firsthand knowledge of Demora is very useful to your delegation," he said.

"My queen would be foolish to ignore it."

The exercises had ended, and platoons began to divide up into combat instruction and practice. The newcomers were divided evenly among the Norsari, who were apparently not jealous of sharing their skills. Quinn glanced at them before turning back to Huzar. "You were watching us last year, weren't you? We found a place where someone had camped for weeks on a bluff overlooking our training grounds."

"Yes." There was no sense in denying it.

Quinn appeared to appreciate the honesty. "I'd be very interested to know what else you did while you were in Demora."

Huzar shrugged, never looking away. "Mostly wandering, advising my men on how to stay hidden, trying to think of ways to get us all home. That was only ever my goal."

"I suppose that's easy to believe, given how little trouble you caused until the end." Quinn smiled ironically and relaxed his arms—but only a little. "I would've done the same in your situation." He turned to watch the Norsari. "And I'm grateful for your help in the mountain pass."

After the landslide of earth and fire, Huzar had found Quinn cradling the badly burned and unconscious body of the woman who had caused it all. Knowing the Demoran wouldn't trust him to help in other ways, Huzar had given Quinn his cloak to help in carrying her. "I'm glad to see Sage Fowler survived," he said.

Quinn glanced at him sharply. "You know her name?"

The reaction—instant but controlled—told Huzar much, though he'd already suspected the Demoran's attachment to her. "I recognized the ambassador. Your Lieutenant Tanner told me her name."

Quinn pursed his lips but said nothing.

"She's important to you," ventured Huzar. "And not just as a diplomat you are obliged to protect, yes?"

"More than my life," Quinn said softly. He gazed out over the battalion as though not truly seeing them. No shyness, no attempt to deny his feelings, but there was a touch of regret. Perhaps she didn't return his affection.

"Sage once told me this fighting would never stop until people like us said, *Enough*," Quinn continued. The men he watched had paired off and begun sparring, some with weapons, some without. "Have you had enough, Captain Huzar?"

"I believe I have, Major."

Quinn nodded once and dropped his arms. "Then let this be the beginning." He drew his sword and gestured to the weapon at Huzar's side. "Let's see what you can do."

As he set his feet, facing his adversary of two years, Huzar considered that this, too, might be a deliberate attempt to gain advantage by making a personal connection.

But it wasn't as though that didn't work both ways.

26

SAGE PACED UP and down the clear area in her tent as Lani lounged in a long chair by the stove. "You will need more rugs if you do not stop soon," the princess said dryly. "There is already a bareness beginning to show."

Sage halted and lifted her skirt to frown at the carpet. She'd opted to wear a dress, though a simple one, thinking breeches would be a distraction when she was here precisely because she was a woman. And she liked dresses sometimes, to be honest, now that she wasn't trapped in them. "Where?"

The Casmuni princess rolled her eyes. "Do not tell me you have lost your sense of when I make a joke."

"This isn't a time to joke," Sage snapped. "Today is the most important day for Demora, and the success of it sits on my shoulders."

Lani shook her head. "Not today. Today everyone will test each other. Before any demands are made, all complaints of the last ten lifetimes will be tallied in hopes of establishing why they deserve what they want. Do you not know this?"

"No! I don't know anything!" Sage sank onto a couch across from the princess and put her face in her hands. "I don't even know why I'm here!"

"You should have studied past treaties," said Lani.

"I have! You've watched me every night since we left Tennegol!"

"Perhaps you should have taken lessons in diplomacy and brought a friend trained in such things," said Clare, pulling back the tapestry from her area and joining them by the stove.

Sage scowled. "You know I've been paying attention."

"Huhn," said Lani as she exchanged a sly glance with Clare. "Then you should have taken time to learn what happened at your Tegann and at the Norsari camp and the Battle of Black Glass."

"I. Was. There," Sage said through gritted teeth. "I know very well what happened at those places. Better than anyone else here."

"Sage is right," Clare told Lani. "She's not ready for this at all. She doesn't even speak Kimisar or have experience dealing with kings and queens, let alone foreign ones."

Lani nodded. "Your king could not have made a worse choice."

They were teasing, of course, but Sage pulled a cushion onto her lap, holding it tightly against her churning stomach.

"Am I interrupting?" The three women turned to see Alex standing at the entrance. He looked amused, but also slightly concerned.

"*Wohlen Sperta!*" said Lani, thanking the Spirit in her own language. She hopped to her feet and waved a hand at Sage. "Perhaps you can talk sense into her."

His eyes had never left Sage. "I don't know if I've ever been able to. But it's time to meet with the Kimisar delegation. Are you ready?"

Clare nodded and stood. "I've sent everything we wished to have on hand ahead." She joined Lani and the two of them walked past Alex on their way out. "I think there are ways only you can reassure her, though. We'll be outside, waiting."

The hanging door dropped closed behind them. Alex didn't move from where he stood. "Are you all right?"

"No." Sage stared at her hands clutching the pillow in her lap. "What am I doing here?" she whispered.

He came and knelt in front of her, taking her cold hands in his warm ones. "You're here because there is no one the king trusts more to make these talks successful," he said.

"And what if that trust is misplaced?"

"No one who knows you thinks it is. Not Clare. Not Lani. Not Prince Robert or the king. Father and Colonel Traysden believe in you, too." He smiled tentatively. "Surely they can't *all* be wrong."

Sage drew a long shaky breath and raised her eyes to meet his, which were full of sympathy. "Is this how it feels?" she asked, finally understanding some of his fears. "To be promoted beyond what you think you're capable of?"

Alex was quiet for several seconds. "Yes," he whispered.

"But you believe in me."

"I do," he said firmly. Alex lifted her hands up to his mouth. "Ironic, isn't it?" he said, kissing her knuckles when she didn't pull away. "My problem is few outside believe I can do my job, and you're the only one who doesn't believe you can do yours."

Sage had heard the whispers that followed him as they walked through the camp yesterday, the snide comments from several officers at dinner as soon as Alex left. She suddenly understood why those opinions carried so much weight—perception was often what determined reality. Marrying her now could have damaged his image beyond repair, and the future of the Nosari—and the nation—quite possibly depended on it.

Last year she'd nearly broken him by refusing to consider his needs and feelings, and she'd sworn never to do that again. Yet here she was, holding him at arm's length and acting resentful, when nothing had truly been taken away.

Alex squeezed her hands. "I promise you can do this."

There were some things that were more important than getting what she wanted right now. Alex was here, supporting her in every way he could, and that was what mattered. Sage leaned forward and kissed him. "I love you."

For a moment he was surprised. Then Alex pushed the cushion in her lap away and pulled her against him, kissing her back. "Just don't ever forget who said it first."

27

AT PRINCE ROBERT'S insistence, Sage walked into the negotiation tent at his side, followed by Clare and Lani. Alex had entered ahead of everyone and posted two guards in bright green-and-yellow Demoran livery inside the doorway. The first thing Sage noticed was that the carved, throne-like chair they'd placed for Queen Zoraya had been moved back from the table to sit several feet behind the others. She frowned. It suggested the Kimisar regent intended to watch the talks more than participate.

Her own seat was on the crown prince's left, with Clare on her other side. A bubble of panic burst in Sage's chest when she saw the Demoran chairs were not centered off Robert, but rather off Robert *and* her. That tiny detail declared she was on par with the king's son, and she gripped the high back of her chair with white knuckles as she waited for the others to file to their places.

To Robert's right was the Duke of Crescera, a burly man with thinning red hair by the name of Welborough. Sage's uncle William had claimed to have a friendship with the duke, but when she'd been introduced to him last night, she'd been too embarrassed to bring up that connection, worried Lord Broadmoor might have exaggerated their relationship. Next to Welborough was Baron Underwood, whom Countess Sophia so feared. He was the highest-ranking D'Amiran loyalist remaining in Tasmet, but he'd never been arrested, seeing as nothing he'd done for Morrow D'Amiran was beyond what a vassal reasonably owed his overlord. Sage had met him before, on the Concordium journey, though he didn't recognize her as he had Clare. Both he and the duke were there voluntarily, representing their own interests.

Lani glided to the far end of the table, a placement that emphasized she was only an observer here. Knowing Sophia's predicament, the princess also intended to keep a close watch on Underwood for Sage. As the last Demoran representative, the minister of foreign affairs, reached his seat, Sage expected the prince to sit, but he stayed behind his chair. She looked at him questioningly, and he shook his head, causing some of his dark brown hair to flop over his forehead.

"This Zoraya is a queen, so I'm expected to stand in her presence, and therefore all of you must as well," Robert explained quietly, pushing the wet hair back into place. He must have washed up right before coming. "Rather than rise when she enters, I prefer to stand, so it's less of a reaction."

Sage nodded, understanding, but feeling more overwhelmed. The tiniest actions had political meaning here. It was like sparring, where a twitch of anticipation could win or lose the fight. Except their opponents had yet to arrive. "Are they trying to make a point by being late?" she whispered.

"Probably," answered Robert. "But I made my own by being early." He smiled. "Patience, Sage. First there will be an hour of everyone thanking each other for coming and reciting all their titles." He tapped the center of her forehead lightly and winked. "Use the time to fill your mental ledger. Just don't go matching anyone."

He was referring to the work she'd done for the high matchmaker, observing and recording personalities and characteristics of almost everyone they met, filling pages of blank books for use in creating stable and prosperous unions. Somehow the thought calmed her. This was something she knew she was good at. Though it wouldn't be for marriages, the principle was the same.

Robert's eyes suddenly shifted to focus behind her, and he dropped his hand awkwardly. At first she thought maybe he'd caught Alex watching and was afraid their close conversation looking like flirting, but when she turned, it could only have been Clare he was embarrassed about.

Seeing the puzzled expression on her friend's face, Sage quickly relayed what the prince had said, and Clare nodded, like it was common sense.

The Kimisar delegation arrived then, all striding straight to their designated seats. Like the Demorans, they remained standing. Queen Zoraya entered last, wearing a full-skirted dress dyed a deep violet color—expensive—and threaded with silver designs. Her crown, too, was mostly silver, and her shiny black hair was woven around and through it in places, as if she feared losing it. When she stopped in front of her chair and faced Sage and the prince for the first time, the brilliance of her blue eyes hit Sage almost physically. The queen didn't possess the same exquisite beauty as Princess Lani—her nose and lips were thin, and her eyebrows nearly straight rather than delicately arched—but there was something striking about her all the same.

Without saying a word, Queen Zoraya abruptly sat. Robert moved around to sit in his chair, taking his time. Sage followed his example and didn't rush, aware the queen's focus had never left her. There was no surprise in her gaze, however. Someone must have warned Zoraya about her, and it made Sage nervous to think that could include Black Glass. The queen studied her like Father used to watch fledgling hawks in a nest, trying to decide which to take for training as a hunting bird, and when.

Sage forced herself to look away, tallying observations on the Kimisar ministers and brazapilla—landowners—instead. The first introduced was General Oshan, minister of war, a man of more than sixty years and fewer than sixty wiry white hairs on his head, most sprouting from his ears. His eyes had the blue-gray ring around the iris associated with old age, but his teeth were in remarkable shape, especially for a professional soldier. Sage suspected they were not his own. On the general's left was Brazapil Donala—half his age but more than twice his wealth, if the list of estates he recited was any indication. Hanging on Donala's every word was a man named Nostin, who said he was a brazapil but did not name any property. A high-strung type, judging by his ragged fingernails. Several other ministers—notably agriculture, treasury, and trade—flanked Oshan, Donala, and Nostin, but those three were the most important, so Sage concentrated on them.

They all had one thing in common, however: none of them wanted to be here.

Prince Robert introduced the Demorans but didn't elaborate beyond their names and titles. He ended with Lani, who was definitely a surprise to them, and an unpleasant one, as Casmun and Kismara had an even longer history of animosity. He finished so quickly that the Kimisar didn't seem prepared to reply. The prince took their silence as a chance to begin on his terms.

"The last time our nations met like this, my father was my age," said Robert. "Kimisara's actions in the last two years have nullified the terms of those agreements, and we do not hold ourselves bound to them any longer." That was mostly a reference to the prior disbanding of the Norsari Battalion. The prince leaned back in his chair. "What is it Kimisara wishes to discuss?"

Almost every man on the other side of the table glanced away. Only Donala and Oshan met Robert's eyes, and it was the general who spoke, though his words appeared to taste like dirt.

"Kimisara permanently surrenders all its claim of Tasmet and asks for peace."

28

THE STRAIGHTFORWARDNESS OF General Oshan's opening statement was shocking, but there was no question about what he meant.
Tasmet had been reluctantly ceded to Demora over fifty years ago, but
Kimisara had always made it clear they considered the territory theirs,
and they would someday reclaim it.

Now they were surrendering it? Permanently?

And *asking* for peace. Not requesting or demanding.

Asking for *peace*. Not a truce or renegotiated terms.

Nothing was that easy. Not after so many generations of fighting.

Sage realized her mouth had fallen open and snapped it shut. The
queen was still watching her, wearing an unreadable expression.

Robert hadn't moved an inch for the last half minute; now he raised an
eyebrow and his lips twisted in skepticism. "Is this an unconditional surrender?" he asked in Demoran, the agreed-upon language for these talks.

"No," said Brazapil Donala. "We have terms."

"Of course you do." One side of prince's mouth quirked a bit.

Then, as Lani had predicted earlier that morning, the listing of griev-
ances began. Donala started with an incident 247 years ago, and Sage realized it was going to be a very, very long day.

For the next several hours, the Demoran side matched Kimisara's complaints
one for one, and Sage's knowledge of history was most useful here. Though

she was careful not to step on the crown prince's toes, he soon was letting her do most of the talking, countering claims with Demora's version of events or a time they'd been provoked. Demora wasn't entirely innocent over the last few hundred years, however, and neither side was able to gain a clear moral high ground. It was like a chess game played with a thousand pieces.

Prince Robert's attention had a tendency to wander, which annoyed Sage at first—until she realized where that attention always went. At dinner the night before, he'd been seated close to Clare, and in her own nervousness, Sage hadn't attached any meaning into how much the two of them talked. Now whenever he shifted or scratched, it was in a way that gave him a chance to look in Clare's direction. Sage found herself leaning back in her chair to give him a better view of her friend. Clare was focused mostly on recording what was said, but at least twice she glanced up and met his eyes. Maybe she wasn't quite as interested in him as he in her, yet she didn't appear uncomfortable.

When the official conversation finally reached Sage's lifetime, Robert brought up Rewel D'Amiran first. Sage let him talk when she noticed how pleased Clare was by the prince's determination to bring her sister's husband to justice. On the other side of Duke Welborough, Baron Underwood suddenly sat forward, also invested in this topic. Count D'Amiran had been missing for over a year, and it seemed obvious that the traitor had found shelter with his brother's former allies, yet the Kimisar claimed he had not.

Brazapil Donala and General Oshan appeared earnest, but Queen Zoraya, who'd been silent the entire morning, altered her posture, a smug smile passing over her features before vanishing as quickly as it had appeared. Sage scratched a note on a piece of parchment where only Prince Robert could see.

The queen knows where Rewel is. They don't.

Robert raised an eyebrow. Sage folded the note and tucked it in her sleeve. A few minutes later the prince yawned. "I'm calling for a recess," he said in a bored voice and with a lingering glance at Clare. "I imagine that's one thing we can agree is needed."

Everyone sat back in their seats sullenly, but no one objected. The prince stood, causing the other men to scramble to their feet. Zoraya remained in her chair, locking eyes with Sage as Robert strode out. After an awkward silence, the other men moved away from the table, muttering and stretching.

"Your Majesty's dress is lovely," Sage said loudly enough to be heard over the noise. "I've been admiring it all morning." At least one Kimisar representative rolled his eyes, but Zoraya's lips flirted with a smile.

"The silver is for my late beloved husband," the queen said in crisp, accented Demoran.

"May his name be untarnished," Sage said gravely.

Zoraya looked pleasantly surprised. "You have studied our customs."

"I should not be here otherwise." Sage stood. "Does My Queen need to refresh herself?"

"We will provide for that," interrupted Brazapil Donala, stepping beside Zoraya. "What is it My Queen wishes?"

Annoyance tightened Zoraya's cheeks. "Nothing at this moment."

Sage hesitated. The queen regent appeared open to speaking with her, but there wasn't a tactful way to push for private conversation. Lani, who hadn't spoken before now, rose from her seat at the far end. "Well, I have need of refreshment," she said.

Clare also stood, and they headed for the exit. Lani paused and glanced back. "Are you coming, Ambazzador?" The princess's tone was casual, but her eyes indicated Sage should follow. When Sage again hesitated, Lani added, "We will return soon enough."

Her message was clear: the talks were only beginning. More opportunities would come.

Sage nodded soberly to Zoraya and followed her friends out.

Prince Robert was waiting in Sage's tent. Lani brushed off his polite move to help her sit and winked at Sage as he immediately turned to assist Clare, then chose the seat next to hers. Sage wasn't the only one who had noticed the prince's wandering gaze. Alex waited until Sage was settled and whispered in her ear that he would be back after checking on a few things. As he slipped out, Lani's maids brought in trays with food and drink.

"Brazapil Nostin will be the loudest voice," Lani said, pouncing on an iced pastry. "It is usually so with the least powerful men."

Robert rolled his eyes. With his dark hair and tanned complexion, the prince looked distractingly like Alex, though sometimes Sage wondered if that was more because she'd first attached Alex's name to Robert's face than from family resemblance. He'd lost much of the playfulness she'd observed two years ago, becoming more cynical, but his sense of humor wasn't completely gone. Robert leaned forward to grab a cake. "His family lost the most land when Tasmet was taken, which is why he has almost nothing now." His hands brushed Clare's as they reached for the same slice. "Oh, sorry, my lady. You can have that. I, ah . . . what was I saying?"

Sage sipped fruit juice to hide her smile. "Brazapil Nostin."

"Right." The prince fumbled with another piece. "Expect him to be especially bitter."

Sage lowered the cup to her knee. "I feel like we've made little progress."

"Nor will we until both sides have brought up every slight for the last three centuries." Robert shrugged. "Then come demands neither side will find acceptable. It could be a week before anyone makes a reasonable proposal."

Lani didn't look surprised, but Sage groaned inwardly. She'd read of peace accords that had lasted as long as two months—the average was four or five weeks—yet she'd assumed the whole of that was full of logical discussion.

"Did you manage to speak with the queen after I left?" Robert asked, brushing crumbs off his lap.

"Not really," admitted Sage. "I complimented her dress, but didn't get much further than that before Brazapil Donala stepped in."

The prince nodded. "Watch out for that one. He's the real power in that group."

"Not General Oshan?" The minister of war was the highest-ranking council member present.

"Oshan may have the army," said Robert, "but Donala made a show of supporting Zoraya as regent last year, and the people love her." He grabbed a handful of mixed nuts and tossed a candied almond in his mouth. "And armies are made of people."

29

AFTER THAT FIRST morning, Sage never had a chance to converse with Zoraya directly. Though the queen was thoroughly attentive to the discussions, she never spoke even when Sage tried to address her. Brazapil Donala and General Oshan rushed to answer any question posed to Her Majesty, almost like they were fighting over her. When that happened, Zoraya would meet Sage's eyes and smile ever so slightly. If the queen had been the primary mover behind Kimisara in asking for these talks in the first place, Sage wondered why she allowed her councillors to walk all over them.

Meanwhile, Sage's inability to tolerate what she considered nonsense often drew her into speaking up—that and the way Prince Robert readily listened and silenced anyone who tried to cut her off, including Baron Underwood on their own side. By the end of the second day, she wasn't hesitating to counter the false and often outrageous claims of the Kimisar ministers. As Robert had predicted, Nostin was the worst, and on the third morning the brazapil came ready to fight.

Sage was ready, too.

The point of contention was the damming of the Nai River by Demora, which had created a pair of lakes upstream, deep in Tasmet.

"You Demorans sink your hooks deeper into the country that used to be ours." Nostin moved a candle aside and jabbed his finger at the map laid out on the table. "These lakes displaced thousands of Kimisar and destroyed my family's ancestral home."

Now Sage understood why Nostin was so belligerent. Though his age told her the brazapil could never have known the land himself, this was personal. His title said his family still owned land in Kimisara, yet it couldn't be that much, given how beholden Nostin was to the much richer Donala.

While she was confident enough to address this matter, Sage glanced at the crown prince before responding. Robert sat back in his chair and raised the fingers of his left hand slightly, telling her to go ahead. Duke Welborough of Crescera also didn't look inclined to get involved, but Baron Underwood puffed out his chest a little. Before the baron could jump in with one of his typical insults, Sage stood straight to face Nostin, taking a deep breath to keep her voice even. "That may have been an unfortunate effect, but it was never the intent," she said. "Damming that river has prevented hundreds of deaths from seasonal floods downstream, and all those who lost land or property were compensated."

"My family was not," spat Nostin.

"They would've been if they'd stayed in Tasmet," Robert pointed out. "Many Kimisar did."

The brazapil's eyes sparkled in the candlelight. "On the condition that they submit to the very family and nation who conquered them."

Duke Morrow D'Amiran's father had been awarded the province as his duchy for his service in that war. The family had then used it as a stepping-stone in their quest to take back the crown they'd lost to the Devlins generations ago.

"Yes," said Robert Devlin calmly. "That is traditional when your overlords have changed."

True as the statement might have been, Sage didn't think the prince's cold response was going to help. Her eyes darted to Zoraya, who had leaned forward. The queen's fingers, which had been tapping the arm of her chair for the past few minutes, suddenly stilled. Was she insulted? Sage cleared her throat. "And if we offered you compensation now?"

Robert pursed his lips in silent protest, but this was the first chance they'd had in three days to make some sort of concession. Sage also didn't expect Nostin to accept the idea—or if he did, he'd name an outrageous sum.

"You reduce my family to destitution, and now you insult me?" The veins in Nostin's neck bulged.

"I offered you what I thought you said you wanted," said Sage. "I cannot give the land back. As you've pointed out, it's underwater. What *would* satisfy you?"

"Dismantle the dams."

Sage crossed her arms. "We've already explained they solve a problem that costs lives annually, and how thousands would be possibly be displaced *again*." She glanced at Robert. "If Tasmet is permanently ceded, as General Oshan said in his opening statement, that land is still in Demora, underwater or not."

She resisted the sarcastic urge to offer him fishing rights, though if he demanded them, she'd give the idea honest consideration. Sage forced herself to lower her voice. "The world constantly changes, Brazapil Nostin. Sometimes the best we can do is adjust to what is."

"Ironic, when spoken by one so young," the brazapil sneered. "How old are you again, oh wise Ambassador?"

"Old enough to have spent more time in Tasmet than you have, Brazapil," said Prince Robert coolly. "And more experienced in battle, I'd wager." He nodded at Nostin's thick waist and the spotless, empty scabbard that hung from his right side, which he wore to make a point of how he'd left his sword behind for negotiations. The man was right-handed, though, making it obvious how little he wore it under normal circumstances.

Sage shuddered involuntarily at the mention of her experience in battle. She couldn't help glancing at Alex, who stood in the shadows off to the side, speaking quietly with a Kimisar guard. The weather was overcast—hence the use of candles in the middle of the day. Shadows dominated the area outside the table, and she couldn't clearly see the other man. Despite his conversation, she knew the majority of Alex's attention was focused on her. The other soldier, too, appeared to be watching her when he wasn't appraising Queen Zoraya's situation. He'd always been present, but she'd never gotten a good look at him.

"Enough," Zoraya said suddenly. "One more insult to the Demoran representative, and I will remove you myself, Brazapil."

Sage was glad to finally hear from Zoraya—and in her defense—even though men like Nostin did not take kindly to such correction. It would likely make him less cooperative than ever, but perhaps the queen was setting up to expel him as a concession of her own. Sage turned her attention to the map, reaching across for the stick of charcoal, which had begun to roll away.

Nostin defiantly yanked the parchment toward him. The candle he'd moved earlier tipped over, arcing down onto her outstretched arm. Time suddenly slowed, and Sage froze, unable to react as the melted wax on the top spilled onto her sleeve and then the flame itself landed against her elbow.

She screamed.

Alex was at her side in an instant, slapping the fire out. It barely singed the fabric before dying, but it didn't matter. "Get it out! Get it out! Get it out!" Sage shrieked.

"It's all right," Alex was saying. "You're all right." He tried to hold her arms down as Sage flailed and cried out.

She felt the warmth of the wax through her sleeve. A rational corner of her mind recognized that it was minor, barely more than nothing, yet her hysteria continued to rise. Waves of heat and pain swept over the left side of her body, and flames surrounded her. The roar of fire was deafening in her ears. She writhed in agony, searching for a way out.

Alex was suddenly in her vision. "Sage," he said loudly. "You're all right. Look at me." He seized her chin in one hand. "Look. At. Me."

The panic receded a bit as Sage focused on his dark brown eyes, and she gasped, inhaling so deeply her head started spinning.

"That's it," he said, voice dropping to become more soothing. "Breathe, love. Slower. You're all right. It's over. There is no fire."

There is no fire.

Sage was back in a dimly lit tent, surrounded by faces. Her knees buckled, and Alex caught her. She gripped his jacket with hands that shook so hard Sage worried she might tear something loose. Stars danced in the corners of her vision as she tried to regain her footing, but her legs, especially the left one, wouldn't work. "I'm all right," she mumbled. "There is no fire."

"Negotiations are ended for the day," Alex snapped. His arm around her waist propelled her toward the exit. "Walk, Sage," Alex whispered in her ear. "Don't let them see you fall."

One foot in front of the other. Sage concentrated on each step until she was outside. A light rain had begun to fall, and she closed her eyes and turned her face up to it.

"Almost there," Alex said.

Sage couldn't muster the will to force her eyelids back open, especially when sweet unconsciousness beckoned. She managed a dozen more steps before everything suddenly grew darker. Her right toes tripped on the edge of a soft rug, and her left leg gave out.

"You made it." Alex knelt as he caught her. One hand tilted her face up. "Stay with me, Sage."

It was too late. "There is no fire," she murmured, then fainted.

30

"THE BASTARD DID it on purpose."

Alex hadn't moved from Sage's side in the last hour as she lay on the bed. He didn't like the way her eyes twitched under her closed lids, or her grimaces and moans. She was dreaming, and that was dangerous.

Lady Clare shook her head as she sat on the opposite side of Sage. "It was an accident. Nothing more."

"Like hell it was," Alex snarled. "Nostin knew *exactly* where to knock that candle. I saw him move it right before he tipped it over."

"I doubt he truly intended to harm her," said Clare with a sigh.

"It doesn't matter. The next time I see him, I'm putting a knife to his throat and making him piss himself."

"Really, Major. That won't make anything better," Clare scolded, though there was no anger in her tone.

The sound of someone entering the tent made Alex lean to peek outside the curtained area. Casseck stood there, looking solemn. "Is she all right?"

Alex glanced back to Sage's pale face, her freckles standing out against the stark white of her skin. Clare took Sage's left hand. "You can go, Major. I'll stay here with her."

He leaned down to kiss Sage's forehead, then stood with a nod of thanks to Clare. "I don't think she'll ever fully be all right," he told Cass. "Do you have something to report?"

"Captain Huzar wishes to speak with you."

Anger surged through Alex's veins. His hand went to his sword belt but came up empty. He'd removed the weapon for the negotiations. "What does *he* want?"

Cass raised a blond eyebrow. "I thought you liked him."

Alex *had* liked him, and that was the problem. The man had saved Sage's life back in Casmun, and he'd reach out to Alex a few days ago. He wouldn't call it friendship, just perhaps a mutual respect. But there was no one else who could have told the Kimisar delegates about Sage's history. Huzar was the reason they knew knocking that candle over onto her would be catastrophic. Alex's hands clenched into fists. "Where is he?"

As soon as he'd retrieved his weapons, Alex headed to the south edge of camp where Cass had indicated. On the other side of the Jovan Road, the rocky landscape gave way to a forested area, and he plunged into the trees, following a worn path to a spring he'd visited many times over the years. The last had been to clean the blood and dirt from his hands after killing and burying a trespassing squad of Kimisar two years ago.

Huzar stood from where he half sat, half leaned against a boulder. He didn't appear to be armed, but Alex assumed he was. The surrounding woods were still bare enough that Alex could see several yards in every direction. "Did you come alone?" he asked Huzar.

The man nodded, and Alex took three long, rapid strides toward him, seizing the front of Huzar's jacket with his left hand and pulling the Kimisar to meet his right fist. He didn't hit Huzar as hard as he could have, but only so he wouldn't lose consciousness right away. Alex then whirled around and slammed the soldier against a tree, pressing his forearm across Huzar's neck to hold him. "Give me one reason I shouldn't gut you like a deer right here," he said.

Up till now, Huzar hadn't resisted. He calmly licked blood off his lips. "Because I could do it to you first."

Sharp prodding made Alex look down. A blade pressed against his gut. He released Huzar and backed away. The knife disappeared, and Huzar relaxed against the tree. "Your anger makes you sloppy."

He was only half right. "I could have killed you rather than just hit you first," said Alex.

"This I know." The Kimisar wiped his face with the back of his hand. "But I also knew you would not."

"Let's talk about what else you knew," said Alex. "You told your ministers what happened to her. Because of you, they knew exactly how to torture her."

"And for that I apologize. Most of what I told them was intended to make them treat her with respect." Huzar shook his head. "Brazapil Nostin is an ass, but I did not think he would do such a thing. Perhaps because I could not imagine doing it. It was truly horrible."

Alex took a long, slow breath as he stared at Huzar. The other man never broke eye contact, and Alex exhaled, releasing some of his anger as he did. He knew an honest man when he saw one. Not to mention Huzar *had* saved her life in the valley. "That is your weakness," Alex said, pausing to breathe deeply again. "Lack of imagination."

Huzar smiled ruefully. "It has damaged me more than once." He shifted his weight off the tree and stood straight. "Yours is impatience, I think. And the ambassador herself."

"Two weaknesses to one. You have the advantage."

The Kimisar shook his head. "I have another. I protect her as you protect your Sage Fowler."

Queen Zoraya? Alex narrowed his eyes. "Why would you tell me this?"

"Because I want us to understand each other." Huzar wiped his mouth again, but the bleeding on his lip had slowed to an ooze. "And she is the one who sent me here. She wishes to speak with the ambassador. Alone."

31

WHEN ALEX RETURNED to Sage's tent, he found Lani seated with Clare and Robert, the three of them talking quietly. He bowed to the Casmuni princess before asking Clare, "How is she?"

"Awake," said a raspy voice, making everyone turn. Sage stood in the opening to her room, holding the curtain to keep herself steady. She was pale almost to the point of translucence, and Alex rushed to her side, afraid she would collapse if she let go. As he slipped an arm around her waist, Sage gave him a tiny, grateful smile and took a few shaky steps. She grew steadier as she walked, but still sank heavily onto the couch across from Lani's. Alex sat next to her and let her lean against him.

"I'm ending the talks," said Robert, shifting to address Sage, resting his forearms on his knees. "What happened today shows they aren't serious about coming to any meaningful agreements."

Sage twitched her skirt around her legs, giving more slack to the left side. "You can't destroy our first chance at peace in generations over something they can claim was an accident," she said dully.

"We all know it wasn't, though," said Rob. "They've never taken you seriously. Father thought you might be a better choice for speaking with their queen, and I agreed, but she's hardly said a word."

"She wants to change that, though," said Alex cautiously. Even if he trusted Huzar, it would be a tougher sell to his cousin, who was technically in charge of everything here. "I've just spoken with Captain Huzar. Queen Zoraya sends her sincere apologies and invites Sage to meet with her alone, for more private negotiations." He looked down at Sage, who stared blankly ahead.

"That will not sit well with her ministers," said Lani. "They are the reason she has not been able to speak with Sage in private now."

Alex nodded. "That's why she proposes a place far from here, without their knowledge." Sage was frowning now, but more thoughtfully than anything else.

Rob snorted. "Sounds like a trap to me."

"A trap? To what end?" asked Clare.

"It could make us appear like we are trying to take advantage of her," said Rob. "Or worse, that we lured her away to kidnap her."

"Possibly," admitted Alex. "But I don't think so." Huzar had seemed almost hopeful they would refuse. He obviously disagreed with his queen's offer.

"Where?" asked Sage, looking up at him. "When?"

"Bey Lissandra in nine days," said Alex, naming a trading port in the southwest corner of Demora. It had a degree of independence that other Demoran cities did not, as well as a high Kimisar population, making it effectively neutral ground. Alex knew the city well, too, which gave him a small amount of confidence. "The queen regent also says in gratitude for this meeting, she'll bring something we've been looking for." He glanced at Rob. "Do you know what that means?"

Sage met the prince's eyes, and he nodded to her. "It could mean Rewel D'Amiran," she said.

"They've repeatedly claimed they don't have him," said Clare, frowning.

Sage smiled a little. "And maybe they believe that. What if Zoraya has been hiding it from them?" Alex felt her sitting up straighter, a spark of light in her eyes.

"Why would she do that?" asked Clare.

"To give her leverage over her council, should she ever need it," said Lani, catching on. "The people support her, according to our spies, but she has been struggling to hold on to power."

Robert nodded. "And it was she who sued for peace, against her council's wishes. Perhaps she thought if she could get everyone here, she could force the outcome she wanted."

"And you think what she wants is peace?" said Clare doubtfully. "You truly think that is her goal?"

Everyone turned to Sage, acknowledging she was the best at reading people's intentions. She picked at the dried wax on her sleeve before finally saying, "I do, but if she's circumventing her own council, it's because she's concluded these talks will fail with the brazapilla present. And that could be dangerous if they find out too soon."

"How is that different from finding out later?" Clare asked. "They have to eventually."

Sage shrugged. "It'll be too late to sabotage, and if we come out with mutually beneficial agreements, they'll be difficult to argue with."

Everyone was silent as they considered. Even if things went well with this meeting, the road forward would still be rough. No rougher than it was now, however.

Alex turned to his cousin. "But will it bother you, Rob, to essentially stand aside while the real talks are held without you?" he asked.

Rob shook his head. "Sage has been running circles around everyone, which is why Nostin and the others want her gone. Either Zoraya thinks she can push Sage around—which I doubt—or she thinks she can reason with her. She'd be mistaken in the first case, and right in the second—both are wins for us."

Color flooded into Sage's cheeks at the prince's compliments. She looked up at Alex again. "What about this Huzar? Can we trust him?"

Alex thought of the man who appeared out of the smoke, offering the cloak off his back. *Take it. Carry her away.* And then after the battle, how he'd approached Alex and King Banneth to ask about her and beg the return of the Kimisar prisoners they'd taken. "I believe we can."

"How do we go about doing this, then?" Sage asked. Alex was relieved to see the color stay in her face and her posture remain steady. "If she doesn't want her council to know."

He took a deep breath. "Zoraya proposes you act as though you're returning to Tennegol, or that Rob is sending you away, but he's going to stay here, keeping the talks going. I and some of the Norsari will escort you and your caravan east before turning back with only a trusted few. The queen will leave a couple days after you. Huzar said she's already planted the seeds of being impatient to return to her son in Kimisara."

"This may have been her plan all along," said Lani. "Seeing as it has so quickly developed."

"In that case," said Rob, "meeting with her is exactly what Father would want you to do." He grinned. "I'll keep Donala, Nostin, Oshan, and the others occupied, which will be easier if Queen Zoraya orders them to stay as long as I'm here." Alex nodded to indicate he would pass that on to Huzar. "Where Sage is really going will stay between us, though. Duke Welborough and Baron Underwood certainly don't need to know, otherwise I won't be able to keep them here and the whole thing will fall apart."

"My father should know," said Alex. "And Colonel Traysden." It would be impossible to hide from the spymaster anyway.

"Well, yes, obviously," Rob agreed. "But no one else."

Princess Lani stood, shaking out her skirt. "It is settled. You know of course that I am coming."

Clare sighed and rose to her feet as well. "I'd better write to Sophia, even if it will only be our entourages arriving. Perhaps they can wait for us there during this meeting at Bey Lissandra. Having them at Jovan will make her feel safer."

Alex glanced up. Did the countess think she was in danger? His father should have addressed any of her concerns.

"If you want to do this right, you have to leave quickly and in a huff," said Robert, his gaze following Clare as she and Lani left. "I'll call for a three-day recess and act like I must consult with General Quinn before proceeding to buy you more time. Meanwhile, I'll also reduce the daily hours of our meeting and skip Chapel Days." He stood and stretched, looking thoughtful. "The general could apply pressure, too. Maybe lock down their camp."

Sage smiled slyly. "That might even make them more eager to get Zoraya away."

Robert winked one hazel eye before ducking out. "Don't ever wonder if you're the right person for this job, Sage. You're a master strategist."

As soon as they were alone, Alex pulled Sage onto his lap and held her tightly. "Are you all right?" he whispered into her hair. Sweat from her restless sleep had made the short, loose strands curl at the top of her neck. "*Really* all right?"

She leaned into him, relaxing. "Thanks to you."

"I'll be right there with you, through all this. I promise."

"I know." He felt her smile. "That's why I'm not worried."

Alex sighed a little and kissed her temple. He would worry enough for both of them.

32

FROM WHERE THEY sat astride their horses on a gentle slope overlooking the city, Sage could easily see how the port of Bey Lissandra radiated from three main shipyards, the cut stone streets stretching outward from each like spokes on wheels. Though it had become part of Demora when the country was unified over five hundred years ago, it had hosted trade from other nations the entire time, Demora, Kimisara, and Reyan laying claim to their own dock areas and wedges of homes and markets. The people spoke a unique mixture of three languages. As Sage and Clare spoke all of them, they hoped it would be easy to get along.

From Sage's right, Alex pointed out the Demoran neighborhood—a wide swath of golden-toned buildings and streets that extended to surround the city as a whole, arcing around the districts to its left and right. On the north side, Reyan conducted most of their commerce, and the hues were more red. To the south, the colors were blue—the bustling markets demonstrating what was possible if the rest of Demora and Kimisara could get along. Where the districts met and mingled, the streets grew even more colorful, giving the city as a whole a rainbow appearance. Behind it all, the glittering blue-green waters of the Western Sea extended to the horizon in a plain flatter than any Sage had seen in Crescera.

Even Lani was impressed.

The view couldn't distract Sage from the task before her, however. Somewhere in the city, the Kimisar queen waited, risking her crown and her life to talk to Sage alone. This meeting had a better chance of succeeding than the one they'd left behind, but that didn't mean it would be easy. It bothered Sage, too, that she didn't have the royal authority of Prince Robert—or even Ash Carter—with her. What if she returned to Arrowhead, agreements in hand, only to have them struck down? She'd almost rather be caught here by the Kimisar council than fail in that manner.

Lani wrinkled her nose. "What is that smell?"

Sage tilted her face up and inhaled deeply, detecting a vaguely familiar tang on the wind. "It smells like . . ." She paused and sniffed again. "That dried seagrass you sent me from Mondelea," she told Clare.

Her friend nodded and smiled. "Kelp chips. I hope they eat them here, too. I haven't had any in forever."

The Casmuni princess made a face. "I hope they taste better than they smell."

Alex leaned forward to address Lani. "What you smell is the sea."

Lani grunted unenthusiastically but then brightened as Captain Casseck came riding toward them from the city. He saluted Alex and gave his report.

"I've got everyone in place where you wanted them, sir," he said. "Nothing out of the ordinary so far."

"Very well," said Alex. "No more salutes and formalities. It will draw attention I'd rather not have."

"Which means you must now call me Lani," said the princess loudly, her brown-and-green eyes focused on Cass. "No more of this Palachessa nonsense."

Sage stifled a giggle. Lani had been trying to get Cass to call her by her nickname for the past week, but ever the polite soldier, the captain hadn't managed to do it. Alex glanced over his shoulder at Sage with a don't-encourage-her look. Honestly, though, Lani's attempts to flirt with Casseck over the past week had been hilariously inept. Sage wasn't sure which of the two was more clueless.

She studied Alex. All remaining tension between them had eased since the candle incident and leaving the army at Arrowhead. Avoiding inns, they'd slept outdoors, around a campfire, and Alex always lay between her and the flames, blocking the flickering light and heat that gave her nightmares. Most evenings she curled up against him to stay warm, wishing there weren't two dozen others sleeping around them in their camp. Last night he'd held her tighter than ever—he was worried about this meeting. Maybe even afraid. The last time she'd seen him like this was in the hours before the Battle of Black Glass, where they'd waited outside the pass for the invasion force they knew was coming.

Sage met Alex's frown, trying to quell her own fears, as Snow stamped and shifted restlessly beneath her with an innate sense of his rider's emotion. They had only ten Norsari with them in addition to him and Cass, and eight Casmuni guards—barely more than half of what he'd had with him on the Concordium mission, and now the majority were in the city, watching for signs of trouble. Everyone else, including Lani's maids, had continued to Sophia's home at Jovan to wait for them, as had most of their clothes.

The last thing their group wanted now was to be noticed, so Sage, Clare, and Lani all dressed in breeches, with swords and daggers at their waists, though Clare only had the latter. Clare's tunic was also longer than average, but her friend couldn't stop tugging the shirt low over her backside. All wore hoods and caps typical of commoners over their hair. Additionally, the past weeks of minimal grooming and no face paint had Lani looking less refined than Sage had ever seen, but lovely as ever. It probably wasn't possible for her to be anything less than beautiful.

"When will this Huzar show up?" she asked Alex.

"He's here."

Everyone looked around, bewildered, and Alex tilted his head in the direction of a copse of fir trees. A shadow within moved.

"Why didn't you say anything earlier?" Sage asked as Alex dismounted.

"Because he came alone."

Sage scowled as she tossed her leg over the horse's neck and slid to the ground. Alex walked by her side to the tree line as Clare came up on her left. Lani and Casseck held back a little, and the princess conspicuously loosened her curved sword in its scabbard. A shape detached itself from its surroundings and walked toward them, shedding a worn cloak that had provided perfect camouflage. From his height and with the queen's guard uniform now visible, Sage recognized him as the man she'd seen Alex talking to before, but this was the first time she was able to see his face.

She'd seen it before.

In a flash, Sage had her dagger out and was in a defensive crouch. "*This* is Captain Huzar?" she hissed.

Alex stood between them, arms outstretched. "Calm down, Sage."

"I will not," she snarled. Huzar didn't appear surprised by her reaction. "It's a trap. He's the one who came after Nicholas last year." Sage swept Clare behind her and backed away. "I saw him in the camp that night. He was in charge of the attack." She couldn't understand why Alex was just *standing* there.

Alex took a cautious step toward her, like *she* was the dangerous one here. "Yes, I know. I didn't realize you'd seen him then."

Huzar moved forward, gliding silently over the pine needles on the ground. Sage raised her knife to make him stop. "I recognize you as well," he said. He had only a trace of an accent, which raised her suspicion more. He must be a spy.

"Sage," said Casseck from where he stood a few paces behind, next to Lani. "He helped us get you away from the waterfire. He saved your life."

"Not good enough," she retorted.

"I spared it a few times as well," Huzar said, folding his arms.

The way he stood, feet wide and braced, shoulders back, was also familiar. Sage blinked, another memory coming to the surface as she took in the swirling tattoos on his forearms. "You were at Tegann," she whispered, and he nodded once. "I killed your hawk."

"I could have put a crossbow bolt through your throat then," he said. "It would have saved the lives of two of my men last year if I had."

"Three," Sage said tersely. "Two on the river and one in the camp." A stone from her sling for the first and her knife in the throat of the second while being pursued. The other had already been on fire when she cracked his skull with an iron pan and left him to die. There had been still another man she stabbed through the hand as he tried to climb in her boat, but she suspected he must have lived.

Huzar nodded again. "Not to mention all those you poured fire on at the Battle of Black Glass."

Her stomach roiled with self-disgust and guilt. "Why are you here, then, if I'm to blame for so many deaths?"

"Because I respect your courage." His eyes were like Alex's, a brown so dark they were nearly black—intense with purpose, yet aged and weary beyond his years. Their earnestness threatened to disarm her in the same way, too, as they flicked to Alex and back to her. "And because I would say there has been enough killing. It's time for this fighting to end."

She stood straight from her crouch, glaring at Alex. "You told him I said that?"

Alex raised his eyebrows. "I was only taking your advice. Perhaps you should, too."

Sage lowered the knife in her hand, but did not put it away. "All right," she said. "Start talking."

33

SAGE, CLARE, LANI, Alex, and Cass chose to ride, but Huzar walked to the gates of Bey Lissandra, where they met one of the Norsari assigned to stand a watch in the area who took their horses. They followed the Kimisar captain to the polished streets of the upper-class and noble neighborhoods. The contrast between the first few city blocks and where they now walked was startling, especially considering what kind of establishments were in their midst.

In the grove outside the city, Sage and Alex had listened to Huzar describe the meeting spot Queen Zoraya had chosen. Alex had raised his eyebrows when Huzar named the place—it was in a wealthy Demoran area of the city and had a strict no-weapons policy, several secret rooms, and multiple entrances and exits. "How can we be sure those things won't be used against us?" Alex had demanded.

"You will have to simply trust," said Huzar. "I might also point out that should it be known My Queen is at such an establishment, it would endanger more than just her own power and position."

Sage had torn her gaze away from Huzar for the first time to look at Alex. "It's a brothel?"

"At that high of a level, it's technically called a pleasure house," answered Alex. "Huzar is right, though, when he says it will be discreet and secure. It couldn't function otherwise."

"The food will be good, too." Huzar offered her a tentative smile, and Alex nodded in agreement.

She sighed and put her dagger back in its sheath. Alex had long ago said he'd never visited such places, but it was disconcerting to hear how much he knew about them. "Lead on."

As they navigated the city streets, Sage spotted Norsari among the population on two occasions, but she had no doubt there were several more. Every time they turned, Alex glanced around for a confirmation she couldn't see. He was tense, but his alertness never increased, which she took as a good sign.

Huzar led them down a side street and directed them into a dress shop. Sage was puzzled until a drapery was swept aside and they were ushered down a passage and into a building nearly a block away. A discreet way to enter the establishment, then, though the use of a women's tailor as a front was puzzling. Wouldn't it draw attention to have men entering the store? Alex didn't appear surprised, but neither did he look like he knew the area.

The door was opened by a handsome man dressed in loose trousers and a vest. Sage gaped and then blushed at the amount of bronze skin and muscles the man showed. Clare was positively mortified, but Lani smiled as though she appreciated what she saw. The man bowed and led them into a receiving room of sorts, where several other scantily clad men lounged about. One of them gave the princess a lusty wink, and Lani returned it.

"This place," Sage whispered to Alex, feeling her cheeks flame, "it caters to women?"

"Mostly." Alex looked amused. "You didn't think men were the only ones who pay for this kind of diversion, did you? And some men come here, too."

Sage glanced at Lani. Their friend Darit preferred the company of men, which made Sage's accidental proposal to him last year extra humiliating. She'd given him a dagger—though it was more of a loan—that had her initials on it, not realizing what such a gift meant to the Casmuni. Fortunately, both Darit and King Banneth had been amused rather than insulted.

Alex's fingers squeezed her waist. "That one over there in red is eyeing you," he teased quietly. "Should I be jealous?"

"No!" She smacked his chest with the back of her hand, still flushing.

Thankfully, the master of the house came to greet them then, bowing low. "It is our honor to serve as host for this royal meeting. Please know you may count on our discretion. Anything you require will be promptly provided."

"He makes it sound like he does this all the time," murmured Sage as they followed him up a richly carved and carpeted staircase.

"Maybe he does," replied Alex. "It would be a way to make extra money, hosting clandestine business meetings."

Alex's musing had merit. The room in which Zoraya waited for them was furnished with a table and chairs, as well as shelves lined with books and maps. The Kimisar queen rose as they entered, and her face, normally passive and immobile, brightened with a half smile of relief, though if Sage wasn't mistaken, much of the happiness was directed at Captain Huzar. Interesting.

The queen regent approached them all individually and clasped their hands, expressing gratitude, but never quite thanking them. "I know coming required a great deal of trust for you," she said in crisp Demoran. "It is my goal to make you not regret this."

She'd already shared water with Lani on the first day of negotiations at Arrowhead, but she offered the Casmuni princess a cup now. "To a new beginning," she said, after taking a sip. Lani nodded and drank.

Sage and the three other women took their seats around the table, with Alex, Cass, and Huzar standing behind them. Zoraya cleared her throat. "Now it is time for me to tell you some of the things that my ministers have not."

Some of the things, thought Sage. It was best to remember that choice of words.

"First, however," said Zoraya. "I promised if you would come, I would bring a gift." She nodded to Huzar, who slid back a panel of the wall behind him, revealing a tiny, hidden room. Inside sat a scrawny man with dark hair and sharp blue eyes. His wrists and ankles were shackled and additionally chained to each other, and Huzar took him by the elbow and lifted him to his feet. Had Sage not already seen the family resemblance, Clare's pale hand clenching into a fist would've told her who this man was.

Rewel D'Amiran.

34

SOPHIA'S TRAITOR HUSBAND, the Count of Lower Tasmet, stood straight and glared at each face around the room. "I thought this was a diplomatic meeting," he said defiantly. "It looks more like a tea party."

"I am sure we will have tea later," said Zoraya calmly. "If you are good boy, perhaps you can have some."

Sage suppressed a smile by pressing a forefinger to her lips.

"You will address me with the respect of my rank," spat Rewel. "I am Duke of—" The words were cut off by a gag yanked across his mouth. Huzar appeared to be enjoying himself as he tied it down.

"Yes, we know who you are," said Zoraya. She glanced to all the Demoran faces. "I give him to you unconditionally. Unless there is anything you wish him to answer now, I suggest we put him aside."

"I have a question," said Clare. The queen gestured for her to go ahead, and Clare stood, taking two steps around the table to face her brother-in-law. Once in the light, the grayness growing out of his black hair became visible. "Do you even know her name?" Clare asked, her chin high.

Rewel's ice-blue eyes darted back and forth, but Clare gave him no hint as to whom she referred. "Who?" he asked around the gag.

"Your daughter." Clare waited a few seconds, but he said nothing. "I just thought it was relevant because you did come to Kimisara to offer her in marriage to their king, did you not?" Still Rewel had no answer.

She leaned forward, her normally soft brown eyes fierce. "It's details like that which reveal your true character. And I will not forget it."

Clare turned away and went back to her seat. "I am finished, Your Majesty," she said coldly.

As Rewel was passed to men of the establishment waiting outside, Sage leaned over to her friend. "How did you know he tried to do that?" she whispered.

"Sophia told me."

Sage frowned. "I wish she'd told me."

The countess had acted ignorant of her husband's plans and intentions in fleeing Demora, but perhaps she hadn't trusted Sage enough to tell her. It *was* rather humiliating to be used that way.

Once again, the women faced one another across the table. Zoraya sat forward, her eyes on Clare. "I have no use for a man who would abandon his wife and child as he did," she said. "I never considered anything he offered."

Sage raised her eyebrows. "What *did* he offer?"

"Half of Tasmet, including Shovan Fortress," said the queen, referring to what the Demorans called Jovan. "Also much grain from Crescera, which his wife had as dowry, and the promise to raise an army in the future from those loyal to his family line."

Clare opened her mouth to object, but Zoraya waved her hand. "None of which matters. I have little use for Tasmet, to be frank, as we can barely feed or manage the territories we hold now, given our crop blight of the last years. However, some issues brought up at Arrowhead have merit."

"Such as?" said Sage, surprised by the admission of Kimisara's vulnerability.

The queen pulled a map from a nearby stack. "Brazapil Nostin complained about the damming of the Nai River. I understand how it prevented seasonal flooding downriver and saved lives, as you pointed out, but we have always depended on the spring floods. For over forty years now, we have not had adequate water for crops in the lower valley, which has caused many there to cross into Tasmet searching for food. My husband and his father before him encouraged such raiding parties. If you wish to end that, the dams must be eliminated."

Sage exhaled heavily. Something that had seemed like a matter of

Kimisar pride was the cause of legitimate problems. "I don't know that I can do anything about the dams," she said. "Especially as it's been King Raymond's intention to build mills there, to harness the power of the water to grind grain from Crescera. The only thing that's stopped him was the instability of the region. Otherwise, the location is ideal."

"Ideal for you," snapped Zoraya. "You will have even more food while we have less still."

"But if Demora produces more flour, we will have more to trade," pointed out Sage. "And would this not be an ideal way to transport it?" She traced the path of the Nai River south through the Kimisar border to the small seaport at its mouth.

Zoraya tapped her lacquered fingernails on the table thoughtfully. "That still does not make the land usable. We have so little that can be farmed."

"Perhaps what you need are crops that require less water," put in Lani. "I happen to represent a nation practiced in such farming."

"Demora, too, might be open to adjusting the water flow if we can see the damage we've caused," said Sage. "Would you be willing to let us survey the area? Perhaps we can offer advice in irrigating the land."

Everyone waited while the queen considered. Finally she half smiled. "It will take a great deal of thought and consulting with experts," she said. "But I think we have made more progress in three minutes than we had made before in three days."

They talked late into the night, taking breaks only for meals, covering more ground than Sage ever would have thought possible. Zoraya had a sharp mind and the ability to see issues from both sides, and for the most part Sage let her move from topic to topic in the way she wanted. In terms of the dams especially, nothing could be set in stone, but Lani pledged Casmun's help, though now that the southern pass between her country and Kimisara was effectively blocked after the Battle of Black Glass, what she could offer was limited.

"That reminds me," said Sage. "There was a seasonal river that flowed out of that pass. What do you think the wall of black glass will do to it?" She suspected she knew the answer, but Lani was better qualified to give it.

"We already have seen some effect," the princess said. "The water is blocked and a lake is forming. It is expected much of it will be turned back to Kimisara, into the river that flowed to the west side." She tilted her head to Zoraya. "You may be getting more water from that, though it will take years to tell how much."

"It will be welcome in that region," said the queen. She rubbed her eyes and glanced at the time candle, which had burned more than two hours past midnight. "I cannot think of anything left to discuss. Shall we adjourn?"

"I have one main concern," said Sage. "When we return to our ministers and nobles with our terms, how much of what we have done today can come to fruition?" She met Zoraya's bright gaze, asking the real question with her eyes. *Do you have enough power to make this happen?*

"If you set a mouse in an open field, he will wander about, looking for fallen grain and all the while fearing predators," said Zoraya. "But if you set a mouse on a straight and sheltered track, with food laid out in one direction, the mouse will go where you want without fear." She smiled. "The Arrowhead talks began like the first. With this framework, our future negotiations will be the second."

Sage nodded, knowing she would have to trust the queen, and so far she had no reason not to. "What about Rewel D'Amiran?"

"He is yours. I can hold him until you are ready to take him." Zoraya glanced at Huzar. "You know of course you were followed into Bey Lissandra."

Alex narrowed his eyes. "By whom?"

"That I do not know," said Huzar. "But it may not be safe to take him back the way you came, if there are still those loyal to him in Tasmet. Your party is small."

"We'll go by sea, then," said Sage. "A ship can take us north to Crescera."

Clare shook her head. "No, Reyan is better. I can get us an armed escort with Papa's connections." Her voice only wavered a little when she referred to her love Luke Gramwell's father, who was the former ambassador to Demora's northern ally.

"Reyan, then," said Sage, looking to Alex. "How long do you think that will take to arrange?"

"A day at least."

Zoraya stood. "Keep us apprised. When you are ready, we will bring the traitor to you, along with a summary of my proposals for your king. Please be swift. I have told my council I am visiting my son in Kimisara. I should like to do so in reality."

"How many guards do you have with you here?" asked Sage curiously. She'd only seen Huzar, but there had to be more.

The queen exchanged glances with her captain, and something passed between them Sage couldn't decipher, though it contained fear. Huzar answered, "I have twelve of my most trusted men here in the city."

"Odd," said Alex. "We only accounted for ten, and four of them were within a hundred yards of each other. Almost like they were guarding something." He crossed his arms. "You wouldn't happen to have more leverage on hand to be used if things started to go badly with us, would you?"

"No," said Zoraya sharply. Fiercely. "They watch my place of lodging. Now it appears I will have to find a new one."

Sage saw the twitch of her eyes and knew the queen was lying. She also recognized the clench to her jaw. Queen Orianna did the same thing any time she felt one of her children was threatened.

Did Zoraya have her son, Mesden, with her?

35

TWO MORNINGS LATER, Sage stood on city docks in the early light of dawn, watching Alex return from a ship anchored in the harbor. The water here was warmed by southern currents, and mist drifted across the bay in patches, occasionally covering the progress of the longboat. Beside her, Lani shivered and hugged her cloak tighter. "I thought you were finally used to the cold," said Sage.

"It is not the cold," said Lani. "Something feels wrong."

Sage couldn't help but agree. It was too quiet. Even the sea was still.

"This is called slack water," said Clare from Sage's other side. "There's often a strange calm before the tide changes to come in or go back out. Sailors consider it bad luck to do certain tasks in this hour."

Now was the time to bring the horses out to the ship on a barge, while the water was calmest or drawing slowly out to sea. They also intended to board themselves, as soon as Huzar delivered Rewel D'Amiran. Clare had told them the best time to sail was with the afternoon ebb tide, and the ship would weigh anchor and tack into the north wind. She kept using terms Sage barely understood, ones she'd learned in her time at the northern seaport of Key Loreda. Sage wondered if she was showing off. Throughout the day of negotiations, Clare had spoken little, and later she'd confessed how inadequate she'd felt as Sage and the queen discussed farming methods, geography, and resources. Any historical points she'd been able to offer were only as much as Sage knew. Going through Reyan to return home was probably a way she felt she could add to their mission, but it was a good idea, and Sage was glad to go with it. Sage only wished Clare understood how indispensable she was.

Despite the deathly calm and the tingle in her spine, Sage thrilled as she imagined riding triumphantly into Tennegol, carrying Zoraya's proposals and tentative agreements in addition to a shackled traitor. She'd achieved everything she'd set out to—and more, seeing as Casmun was also engaged in these solutions. Clare's sister, Sophia, would finally be free. Perhaps this could be the beginning of letting women have more say in Demoran affairs in general.

Alex came into view again through the last patch of fog, and Sage smiled. She'd be more than glad to share this success with him. Maybe it would be the proof everyone needed to see him as deserving of his rank and command.

Maybe then they could be married.

The boat bumped against the dock, and Alex climbed up, tossing a looped rope over a wooden post. "All is prepared." He'd insisted on inspecting every inch of the vessel and interviewing all of the crew. "Your rooms are cramped but adequate."

"Cabins," murmured Clare, but Alex didn't hear her.

"I'll take care of the bags," said Casseck. He scooped up the packs at the women's feet and handed them down to Corporal Duncan waiting in the boat. On another dock nearby they could hear the horses being walked onto the barge. All but two Norsari were coming with them. The remaining pair would ride back at speed to update General Quinn and Prince Robert.

"Do you want to go now or wait for Huzar?" Alex asked Sage.

"I think he's here," she replied, nodding toward a side street. The cloaked form of the Kimisar captain stepped from the alley, holding the arm of Rewel D'Amiran with a grip as strong as the irons on his wrists. The duke's ankles were unshackled so he could walk. To Sage's surprise, Zoraya herself followed on his heels, carrying a bundle of parchments. It was quite a risk for her to appear in the open, even at this silent hour, but perhaps it was an effort to show the mutual trust they'd built. She came to meet Sage where the stone street ended and the wooden docks began.

"I wanted to say good-bye myself," the queen said, offering the documents she'd brought.

Sage accepted the bound packet. "I'll do my best, but you know I can promise nothing, as this wasn't how my king expected us to meet. I don't have royal authority without Prince Robert."

Zoraya nodded. "Yet I feel we are much closer than we were before. I eagerly await news from you." She even sounded like she meant it.

Alex stepped forward. "Rewel D'Amiran," he said formally. "As an officer of King Raymond the Second, I hereby place you under arrest for crimes of treason against the crown. All your actions from this moment forth are subject to record and can be used against you in your trial."

The count sneered. "Can I expect a fair trial?"

"Fairer than you deserve, I'm sure," Clare said.

Alex took his arm and Huzar let go. "Which is why you should be very afraid right now."

Rewel opened his mouth to retort, but the words never left his lips. An arrow burst through his throat. Blood splattered all over Clare, and she screamed.

"Get down!" Alex's hands were on Sage's back, pushing her down, but she was already lunging at Clare, angled to knock her into Lani. The four of them tumbled to the ground as more arrows whistled through the air. Alex was on top of Sage, shielding her and Clare as he looked around for the source of the attack. Cass leapt from the edge of the dock and covered Lani with his own body.

"Where?" shouted Alex. "Where did that come from?"

Norsari soldiers came running from where they'd been loading horses, pointing up at the buildings nearby. Sage caught a glimpse of a form ducking behind a dormer, then scuttling back over the rooftop. A gurgling sound made her turn her head to see Rewel D'Amiran mere feet away, sputtering and clutching at his bloody throat. Clare was staring at him, eyes wide enough to see white around the whole brown. Sage grabbed her friend's chin and pulled it around to her. "Don't look," she said, taking her own advice. She'd seen men die up close, and it wasn't something she ever wanted to see again.

But they couldn't help hearing.

The duke choked and gasped as shouts sounded around them. "Everyone, stay down," Alex commanded, at last lifting himself off of Sage. "Are you hurt?" he asked.

"I'm fine," she answered, shifting into a more comfortable position but keeping low to the ground. Alex wasn't bleeding that she could see. Sage turned to her friends. "Clare?"

Rather than reply, Clare leaned away from the expanding pool of blood and vomited.

"I saw six arrows," said Cass. "The others hit . . ."

Sage and Alex turned to where Cass pointed. Captain Huzar was lying over the queen, blood streaming down his face. From the looks of it, half of his left ear was gone. Beneath him, Zoraya moaned. Lani was already comforting Clare, so Sage crawled toward the Kimisar before Alex could stop her.

Huzar rolled back, cradling Zoraya in his arms. Blood flowed down the front of her dress from a razor-sharp point protruding from her collarbone. The shaft of the arrow came up out of the back of her shoulder. Only a few inches had separated her from a fate like Rewel's. Bad as it was, the queen was lucky, for now.

"Malkim," Zoraya whispered in her own language, looking up at Huzar in a daze. "I cannot move my arm."

Sage drew her dagger from her waist. "We need to get her away from here," she said as she sawed at the arrow shaft a few inches above the entry wound. Alex stood over them, bellowing orders to the Norsari and Casmuni running after the shooters.

"The assassins are in the city, Spirit knows where," said Huzar.

"Then we'll take her to the ship. No one will be able to harm her there." The cut was deep enough now that Sage resheathed her knife and snapped the shaft the rest of the way, murmuring an apology when Zoraya cried out in pain. The queen's bronze skin had turned sickeningly pale, almost green, and was sheened with sweat.

"Everyone, into the boat!" Sage yelled, moving around to support Zoraya's uninjured side. Lani heaved Clare up by her elbow and half dragged her toward the water. Together, Sage and Huzar carried the queen to the edge of the dock while Alex, sword drawn and constantly scanning the rooftops and the streets, brought up the rear. They started to lower Zoraya into Casseck's and Corporal Duncan's waiting arms. Lani jumped down beside them to help.

"No!" shrieked Zoraya, sitting up and clutching at Huzar with her right hand. "You must go! They will come for him!"

"Stop!" yelled Sage at the queen in Kimisar. "You will make things worse!" A surge of blood came from the wound, soaking her hand.

Huzar froze, eyes wide, then shook his head. "I cannot leave you."

"Malkim." Zoraya held him close to her face. "He is the only thing that matters."

Sage stared at the two of them, her mouth dropping open. Mesden *was* here. Queen Zoraya trusted her own council far less than anyone had realized.

Huzar shook his head again. "My Queen—"

"You are sworn to me, and I order you to go." Zoraya's forehead creased, eyes suddenly pleading as her voice fell to a whisper. "If you love me, you will do as I ask."

Huzar swallowed and nodded. The queen's hand relaxed, and she sagged into Casseck's arms, looking faint. "I know you will not fail me," she mumbled, her eyes drawing closed. Zoraya's body went limp, and Sage continued to help lower her into the waiting boat. The queen's head was settled into Lani's lap, and Cass then reached up to help Clare, who was pale as parchment and shaking all over.

"What do we do about Count D'Amiran?" Sage asked.

Alex glanced at the still body, lying like a heap of wet clothes. "Leave him. Retrieving him isn't worth losing any of us."

Before Sage could say anything, Huzar stood straight and seized her by her collar and lifted her off her knees, yanking her close to his face. "How do I know this isn't a Demoran plot?" he growled.

A sword point came to rest on Huzar's neck, immediately collecting blood that trickled down from his torn ear. "Unhand her, Captain," Alex ordered, his voice deadly calm.

Huzar released his grip, and Sage straightened her clothes while fiercely returning his gaze. "Now you know how I've felt since meeting you," she said.

Alex lowered his sword and tilted his head toward the city. "Go," he told Huzar, almost kindly, as though he hadn't been ready to cut his throat seconds ago. "We'll keep her safe, I swear it."

Huzar backed away, never taking his eyes off Sage. "Do not make me regret trusting you, Sage Fowler," he said, then turned and ran.

36

SAGE KNEW WHEN the longboat passed out of crossbow range because Alex's breathing slowed noticeably, and his shoulders lowered a couple of inches. There was no possibility of relaxing fully with a wounded Kimisar queen in his custody, however. A silence had fallen again, though the fog had lessened, and Sage shivered as the rowers propelled the boat swiftly across water smooth as glass. She wanted to tell Alex where she believed Huzar had gone, but shortly after they shoved away from the dock, Sage recognized that Zoraya wasn't unconscious at all—she'd pretended to faint, probably to stop her captain from arguing further.

The queen's shoulder was bleeding from two places, which worried Sage, thinking about the soldier she'd killed at Tegann. He'd bled out so fast he'd lost consciousness right after her. Alex assured her the darkness of the blood was a good sign, though. Had an artery been severed, the color would've been much brighter. It was the thought of assassins going after an innocent little boy that made her queasy, though. What if Huzar ended up leading them straight to the king?

The packet of letters from the Kimisar queen lay in Sage's lap, the bottom soaked with Rewel D'Amiran's blood and the top with Zoraya's. She doubted much of it was readable anymore. It felt symbolic: all that work—all their hopes—washed away by blood and violence. Worse, if Mesden was harmed, Demora's chances of peace were effectively shattered for another hundred years.

Maybe that had been the goal.

Who was trying to start a war? Not Demora, she was sure, but the alternative meant Kimisara had tried to murder its own queen. There had been other arrows, too, meaning someone else among them had also been a target. Sage was inclined to believe it was her. If Huzar knew what role she'd played at the Battle of Black Glass, so did other Kimisar. That might also explain the attempt to kill Zoraya—she was consorting with her nation's greatest enemy.

When they reached the ladder hanging over the side of the ship, Alex slung the queen over his shoulder and climbed up without assistance, which was a marvel to Sage, as it was difficult for her with two hands and carrying nothing. Clare was too shaky and had to be lifted up in a sling of sorts.

The ship's captain directed Alex to take the queen to his own cabin, and Sage followed him after Lani assured her she would tend to Clare. They placed Zoraya on a long chair near a window for better light, and carefully cut her dress away from her shoulder. Casseck gritted his teeth and shook his head as he wiped blood away from the entrance and exit wounds. Shards of white bone jutted out from the head of the arrow, which could barely be seen.

"Not completely broken, I think," murmured Alex, pouring a little water over the queen's shoulder. "That will make removal difficult, but it will heal faster."

Sage swallowed a mouthful of bile. "What can I do?"

"The ship's captain will bring bandages and water soon," Alex said. "Are you up to sitting by Her Majesty and wiping away blood as needed?" She nodded, and after a wary glance at her, Alex addressed Casseck. "She may start bleeding beyond what we can control, maybe even before we can get the arrow out."

Cass acknowledged him and hurried from the room. He was the best at stitching wounds—he'd done the sutures in the scar on Alex's temple—so he must have gone to get supplies for that. The ship's captain entered, carrying a surgery kit. Alex and Sage were sorting through it as Casseck returned and set a cloth-wrapped metal box off to the side.

Zoraya moaned, and Sage stepped around and took her hand. "I'm here, Your Majesty," she said. The queen shifted against the cushioned chair back.

"Lie still," Alex told her. "Or I will have to restrain you."

Zoraya's eyes opened, no trace of unconsciousness in her defiant gaze. For a second she looked ready to snap at him but then apparently thought better of it. "Tell me about my wound," she said.

Alex's mouth twitched in what Sage recognized as admiration. "The head of the arrow is embedded in your collarbone, Majesty," he said. "We will have to back it out and then push it forward. Once it is free, we will cut it from the shaft and pull that back out here." He gently touched the entry wound and Zoraya hissed in pain. Sage wondered if he had done that as a test of what she could feel.

"That explains my arm," the queen muttered. "I cannot lift it."

"Nor will you for several weeks," said Casseck. "We will press the bone back together and put you in a sling."

Zoraya focused on the ceiling and exhaled slowly as sweat formed on her upper lip. "When will you begin the removal?"

"We need a few more minutes," replied Alex. "Everything must be ready before we can start."

"Very well." The queen looked at Sage. "I birthed a baby of eleven pounds. This shall be nothing." The brave words were said with a noticeable quiver, and a silent plea was in her eyes. *Don't leave me.*

Sage brought Zoraya's hand to her chest and squeezed it reassuringly. "It shall be nothing," she agreed in Kimisar. "Let us talk of pleasant things. Tell me about your son."

The queen frowned at her suspiciously. "Why?"

Sage's belief that Huzar had gone to protect the young king wasn't the primary reason she'd suggested that topic. "I thought mothers loved to talk about their children." She smiled in innocent bewilderment, and when Zoraya relaxed slightly, Sage asked, "Why did you choose the name Mesden for him?"

"The king chose it." Zoraya focused on Sage, away from the dagger blade Alex held in the flame of a candle to sterilize it. "It is a name from legend."

Though she knew the history already, Sage encouraged the queen to keep talking. As she'd hoped, the subject quickly became Mesden himself. Zoraya was closely involved in his care and education. It reassured Sage that the queen may have kept her son close for maternal reasons rather than mistrust of her own country.

With one eye on Zoraya and another on wiping blood away from Alex and Casseck's work, Sage managed to watch them through the steps they'd described, holding down her breakfast with some effort. The amount of blood was unnerving yet manageable, but after they sawed off the arrow's point and yanked the shaft out from the back, the flow increased.

Alex swore, but he'd obviously been expecting it. He gestured to Cass, who opened the metal box to reveal not needle and thread but hot coals. "Don't watch, Sage," Alex said.

She held up the bloody towel. "But she's bleeding—"

"We're about to stop the bleeding. Look away."

Spirit above, they were going to cauterize—*burn*—the wound to end the flow of blood. Sage squeezed her eyes shut and turned to her left. Zoraya screamed around the piece of rope they'd put in her mouth, and Sage might have made it had it not been for the smell. Suddenly she was back in the valley, surrounded by screams and men on fire, crawling through a river of flames. The sharp pain of her temple hitting the edge of the table brought her back into the current moment for only a split second before everything went dark.

The next thing she knew, Alex was crouched over her, feeling her head and apologizing. "I'm so sorry, Sage. I should've known what would happen, but you were doing well, and the queen needed you."

Sage sat up, dizzy. The scent of charred flesh lingering in the air made her gag, and Casseck barely got a bucket under her before she vomited. She waved Alex away. "I'm fine. Get back to Her Majesty."

Alex and Casseck returned to their work, and Sage fumbled to the stool, trying to remember what she and the queen had been talking about. "You said Mesden already knows his letters," she said, wiping her mouth. "Can he read yet?"

Zoraya was hoarse from the last few minutes. "We are quite a pair, no?" She smiled weakly at Sage before answering her question. "Not yet. We are focused on learning Demoran speech first."

A half hour later, Queen Zoraya rested in a hammock, eyelids twitching from dreams under the influence of drugs Casseck had mixed as soon as he and Alex had finished bandaging her shoulder. Sage had watched Cass administer the opiates with a hunger she'd almost forgotten, suddenly aching for the foggy bliss they'd given her in the aftermath of the Battle of Black Glass. Her mouth went dry, and the bruise on her head throbbed. When Cass set the bowl down, she reached for it without thinking. What was left shouldn't go to waste.

Alex snatched the bowl away.

She started to object, reaching for her temple. "But my head—"

"No, Sage," Alex said firmly. "You don't need it."

Her hands shook as she clasped them together. "Alex, please!" Tears streamed down her face as he poured the remainder in the bucket she'd been sick in.

Rather than scold, Alex folded her in his arms, rocking her as she shuddered and cried uncontrollably like she had in the days after he denied her the medicine last year. "It's all right," he soothed. "It'll pass. You're stronger than you think."

No, she wasn't; she was weak. Sage sagged against his chest, weeping and shivering, until the world slowly became reasonable again. She realized Casseck must have left, which was even more embarrassing. "I'm sorry," she mumbled.

"Don't be," Alex said into her hair.

"Will it always be like this? Will I always want that stuff?"

"I honestly don't know." Alex loosened his arms and kissed her forehead before gazing down at her sympathetically. "But I don't think it was the only thing that shook you. Most was shock from what happened this morning. Seeing the medicine just broke the dam."

The events of the morning came crashing down on her. She sat back, looking at the Kimisar queen covered in blood. Back on the city docks lay the body of a traitor the king had wanted to bring to justice. It was hard to imagine a worse situation for peace now. "Spirit above, Alex," she whispered. "What are we going to do?"

"I'm going to find out who did this," he said. "But I need to talk to Huzar first. Hopefully he'll be back soon."

"He's here." They turned to see Casseck standing at the door. "The captain arrived with the first of the horses." He looked at Alex. "And we have a serious problem."

"More serious than being in possession of the half-dead queen of our historical enemy?" Alex asked. "Without Huzar we have no way of proving we didn't just *take* her."

Cass stepped back, and the man behind him came forward. Even before she could see clearly, Sage knew what—who—Huzar carried in his arms. A plainly dressed child with curly black hair craned his neck around to look at them, his blue eyes wide.

Alex's mouth dropped open. "Is that . . ."

At the sight of the queen, the boy twisted to get free, screaming, "Mama! Mama!"

Huzar set him down, and as the child ran across the cabin to the queen, sobbing, Alex closed his eyes and covered them with a bloody hand.

"We are in deep shit."

37

SAGE GRABBED FOR Mesden before he could jump on his mother. "You must have care," she told him in Kimisar. "She is hurt."

Once she'd stopped his momentum, she guided him gently to the queen's side. He halted and stared, and Sage was glad they'd bandaged Zoraya enough that he couldn't see her wounded shoulder and the exposed bone. "Will she die?" Mesden whispered with quivering lips.

"No," she assured him. "But she needs rest. We will wake her soon. I know she will be glad to see you."

Mesden gawped at Sage's bloody clothes. "Are you also hurt?" he asked.

"No, this from helping bandage your mother."

The boy threw himself into her arms. Sage sat on the stool again and rocked him as Alex and Casseck described to Huzar what they'd done for his queen. The Kimisar captain listened with a face of stone, arms folded across his chest. When they were done, he nodded once. "I thank you," he said in Demoran.

"What's going on in the city?" Alex asked him. "Have your men caught any of the assassins?"

Huzar frowned. "No, their priority was protecting the king. Once I had him, they went to pursue, but they are far behind."

"I'm sure the Norsari and Casmuni with us are closer to catching them," said Alex. "We'll share anything we find with your men." Huzar only grunted, and Alex took a deep breath. "While I'm glad to see your king is safe, you have to know this complicates the situation even more. If the Kimisar council learns we have both the queen regent and the king, they'll assume the worst, which is that we captured them. That's an act of war."

The captain sighed as though he agreed. "She can never bear to have him far away."

"But if the council doesn't know Her Majesty is here," said Sage, "they don't know he is, either. Where do they think he is? And how long before they discover he's gone?" she asked.

Huzar worked his jaw a few times before answering. "They think he is at a country estate about three days south into Kimisara, but they may never realize he is not. There is a decoy child in his place."

Sage stole a glance at the sleeping queen. Clever. And paranoid. Not that the latter was unjustified.

"His nursemaid and my guards are the only ones who know the truth," Huzar continued, then added, "And the boy himself."

There was a reason Zoraya had been so personally involved in Mesden's education. "If Her Majesty has set this up," said Sage carefully, "it must be because she doesn't trust her own council and brazapilla."

Huzar's expression darkened. "You seek to blame this on my country?"

"The fact that you left your queen in our care indicates you did not truly believe it was our action, either," Sage retorted.

"Perhaps not you, Sage Fowler, or you, Major," Huzar said with a nod to Alex. "But that does not mean others in Demora are innocent."

Though he likely didn't understand them, Mesden looked frightened at their fierce words, and Sage tried to speak calmly. "I seek only to create a list of possibilities. I will not leave Demora off of it."

No one she could think of made sense, though. Even the D'Amiran loyalists who objected to the peace talks wouldn't have wanted Rewel dead. "Who gains most from the queen's death on both sides?" she asked. "Who has challenged her? Brazapil Nostin?"

Huzar's mouth tightened. "Nostin is a coward. He does nothing without Brazapil Donala's permission or guidance."

"And Donala himself?" Alex said.

"He was a primary candidate for regent. My Queen had the support of the people, and he conceded. But he would be the leading choice again if she were to disappear," Huzar admitted. "And he is wealthy enough to stand against General Oshan, who would challenge him."

Sage nodded. "Then he belongs on the list."

Huzar turned his eyes on her. "What of the Casmuni?"

She blinked in surprise, having expected him to ask about Demorans. "What of them?"

"Chessa Alaniah was at the negotiation table," said Huzar. "Casmun has interest in the outcome."

Sage shook her head. "Her presence was coincidental. She was already in Tennegol and decided her brother the king would want her to attend."

"She was there to strengthen Casmun's alliance with Demora while Kimisara was weak," countered Huzar. He shifted his crossed arms. "Convenient."

It went against everything Sage knew about King Banneth. "No," she said firmly. "The Casmuni gain nothing."

There was an uncomfortable silence, and Huzar gave Alex a pointed look. Alex cleared his throat. "Sage," he said hesitantly. "I know Lani's your friend—"

"No." Sage cut him off. The Casmuni king had been willing to marry her to force his ministers to talk to Demora after two centuries of isolation. No one was more dedicated to making peace. "It has nothing to do with friendship. I know Banneth. I won't even consider it."

Huzar didn't look happy with Sage's refusal, but he moved on. "Then which Demorans do you suspect?"

Sage had been working through that in her mind before Huzar's distracting accusation. With Rewel gone, Sophia's daughter was the legal heir to Tasmet. If the strongest D'Amiran loyalist, Baron Underwood, wanted control of the province, the chaos between Demora and Kimisara caused by the assassination would be the perfect opportunity to take Aurelia D'Amiran. He might try to force Sophia to marry him—and Sage suspected the now-dowager duchess would if it meant protecting her daughter.

"Baron Underwood," Sage said, then explained her logic.

"Isn't he already married?" asked Casseck.

"Watch for that to change," said Sage, arching an eyebrow.

"Yes, but he'd only do that if the attempt on the queen's life was successful," argued Cass. "We'll never know now."

Therein was the problem: the queen's survival, while fortunate, would make it almost impossible to uncover who had sent the assassins and why.

"Well, then that's our solution," Sage said. "We let everyone think she's dead and wait for the traitor to make his move."

38

FOR A LONG moment the cabin was silent, save the creaking of the unlit lantern hanging from the ceiling, swaying with the motion of the ship. Sage shifted Mesden on her lap as she watched the others, whose reactions were all different—and disheartening. Cass's mouth dropped open in shock, and Huzar looked sick at the idea of pretending his queen was dead—then he turned angry. And Alex . . . the merits of the plan felt obvious. Sage couldn't understand why he didn't agree right away. His expression of doubt was like a knife in her stomach.

"Just like we did in Casmun," Sage said, ignoring Huzar's scowl and focusing her argument on Alex. "You were there when the *dolofan* came for King Banneth."

The *dolofan* were Kimisara's branch of spies. They specialized in assassinations. Huzar dropped his crossed arms and balled his fists. "This is the first I've heard of such a plot."

"It was an agreement between the Casmuni minister of finance and your king Ragat," explained Alex. "After Banneth's death, Minister Sinda intended to marry Princess Alaniah and rule for Banneth's young son. In return for the assassination, the guards at the southern pass stood down to let the Kimisar through to invade Demora from the south."

"Yes," said Sage, flinching at the indirect mention what she'd done to stop that invasion. "The only way we could prove Sinda was behind the plot was to make it appear as though it succeeded. When he tried to blame me before the council, his plan fell apart."

Lani had been there, too, and Sage was sure the princess would support her plan. Where was Lani when she needed her?

Alex shook his head. "This is different, Sage. We didn't have time for anything else."

"But it worked," Sage insisted.

"With power-hungry ministers in a locked room," said Alex. "Not two armies ready to fight. Imagine the chaos news of her death would bring."

"It will be chaos no matter what, but this way it can be controlled," said Sage. "If we return to Arrowhead, word of what happened will travel ahead of us." She gestured to the unconscious queen. "Her Majesty will travel slowly. By the time she gets there, everyone will have been at one another's throats for days, and her arrival will change nothing."

Huzar was the first to grasp her point. "You're saying if the report is of the queen's death, there will be pandemonium, but that will end when she returns."

"Yes," said Sage. "When they see her alive and under our protection, everyone will stop and reassess. Meanwhile, the traitor will have acted, and we'll have some idea what he wanted to accomplish."

Alex had one arm across his stomach, bracing the other upright so he could tap his bottom lip, as he often did when he was thinking. He shook his head. "There's still the problem of getting the queen back to Arrowhead in one piece. All of us together aren't enough to guard you, her, Mesden, and Princess Lani over that distance. One of those arrows was aimed at you, Sage. I won't take that risk."

"So we'll stay here," replied Sage. "We'll wait until the Norsari can come and get us. It will give Her Majesty time to recover."

"Stay in the city where someone tried to kill you? Not a chance," said Alex flatly.

"Nor would I agree to that," said Huzar.

Sage pointed to the floor. "I meant here, on the ship." When Alex hesitated, she asked, "Can you think of anywhere safer?"

"Reyan," offered Cass. "As we planned."

Alex shook his head. "Too far. And with the ship no one can sneak up on you." He glanced at Huzar. "You'd have to take the news to your council yourself, otherwise we'll have no idea how any of them react."

The captain recrossed his arms, the tattoos lining up to create a single design. "As well as making the claim convincing," Huzar said, though the idea obviously pained him. "They know I'd never leave her side if she were alive."

"We'll protect her life with our own," promised Sage.

Alex raised his eyebrows. "Then you like this plan?" he asked Huzar.

"I do not like it," the captain replied. "But it appears the safest for My Queen." He locked eyes with Alex. "I will agree on one condition."

"Name it," said Alex.

"*You* will also return to Arrowhead."

Sage's shoulders slumped.

"Done," said Alex.

"Why can't Captain Casseck go?" Sage asked. "General Quinn would believe him."

"It's only fair, Sage," said Alex, keeping his eyes on Huzar. "And I should be there to assess the situation for myself. But I'm telling my father and Colonel Traysden the truth. Robert, too."

Huzar considered for a few seconds. "Robert is your crown prince and Traysden is your minister of intelligence?"

Alex nodded. "You may also tell those you absolutely trust. We can't each uncover the traitor alone." Huzar acknowledged with a grunt, but said nothing.

"I assume that means I'm staying," said Casseck.

"Yes." The muscles in Alex's jaw clenched; he wasn't happy about it, even if he knew he had to do it. "You, a few Norsari, and all the Casmuni—they won't want to leave the princess anyway."

"What about Mesden?" Sage asked. The child looked up at his name, and she smiled to reassure him.

Huzar swallowed. "He will stay. My Queen would not have it otherwise, and taking him anywhere else risks exposing the decoy king." He came a few steps closer and knelt before the boy. "My friend," he said in his own language. "The time has come to play the game, this time with many people."

Mesden's blue eyes widened. "The hiding game?"

Sage and Alex exchanged glances. *The hiding game?*

Huzar was focused on his king. "Yes. Are you ready?"

The boy smiled a little smugly. "I will win."

"See that you do." Huzar ruffled Mesden's dark curls and stood, addressing Sage and the others in Demoran. "My Queen has prepared him for hiding. He believes it is a game to pretend he is someone else, and he is well practiced."

Sage's arms tightened around the child unconsciously. For all the fear Clare's sister, Sophia, lived with, Queen Zoraya had it much worse, but she had been ready to wrest her child's fate away with her own hands. Horrifying, but admirable.

"May I have a moment alone with My Queen?" Huzar asked quietly.

Sage stood, putting Mesden on his feet. "Of course." She propelled the young king toward the door with the promise of food and a quick return. Alex and Casseck followed her out, where Lani waited in the passage, wearing a scowl.

"Were you going to consult me in any of your planning?" she asked haughtily, her hands resting on her hips.

Sage grimaced. "I'm sorry, Lani." After her initial wish for the princess's support, she'd completely forgotten about her and Clare.

Alex turned away. "I need to talk to the ship's captain."

"Where are we going?" Lani demanded as Alex headed for the door leading outside. "Since it is decided."

"We're not going anywhere," said Casseck, gesturing to Lani and Sage. "Major Quinn and Captain Huzar will return to Arrowhead with the news that Queen Zoraya was assassinated."

All the color drained from Lani's face, though she was pale already. "The queen is dead?"

"No," said Sage quickly. "We think the only way to find out who is behind this is to make them think they succeeded."

Lani pursed her lips. "So to know them by their actions? Like . . . ?"

"Like Minister Sinda, yes," said Sage.

The princess clenched her fists at the mention of her ex-lover's name. Her eyes, now dominated by their green hues, darted to Casseck. "And we will stay here while the Maizshur goes to find the guilty?"

"I'll keep you safe," said Casseck, reaching for Lani's arm. "You needn't worry."

Color rushed back into Lani's pallid cheeks as he touched her, and she smiled at his back as he followed Alex. When he was gone, she quickly turned a frown on Sage. "I am surprised to hear you are content to wait while others act," she said.

It hadn't felt like waiting when Sage came up with the plan, but she'd also expected Alex to stay with them. Now she realized how little she'd be doing. She held Mesden's hand out to Lani. "Can you take him to get a bite to eat? I need to speak to Alex."

Lani huffed but took him. She bent over to address the boy. "What is your name, handsome?" she asked in his language.

The smug smile returned to his face. "Victor," he said. Apparently, he believed this was his first test in the hiding game.

As Lani led him off, Sage went the way Alex and Casseck had left. Outside the stuffy cabin, the fresh air made the smell of blood on her clothes more obvious and sickening. Alex and Casseck were talking to the ship's captain.

"If you want some of the th' horses sent back, Major, I can't unload them till th' next slack," the man was saying. His white-whiskered jowls framed a face brown and wrinkled as a walnut shell. "That's about an hour. We can set sail as th' tide goes out right after that."

Sage raised her hand to shade her eyes. It was about noon, and the ship had swung around so its rear was toward Bey Lissandra, pointing the front into the current. From here she could see the water had risen several feet against the city docks. Almost high tide. After it peaked and turned, the ship would leave.

Leave Alex.

"Time and tide wait for no man," came a soft voice behind her. Sage jumped and turned to face Clare, who was pale but steady on her feet, which was more than Sage felt with the heaving deck.

"What was that?" Sage asked.

"It's a sailors' expression," said Clare. "Meant to remind them they cannot choose their time of departure."

Sage's lips twitched. Alex's impatience and unwillingness to let invisible forces dictate when he could act would have made him a very poor sailor. As he and the captain continued discussing details, Sage explained everything to Clare, who frowned and muttered that she should've been in on the plan. Sage resisted pointing out Clare had been on the edge of fainting the last time she'd seen her, and not likely to have been much help in the room.

"Can't we go to Reyan as planned?" asked Clare. "I have Papa's connections. We would be safe there."

Still watching the other conversation, Sage shook her head. "Alex says it's too far."

"And you agree with him," said Clare.

The hostility in her friend's tone made Sage glance at her. "It's a fact."

Alex parted from the captain and crossed the deck to them. "It's all arranged. Still some details of this ruse to discuss with Huzar, and a few other tasks before we can head back." Getting some of the horses to shore and gathering supplies for the journey, obviously, but Sage suspected one of those tasks was dealing with Rewel D'Amiran's body. Alex gave Clare a respectful nod. "My lady, will you please excuse me while I say good-bye to Sage?"

He was leaving now? Sage suddenly couldn't breathe. She barely noticed Clare's retreat.

As if understanding, Alex took her hand and looked her in the eye. "I need to get back to the city to see what the Norsari have found. By the time I know anything, you'll be gone. I don't like it, but that's the way it is."

Time and tide wait for no man.

The world was always conspiring to drive them apart and separate them. How long would it take to discover the traitor? The Norsari would come for them as soon as possible, but she, the queen, and everyone else would be stuck on this ship for weeks. It would be worse than sitting at Vinova as she had for months, waiting for something to happen. Meanwhile, Alex was heading straight into the hornet's nest with the news that would rattle it. She dropped her gaze, clenching her jaw in frustration.

"Sage, this was your idea," Alex reminded her gently, nudging her chin up to face him. "And we're going make it work." He leaned down to kiss her softly. "Trust me."

She threw her arms around his neck and kissed him back, trying to fit Spirit knew how many lonely days and nights into it. He held her tightly until Huzar called him, and then he was backing away to the longboat, saying he loved her. She watched Alex climb down, waiting for him to tell her he would see her soon, that they would be together again and everything would be all right.

But he didn't. He was too honest for that.

39

SAGE WASHED HER hands and face, but didn't know where her spare clothes were to change. She and Clare sat by Zoraya, as there was nothing helpful they could do otherwise. Lani brought Mesden back, and together the three of them decided cutting the boy's hair would help with "the hiding game." As they finished snipping away his babyish curls, he began to doze off in his chair.

Clare tucked the boy king into the captain's bunk for a nap, and Lani retreated to her own cabin, her rosy cheeks having taken on a greenish cast due to the constant motion of the ship. The sunlight coming through the windows had moved across the floor, indicating the ship had drifted around again with the changing tide, and the queen swung back and forth with the steady rhythm of the waves. Sage and Clare sat together, watching mother and son sleep, listening to the sailors outside preparing to set sail. The last two hours had passed so slowly that the thought of the many yet to come felt unbearable.

"I wonder if she will be angry when she learns of our plan," Sage said.

"As long as we keep her son safe, I think she'll forgive us," replied Clare.

Sage frowned. "She's not the type to sit around and wait for what she wants to happen."

"You're thinking of yourself, Sage," Clare said dryly.

"No, truly." Sage shook her head. "She forced the peace talks against the wishes of her own council and brazapilla, and she found a way to make us leave the negotiations so we could meet her at Bey Lissandra."

"Brazapil Nostin did that," Clare reminded her. "Her Majesty had nothing to do with that candle."

But Sage had been thinking about that, and she wasn't so sure. Nostin never had original ideas; someone else had to have put that in his head. He followed Donala's lead, so maybe the stronger brazapil was the source, but it was the queen who'd been ready to take advantage of it. Sage glanced at Zoraya, realizing the woman wasn't actually asleep anymore. She was listening to their conversation, just as she had on the longboat.

Always cautious, this one. Manipulative, too.

That didn't necessarily turn Sage away. She herself had learned from one of the most cautious and manipulative women in all of Demora, Darnessa Rodelle. The matchmaker's line of work required those qualities, guided by a sense of loyalty to the good of the nation. It also meant she'd seen those very qualities in Sage.

After several minutes of silence, Zoraya slowly opened her eyes. "Mesden . . . ," she mumbled.

Clare hopped up. "He is safe, Your Majesty. Sleeping right over there."

The queen barely glanced at her son, nor did she comment on his shorn hair, which signaled to Sage that she was right to think Zoraya had been aware of her surroundings for quite a while. Sage rose from her seat and went to the queen's side. Zoraya met her gaze steadily, then licked her lips before saying in her own language, "I thirst."

Sage had a cup of cool water ready. "Drink slowly, Your Majesty," she said in Demoran as she lifted it to the queen's mouth. "Your stomach may not tolerate much after the medicines you were given."

She knew that from experience.

After several small sips, Zoraya leaned back and blinked at Sage. "I would not have expected the ambassador herself to sit with me." Again she used Kimisar words, but it couldn't be to hide their conversation because she knew Clare spoke her language. Sage suspected it gave the queen a feeling of control, however, in a situation where she was helpless.

"We're rather low on servants," Sage replied as she returned the cup to the heavy pewter tray nearby, still speaking in Demoran. "Did Captain Huzar tell you of our plans?"

"Yes." The queen gave no opinion, however, and still refused to switch her speech.

Clare wiped Zoraya's sweaty face with a cool, wet cloth. "Is Your Majesty in pain? Would you like me to get Captain Casseck for more medicine?"

"Yes, please." The queen did not take her eyes from Sage's as she nodded. Sage wondered if she'd been awake enough to overhear how Alex had kept the opiates away from her. Zoraya waited for Clare to close the door behind her before finally speaking in Demoran. "Will I be kept for ransom?"

Sage tried to suppress the irony in her voice. "We are not in the business of taking hostages, Your Majesty."

"And you are not sure Kimisara would pay," Zoraya said frankly.

"Not to put too fine a point on it, Your Majesty, but you yourself don't trust your own ministers." Sage dragged her stool closer and sat. "It's not a good idea to let your country know we have you yet. They may believe we kidnapped you and use that as an excuse to declare war."

"If they can blame Demora for my death, they will declare war anyway."

Sage tapped her fingers on her leg, trying to remind herself that violence was likely to erupt no matter what, but their plan was the best chance of containing it. Somehow it didn't feel as convincing as it had earlier. "Either way, staying here is the safest and easiest solution," she said.

The queen's mouth twisted up in an ironic smile. "Easier than dumping me in the sea and pretending we never met?"

"That was never an option."

A look of shame crossed Zoraya's face, and Sage guessed the queen was thinking if their positions were reversed, that possibility would not have been automatically discarded. "Do not think me ungrateful," Zoraya said, turning her head to her sleeping son. "But this is a bad plan. In my country, as I expect it is also in yours, it is easier to hold power than take it—or take it back. Whoever seizes control will be difficult to defeat once they have it. Why else do you think I act the way I have?"

"You must leave that to Captain Huzar," said Sage. "Don't you trust him?"

The queen blinked, still looking away. "I trust him more than any other."

"Why is that?"

"He is a loyal son of Kimisara who has proved his worth several times."

"So I've heard." Sage brushed a wet clump of Zoraya's blue-black hair away from her face. "I think he cares for his queen in ways beyond simple loyalty, however." When Zoraya wouldn't answer, Sage continued. "Of course, I was trained to see such things in my work as a matchmaker."

She'd only been Darnessa's apprentice for seven months, but that was plenty.

"Matchmaking," said Zoraya slowly. "An interesting Demoran custom."

"One which has held together a nation of many languages and customs for hundreds of years," Sage said. When she'd taken the job, she'd detested the idea and only did it to escape her uncle, but over time she appreciated how careful and forward-thinking it was in practice. "Does Your Majesty have deeper feelings for him?"

Zoraya stared at the lantern swaying from the ceiling. "A queen does not have the luxury of such emotions." She pressed her lips together for a few seconds before saying, "But I am aware of the captain's affections."

"Of course you are. You used them against him."

The queen's sharp eyes came back to Sage. "I did what was necessary to get him to obey orders when he was conflicted. My son's life depended on it."

"I know," said Sage. "And I will not forget it."

They stared each other down until Casseck knocked on the door. Sage called on him to enter, which he did, bearing a tray. "How is Your Majesty feeling?" he asked as both women settled back and broke eye contact.

"Helpless," said Zoraya, using a tone that indicated frustration, though Sage saw the way her lips trembled with the fear she would not allow herself to acknowledge, let alone express.

Casseck spooned broth laced with sedatives into the queen's mouth, but this time Sage was too distracted by her own thoughts to give any to the opiates.

Fear is more dangerous than anger, Father had told her years ago. *Because it doesn't know what it wants, other than to not be afraid.*

The queen would do whatever it took to keep Mesden safe, and that meant keeping him—and herself—in power.

A person consumed by fear is just as likely to turn on you as to accept your help.

What would Zoraya be willing to do if she thought Sage was standing in her way?

Cass finished and checked the queen's bandages before nodding to Sage and leaving. The medicine was already taking effect, and Zoraya's eyelids drooped. Before she could drift away, Sage asked, "What would you have me do, Your Majesty? We don't have enough soldiers to protect you off this ship."

"You said you have allies in Reyan you expected to provide troops for your return to Tennegol before. Could they be persuaded to march for me?" Zoraya's words slurred a little, but the meaning behind them was clear. The woman had already begun plotting a way to return, and she expected to need force.

"I don't know," Sage admitted. Reyan had always remained neutral in Demora's conflicts with Kimisara. Even if they agreed to help, it would take weeks to assemble troops and then march—or sail—back. The situation back at Arrowhead could have changed two or three times by then. Reyan was too far.

She frowned thoughtfully, then turned around as the door opened, and Clare reentered the room, dressed in fresher clothing.

Clare.

Clare's father owned a huge swath of land north of Sagitta Crossing and quartered his own private army at the Western Strong. If the ship took Sage and the others to a place up the coast, they could head inland

182

and be at Baron Holloway's within—Sage closed her eyes to envision the map and distances—five days, give or take. News would only just be reaching Arrowhead then. They could be halfway back with Zoraya before Alex's Norsari would be expected to make it to Bey Lissandra to retrieve them, bringing this to an end much sooner. She reopened her eyes and jumped to her feet, excited. "Can you sit with the queen?" she asked Clare.

"What are you up to, Sage?" her friend asked suspiciously.

"I need to speak with the ship's captain," said Sage, biting her lip to hold back a grin. "Will you stay?"

"I don't need a nursemaid," said Zoraya, almost drunkenly. "I need an army."

"And I'm going to get you one, Your Majesty."

40

EVERYTHING IN BEY Lissandra was a mess, and without Cass, Alex had to arrange all the details himself. Huzar disappeared almost as soon as he was off the boat, charging down an alley to find his own guards. Alex gestured for one of the Norsari, Sergeant Gaverson, to follow the Kimisar captain. He trusted Huzar; he just wasn't sure he trusted the man to tell him everything. On the way back to the docks, Alex had criticized Huzar for not having told him Mesden was with the queen, but the captain had only fiddled with his ravaged ear and said it wasn't something the Demorans had needed to know.

By the time Alex sorted all the horses and sent four Norsari back to the ship, over two hours had passed. All the Casmuni had insisted on staying with their princess, which made that easier. Another hour later, he was securing Rewel D'Amiran's wrapped body on a wagon when a pair of Norsari returned to the docks from the city, dragging a corpse between them. They dropped the dead assassin at Alex's feet, faceup. Dust and grime coated the man's hair, making it difficult to judge its true shade of brown. One of the Norsari tossed a broken crossbow down next to the body.

Alex used the toe of his boot to turn the assassin's head, studying the angle of the wound in his neck. "Self-inflicted?"

Private Busker on his right nodded. "We had him cornered, and he was wavin' his knife around. Next thing we knew, he was bleedin' all over."

"Damn," Alex muttered. "Where's the knife?"

Busker produced a short dagger crusted in dried blood, and Alex took it and studied the design. Nondescript—no Demoran family crests, no initials, not even the four-pointed star of Kimisara. The man's clothes, too, were of a style that would have blended in among Tasmet or Kimisara, and his features weren't distinctly northern, like Cass, or southern, like Huzar. The crossbow was simple and had no distinguishing marks, also telling him nothing. "Anything else on him?" Alex asked, though he was sure Busker would've said if so.

"No, sir, but we heard the Kimisar found another assassin. They were nervous at first, too, but loosened up after a couple hours."

After their boy king was relatively safe. Alex squinted across the harbor at the anchored ship. Sailors were climbing up the masts and out onto the yardarms, letting down sails. "Where are the Kimisar guards now?"

"Right behind us." Private Busker jerked his head over his shoulder as a half dozen civilian-dressed men came down the main avenue running east, Huzar leading them. From a side street, Sergeant Gaverson, who'd followed the captain, appeared, giving Alex a slight nod. Busker stepped back as Huzar strode up to Alex.

"Find anything?" Alex asked. It frustrated him to beg for information rather than be out there searching for it.

"One more assassin who no longer lives," said Huzar. Congealed blood still crusted over remaining chunk of his left ear. "But there were at least three. The rest of my men are still searching."

So one had gotten away for sure. "Where is he?" Alex said. "I want to examine the body."

"*She* is a little too messy to be carried around," Huzar replied. "Fell off a high roof. Or jumped. We're not sure." Over his shoulder, Alex saw his sergeant nod, indicating Huzar wasn't leaving something out. "We did find one interesting item on her." Huzar pulled a scrap of parchment from his jacket and held it out.

Alex took it and grimaced at the ink smeared and spread by the blood that soaked the note almost beyond reading. He held it up to the sunlight now streaming almost horizontally across the water behind him. It was a list of names.

Rewel D'Amiran
Queen Regent Zoraya
Sage Fowler
PL Lady Clare Holloway

His stomach rolled over. Alex had assumed Sage was one of the targets, but seeing it in writing—knowing someone had taken the time to assign her death—was something else. He snuck a glance at her ship again. The anchor was being raised.

"What is this?" he asked, pointing to the letters *PL* next to the barely legible name at the bottom.

"It is a Kimisar code phrase used by *dolofan*," said Huzar. "*Pesta lundamyetsk.*" He paused. "Your death for this one."

"Meaning?"

"If Lady Clare was harmed, the assassins themselves would become their employer's next targets," Huzar replied.

Alex pursed his lips. "So this is *dolofan* work."

Huzar shook his head. "If they were *dolofan*, it would have been done up close, by the blade, and they would not have failed."

"Hmph," Alex grunted. He'd seen Kimisar assassins fail in Osthiza, but he was inclined to agree on the closeness aspect.

"The *pesta lundamyetsk* for Lady Clare tells me this is a Demoran plot," said Huzar. "Why else would she be spared?"

Alex raised an eyebrow. "I think the use of a Kimisar phrase indicates otherwise." He shook his head. "She's extremely rich. Duke D'Amiran had planned to marry her for her dowry. Sounds like someone doesn't want to piss off her family."

"Or that her family is involved."

"Perhaps," Alex conceded. "Her father had arranged Lady Clare's sister's marriage to Rewel D'Amiran, but it appeared to be based on greed rather than treachery on his part." He gave the parchment back to Huzar, not wanting to hold Sage's death sentence in his hands any longer. "I don't think this tells us much more than we already know."

Huzar folded the note in his hand. "And what have you found?"

"Almost nothing." Alex offered him the dagger and waited as the Kimisar studied it. Finally, Huzar handed it back, shaking his head, indicating he saw nothing worth mentioning. His brown eyes were drawn to the sea, and he clenched his jaw. Alex followed his gaze to the ship now turning northwest to catch the wind.

"It is time, then, to return to Arrowhead," Huzar said, "and tell them My Queen is dead."

Alex had no intention of lying to Robert, but the other nobles at the talks were suspect. It was probably too risky to send even a coded message with the truth to the king. General Quinn and Colonel Traysden wouldn't like that, but Tennegol's reaction would be too late to matter. "Is there anyone among your council or army you can trust?" Alex asked, watching the ship—and Sage—sail away.

Huzar considered. "Perhaps General Oshan, but I will wait to see his reaction to the news before I decide whether to tell him the truth."

"Is there anything else I should know?" Alex asked.

The captain hesitated. "My Queen's belongings were searched after I took the king. I had sent his guard out to find the assassins, and they left her room unwatched. When I returned later, things were missing."

"Like what?"

"Her private papers," said Huzar. "Everything she'd written about the meeting here, all that was agreed upon."

"Anything about the king or his decoy?"

Huzar shook his head. "That is too important to be committed to writing."

"That actually sounds like good news to me," said Alex, pivoting a little to face the water as Huzar did. The last rays of sun faded rapidly, causing the sea and sky to merge into one solid and deepening shade of violet. "Your king wasn't on the list, either, meaning the culprit wants him alive or didn't know he was here. Mesden is safe, and whoever comes forth with knowledge from those documents will be the guilty party."

"Perhaps, but I doubt it will be that simple or easy."

Alex smiled grimly. "It never is."

"I hope this works, Demoran," said Huzar, crossing his arms and focusing on where the ship's silhouette now faded against the clouds on the horizon.

Alex imitated the other soldier's stance, watching the last of the shape disappear. "As do I, Kimisar."

They were both heading into what could easily become a war zone, but at least Alex had put Sage where no one could reach her until it was safe to come back.

41

SAGE RETURNED FROM the deck triumphant. She had gone to the captain and explained that she wanted to pull into shore a few miles up the Demoran coast. The captain had scratched the white whiskers growing thick from his sideburns, and said, "That we can do. There's a place we can get fairly close to shore. Could be there by tomorrow afternoon." She wondered how much Alex had paid or promised this man for his trouble. Probably a lot, given they'd also demanded secrecy.

Clare was waiting inside the cabin with arms crossed and an expression as angry as any Sage had seen on her. "What in the name of the Spirit do you think you're doing?" she demanded. "What army are you talking about?"

"Yours," Sage answered. "Or rather, your father's."

Clare's face went white as parchment. "*What?*"

"We'll sail north for a day and then go ashore and head for the Western Strong," said Sage.

"Why?"

"The reason we're stuck on this ship is because there's no other way to protect us," Sage said patiently. "Your father has over a thousand troops at his disposal." She was puzzled by Clare's distress. "What's the matter? We'll be safe there."

"*You'll* be safe!" Clare cried. "What about me? The only reason Father hasn't married me off is because I was out of his reach."

Spirit above, in her eagerness to be *doing* something, Sage hadn't even thought of that. She shook her head. "I won't let him—"

"He has the legal right!" Clare shouted. "I'll end up like Sophia, with whoever he thinks will gain him the most!" She burst into tears.

Sage had always watched over Clare, as far back as the Concordium journey, when she'd tearfully confessed that her father had lied about her age. The implication that Sage couldn't—or wouldn't—protect her now hurt. Her original plan was the only safe option a few hours ago, but once Sage realized they could go to the Western Strong, staying on the ship felt like doing nothing. They could bring Zoraya home sooner. "I'm not sitting around and waiting for weeks to hear from Alex that it's safe to come back," she snapped. "I can't."

"So this is about staying close to him!"

"No!" Her friend was being ridiculous. "This is about keeping Kimisara's rightful ruler on her throne."

"She's only the regent." Clare pointed to the sleeping boy on the other side of the cabin. "*He* is the rightful ruler."

"I see no difference."

"No?" Clare lowered her hand. "Because she makes you feel important? Because our king can manipulate her trust by sending you to deal with her?"

Sage shot a glance at Zoraya, who looked to be genuinely unconscious. "It's not like that! He only thought she would respond better to another woman."

"I see no difference." Clare crossed her arms again, her eyes dry and furious. "And now you're using me to get what you want, with no concern as to what *I* want, as to how *I* feel."

"Clare," Sage begged. "I'll protect you from your father, I promise."

Her friend made a noise of disgust and turned away, heading for the door. "Make your plans with the queen regent." Clare paused with her hand on the latch. "I don't need your protection, Sage." She jerked the door open and went through without a backward glance. "And I don't need your promises, either."

Sage stood rooted as the latch clicked shut behind Clare. Her friend was right. She hadn't considered how Clare would feel about going home to the man who'd sent her to the Concordium illegally after practically selling her sister to a traitor. Sage *did* have an idea on how to get what she needed from Baron Holloway, and maybe she could have talked Clare into it, but she hadn't consulted her, just acted.

"If it makes you feel any better," mumbled a voice off to her side, "I approve of this new plan."

Sage turned to face Zoraya. The queen's blue eyes were glazed and unfocused as she smiled. "And your king is not as clever as he thinks if he believed I would trust you because you are a woman." She blinked slowly. "I trusted you less."

"Do you trust me now?" Sage asked her, taking a few steps closer.

"I trust your intentions." Zoraya leaned back, eyelids heavy. "Your judgment is suspect."

Sage's face warmed at the queen's opinion. She could probably ask any question right now and get an honest answer, thanks to Casseck's heavy dose of medicine, but she wasn't sure she wanted to know what Zoraya really thought. Her arm itched, and she scratched it. She hadn't been able put any lotion on her scars today.

Even in her drugged state, the queen noticed the movement. "Malkim told me about you," she said. "About your burns. He said he thought you might have died."

"Well, I didn't." Sage wished the woman would go to sleep.

"It was my idea, you know."

Sage frowned. "What was?"

"The candle." Zoraya closed her eyes. "I didn't tell Nostin to do it, but I put the idea in his head. I knew you'd anger him enough sooner or later." She sighed and shook her head. "But I needed you to leave so we could meet."

Not quite an apology, but Sage didn't think the queen was in the habit of making them. She probably considered it weakness. In her position maybe it was. Sage could think of nothing else, so she said, "I wasn't harmed."

Unless one counted the nightmares, which had surged in frequency. Alex had been with her since then, usually sensing them and waking her before they reached their peak. He wasn't here anymore, though.

Zoraya reopened her eyes and turned her head to Mesden. A sad smile teased her lips. "He looks much older now. I shall miss those curls."

"I think he's rather handsome," said Sage, relieved at the change of subject.

"He is." Moisture gathered in the queen's eyes. "He looks like his father now."

King Ragat had been nearly sixty, so Sage suspected the resemblance had much to do with the lack of hair. "I never met His Majesty to know," she said.

A pair of tears streamed into Zoraya's black hair. "Not Ragat," she whispered, almost inaudibly, as her eyes closed one last time.

42

SAGE STAYED WITH Zoraya all night, but the queen never said another word about Mesden's real father, and Sage was afraid to ask. The next morning, Casseck came to check on them. He was greatly encouraged by what he saw of the queen's wounds, and after replacing the soiled bandages, he told Her Majesty he would make her a brace to hold her shoulders in place while the bone healed in addition to a sling for her arm. Then Cass looked at Sage and said, "Which apparently I must do now, seeing as we'll be getting off the ship in the afternoon."

Cheeks burning, Sage tried to explain, but Cass turned away again, plainly not interested in what she had to say. It surprised her, though, that he hadn't tried to change the ship captain's mind when he'd learned of Sage's new plan. After a few seconds of embarrassed silence, Sage asked if he could watch over the queen while she stretched her legs for a few minutes. All she got was a curt nod.

Sage fled to the open air, queasy for reasons other than the constantly tilting floors, though they didn't help. First Clare and now Casseck hated her. Honestly, she couldn't blame them.

Sailors above and around her went about tending to the ropes and sails, using a lingo she barely understood. Under normal circumstances, Sage would have been wild to learn about this new world, but she couldn't bring herself to care. For a few minutes she stood by the rail, watching the ship head into the sunrise, letting the salt spray sting her eyes. She couldn't see land yet, but it would be several hours before that, she expected. Out of the low, white-capped wake created by the ship's movement, tiny, finger-length fish spread fins like dragonfly wings and skipped from wavetop to wavetop. Flying fish. Clare had told her about them once, but Sage had hardly believed her. Some friend she was.

Sage scratched her neck, noticing a stiffness in her clothes. She looked down, remembering she was covered in dried blood. Her spare shirt must be in her bag in the room she was supposed to have shared with Clare and Lani. The sun was high enough that Clare was probably up and about, so Sage headed for the cabin. Clare opened the door as she reached it, and Sage stepped back, embarrassed. "I, ah, just needed to get my pack," she said.

Clare shrugged. "Lani's in there. She's been vomiting all night, which you would know if you'd bothered to check on her." Sage opened her mouth to protest that she'd been occupied with the queen, but Clare turned to slip by her in the narrow passage. Once she was past, Clare called over her shoulder, "I'll take care of Mesden, seeing as someone should think of him."

That was just uncalled for. Sage made a face at her friend's back, then immediately felt rotten about it. With a sigh, she entered the cabin, which was dark and stuffy and smelled horrible. The princess peered out of her hammock at her, a greenish tint to the hollows under her eyes. "Please tell me land is in sight," she groaned.

Sage sat in the canvas chair by her friend. "I guess Clare told you we're landing this afternoon."

"Yes." Lani tugged the blanket up to her chin. "And I am glad for more than one reason, though she is not glad at all." She glared at Sage. "Clare says you told the queen you are gathering troops for her. Do you intend to march her back to Arrowhead yourself? Can you not wait for the Norsari?"

"Pretending the queen is dead may uncover who tried to kill her and why," said Sage, "but whoever comes out on top may be unwilling to concede his power when she returns. If we have to force them out, a Norsari escort won't be enough."

Lani frowned. "And you did not think of this when you made the plan to pretend her death?"

Sage thought of Zoraya's drugged confession, but the fewer people who knew about that, the better. "The idea of getting troops from Lord Holloway hadn't occurred to me then. Now that it has, I prefer it to sitting on this boat and waiting."

"Clare seems to believe her father will not help."

Sage had thought Clare was only wrapped up in her fear, but her father could easily refuse to lend soldiers. Or he might offer them on the condition that Clare marry the nobleman of his choice. Sage frowned. "She didn't tell me that."

Lani raised an eyebrow. "You did not think to ask her."

"No, I didn't," said Sage. "I'm sorry."

"I am not the one you must apologize to."

Sage sighed. "I don't think she'll listen yet." She grabbed her bag and dug through it for a clean shirt. After changing, she looked back to Lani, who now had her eyes closed.

"The waters are calm at the moment," said Sage. "Would you like to get some fresh air? It might help."

The princess moaned. "I thank you, no. With my luck I will vomit *on* Captain Casseck rather than in front of him this time."

Sage was pretty sure she herself had thrown up on Cass during the week she was coming out from her dependence on pain medicines, but she decided not to mention that. "But then you'll miss the chance to faint and have him carry you back down here."

Lani shot her a poisonous glare. "I am not some delicate flower, nor am I desperate enough for such a ruse." Then she sighed and rubbed her forehead. "Saizsch, I do not understand him. He is kind and caring, yet there is no difference in the way he treats me from Clare."

"Or me?"

"No, I believe he is a little afraid of you."

Cass was probably more than a little afraid of Lani. Sage shrugged.

Lani pushed her lower lip out in a pout. "He will not even tell me his common name. When I ask, he pretends to misunderstand and says his short name is only Cass."

"Oh, well"—Sage grimaced—"that's actually because his first name is pretty awful."

"Really?" The princess leaned forward. "What is it?"

Sage held up her hands. "Oh, no. He'll know it was me who told you."

"No wonder you stopped being a matchmaker." Lani raised her eyes to the ceiling. "You are terrible at it." She looked back at Sage. "How is the queen?"

"She should recover," said Sage. "She needs rest, though."

Lani raised an eyebrow. "She will not get much in the next few days if we are to travel by horse to Clare's home." Sage didn't answer, and the princess continued, "But she has fortitude and little fear from what I have seen."

Sage sat back in her seat. "Her fear is reserved for her son."

"To be understood. She is a mother."

The Casmuni had long spied on the Kimisar. Sage wondered if they knew anything about Mesden's true father. "Do you know much about her?"

Lani shifted a little to better face Sage. "She was Ragat's third wife. Of the first two, one killed herself and the other was executed for some kind of treason—I can never remember which was which. We in Casmun have always suspected their deaths had to do with their lack of children."

Sage nodded. "Similar things have happened in Demora's history, I'm sorry to say."

"Zoraya was selected by the king at the age of seventeen. She came from a large family in a region known for hardy life," Lani continued. "Very fertile family, if you forgive the expression. Yet it was six years before she became pregnant."

"Sounds like the problem was with Ragat," said Sage dryly.

"Which he probably knew," agreed Lani, "and would also explain why he felt the need to pick fights with Demora and Casmun after many years of truce."

"But he did have a son eventually. Mesden." Sage tapped her lip as she thought, a habit she'd picked up from Alex. "Which likely saved Zoraya from the same fate as her predecessors."

"Yet it only kept her one illness or accident away from disaster," said Lani. "I think you can imagine the strain she must have lived under these years."

It was obvious now that Zoraya had taken matters into her own hands in conceiving an heir. Perhaps the assassination attempt had been motivated by someone who knew Mesden wasn't actually Ragat's son. Except . . . "As chaotic as Kimisara is right now, losing Mesden would be a disaster. A civil war would break out over the succession," said Sage.

"That is obvious. Why do you bring it up?"

"Getting Zoraya out of the way could be helpful to many who want more power," Sage replied. "But I don't see much advantage to killing Mesden. He's a child, easy to shape and manipulate."

It would be easier to seize control with him in place, true heir or not.

Lani nodded. "You believe the next move of the plotter will be to hold the child king, or rather, the false child king."

"Probably." Sage stood, shouldering her pack. "I'll need to send a messenger to General Quinn when we reach land, both to tell him where we've gone and about what to watch for."

"And to apologize to Ah'lecks for not doing what he has expected," said Lani, closing her eyes and settling back in the hammock.

"And that." Add Alex to the list of people with reasons to be angry with her.

Sage left Lani and headed back to Zoraya's cabin, trying to sort in her mind how Mesden's origin could affect events. Did the plotter know and simply want the queen out of the way? Or would it make more sense to use the truth against her?

Casseck stood when she entered the room and left with only a nod, but Sage barely noticed. All her attention was on the sleeping queen. In some ways, Sage admired the woman for taking fate into her own hands, but it also made her wonder if Zoraya kept her son close out of love or more out of fear her secret would become known.

In any case, returning the king and queen regent to Kimisara just became a whole lot more complicated.

43

ALEX RODE INTO the Arrowhead camp under the cover of darkness, noting the Kimisar side didn't appear to be any more active than usual. Hopefully, that meant they didn't know anything about Bey Lissandra yet. The Norsari detachment rode straight up the wide path in the center of the tents, and by the time Alex's feet hit the ground, the crown prince was at his side.

"You're back much earlier than expected," Robert said. "Tell me that means something good." He glanced at the six men dismounting behind Alex. "Where's Sage?"

"Not now." Alex handed Surry's reins to a sleepy page and patted the horse on the neck. The mare was exhausted after three days of hard riding. "I need to see the general."

Outside Rob, Father and Colonel Traysden had been the only ones who knew of the meeting in Bey Lissandra. After updating them, Alex's priority would be finding out if that information had somehow slipped outside the tight circle.

They headed in the direction of the command tent, his cousin filling him in on the last few days. "I insisted on a three-day recess, and then another day off the next Chapel Day. The past week was hell. Everyone always ended up shouting. It's like they have no interest in making this succeed. I would've called an end to all this days ago if I weren't covering for Sage's meeting."

Alex nodded grimly. That fit with Queen Zoraya's assessment.

"And speaking of ending things," continued Rob. "Underwood and his friends left three days ago. Not that I was sorry to lose them."

Alex stopped in his tracks. The timing was more than suspicious. "And my father let him go?"

"Seeing as the baron wasn't invited in the first place, there was no reason to stop him." Rob grinned. "Though the general did send a Norsari company to follow."

"Who's leading it?"

"Captain Nadira."

Alex nodded and continued walking. Ben Nadira would have been his choice, but with Cass staying with Sage and Lieutenant Hatfield continuing to Jovan as her false escort, the only experienced officer he had left with him was Lieutenant Tanner. "How did the Kimisar react to our baron and his underlings leaving?"

"He contributed little, so I don't think they miss him." The prince trotted to keep up. "But I was so tired of arguing with Nostin that I played sick yesterday and canceled talks." Rob glanced back at the six Norsari. "How did your meeting go? Is Lady Clare with Sage?"

"Not now, dammit."

They reached General Quinn's tent and swept inside without waiting for permission or announcement. Alex's father jumped to his feet from his chair at the long table, and after salutes and a few seconds of searching Alex's face, he looked relieved. "When I heard you were coming without certain members of your party, I was concerned," the general said. "But they're well?"

His father been worried about Sage, which was gratifying. "I left everyone in good health," Alex said simply.

The general nodded, and Alex glanced around. Colonels Traysden and Murray were present, as well as the Duke of Crescera and the man who attended every meeting with him. Alex would have to withhold the truth until both men left, though it would be handy to see the duke's reaction to the news. Robert edged forward to be part of the conversation. "I can only assume your swift return means plans did not go as intended," said Alex's father.

Alex waited until all the Norsari had formed up behind him. "Queen Zoraya is dead," he began. "As is Count Rewel D'Amiran." He paused, pivoting a little to make it appear he was including Welborough, though it was more to watch his expression. "Assassinated by parties unknown."

There was a long, shocked silence. Colonel Traysden spoke first. *"Unknown?"*

He was asking why the Norsari hadn't caught the assassins, but Alex didn't want to let the duke know more circumstances than necessary. "We caught two," he said. "Both died."

"Where did this happen?" the duke demanded, puffing his chest out like an angry rooster. With his reddish hair styled to appear fuller than it was, he rather looked like one, too.

Alex focused on his father, trying to tell him there was more than he could say in present company. "Bey Lissandra."

"What were you doing in Bey Lissandra, Major?" Duke Welborough asked.

"I have every right to be in a Demoran city, Your Grace," said Alex. His right hand clenched with the urge to knock the man out of his shiny boots.

The general frowned. "This has now become a strategic military meeting. I must ask Your Grace to leave."

To Alex's surprise, Welborough didn't object. The Cresceran duke merely gestured to his attendant and strode to the exit, giving no bows of respect.

"Your Grace," called General Quinn. Both men stopped inside the doorway. "What you've just heard does not leave this tent. If any word of this report gets out, you will be arrested for treason."

The duke only smirked and swept out.

Alex's father eyed the Norsari. "I trust your men's silence, but I think it best if they leave now, too," he said.

"Dismissed," Alex said over his shoulder. "Get some rest." They all came to attention as one, then pivoted and marched out.

Neither Colonel Traysden nor Lieutenant Colonel Murray made a move to depart. Robert folded his arms and stayed in place like he was daring his uncle to order him to go, too.

The general ran a hand through his iron-gray hair as he sat back down. "All right, Major. Tell us everything."

Alex began with a question of his own. "Who else knew?" he demanded.

His father frowned. "Knew what?"

"Who knew where the ambassador was really going?"

The general glanced at Alex's clenched fists. "If you are angry about the danger, I might remind you that she knew exactly what risks she took by going. As did you."

Alex forced himself to relax and breathe evenly. Sage was safe. Getting angry now wouldn't help the situation.

"What happened, son?" his father asked quietly.

"Queen Zoraya was giving us Rewel D'Amiran," said Alex. He explained the plan to travel through Reyan rather than Tasmet, and his father nodded his approval. It was always reassuring to know he'd done—or had planned to do—the right thing. "The attack came three mornings ago, when Her Majesty met with us to turn over the count and give the ambassador a summary of all the agreements they'd come to."

Traysden glanced at Lieutenant Colonel Murray's quill scratching across his parchment before leaning his forearms on the table. "Was the ambassador also a target of this attack?"

"Yes." Alex described the list Huzar had found. "Captain Casseck, four Norsari, and the eight Casmuni guards are with them. I'll send a Norsari detachment to retrieve them, with your permission."

General Quinn tapped his fingers on the table. "I find it hard to believe Ambassador Fowler and Princess Alaniah agreed to hide for that long."

Alex hesitated, knowing this wouldn't go over well, at least at first. "I lied. Count D'Amiran is dead, but Queen Zoraya was only wounded. She's with the ambassador."

Alex's father sat up straight in his chair. "*She's what?*"

"On a ship off the western coast, waiting until it's safe to return," said Alex.

General Quinn lowered his voice with a great deal of effort. "The Kimisar queen is in Demoran possession? Are you insane? *Why* did you tell us she was dead?"

"Actually, I just told Welborough, because it's what everyone else is meant to believe." Alex folded his arms. "And I prefer to think of the queen as being under Demoran protection. Unless you think I should've left her wounded and unconscious in a city where someone tried to kill her."

His father ignored the insolent tone that had crept into Alex's voice. "What about her own bodyguards? Could they not escort her safely home?"

"Her wounds were enough that it was too dangerous." Briefly he described the queen's injuries and what was done to treat them, mentioning Huzar's as well.

General Quinn exchanged a skeptical look with Traysden. "Tell me you considered all this may have been a trap. Now they can claim we've kidnapped their queen."

"Not if they don't know we have her." Alex dropped his arms. "After dealing with the queen and captain for several days, I'm almost certain this was not their plan, and the ambassador concurred. Huzar agreed to leave Queen Zoraya in our care, but it was not an easy decision for him to make."

"He's her lover. Did you know that?" asked Colonel Traysden. It was his business to know such things as minister of intelligence, but that he hadn't told Alex earlier was annoying.

"I came to suspect it," said Alex. "But that doesn't change my assessment of the situation in any way." He took a deep breath. "There's more," he said, bracing himself before telling them about Mesden.

Everyone was silent when he finished, watching as the general pinched the bridge of his nose and thought for a minute. "You came in saying the queen was dead," Alex's father said finally. "I assume there's a reason."

Alex nodded. "The plan is to let whoever is behind this think he succeeded, then by his actions we can determine who that is."

"By who tries to seize power," his father said quietly.

"Probably, yes."

The general frowned. "The Kimisar will blame us for the assassination."

"They'd point the finger at us even if they knew she was only wounded," said Alex. "But if they think she's dead, their first concerns will be internal, which gives us an advantage. We now have a chance of discovering the culprit, which is why I lied to Duke Welborough. A Demoran could be the one behind it."

"Perhaps," his father admitted. "What's your opinion, Kristor?"

"I think it will be chaos no matter what," said Traysden. He rubbed his shaved head with one hand and sighed. "Who is going to bring the Kimisar this news and when?"

"Captain Huzar," answered Alex. "He's following, but only travels at night to avoid notice, so probably the day after tomorrow."

"Not much time," muttered the general. "I need a map." His aide placed one in front of him and he frowned at it for several seconds. "Murray, get all the battalion officers here in ten minutes."

The staff officer jumped up and ran to tell the messenger outside. Colonel Traysden handed General Quinn a charcoal pencil. "Seven miles would be a good perimeter. We can manage that by sunset tomorrow."

"Agreed." Alex's father sketched a light circle around their position. "And I want your number of scouts doubled by sunrise."

"Consider it done," said Traysden.

Murray returned and took his seat again on the general's left. "What is the plan, sir?"

"We're going to spread out and surround the Kimisar at a distance of seven miles—close enough to react to their movements but far enough out for them not to notice." He paused to glance at the aide, who'd pulled up a stack of small blank pages. "No written orders this time, Murray. It's too sensitive."

"Very good, sir," said Murray smoothly, sliding the parchments back to their previous place. Alex wondered if the staff officer was ever frustrated with the general's constant stream of changing plans and orders.

Alex dropped heavily into a chair, the last few days suddenly catching up to him. His father hadn't said it outright, but Alex could tell he disliked their plan to uncover the traitor. It was just too late to change their path now.

44

THE MORNING STARTED with bad news. Almost first thing, Alex learned that sometime in the commotion of the battalions preparing to march at first light, Duke Welborough had departed, leaving behind at least half of his retinue. Those remaining then spent the morning packing everything and following him north up the Span Road. General Quinn ground his teeth, but he couldn't do anything to stop them. Like Baron Underwood, the Duke of Crescera had come of his own accord and was free to leave whenever he chose. He'd been fairly reasonable at the table, though, and his presence would be missed, unlike the baron's.

The timing didn't sit well with Alex, making it seem as if the duke had been waiting for the news of Zoraya's death, but Prince Robert was more pragmatic. "He's been grumbling about leaving since Sage did," he said. "The chance for peace is pretty much gone; why would he stay?"

It was the *pesta lundamyetsk* note on Lady Clare that bothered Alex most in this case. If anyone at the talks had reason to stay on the good side of Clare's father, Baron Holloway, it was Duke Welborough—the man who collected his taxes and depended on his private army.

"Maybe," said Rob when Alex explained. "But I can't think of any reason Welborough would be behind this, and about a thousand why he wouldn't."

Alex had to agree there. The duke had heavily financed the mills King Raymond wanted to build on the Nai River in Tasmet. As his province produced most of Demora's grain, Duke Welborough stood to profit a great deal from peace. Baron Holloway would, too, for that matter. That meant the primary suspect on the Demoran side was still Underwood.

The baron's early departure implied he might have been worried about being trapped here. Sage had said she believed he wanted to take power in Tasmet by marrying Countess Sophia, which he might move to do while the nation's focus was elsewhere. Using the chaos to his advantage might not prove he was behind the assassins, though. And if not Welborough or Underwood, the traitor was likely among the Kimisar. Someone who wanted to take Zoraya's place and blame the Demorans while he was at it.

Nevertheless, Alex had little trouble convincing his father to let him send a Norsari platoon to follow Welborough and keep an eye on him. As it was a relatively easy mission, he put one of his newer lieutenants in charge and focused on arranging another detachment to retrieve Sage and the queen. After sensing his father's disapproval last night, Alex knew he had to see the plan through on this end, which meant he would not be going back to Bey Lissandra. Meanwhile, Rob spent the morning in the negotiation tent.

Sometime around noon, his cousin found him. "Not a whisper," he said. "Today went the same as the last two weeks, which is to say nowhere. The idea Donala put forth today was to wed Rewel's daughter to Mesden."

"She's not even two years old," said Alex.

"I know. He said it would guarantee neither of us would attack the other, but it really only gives the Kimisar a legal claim to take Tasmet back in a few years." Rob rolled his eyes.

Alex frowned. "What concerns me is where they got that idea. Queen Zoraya said that's what Rewel offered her when he fled to her protection."

"I wouldn't worry too much," said Rob. "Yesterday they were suggesting my sister Cara, who's several years older than Mesden." He shook his head. "It's as if they're throwing out ridiculous ideas in the hopes that we'll toss our hands up and leave, but they aren't willing to be the ones to walk away from the table."

"It's worked for at least three negotiators," grumbled Alex. "You're the only one left."

Rob only shrugged. He never appeared to worry, which was a bad thing without his half brother Ash Carter around to counter the crown prince's laid-back attitude. "Where's Ash?" asked Alex. "I thought your father was going to send him out here to check on our progress. Shouldn't he be here by now?"

"We got a message a few days ago saying he was delayed, but he didn't say how." Again he shrugged like there was nothing to worry about. "There weren't any code words in the message that indicated distress, though."

As if in response, the herald sounded to indicate someone important was arriving. Either it was Ash or more bad news, so Alex and Rob trotted to meet the incoming party. Even from a distance they could tell it was a bigger retinue than Ash's group would've been, and Alex's gut clenched in anxiety. When they rounded the last row of tents, Alex saw a lady, sitting sidesaddle and holding a small child. The man helping them down was Lieutenant Ash Carter.

As soon as the woman was on the ground, she held out her arms for the little girl, and Ash handed her back. She clutched the child and looked around with wide eyes, relief plain on her face. Alex had never met her, but the family resemblance was obvious—this could only be Countess Sophia, Lady Clare's sister. Robert, who had been at her wedding, strode up to her and kissed her hand, offering his welcome. Still holding her daughter, Aurelia, she curtsied and then burst into tears.

Sweet Spirit, what could have happened to drive the countess and her child into what was about to become a war zone?

Rob looked helplessly back at Alex as she sobbed on his shoulder. "I think I'll take Her Ladyship to the ambassador's tent, as it's still up."

Alex nodded. "I'll get the general."

After thirty-nine years in the army, General Quinn walked everywhere like a soldier, nearly marching, posture erect, paces even and measured, never running. His right arm swung back and forth with his steps, but the way his left gripped the hilt of his sword told Alex his father felt as agitated as he did. Alex followed, keeping pace with Lieutenant Colonel Murray. Ash Carter walked beside Colonel Traysden. He'd confirmed that Countess Sophia was the reason for his delay, but said little else.

In the ambassador's tent, Sophia was calmer, though she leaned on the prince's shoulder for support. Little Aurelia lay with her head on her mother's lap, her thumb half hanging out of her mouth as she dozed. The general bowed as soon as he entered the tent, as did everyone behind him. "My lady," he said briskly. "Your visit comes at an inopportune time. I wish you'd sent word that you wanted to come."

The countess sniffed and wiped her cheeks. "I apologize, General, but this is the only place I felt would be safe."

General Quinn exhaled in what Alex knew was a suppressed sigh. He took several steps and sat across from her on a backless couch, then leaned forward with his elbows on his thighs. "Please tell me what's happened that you feel you're in danger." When Sophia glanced at Alex and the others, he said, "You may speak freely, Your Ladyship. Every man present has my absolute trust."

Sophia took several deep breaths before whispering, "They want my daughter."

The general glanced at the sleeping child. "Who wants her?"

"My husband's allies in Tasmet," she said. "They act on his behalf. I have seen an unusual number of travelers passing through Jovan, only to return a day or two later. We are being watched."

"My lady, Jovan is a nexus of trade. Such back and forth movement is common."

"I am not imagining this!" Sophia cried. Aurelia stirred on her lap but did not wake. "My guards have found evidence of attempts to get inside the fortress. One person may have even made it into my private living quarters!"

The general's eyes widened, and he turned to look at Ash Carter. "Did you see anything like what the countess claims, Lieutenant?"

Ash stepped forward. "Some of the evidence was . . . inconclusive, but I do believe she had reasonable cause for concern."

"Very well." Alex's father refocused on Sophia, speaking kindly. "Be that as it may, my lady, Jovan would be a far safer place than this camp."

Sophia shook her head. "No, General. My husband knew the ins and outs of Jovan. There are secret passages and hiding places I am always discovering. His allies are testing the weaknesses of the fortress and its guard. They are coming for my daughter, the last link in the D'Amiran chain." She swallowed, her back stiffening. "They shall not have her."

The countess was describing exactly what Sage had predicted about Underwood, and it had to have peaked around the time Sage and the queen were in Bey Lissandra.

General Quinn tapped his fingers together. "Have you heard from your husband, my lady?"

"No. Not since Aurelia was born. When he left us." Her eyes widened and her hands began to tremble. "Have you?"

General Quinn frowned, then glanced up as two maids entered the tent, curtsying. "I think Your Ladyship needs to rest. These women will attend to your needs while you're here." He stood, making eye contact with Alex and the other officers.

"Are you going to send me back?" cried Sophia.

"Not until I better understand what the situation is," he assured her. The general bowed and walked out. No one needed to be told to follow him—or to stay silent. Back in his own secure tent, Alex's father rubbed his face tiredly. "This is exactly what I didn't need."

"My apologies, sir," said Ash Carter. "I believed it best at the time to bring her, and I thought her sister was here."

Alex frowned. Lady Clare hadn't arrived at Jovan, but the Norsari escort under Lieutenant Hatfield would have. Their presence should've made the countess feel more secure.

"No, you did the right thing," the general told Ash. "It just complicates an already dangerous situation." Everyone took turns bringing the lieutenant up to speed, describing the Demoran soldiers now quietly moving to surround the Kimisar.

Ash gave a low whistle. "And the Kimisar still know nothing about this?"

"So it would seem," said Robert. "This morning's talks were no different, minus the Duke of Crescera."

"They'll know soon," said Alex. "Huzar will bring them the news."

"And then all hell will break loose," said Ash.

Alex nodded wearily. That pretty much summed it up.

45

ASH ATTENDED THE afternoon talks, and Alex decided to go along, wanting to see—and be seen by—the Kimisar delegation. As he was known to be assigned to the ambassador's protection, Alex expected some kind of response to his presence, but the one he got only left him confused.

Alex had taken a position off to the side as he had when Sage was at the negotiations, and everyone was making their way to their seats when General Oshan stepped around the table to speak to him. "Has your ambassador returned?" he asked quietly.

"No." Alex shook his head. "I left her at Jovan."

"I hope she is well."

"She was when I left her." The minister of war's earnestness disarmed him a little. "And how is your queen?" Alex asked, hoping for a reaction. "I'm told she left shortly after the ambassador."

Oshan nodded absently. "She went to visit her son; My Queen cannot stand to be away from him for long. But I am hopeful she may return. We have missed her calm presence."

Alex blinked, the simple, open statements surprising him. "I hope for your sake she does return," he said.

Oshan lowered his head in a slight bow and went to take his place next to Brazapil Donala, who shot him, and then Alex, a suspicious glare before turning to Prince Robert. "Where is the Duke of Crescera?" he asked loudly. "He was also absent this morning."

"Duke Welborough has decided to return home," Robert said smoothly.

"And you did not stop him?" said Nostin, picking up Donala's line of thought and continuing it, as he had in the earliest days of negotiation. That tendency had irritated Sage to no end, especially as Donala appeared to use it to slander and accuse by proxy, while keeping his own hands clean.

"The Duke of Crescera was here of his own accord, and was free to leave at any time." Rob kept his tone light and pleasant.

"Unacceptable," snapped Donala. "First the ambassador, then Baron Underwood, and now the duke. You have steadily replaced every member of your delegation with soldiers." He gestured to Alex. "Even your Norsari commander has returned."

Alex's fist clenched behind his back, remembering the candle that they'd used to make Sage leave.

"I'm here," said Robert. "Fortunately, my half brother joins us now. Gentlemen, this is Ash Carter, representing the ministry of intelligence and also the crown." Ash nodded from his seat at the prince's right, his stocky frame taking up much more of the chair than Rob did in his.

"And while neither of you wear your rank here, Your Highness, we all know you are both officers in the Demoran army." Donala narrowed his fog-blue eyes.

"If you like, we can invite other Demoran nobles to the table," said Rob. "It'll take a few days, but I'm willing to wait if you are."

"The Countess D'Amiran will do."

That took Rob by surprise. "What do you know of Sophia D'Amiran?"

Donala's mouth twisted up. "We know she and her daughter are heir to Tasmet." His smile widened. "And we know they are here."

General Oshan's head jerked around to look at the brazapil. His nostrils flared, making his already-hooked nose curve down like a beak. The countess's arrival was apparently news to him.

Alex watched his cousin weigh his next words carefully. "Countess Sophia may not be interested in participating, and even if she is, she's still recovering from her journey."

Brazapil Donala stood, contempt and anger darkening his eyes. "We will be here when she is." He turned and stalked out of the tent, followed quickly by General Oshan, who looked furious but for different reasons. Nostin and the others left a few seconds later.

Robert waited until they were gone for a full minute before slumping against the back of his chair and exhaling heavily. "I guess that's it for the day."

"Who were those men?" said Ash. "I never got introductions."

"The demanding one is called Donala. He owns more land than any other brazapil." Rob rubbed his face tiredly, not looking optimistic for once. "The general, Oshan, is minister of war. And then there's Nostin. Mostly inconsequential, though he was the one who knocked the candle over on Sage."

Ash glanced up at Alex. "Did you see that Oshan didn't know about the countess?"

"Yes," said Alex, half smiling. "Never seen him so pissed."

"Why would Donala not tell Oshan what he knew before coming in, though?" asked the prince.

"Because Oshan has the army," answered Alex. "Donala was telling the minister of war that he's not to be trifled with, that he has information sources the general doesn't."

Ash nodded his agreement and leaned his elbow on the table, pointing at the way the delegation had exited. "Their power struggle will be between General Oshan and Brazapil Donala. It's ready to boil over as it is, and they don't even know about the queen's death yet."

"And we apparently have a leak," Rob muttered. "Someone in our camp told Donala about Sophia—and quickly."

"I never should've brought the countess here," Ash said, shaking his head. "But I could hardly blame her for being afraid."

"It must have been bad if Lieutenant Hatfield and the rest weren't enough to make her feel secure," said Alex.

Ash looked up at him, puzzled. "Hatfield went to Jovan?"

"He led Sage's escort group there," Alex said. "A dozen Norsari and about eight Casmuni. The rest turned back with us to Bey Lissandra."

"When? We never crossed paths on the road."

"They would've gotten to Jovan before you," Alex said, wrinkling his forehead. "Maybe they were already out investigating the countess's fears." Norsari were supposed to take the initiative in such matters, and Hatfield was a good man. Alex was putting him in for promotion as soon as this mission was over.

"No, Alex," Ash insisted. "They never arrived."

46

ALEX WANTED TO ask the countess about the missing Norsari, but Robert started their conversation with the Kimisar demand that she attend negotiations.

"But I do not know enough to help!" cried Sophia, her voice quavering.

General Quinn wore a helpless expression, and the prince stepped forward and sat next to her on the couch, taking her hand. "I'll be there with Your Ladyship. You needn't say anything if you don't want to, but your presence could help us move forward."

"You have been here for weeks," sniffed Sophia. "Why do you keep trying to make peace with a nation that so obviously does not want it?"

"Begging my lady's pardon," said General Quinn. "But weeks are nothing in comparison to the years I've spent in Tasmet, trying to prevent war."

"I wish I had never come here!" Sophia leaned her head on Rob's shoulder, tears spilling down her cheeks faster than she could wipe them away. "Where is my sister? No one will tell me where she has gone. I need her."

"Somewhere safe." The general exchanged glances with Alex.

The countess lifted her head from Rob's shoulder, and her spine stiffened. "I will not help you unless you tell me the truth." She set her mouth. "Bey Lissandra is the nearest city of any size. Is she there?"

"No, my lady," Alex's father said quickly. "She isn't, and you must never imply that she was or is there."

"Why not?"

Prince Robert looked up at the general. "If she's coming to the table, we have to tell her what the situation is, sir."

Alex had to admit that Rob was right, or they risked her saying the wrong things. General Quinn sighed. "Very well. You may give her the details Duke Welborough had." Alex's father apparently wanted to keep it quiet that the queen was still alive. He tilted his head at Alex. "Speak with me in private, Major."

They moved to a corner of the tent while Rob spoke earnestly to Sophia.

"What was your message from Lieutenant Nadira?" the general asked quietly.

Alex dug the scrap of parchment from his pocket. A messenger had given it to him just before this meeting. "Underwood's party's trail has split in several directions, and there are far more men out there than left here."

"Meaning Underwood had troops waiting for him. Perhaps in case we tried to keep him here," his father said, and Alex nodded in agreement. The baron was looking guiltier every hour. General Quinn shook his head in disgust. "Dammit. How could I have not noticed them?"

"You can't see everywhere."

"Doesn't matter. I should've known." Alex had never seen the general so frustrated. "And now I have to spread out here to contain the Kimisar. I don't have the manpower to do anything but watch my back."

The all-powerful image of his father that Alex had held most of his life was slowly becoming more human, but surprisingly, he didn't feel the loss. Rather, it made Alex more confident in offering his opinions in support. He raised his eyebrows. "Good thing you have a ready-made force for reconnaissance and tracking."

The general nodded. "Get word to your men waiting at Jovan. I want them back here as soon as possible to guard the bridge over the Nai River."

"We have a problem," Alex said, hating to give his father more bad news. "Ash Carter said Lieutenant Hatfield's group never arrived at Jovan."

"And I always assumed she was overly paranoid," Alex's father murmured, watching the countess bury her face in her hands as Robert comforted her. He shook his head sadly. "What did Countess Sophia say about that?"

"I haven't asked her yet."

The general sighed. "Best not; it will only upset her more. We can trust Lieutenant Carter's word."

"I want to lead a search party to find them," said Alex. "Just a couple squads; you can order the rest where you need them. We'll be back in a few days."

"Very well."

Alex moved to leave, but the prince came over to them. "She's agreed to come to the talks, but I want to give her at least one more day to prepare."

"She may not have to go," said Alex. "If Huzar gets there tomorrow with news the queen is dead, you can expect the Kimisar to either leave or come charging at us."

General Quinn shook his head. "Our numbers are far superior," he said. "They'd be foolish to take up arms."

Robert looked thoughtful. "I'll send the Kimisar word that she needs a couple days to recover from her journey. Hopefully they'll forget all about her once they get their news."

The general nodded and turned to address Alex. "Get going. The sooner you leave, the sooner you can return."

"Yes, sir." Alex saluted and hurried out. All the preparations he'd begun for retrieving Sage would have to be put toward this mission. It was far too dangerous for her to return now.

47

SAGE AND THE others were back on Demoran soil by sunset the day after leaving Bey Lissandra, headed northeast to Clare's home. Few in the party spoke to Sage: Clare because she was angry, Casseck because he was embarrassed—and angry—Sage had gone around him, Zoraya because she was in pain, and Lani because she didn't want to take sides. The princess may have favored their action, but she wasn't sparing in her disapproval of how Sage had made the decision without consulting anyone else. It struck Sage as tragically funny that only a few years ago, being surrounded by people who held her in contempt felt like a badge of honor; now it kept her awake until the wee hours of the morning. That and nightmares which included everyone ignoring her while she burned.

As for Captain Casseck, when Sage asked him why he hadn't put up more resistance once he'd learned of her plan, he simply stated that Alex had left her in charge.

"I would have tried to talk you out of it, Ambassador," he said. "But I ultimately would've followed your orders."

Ambassador. The title was like a punch to the stomach. He wouldn't even call her Sage anymore—and it wasn't because Alex had put her over him. After they sent one of the Norsari back to Arrowhead with coded updates for Alex and the general, Cass rode by Lani's side. Under normal circumstances that would've made Sage happy, but she knew it was done mostly to avoid her.

Clare assumed Mesden's care, which left Sage to stay by the queen.

Her Majesty no longer took medicines, and as she needed all her concentration and energy to steer her horse with one arm, Zoraya spoke only when she couldn't avoid it. After the night the queen had confessed that King Ragat was not the father of her son, Sage didn't know how to bring that up again, or even if she should. Such a secret could tear Kimisara apart, let alone the fragile peace process.

In all, it was a tense and silent journey to the Western Strong.

Sage's initial plan to coerce Baron Holloway into helping them had hinged mostly on letting him know how much he needed to prove his loyalty to the crown after wedding Clare's sister, Sophia, to a family of traitors. Too late, she'd realized another way he could achieve that was by marrying Clare to a supporter of the royal family. Since then, Sage had focused on finding a way to prevent that. She had a lot of time to think while they traveled, allowing her to develop a better strategy and a failsafe plan. Both involved going back to something she'd never expected.

They entered Holloway lands in the late afternoon of the fourth day, and after another hour they came within view of the fortress that overlooked the family's sprawling estate and the nearby town. The setting sun gave the white buildings a golden glow, with dazzling light reflecting off dozens of glass windows. Sage studied the layout with a bit of fascination. With the annexation of Tasmet over fifty years ago, fortified homes were no longer necessary, and apparently Clare's family and the local people had taken full advantage of that in the last two generations. Rather than build tall and strong structures behind high walls, they now spread the same amount of living space over the ground. Silly, in a way, as it took up some of the land that could be farmed, but it did look grand.

The fields themselves stretched as far as the eye could see, bordered by copses of trees and roads wide enough to accommodate heavy wagon traffic. Sprouts of green had begun to show in the tidy, groomed rows, and when Sage compared what she saw to the memory of how much her uncle's modest lands yielded, the amount of profit was dizzying. The prosperity and its vulnerability reminded Sage how much was at stake for those with whom peace had become a way of life—and how much could be gained in the lands where war always loomed.

Some of the anxiety on Clare's face actually lessened at the sight of her home, and she pointed out the fields being seeded for oats and wheat. Or rather, she pointed them out to Lani and Casseck. Sage was still being ignored.

A half dozen riders were coming up the road, led by a young man who could only be Clare's brother; he had the same wavy hair and brown eyes framed with thick lashes. As the group came closer, he scanned the travelers, appearing to take two full looks to identify his sister, and then his jaw dropped. Clare was riding astride rather than sidesaddle, her tunic barely covering her thighs. From the expression on his face, one would think he hadn't ever realized his sister had legs. But then, Sage considered, she herself had been shocked the first time she saw Clare not wearing a long dress fit for royalty.

"H-how are you?" he stammered, staring at her rumpled and dusty clothes and the torn knee of her wool hose.

"Much better than I look, I assure you." Clare turned to Sage and the others. "This is my brother Edmund." He made awkward bows from his horse as she introduced everyone, simply referring to the queen as Raya. They'd decided to hide her identity from Clare's family and attribute her broken collarbone to a fall from her horse. "Where is Father?" Clare asked.

Her brother flushed. "He went to check on the Morannet manor. Won't be back until morning."

"Hasn't changed, has he?" Clare shook her head sadly.

"No, but at least that will give you time to clean up and dress presentably," Edmund said. He turned his horse around and began leading them up the road. "It looks like you could use some rest, too."

Lady Holloway was bedridden, but she managed the household from there. Everyone had baths and rooms prepared within the hour, and a healer was called for Zoraya. Lani helped Casseck tend to the horses, something she'd been doing at every stop along the way, though she didn't appear to have ever made anything more than friendly conversation with him. Clare intended to spend most of the night talking to her mother, and the Kimisar queen and her son were asleep soon after settling, so Sage cleaned up alone and dressed in the plainest gown she was offered. As she tied the bodice, she gazed longingly at the bed. It looked as comfortable as the one she'd been given in Casmun—and that had been a queen's. With a sigh she turned her back on the temptation. She still had work to do.

No one stopped her as she passed through the halls. Most servants scurried to get out of her way and bowed as she went by. She might have tried to talk to them if the hour wasn't so late. Sage nearly got lost trying to get to the main doors, but eventually she oriented herself by a painting she'd seen on their arrival. Soon after she was strolling the streets outside the estate. The town was much bigger than the one next to her uncle's manor, larger even than Garland Hill, where Crescera's high matchmaker lived. The one here would be nearly as powerful and knowledgeable.

Again, Sage was overwhelmed by the sheer scale of her surroundings. She'd been in larger cities like Tennegol and Osthiza, and it felt strange to be intimidated until she realized why: she was alone. Clare could have guided her straight to her destination, perhaps taking a side trip to her favorite bakery. Lani would have dallied at every shop they passed. Even Zoraya or Casseck would have made it so *someone* looked at her. Surrounded by the closing markets and last-minute trading, Sage felt even more invisible than she had in the last few days. She was almost afraid to ask for directions, as if anyone she tried to stop would stare right through her.

Fortunately, matchmakers were always located near the main square—the better for keeping an eye on everyone—so Sage headed in that direction. She passed a lower matchmaker's home on the way, indicated only by a familiar wooden sign with two linked rings for those who couldn't read. A few houses down was a fancier place, two stories rather than one, with an alley next to it leading to the bathing room girls used to prepare for their evaluations. Sage shook her head. Her own interview seemed a hundred years ago.

Part of her didn't want to do this. It used the system in the way Sage loathed most, but it was for Clare. Her friend may have said she didn't need Sage's promises or protection, but Sage had dragged Clare into the jaws of the wolf, and she would do whatever it took to get her back out. Even this.

Hoping to avoid attention, Sage ignored the bell out front and went around the back to the kitchen. Luck was with her, and the matchmaker opened the door at the first knock. The woman was perhaps in her midthirties, with a mass of curly red hair and freckles. She frowned at first, probably anticipating Sage was a girl from town trying to curry favor, but after a couple seconds, her expression changed to cautious curiosity. "I don't know you," she said.

Sage met the woman's gaze with only a slight flinch. Did these women practice that shrewd, evaluating expression? She'd not met one matchmaker who didn't wear it. "My name is Sage Fowler," she said. "I apprenticed with Mistress Rodelle."

"I've heard about you." The matchmaker's green eyes widened. "Most stories were beyond belief."

Sage tried not to blush. "If it was Darnessa who told you, then I can assure you it was all true." The high matchmaker wasn't prone to exaggeration, except when dealing with men she wanted to manipulate.

The woman before her shook her head in awe, dropping her critical look completely, which made Sage even more uncomfortable. "What brings you to my door, Sage Fowler?"

"I need your help."

The matchmaker stepped aside and gestured for Sage to come in. "Then you shall have it."

48

BARON HOLLOWAY WASN'T at breakfast with the family. At first Sage wondered if he would arrive late, in the way that some men often did, forcing the room to stop and acknowledge him as he entered, but everyone acted as though his absence wasn't unusual. Clare's face was tense and pale in anticipation of facing her father, and Sage wished she'd had the time—and the courage—to explain her plan. Zoraya looked better than she had since Bey Lissandra, due to a full night's rest in a soft bed. The queen had regained her appetite and ate heartily, which Sage was glad to see. Mesden was dining with Clare's nieces and nephew in the nursery, proudly playing the part of Victor, though his mother had had to specify that he was to say he was visiting from Casmun, not Kimisara.

Lani sat across from Casseck, alternately pushing the unfamiliar foods around on her plate and asking the captain to pass her items. From the way he flushed every time she spoke to him, he finally must have realized the princess's interest in him was deeper than friendship.

Sage was once again mentally rehearsing the threat-laced request she would make to Clare's father, but she grew frustrated as it became obvious no one expected him to show. "What is so important at the Morannet manor that Lord Holloway would visit for so long?" she asked casually.

Both Clare's brothers and younger sister froze, Edmund in midbite. Clare's cheeks went from white to crimson. The woman who'd been introduced as the oldest brother's wife snorted. "Sowing his oats, of course," she said.

"That is a popular crop around here," said Lani as she poured honey on a biscuit. Across from her, Casseck choked on his eggs, making her glance up. She blinked and looked around the table, realizing how uncomfortable everyone was. "Have I said something wrong?" she asked.

Sage's face felt hot as she leaned over to whisper in the princess's ear. "I'll explain later." At the same time, on Lani's other side, the Kimisar queen spoke up. "He is visiting his mistress, which apparently everyone thinks they can pretend away by not mentioning."

Sage covered her eyes with her hand. The woman had no tact, though Zoraya would probably describe it as having no respect for nonsense.

"Oh." Lani's eyes flashed to Casseck, who was almost scarlet from trying not to cough. She turned to Sage. "Now I understand why your country has a tradition for naming children not from marriage, if such a thing is common."

Spirit above, Lani was just as bad.

"It is *not* common," said Casseck, somewhat fiercely. Lani arched an eyebrow at him, and he added, "At least, it shouldn't be."

Lani looked very pleased with his declaration, but Sage cringed, thinking of her cousin Aster, who was being raised alongside her uncle's legitimate children. She opened her mouth to speak when the door to the dining room opened and the steward announced Baron Holloway had returned.

Everyone jumped to their feet except Sage, Zoraya, and Lani, though Sage started to rise out of habit. Lani grabbed her before she got more than a couple of inches up.

Ambassadors outranked barons by quite a lot.

Clare's father strolled in, appearing pleased that he'd caught everyone off guard. To Sage he was nothing to look at. Like most men his age, he had a thickening middle and balding head, the latter of which he tried to cover by growing the remaining hair long and styling it across the bareness on top, fooling nobody. His eyes narrowed at the sight of three women refusing to rise in his presence. "I see no one waited for me."

It seemed everyone felt silence was better than trying to make excuses.

He focused on his newly arrived daughter, who, like Sage, had worn her cleaned and mended travel clothes to the breakfast table. Sage wore them for comfort, but she suspected Clare wore them to appear less marriageable. "So my manservant was telling the truth," he said. "I'd thought I'd never see you again." The baron looked at Sage and the others still sitting. "Who are you?"

Clare answered, "Father, may I present to you Ambassador Fowler, His Majesty's representative in the peace talks with Casmun and Kimisara." She nodded to the others. "This is Princess Alaniah Limistraleddai and Lady Raya of Casmun, representing their national interests." Zoraya's lips twitched, but she did not object. "And this is Captain Casseck, second-in-command of His Majesty's Norsari Battalion."

For a moment, the baron appeared impressed despite himself. Sage doubted he'd ever had a princess, an ambassador, and a Norsari soldier under his roof, let alone at his breakfast table. If he knew he also had a queen, he might have even shown some respect. Instead, he grunted and took his place at the head of the table. "I can see everyone is finished. You may all leave, except Clare, as I wish to speak with her."

The Holloways all moved from the table as one, without argument. Casseck looked as though he were about to go, but Lani caught his eye and shook her head slightly. He sat back down, and Lani then took deliberate bites of her food while Clare's family filed out. Sage followed Lani's example and continued eating, though her mouth was so dry she had to take a drink to wash everything down. Next to Cass, Clare put her hands flat on the table and focused on Sage for the first time in days. Sage again wished she'd tried to apologize before now.

Clare's father loaded his plate high with ham and eggs, then poured gravy over the top, ignoring that Sage and the others hadn't left. As she wiped her hands on her napkin, Lani caught Sage's eye, and Sage nodded.

"Are you finished eating, Lady Raya?" Lani asked casually.

"Yes, thank you," answered Zoraya, patting her lips with her napkin like she had all the time in the world.

Lani stood, and Casseck and the queen rose with her. The princess nodded at Baron Holloway condescendingly. "Please excuse us, Baron." Having established she was leaving on her own terms, Lani sailed out the door like the dress she wore was far grander than it was. Sage covered her smile by taking another sip of water.

"I said I wish to speak with my daughter alone," the baron snapped at Sage.

Sage glanced over at him, then back at her friend. "What concerns Clare concerns me."

"And who are you again?"

"Ambassador Sage Fowler."

"Ah, yes." Holloway chewed noisily and swallowed. "Why have you brought my daughter back?" he said around another mouthful.

Clare cleared her throat. "We need a place to stay. The ambassador's life was threatened, and I assured her that you had the necessary resources to provide for her safety."

Her father sneered at her. "You dare to come here begging for my help after telling me you wanted nothing of mine ever again?"

Sage's eyes widened. When had that happened? Clare hadn't corresponded with her father in months that Sage knew of, not since writing about her position as Sage's companion at Vinova.

"I humbly beg your forgiveness for the words in my last letter," Clare said quietly. "You must understand I was distraught at the loss of my intended. The thought of marrying another was unbearable. And"—here she met Sage's eyes—"the ambassador and Demora needed my service."

Sage's heart squeezed painfully. That was true, but did Clare realize how much Sage depended on her as a friend? Probably not, given Sage was the reason she was now humbling herself before the person who deserved it least.

The baron snorted. "You were to serve Demora by getting married, not sitting in a frozen corner of the country."

"Like your other daughter, Sophia?" Sage said, remembering what she'd planned to say. "The one who married a traitor at your bidding?"

"That family betrayed me, too," he snarled. "My agreement was with Morrow D'Amiran, but he slipped a clause in the contract that said he could pass her off to Rewel. She was supposed to be a duchess, not a countess."

Sage smiled sweetly. "Then it is fortunate that events may still bring her that rank."

The baron looked mistrustful at the sudden pleasantness. "You and your guests may stay, *Ambassador*, only if Clare submits to my choice of husband." He shoveled another dripping piece of ham into his mouth. "I think that fair considering you are the one who kept her from me."

Before Sage could protest, Clare kicked her lightly under the table. Sage bit her tongue.

Clare eyed her father. "You say that like you have someone in mind already."

"I recently received a letter from the Duke of Crescera, who saw you at Arrowhead," her father replied. "He was widowed last year and rather taken with you, though I assume you must not have been dressed like that." Holloway jabbed his fork at her clothes.

"He's twice my age, Father," said Clare. "His son is older than me!"

"And we're already discussing Sophia marrying the duke's son when this is all over."

Sage suddenly understood why Duke Welborough had attended the talks: he'd wanted the first choice of the scraps that fell from the table—notably Sophia.

"No," said Clare, shaking with either anger or fear. "I will not."

The baron shrugged and went back to his food. "Then I'm afraid my answer to your request is the same."

Clare shot a warning glance across the table before Sage could open her mouth and brought her foot down hard on Sage's again. "Then I want my dowry," Clare said, her voice growing stronger with every word. "Five hundred men-at-arms and provisions for two months."

Sage's mouth dropped open. She'd only planned to request thirty to escort them to Garland Hill, where maybe Mistress Rodelle could help them with her connections.

Her father also gaped at Clare. "Ridiculous."

"How so?" demanded Clare. "According to the documents you signed when you sent me to the Concordium, those troops are your gift to me, which I am in turn to give to my husband. That I don't have one is a minor detail. They are mine."

"No." His face reddened with fury.

Sage knew now was the time to apply the pressure she could bring to bear. Unlike Clare, she didn't have any obligation to this man. There was nothing he could do to her, but there was plenty she could do to him. "To which I offer you a chance to reconsider," she said. The baron's eyes shot to her, and she met his stare coldly.

"And why would I do that?"

"To stay in my good graces."

Holloway threw his head back and laughed. "And what use is that?" He took a sudden, serious turn. "It would seem you should be begging to be in *my* good graces."

Sage only smiled until her silence began to make him uncomfortable, and he went back to eating to avoid her eyes. "What is it you think you have to offer?" he said after he swallowed and took a drink.

"I assume you plan to put forth your youngest daughter for the Concordium in three years," Sage said pleasantly. "I can assure that she is selected."

Holloway snorted. "She'll be the richest candidate in the whole conference. Mistress Rodelle wouldn't turn her away if she had a worse reputation than you did."

He probably meant to intimidate Sage by letting her know how widely rumors of her younger behavior had spread, but it only gave her more confidence. "You seem blithely unaware of how you and your family are perceived by the matchmakers' guild." Sage gave her tone a bit of an edge.

The first flicker of doubt crossed the baron's face. "How would you be privy to such information?"

Sage pulled out a gold medallion with the raised design of two interlinked rings. "This belonged to Mistress Rodelle herself," she said, and

Clare frowned slightly, perhaps suspecting Sage was lying—which she was. Sage twirled the coin on the table as she continued. "She gave it to me so I would have the assistance of any guild member in any matter." She set it flat and slid it toward Clare's father. "I can assure you if I say your daughter is unfit, she will never wed anyone, let alone make a Concordium match. The same applies to your son Edmund."

The baron barely glanced at the large coin. "I have no compunction at arranging marriages myself. I've done it."

Sage nodded. "Which is why your name isn't trusted in Tennegol, either." She dragged the medallion back toward her, scraping it loudly across the wood. "Many doubt your loyalty to the crown."

"I had no knowledge of what the D'Amirans planned to do," he snapped. "And they cheated *me*."

From the corner of her eye, Sage saw Clare flush with anger at her father playing the victim, and she kicked her friend—gently—to tell her not to jump in. Yet.

Sage narrowed her eyes at the baron. "Neither the duke nor count was a pairing any respectable matchmaker would've made. Nor any father who cared for his daughter's well-being." She paused and re-pocketed the coin. "That arrangement was one of several that undercut years of careful planning of matchmakers across the nation, not to mention you lied about Clare's age when you sent her to the last Concordium." The legal age of matching was sixteen, and Clare had been only fifteen. Sage shook her head. "You, sir, have made a number of powerful women extremely irate."

She sat back in her chair, relishing both the moment and the admiring look Clare now gave her. "As for your innocence in the D'Amiran rebellion," she said, "I can assure you the duke's own records implicated you." That was true only to a minor degree. The baron had pledged support, but within Sophia's marriage and dowry contract. Sage suspected those negotiations had made Morrow D'Amiran aware of the Holloway family's wealth and how much he could demand if he took Clare for his own wife.

"If that's true, why haven't I been arrested?"

"Yet?" Sage let the word hang for a few seconds. "For Clare and Sophia's sake. The king holds them innocent."

The baron sneered. "And because he knows how much the treasury would lose in taxes." Clare rolled her eyes, but he was too focused on Sage to notice.

"Indeed," Sage said with mocking deference. It was a fair bet that a man who'd lied to get his daughters high marriages wasn't honest when it came to accounting, either. "In these times of strain, His Majesty needs everyone to do their part in supporting the kingdom. He may be inspired to look closer at what you contribute."

The baron paled at the thought of an audit. "His Majesty will find nothing out of order."

"I'm sure he won't," agreed Sage, with a sly glance at Clare. Not after Holloway scrubbed his records clean, anyway. "But between such an investigation and your *allegedly* unwitting support of the D'Amiran family, it may be difficult to find anyone willing to marry your remaining children and future grandchildren, with or without a matchmaker." She wrinkled her brow sympathetically. "I'd hate for your family to fade into obscurity like so many others in our history."

All of them thanks to matchmakers, who could hold a grudge like no other.

Baron Holloway sat rigid in his chair, holding the stem of his goblet with a death grip, seemingly unable to bring himself to ask what it would take for Sage not to destroy him.

"Of course, Father, helping us now could go a long way toward proving your loyalty to His Majesty," said Clare quietly.

"I'll give you fifty men-at-arms," he said in a strangled voice. "And provisions."

"Four hundred," countered Clare.

"One hundred."

"Three hundred."

"Two hundred," the baron snapped. "And I will never hear from you again."

"Done." Clare stood, chin high. "When can they be ready?"

"Tomorrow."

Sage rose from her chair, smiling. "Wonderful. I'm glad you could see reason, Baron." Rather than curtsy, she nodded, all benevolence. "If you'll excuse us, there's much to arrange before our departure."

She headed for the door, pacing herself to get there the same time as Clare. "One question, if you please, *Ambassador*," called Baron Holloway before they could exit.

Sage turned back, suddenly afraid Clare's father had found a flaw in her threats. "Yes?" she asked, masking her anxiety as best she could.

"How old are you?"

She blinked, realizing she wasn't sure. It took several seconds for her to count the days since the equinox. "Eighteen," she answered. "But only for one more day."

Without waiting for his reaction, Sage hooked her elbow with Clare's and walked out. Neither spoke until they were far down the passage. Then Clare abruptly said, "I knew he wouldn't let us stay here, but I thought at least if we had some soldiers when we left, we'd be safer."

Sage stopped and faced her friend. "What you did was amazing, Clare. I don't know how to thank you."

"I'll never see any of my family again, though." Clare shrugged, trying unsuccessfully to make it appear as though it didn't matter. "But that's what I thought when I left for the Concordium."

"You still have Sophia." Sage put her arm around Clare's shoulders. "And me," she added quietly when her friend didn't shrug her away.

"I know." Clare swiped at her eyes with her sleeve. "Now what?"

"We can't stay here, but maybe that's better," said Sage. "We can move closer to Arrowhead, ready to escort Zoraya back as soon as Alex finds the traitor."

Clare bit her lip. "Is two hundred troops enough?"

"To protect us all? Absolutely."

"But you want more than protection, don't you." It was a statement, not a question.

Sage nodded, but she wasn't ready to explain why she suspected they might need force to put Zoraya back in her place as queen, and Clare didn't ask.

49

PROVING HIS EAGERNESS to be rid of Sage and Clare, Baron Holloway spent all that day arranging what he'd agreed. Sage wrote letters to her uncle at Broadmoor Manor and to Darnessa Rodelle, telling them she was coming and asking them to gather any armed men they could recruit—each with their own particular connections. After midday meal, Sage went back to the local matchmaker to return the coin she'd borrowed, asking Clare to come with her. Things were almost back to normal between them, and Sage was eager to strengthen that bridge.

"That story about Mistress Rodelle giving you her guild coin was made up?" Clare shook her head. "Sage, you're bolder than a pickpocket in a room full of sleepwalkers."

"You have no idea." Sage licked her thumb and rubbed it across the surface of the coin, wiping away the gold paint. The metal beneath was silver, which designated midlevel guild members. "But it worked."

Clare sighed. "I suppose you really do have the influence, though. That was the only way to prove it to him."

"Which is why I don't feel bad." That and because Clare's father was a jackass. They walked around to the back of the matchmaker's home. Sage knocked on the kitchen door and Mistress Gerraty let them in.

"Lady Clare!" she said with a wide smile. "I hadn't ever expected to see you again." The matchmaker took her hands and squeezed them. "I heard your intended was lost in a battle. Are you here for another pairing?"

"Oh, Spirit, no!" said Clare. "I don't think I'll ever get married now."

Mistress Gerraty studied her for a few seconds. "You loved him that much?"

"I did." Clare's soft brown eyes misted a little, but she smiled slightly, like the memory of Luke Gramwell had become sweeter—or at least less painful.

The matchmaker leaned forward and patted her cheek. "You're still young, my dear. Don't give up on the world yet." She turned to Sage, who offered her the guild coin back. "Thank you, Ambassador Fowler. I assume it worked."

"Like a charm." Sage smiled and dropped it into the woman's freckled hand. "We're leaving tomorrow, but I need to see your books before we go."

Mistress Gerraty led them toward the front of the house. "Any particular information you're seeking?"

"I'm looking for those who have soldiers among their assets. We may need to borrow some."

They stopped outside the doorway of a room containing a desk and a bookshelf full of ledgers. The matchmaker drew her brows together. "You're not thinking of creating matches for this purpose, are you?"

"Of course not," said Sage. "But anyone who turns down a chance to do their matchmaker a favor would be a fool, wouldn't you agree?"

Mistress Gerraty smiled and gestured to the ledgers on the shelves. "Absolutely. Be my guest."

Sage and Clare worked until sunset, scanning pages and taking notes. In all, they found the potential for another hundred troops at least among minor lords and wealthy landowners who would be up for matches in the next few years. Clare had the better handwriting, so she was compiling a list for Mistress Gerraty, who would then send out very polite requests for them to send men to meet the force Sage would gather near Garland Hill. Darnessa Rodelle could also use her influence to pull in more support. In Sage's experience, people jumped to respond when the opportunity to make a matchmaker happy presented itself.

Now that Duke Welborough of Crescera was apparently in the market for a new wife, he would've been a great resource to tap for troops—especially if he was as interested in Clare as her father had indicated. He might be very willing to do her such a favor. When Sage said something about that to Clare, though, her friend disagreed. "Considering what he wants, I'm not sure I'd want to be in debt to him," she said.

It didn't matter, though. The duke was currently at the Arrowhead talks. There was no possibility of word reaching him in time.

As Clare wrote, Sage flipped through the pages of one of the ledgers. "Would you like to know what your evaluation said?" she asked.

"That's private information," Clare scolded without looking up. Then after a few seconds' pause, she said, "Well, are you going to tell me or not?"

Sage grinned. "Nothing bad. Mistress Gerraty thought you were the perfect lady, and you have a knack for making people feel better about themselves."

"Most people ought to."

"She also thought you should be saved for consideration for Prince Robert, though she had doubts about tying your father to the royal family." Sage frowned at the book. "Right after Sophia's wedding, she made your father think she'd misrecorded your birth year, which he took advantage of and sent you to Mistress Rodelle for Concordium evaluation, though you shouldn't have been eligible. She and Darnessa worked together to spare you from a similar fate as your sister."

"I wish they'd told me," Clare muttered. "I was terrified both of being married and of being found out as too young."

Sage flipped the page. "Not much else on you, but lots on Sophia."

Clare set down her quill and stretched. "She used to be so vivacious. Competitive, too. Soph probably would've scratched my eyes out if she saw that Mistress Gerraty considered me for the prince."

"I remember you saying she was a little obsessed with him," said Sage, peering at the list of attributes. *Fluent in Kimisar and Reyan.* That wasn't a surprise, as Clare had been drilled in both languages. *Intelligent. Ambitious. Bold.* Sage thought of the shell of a woman she'd met at Jovan and shook her head. That was what happened when people were improperly matched.

Her friend sighed. "I knew Sophia was unhappy and that her husband was cruel, but I thought if anyone could bear such a life, it would be her. But now she's so . . . fearful."

"That's what happens when you have a child," murmured Sage, turning to the next page, which was about Sophia's interview. "They become more important than your own life." Father had nursed her through her illness to the point of not taking care of himself. By the time Sage was well enough to realize he was sick, he was already too far gone to recover. For years she'd blamed herself for his death.

"I know you didn't like her, but she wasn't always what you saw at Jovan," said Clare.

"I liked her just fine. Our misunderstanding was blown out of proportion." Sage squinted at the book. The light was getting bad.

"We have to help her, Sage, not just Zoraya," Clare said. "We have to end this so she and Aurelia can live without fear."

The fierceness in her friend's voice made Sage glance up. An arrow of jealousy went through her at how deep the sisterly bond went, especially considering how fragile her own peace with Clare was at the moment. "Of course we will," she said.

"Promise?"

"Promise."

Sage glanced back down, focusing on a single line. *When asked about her sister, Sophia described hidden deformities.*

Clare leaned over to look. "What else does it say about her?"

Sage snapped the book closed. "Nothing."

Clare shrugged and went back to writing notes.

50

AS HUZAR NEARED the Arrowhead camp, he found a Demoran picket line in place several miles out. He knew their soldiers' routines, however. Sneaking past them wasn't difficult, but it took time and meant he had to leave a couple men behind with the horses. The Demorans hadn't been there when he left with Queen Zoraya two weeks ago, meaning this was how General Quinn had reacted to the news Major Quinn had brought him; he expected trouble.

Huzar and the remaining eight of his squad approached the camp in the evening twilight. Once the sentries identified him, he was brought straight to the queen's tent. His fists clenched at the sight of Brazapil Donala at the head of the table, in Zoraya's chair.

Not yet, you bastard.

The captain forced himself to bow respectfully. As he stood straight, General Oshan rushed in. The minister of war frowned at Donala before taking a place on the left, across from Nostin. Huzar resisted fiddling with his torn ear, a habit that had started because the change in his hearing made him feel like he needed to wipe it clean. The other ministers filed in and, after pausing, each took a seat either by Nostin or Oshan.

They were choosing sides. Nostin—which really meant Donala—had more supporters than General Oshan. Not good.

"Your arrival is most unexpected, Captain," began Donala, his left hand clenching the wooden arm of the chair. "I have never seen you anywhere but at the queen's side."

Huzar recognized the declaration under the words. The brazapil knew how close he was to Zoraya, but there was also a note of acceptance. Maybe even a hint of jealousy. The only way to lessen the veiled threat, however, was to face it head-on. "There is only one circumstance that would compel me to leave her."

Donala blinked slowly, and his mouth tightened. Spirit on high, he already knew. Or suspected.

The next words nearly choked Huzar to say. "My Queen is dead."

Donala's cheek twitched, but he said nothing.

"When?" demanded General Oshan, his voice cracking. "How?"

"Five days ago in Bey Lissandra," Huzar said. "Assassinated with an arrow to the heart." A deathly silence descended over the tent as he pulled the queen's personal seal from his jacket and laid it on the table between Donala and Oshan. When he glanced up at the general, the old man had tears in his eyes.

Nostin took up his usual hostile stance. "Why was she in Bey Lissandra, Captain? What reason could you have for taking her there?"

"I escorted her where she ordered me to."

"To what purpose?" Nostin snapped.

Donala spoke before Huzar could. "She must have had reasons we were not trusted to know." The almost-defense of Zoraya's actions took Nostin—and Huzar—by surprise. Donala turned to the minister of war. "Did you have any knowledge of this, General Oshan?"

Oshan shook his head, still unable to speak as he stared at the seal. Donala looked back to Huzar. "Was she meeting with the Demoran ambassador in secret?"

A ripple of shock went through the ministers on either side of the table, but Huzar remained still, having realized a few seconds earlier that Donala had known this, too—and he hadn't shared his knowledge with anyone. Again, Huzar decided honesty was the best countermove. "She was, Brazapil," he answered.

Donala linked his hands and leaned his forearms on the table. "Please give us a full account. If you can." The last was said almost kindly.

The ruse Huzar and Quinn had agreed on involved denying the

ambassador had been in Bey Lissandra, but Donala knew so much that now Huzar had to give more information than he'd planned. He described the attack, starting with Rewel D'Amiran's death and saying that Ambassador Fowler had also been targeted. For now Huzar chose not to mention the list he'd recovered or the *pesta lundamyetsk* on Lady Clare, hoping someone might ask about her, but none did.

"Are you certain the ambassador was meant to die?" Donala asked. Doubt shadowed his eyes for the first time.

From the expression on the brazapil's face when he heard Sage Fowler had been on the docks that morning, that piece of information had actually been a surprise. It would be easy for Donala to blame Sage, so Huzar had planned an answer that would be convincing as to her innocence, which he truly believed in.

"I am certain, Brazapil," he said, pointing on his shoulder where Zoraya had been hit. "An arrow pierced her near the neck, and for a few hours her survival was not certain." Huzar was ready to describe the queen's wounds as the ambassador's, but Donala only nodded, frowning thoughtfully.

General Oshan stood. "I will send soldiers to secure our king. We will end these talks and depart."

"The first is already done," said Donala abruptly. "The second I will not comply with."

Oshan's tanned face reddened all the way to his balding scalp. "Explain yourself, Brazapil."

"Yesterday, I sent some of my personal troops to guard the young king," replied Donala. "They will be there by tomorrow. Mesden will be safe."

Huzar noticed Donala didn't appear concerned that assassins might beat his men to the king, but the move wasn't particularly worrisome. There was little advantage to killing the boy, unless one wanted to lock Kimisara in a civil war. Meanwhile, keeping a young, impressionable king alive—and in one's possession—would be far more advantageous.

In any case, it wasn't Mesden at the royal estate, though Huzar sent a prayer to the Spirit for the innocent boy's safety.

General Oshan turned purple with rage. "You knew about this," he hissed.

"I heard unsubstantiated reports," said Donala. "I did not yet believe them, but I took precautions."

"Why was I not informed?" demanded Oshan.

"Because I wanted to see your reaction when the truth arrived." Donala waited for the general to reply, but he was stunned into silence. The brazapil then looked up to Huzar, wearing an unreadable expression. "You have my gratitude for bringing us this difficult news."

The near-instant trust that it was accurate made Huzar suspicious. Brazapil Donala had more faith in his earlier source than he claimed.

Or he'd ordered the assassination himself.

General Oshan recovered enough to speak. "You will get us all killed!" he shouted, pointing outside the tent. "While you play games with information, the Demoran army is sitting over there, waiting to eliminate us the moment we respond to their treachery!"

"They could have done so at any time in the past three weeks, General," said Donala sharply. "Yet they have not. Why do you believe that is? *Think.*"

Donala swept his eyes over every man at the table, but no one answered. "Until now we've had no reason to doubt Demora's sincerity in these negotiations. That Ambassador Fowler agreed to meet with our queen after a rather unfortunate incident"—here he gave Nostin a poisonous glance—"only lends to that idea. According to Captain Huzar, she nearly paid for it with her life."

"Wait," said General Oshan. "If the Demoran ambassador was there, then so was the Norsari commander, correct?"

"Yes, sir," Huzar answered.

"That *lying* bastard," Oshan growled.

The general's reaction startled Huzar. When had he spoken with Major Quinn?

Donala raised his eyebrows at the minister of war. "And what, pray tell, did the Norsari commander lie to you about?" he asked. "What were you discussing with him yesterday, General?"

Oshan's left hand gripped the hilt of his sword. "Are you accusing *me* of conspiring with the Demorans?"

"I'm merely asking about your conversation with a man who witnessed the death of our queen," said Donala calmly.

Huzar glanced around at the faces of the other ministers and brazapilla, watching them attach new meaning to something they'd all seen.

Oshan clenched his jaw and moved his hand to a more casual place on his belt. "We spoke of nothing consequential. I only asked if the ambassador was well."

"I'm glad to hear that." Donala held the general's gaze for a few heartbeats, allowing the seeds of doubt he'd sown to take root in everyone's minds before continuing. "The presence of Major Quinn tells us the Demorans know what happened. That is significant, and may explain why Baron Underwood and Duke Welborough left, but it does not mean they're behind My Queen's death."

"Who else could it possibly be?" asked Nostin, eyes wide in disbelief. "One of us?" Huzar's gut twisted as suspicious glances were cast at General Oshan.

Rather than answer directly, Donala focused on Huzar. "Where is Princess Alaniah now?"

Mouths on either side of the table dropped open in shock. "The Casmuni?" whispered someone behind Huzar.

"King Banneth sent his sister to make an alliance with Demora," said Donala. "Our queen's attempt to make peace threatens the strength of that union."

Huzar shook his head once. Ambassador Fowler had been absolutely certain the Casmuni weren't involved, and he'd let her convince him. Donala was right, though. It made sense. Huzar suddenly realized everyone was watching him.

"I asked you to confirm that Princess Alaniah was there, Captain," said Donala impatiently. "And unharmed."

Huzar's mouth was so dry it was difficult to speak. "Yes, Brazapil, to both."

Donala nodded, seemingly unaware of Huzar's discomfort. "Having been unable to disrupt the process from within, this assassination could be Casmun's desperate attempt to force us into attacking the Demorans." He paused. "Therefore, we cannot react to this news."

Everyone stared at the brazapil at the head of the table. To Huzar's surprise, it was Nostin who protested first. "You would have us return to the negotiation table as though nothing is wrong?" he sputtered. "As though the queen regent wasn't just murdered?"

"Yes," said Donala. "It is the only way we can keep the upper hand while we're this outnumbered. The Demorans can't tell us or they risk appearing guilty—*which they may be*, but this way we can force whoever has done this to take action again. Next time, we will be ready."

"We need to declare a new regent," said Brazapil Nostin quickly. "I nominate Hanric Donala."

"Not enough of the council is present to decide," protested the minister of trade, from General Oshan's side of the table.

Donala reached for the royal seal. "There are enough here to be the majority in any vote."

Oshan's hand slammed down on the four-pointed star. "Only if I vote for you," he snarled. "Which I will *not*. Until the full council convenes, leadership falls to the commander of the army, and that is me."

The brazapil pulled his hand back, his face blank. "Very well."

Huzar observed all of this without comment, making a mental note of every man's expression.

"Where is the queen's body?" Nostin asked, looking eager to be of some use to Donala after having just failed him.

"I buried her outside the port city," Huzar replied. Imagining it was the truth was enough to make his words thick with grief. "There was no time for anything else."

Donala nodded. "We will recover her later for proper honors." He took a deep breath, and everyone on either side of the table focused on him in anticipation. Kimisar law may have defaulted ruling powers to the minister of war, but it was clear who was in charge. "The Demorans have called for another day of recess, claiming Countess Sophia D'Amiran is not ready to come to the table yet."

Huzar's eyes widened. The Countess D'Amiran was here? What in the name of the Spirit could have brought her into such a dangerous place?

"This is clearly a ploy to delay long enough for us to hear Captain Huzar's news," Donala continued. "But that is no matter. When we do not behave as they expect, the Demorans will be forced to return to negotiations." He smiled a little. "I imagine it will be like sitting on hot coals for them, knowing our queen is dead but being unable to bring it up."

Oshan wasn't quite ready to concede defeat. "This game you are playing will turn deadly," he said. "How long do you propose we dance around each other, pretending nothing is wrong?"

Donala's smile only tightened. "Until we are ready to change the tune."

Huzar's stomach sank as he realized Quinn and the ambassador's ruse had failed. Donala may or may not have been behind the plot to kill Zoraya, but it was obvious the brazapil was the one directing the music now.

51

TRUE TO HIS word, Baron Holloway had two hundred men ready to march by dawn the next day. There was no deception in Clare's father when Sage spoke to him before they left, only the plain desire to be done with his daughter and the trouble she'd brought. "You'll get nothing else from me ever. Do you understand?" he told Clare coldly. "From now on you are someone else's problem."

He turned and stomped away as Clare watched. "Good-bye, Father," she whispered.

Sage put an arm around her. "Are you all right?"

Clare shrugged her off. The forgiveness of yesterday evening was gone in the face of what she was losing. "I think I'd feel worse if I hadn't learned what a real father should be like. Maybe when this is all over, Mama and Papa will take me in again."

Lieutenant Gramwell's parents would probably be more than willing to adopt Clare, but Sage had other plans for her friend. Rather than say any of that, however, Sage gave Clare the space she needed to mourn. "Let's go."

They mounted their horses, Zoraya with minimal assistance. The full day of rest had done the queen much good, and she'd gotten the hang of having her shoulders braced and her left arm in a sling. Casseck had said it would be another six weeks at least before her collarbone was fully healed. "How does it feel?" Sage asked her.

The Kimisar queen grunted. "It itches, but inside the bone, where I cannot scratch. Maddening."

"Sometimes my skin is like that," Sage said sympathetically. "I often have an itch, but when I scratch the skin there, I feel nothing, so I get no relief."

Last night, Zoraya had caught Sage in her room right after bathing and asked to see her burns, and Sage had somewhat reluctantly shown her. The queen had stared at the pink-and-white mottled skin over Sage's left arm and leg for a full minute before nodding and saying, "I am glad to know you have suffered." Then she turned and walked out.

At first Sage was shocked by Zoraya's words, but after some consideration she thought perhaps it was a difference of language that made the phrase sound harsh. "I am glad to know *what* you have suffered" would have been more appropriate, but honestly, either one was believable coming from Her Majesty.

"How far is it to your family's estates, Ambassador?" asked the queen.

"Three days, but I don't intend to stay long," answered Sage. Her plan was to visit her former employer in Garland Hill for the same assistance in gathering more troops as she and Clare had with her matchmaker, and the village was too close for her not to also visit Broadmoor Manor. Sage had sent a courier ahead to Darnessa as well as to her family, though she doubted her uncle would offer any help. When she'd left his home over two years ago, it hadn't been under the best of circumstances. Most of what they needed would have to come through the matchmaker, assuming Darnessa agreed. There was a chance Mistress Rodelle would be angry at the presumption and the steps Sage had already taken.

Sage avoided Zoraya's eyes. "I'm hoping by the time we get there, most of the work of calling for men-at-arms will be done."

Either that or there would be neither soldiers nor any kind of welcome.

The queen frowned. "You plan to gather more troops?"

"I do. These can protect us, but more may be necessary if we are to bring you safely back to Arrowhead."

Zoraya opened her mouth to speak, but Casseck rode up on his dun-colored stallion, interrupting them. The captain's cold treatment of Sage had thawed a bit once he realized that she and Clare had acquired enough troops to protect them, but he was still formal. Lani was beside him on her horse, and Mesden was settled in front of one of the Casmuni riders. "Everyone is ready at your command, my lady," Cass said.

Sage frowned. "You're the military man here." Then she realized Cass was speaking to Clare, who sat astride her dappled mare on Sage's other side.

Clare flushed. "I will defer to another."

"These troops belong to you," said Lani. "I suggest you let them know it."

Cass smiled and held up his arm, indicating Clare should take a place at the front of the company. She bit her lip and urged her horse forward. Sage, Lani, and Zoraya took places on either side of her, and Casseck turned back to ride down the columns toward the rear, calling the preparatory command.

"How will they all hear me?" Clare whispered.

"That is what flags are for," said Lani. "But since we do not have one, you will have to make do with this." She drew the curved Casmuni *harish* from her belt and offered it to Clare, who took it with a trembling hand. When she held the sword high, platoon commanders behind them raised theirs in imitation. Every soldier was silent, waiting.

Sage smiled. Nervous as Clare was, she knew exactly what to do.

"Move out!" Clare shouted. She lowered the sword to point ahead. At the same time, she kicked her horse into a walk. The noise of a two hundred men stepping off echoed behind them.

52

TRACKING THE MISSING Norsari and Casmuni from Arrowhead was easy. Alex and his squads traveled faster and slept less than the average courier, making it to Jovan in only two days. Every manor and village had seen the decoy escort group pass through. The people seemed open and honest, and none reported any trouble with bandits or harassment from Baron Underwood's people, which Alex had expected to hear about. When the search party reached Jovan, however, everyone they spoke to said the same thing: the soldiers never arrived.

Somewhere between the last stop and their destination, the entire company had vanished.

Alex had granted Lieutenant Tanner permission to come, as the leading officer of the missing soldiers, Hatfield, was Tanner's closest friend. Had Casseck been the one missing, nothing would've stopped Alex from leading the hunt. Now Tanner was becoming more and more agitated, to the point that Alex regretted his allowance.

The team backtracked. They must have missed something, but search as they might, they could find no sign of a fight. In fact, there were no signs of the company at all. A group that large usually disturbed the ground on either side of the road, yet the only tracks they found were a week old, likely from Ash's own escort of Countess Sophia, headed west. Alex and his squads returned to the place the missing soldiers had camped outside the last town. Wagons had been there, but it was as if they had never gotten back on the road.

A stone farmhouse stood a few hundred yards away. Alex had ignored it on their first pass through the area because several sources had told them that the Norsari had come and gone. This time Alex knocked on the door, and a young girl of about eight years answered.

"Hello," he said, kneeling to below eye level of the child. "I'm looking for some of my friends. Is your father home?"

The girl shook her head. "He's in the east fields today with my brother. They won't be back until nightfall."

Still a couple hours away. Damn.

Alex smiled. "Maybe you can help me."

Her honey-brown eyes immediately turned suspicious, and she took a step back, gripping the door like she would slam it closed.

"No, no," said Alex, raising his hands. "I just want to ask a few questions."

The girl hesitated. "What do you want to know?"

"My friends were a big group that camped in tents right over there about ten days ago." Alex pointed in the direction. "Do you remember them?"

"Yes."

"Did you see them leave?"

She shook her head. "They were gone in the morning."

Double damn.

"Did you hear anything that night?" Alex asked. "Shouting or fighting?"

"No."

Alex slumped a little. A dead end. Children slept soundly, though. Maybe the father had heard something. "Nothing strange at all?" he asked again, half-heartedly.

"Our wagon was stolen that night," she said.

A few feet behind him, Tanner pointed to a three-wheeled wagon outside the lean-to that served as shelter for goats and a few pigs. "Was it like that one?"

"It *was* that one," the girl said. "Father followed the tracks and found it, broken down."

Alex frowned. Had the Norsari done that? "Where did the tracks go?" he asked.

She pointed at two parallel paths running north. "Up that road."

The road was little more than worn ruts leading into the woods. "What's up that way?" asked Tanner.

"The north field. We're not using it this season."

"Thank you," Alex said, rising to his feet and taking a step back to keep the girl from feeling threatened. "You've been very helpful. May we look at the wagon before we go? Maybe we can fix it for you."

She shrugged. "Father already ordered new parts from the blacksmith."

"We'll check anyway." Alex gestured for Tanner to follow him. The girl closed the door, and they heard her bolt it from the inside. A few seconds later she was peeking out of a window. "Don't act like you see her watching," Alex murmured.

"It's a shame she has to be so cautious," Tanner said quietly.

Together they inspected the wagon for any clues as to who'd taken it and why. The wooden planks were stained, but not with blood—or at least fresh blood. It had probably been used to haul animal carcasses from hunting or the butcher in town. After a few minutes, Alex gave up and signaled his team, which waited by the main road, holding the officers' horses, and they remounted and headed north up the rutted path. It felt like they were grasping at straws, but it was the only lead Alex had.

His gut also told him the group's disappearance was key to Countess Sophia's fears. Alex was grateful she'd brought attention to something sinister they might never have noticed otherwise until it was too late.

It might even be too late now.

The road, such as it was, led into a forested area sprinkled with huge boulders half buried in the ground, like they'd been dropped from the sky by the Spirit. About two miles on the other side of the woods was a field, left fallow for the year so the common weeds and plants could replenish the soil exhausted by crops. Or not. A patch on the far end had been cleared by burning recently and also plowed. Alex ordered Tanner and a few others to continue up the path into another expanse of forest as he scanned the area.

He was running out of time to find any clues that existed. The sun was low and much of its light was blocked by treetops at the far end of the field. Old wagon tracks crisscrossed the ground leading to the disturbed area, but it was such a mess he couldn't make anything of them. The long shadows made something catch his eye, and Alex tossed his leg over Surry's neck and dropped down for a closer look. A few steps away from the compressed line left by wheels, he bent over to pick up a large coin half buried in the dirt, like it had been stepped on. His gloved fingers brushed away the soil, revealing the shape of a bird of prey.

A Norsari medallion.

Alex looked up and across the field, a horrible suspicion building. He shouted for Tanner and the others as he took off running for the burned and plowed area. They charged up behind him, meeting Alex at the edge of the disturbed plot. Up close, he could see the scorched patch hadn't been to clear weeds—it had been a bonfire.

The soil, too, wasn't plowed as he'd assumed; it was turned over in a large rectangular area. A vague, rotting scent hung in the air. A smell Alex knew all too well.

Sweet Spirit, *no.*

Without a word, the men around him dismounted and dropped their packs, pulling out latrine shovels and other digging tools. Alex's was still on Surry's saddle so he only watched, praying. It would be worse to find what he suspected than to find nothing, but he knew in his heart his prayers were useless.

Less than two feet down, they hit something solid.

Several men backed away while others dropped to their knees and flung dirt clumps away with their hands until they uncovered a leg clad in brown.

Norsari brown.

Next to it was a bent arm, covered in the tan fabric of a Casmuni guard. Everyone but Lieutenant Tanner froze.

"No, no! Spirit, no!" Tanner began digging like a man possessed, crying his friend's name. "Sorrel!"

Alex and the others could only watch helplessly as Tanner struggled to uncover the body. The sickly-sweet smell of decaying flesh became stronger with every handful he cast away, uncovering more parts of those who'd been their friends.

The dead man's face was revealed, and it wasn't Lieutenant Hatfield's. Tanner sobbed and sat back on his heels, his scarred face streaked with dirt and tears. He gazed blankly over the disturbed earth of the mass grave. His friend was in there somewhere.

Shovels dropped to the ground. No one wanted to dig anymore. They knew now. Disturbing the dead further was not only unnecessary, it felt like sacrilege.

Alex patted Tanner's shoulder and knelt, trying not to put weight on any of the other body parts sticking out of the ground. A crusted whiteness was still visible around the man's blue lips and down his chin, like he'd been foaming at the mouth. Poison, then. Whatever it was had been swift and powerful. He brushed dirt away from the gaping wound in the corpse's throat. The clothes below were nearly bloodless. The cut had occurred after the man's heart stopped. The killers must have wanted to be sure everyone was dead before they buried them.

His soldiers been slaughtered in their own camp. Nausea roiled in Alex's gut. Whoever had done it had carried every scrap of evidence here, stealing the farmer's cart to help. Then they'd buried the bodies and burned the tents and equipment where no one would find them for another year at least. The group's horses must have been taken, but everything else was destroyed.

Not only that, but it had to have been Demorans who'd killed them. No Kimisar group large enough to do this could have escaped notice this deep into Tasmet. Back at Arrowhead, at Bey Lissandra, the traitor was one of their own.

Countess Sophia had been right to be afraid.

Alex wanted to turn his face up to the sky and scream his rage at the clouds, telling them just what he thought of the Spirit that had allowed this to happen. Nothing—no land, no title, no power or money—was worth the lives left to rot here. He was so damn sick of death and fighting, yet all he could think of was finding whoever had done this and wiping them from the face of the earth.

Everyone was watching him, waiting for his leadership. Alex stood, telling the soldiers to recover what they'd found, and they slowly obeyed, following his example and remaining stoic. He offered a hand up to Tanner, and, in his only allowance of emotion, he embraced the lieutenant long enough to make sure he would be steady on his feet. Then, when the dead were cared for as much as could be managed, he turned away and led the Norsari back to the road.

Back to revenge.

53

CAPTAIN HUZAR WASN'T allowed to attend the talks when they resumed with Countess Sophia D'Amiran present. General Oshan had wanted him there, but Brazapil Donala—rightly—claimed anyone who recognized Huzar would then know beyond doubt that the Kimisar were aware of Zoraya's death. The Demorans were expecting a reaction to the queen's assassination, and the Kimisar council wanted to pretend as though nothing was wrong. Or rather, Donala wanted it. He was waiting for something, but Huzar couldn't decide what. Confirmation that the boy king was now in his control, perhaps.

Somehow Huzar had to let the Demorans know what had happened and that the Casmuni were suspect, but even if he could find a way, telling them about Donala's power grab was a kind of betrayal. The brazapil had done nothing illegal or without reason, and Huzar found it difficult to stand with General Oshan when the minister of war had abdicated all his authority.

Fortunately, Oshan and Donala were keen to have Huzar around for their discussion that evening. He felt like a toy being yanked back and forth between two children. Both men wanted him on their side, though he wasn't sure why he was so important to them.

The general refused to sit as Brazapil Donala took his place at the head of the table. Nostin settled next to him as usual—looking angry. All other ministers were absent. Oshan prowled around the tent, throwing accusations at Donala.

"What in raging hell were you playing at today?" he demanded. "You withdrew our protest of the dams across the Nai? And let the Demorans survey the lower end of the river? How is that *not* two concessions from our side with nothing gained?"

Huzar's breath hitched. That had been Queen Zoraya's first agreement with Ambassador Fowler.

Nostin opened his mouth, but Donala silenced him by raising his hand. "It got their attention, yes?" he said.

"I would listen, too, if Demorans suddenly offered to let our troops march into their territory," snapped Oshan.

"Not troops," said Donala, shaking his head. "Engineers. We will convince them of the damage their dams have caused downstream. Then we can have a reasonable discussion on how to proceed."

The general scowled. "And asking their help in building a new port?"

"That is contingent on the results of the engineering study," said Donala calmly. "And on the Demorans agreeing to ship us flour from their proposed mills on the River Nai. Nothing is set in stone."

Huzar felt the blood freeze in his veins. Donala's proposals were too much of a coincidence. What was he playing at? He cleared his throat. "May I ask how the Demorans responded to such offers, General?"

"With suspicion." Oshan crossed his arms and glared at Donala. "It was also as if the prince and his bastard brother had heard such ideas before, whereas I had not. Yet to keep the appearance of a united front, I could say nothing."

"Then say your piece now," said Donala.

"Why are you doing this?" Oshan demanded.

"I explained this to you when Captain Huzar arrived," said Donala patiently. "The Casmuni have the most to gain by ruining these talks. By continuing—and making progress as our queen had wanted—we will force them to act again."

The general stepped forward and leaned his knuckles on the table. "You also said you expect a reaction, but I'm not waiting for it," he growled. "I own the army, and we are leaving. Tonight."

"I have my own army, General," said Donala coolly. "It is on its way in support of me. Unless you intend to make your men fight mine while we are in Demora and surrounded by its army, you will stay."

"Surrounded?"

"They have built a perimeter around us while *your army* has slept."

Huzar had reported the soldiers he'd run into near the road, to Arrowhead, but apparently they were only part of what was out there. The move made sense if the Demorans were expecting a response from the Kimisar. He hoped to the Spirit the men he'd left out there hadn't been caught. "I have seen this myself," Huzar said. "I had to sneak past a picket line several miles to the west."

Donala nodded his thanks for Huzar's statement, but the captain didn't want acknowledgment for merely being truthful, especially when it was obvious the brazapil was anything but.

"What more proof do you need that the Demorans are guilty?" yelled Oshan. "They killed our queen, and now they will annihilate us. When your army gets here we must turn and fight—if it's not too late."

"I disagree. The Demorans could have wiped us out at any point. They're waiting for something, and I want to know what." Donala sat taller in his chair, as though he were taking complete command of the situation. "But once my troops are here we will have the advantage."

Huzar cleared his throat. "What do you intend to do with this advantage, Brazapil?" he asked.

Donala didn't look as happy, considering he shortly expected to be in a position of greater power than ever before. "Whatever it takes to get answers, Captain," he said.

54

ON RETURNING TO Arrowhead, Alex left Lieutenant Tanner and the other Norsari to guard the bridge over the Nai River as his father had wanted, relieving the regular army company and returning with them to the Demoran camp. The vision of the field he'd found haunted him every step of the way.

Soldiers weren't supposed to die like that, poisoned and betrayed in their own country, then dumped in a shallow grave. That wasn't what kept him awake, though.

It could have been Sage.

She was supposed to have been returning to Jovan with the soldiers, which made him wonder if she had been the target. Then, that attempt having failed, her name was added to the list at Bey Lissandra. Princess Lani and Lady Clare should have been in that caravan, too, so perhaps they were also meant to die, but then the connection these killers had to the ones in Bey Lissandra was tenuous. Lani hadn't been on that list, and Clare had been specifically spared.

Taken all together, nothing made sense. The only thing Alex felt sure of was that what he'd found in that field was too deep in Tasmet to be anything other than the work of a Demoran, or someone closely allied with one. It wasn't a comforting thought.

Alex expected to return to an army camp at least in some sort of stand-off, but the sentries he met and signaled his return said nothing of the sort had occurred. Talks had resumed yesterday with Countess Sophia present, and General Quinn now also attended. Impossibly, it appeared the Kimisar didn't know about their queen yet—which meant Huzar hadn't told them, but no one had seen the captain, either.

A page came running to take his horse as soon as he drew to a halt. "Major Quinn, sir!" the boy said with a salute. "Your presence is requested in the ambassador's tent."

For a split second Alex thought he was saying Sage was here, but then he remembered that Countess Sophia now occupied it. He hurried in that direction, cutting through rows of tents to get there. The camp was half the size it had been before, though what remained was spread out a bit to create the illusion of more troops. Soldiers were lining up outside the mess tents for early-evening rations, reminding Alex he hadn't eaten since leaving the river this morning.

Inside the ambassador's tent, Alex found his father sitting in a wooden chair nestled within the arc of cushioned sofas and chaises. Prince Robert and Ash lounged on couches, looking exhausted, while Colonel Traysden paced around like a restless cat. The general's staff officer, Murray, sat at the table off to the side, scribbling notes and orders. "Welcome back, Major," said General Quinn wearily.

One person was missing. "Where's the countess?" Alex asked, taking a seat next to his cousin.

Robert jerked a thumb at the curtained area in the corner. "It's been a hell of a morning in negotiations. She's resting."

The partition opened and Sophia stepped out, closing it again behind her. "No, Your Highness, I am awake, but Aurelia is sleeping now." She trudged to the last open chaise, her face pale and her eyes lined with dark circles. She clutched her hands to keep them from trembling as she sat. "If there is news from Jovan, I should like to hear it."

All eyes turned to Alex except for Sophia's, which gazed unseeing at the tea set on the low table in front of her. He cleared his throat. "I found the missing escort," he said. "Dead. All of them."

The countess closed her eyes as tears streamed down her cheeks. "Spirit give them rest," she whispered. In response, everyone brought their hands to their chests, two fingers pressed to their hearts.

Everyone was silent, waiting for Alex to continue. "They were poisoned and their bodies dumped a few miles from the road," he said numbly. "Whoever did it must have taken the horses—a number of them were Casmuni bred, so perhaps finding them will lead us to the killers eventually, but the trail was over ten days old, and there wasn't enough for us to follow."

Sophia opened red-rimmed eyes. "Do you believe me now, General?"

"I never doubted Lieutenant Carter's decision to bring you here, Your Ladyship," Alex's father said.

Sophia's mouth pulled into a thin line, but she said nothing.

Rob rubbed his face. "There were at least a dozen Casmuni in that group from Princess Lani's escort. This could ruin the whole process of sending Rose to them."

"Let's take things as they happen with regard to that," said General Quinn. He looked to Alex. "In the meantime, we have a new problem. The Kimisar apparently haven't learned of their queen's death. There's been no sign of any reaction on their side."

"Yet they're trying to provoke us," said Ash, sitting up. "Since yesterday, Brazapil Donala has been putting forth proposals that are suspiciously like the ones you listed from Queen Zoraya's agreements."

"Who knew about them?" asked Alex.

His father swept his hand across the tent, indicating everyone. "Only the people here now."

"Not me," Alex heard Sophia murmur, but no one else appeared to hear her.

"And Captain Huzar," said Alex. "Has anyone seen him?"

"No," said Traysden, shaking his head. "But we caught some of his men west of here, holding on to a number of horses. He and some others must have made it past our picket line."

Alex considered. "Huzar claimed the queen's own papers were missing after the attack," he said. "It's possible Donala has those."

"Who is this Captain Huzar?" said Sophia abruptly. "I have not heard this name before."

"Queen Zoraya's personal bodyguard," explained Alex. "He was wounded in the attack. An arrow took off the top half of his left ear."

Remembering the angles from that day, that was the arrow that had been aimed at Sage.

"And he was the one meant to tell the Kimisar about the queen regent's death?" the countess asked.

"Yes, Your Ladyship," said Alex.

Sophia frowned, clearly frustrated at being ignorant of information everyone else already had. Alex couldn't blame her, but some details—like Huzar—simply hadn't been necessary or relevant.

"I want to go back to Bey Lissandra," said Alex, changing the subject. "What I found outside Jovan is clear evidence that the ambassador's life is threatened. If my job is to protect her, then that's where I should be."

Everyone glanced at one another rather than speak. Alex looked around, a sick suspicion growing at their silence. Rob pursed his lips. "One of the Norsari with them came back two days ago, to tell us she didn't stay on the ship."

"What?" Alex jumped his feet. "Where is she?"

"Your ambassador took my sister back to our father," spat Sophia. Her hands clenched in her lap. "She thinks he will provide them some protection."

"Sit down, Major," General Quinn said. "The Western Strong is not a bad place for them to be, considering."

"Considering someone in Demora wants her dead?" Alex nearly yelled.

"Outrage will get you nowhere, son," said his father calmly. "Sit."

Alex dropped back down and gripped his hair in his hands. *Sweet Spirit, Sage. Why can't you just* . . . Do what? It wasn't like he'd given her orders. But why was she putting herself at risk?

A hand nudged his shoulder, and Father offered him a folded note. "This is from her."

Alex took the parchment and opened it, wondering if his father and Colonel Traysden had already read it. Probably.

This was my idea. Don't blame Casseck. I love you.—S

He snorted in humorless laughter. Poor Cass was probably at his wit's end trying to deal with her. "What now?" he asked.

"We don't know what the Kimisar situation is," said Colonel Traysden. "But I think this plan to find the traitor has failed. We haven't been able to eliminate any suspects on our side, and the Kimisar haven't reacted at all. In some ways that's better because no blood has been shed—yet. But we're all poised for a fight, and this quiet can only last so long."

The general nodded. "Agreed. Nothing has been gained. We should bring the queen back now, before they realize we have her."

Sophia sat up straighter. "What do you mean, General?"

"I'm sorry for not being honest with you before, Your Ladyship," said Alex's father. "We thought we could discover the perpetrator by watching who tried to seize power, but in truth, Queen Zoraya survived the attack."

The countess's mouth dropped open. "You sent me in there to negotiate without telling me the whole truth?"

"I assure you very few knew this, Your Ladyship."

"Everyone *here* knew it!" Sophia cried, rising to her feet. "How can I trust anyone when no one will trust me?" She turned and ran for the curtained area, tears streaming down her face.

Robert shot the general an exasperated look. "I told you we should've let her know, Uncle." He stood and followed the countess, who, after a quiet, heated exchange, allowed him to come in and comfort her.

General Quinn sighed and rubbed his face, then stood. "I'm going to guess she won't be attending tomorrow morning's session, which means neither will Donala. All these damn games are exactly why I became a soldier and not a diplomat." He turned to Alex. "The Norsari are spread out behind us, watching our backs, but there's one platoon left here. Take them to the Western Strong and bring the ambassador and her party back."

"Yes, sir." Alex jumped to his feet, then swayed a little.

His father frowned. "When's the last time you slept, son?"

Not since he'd found the mass grave, and there had only been a few hours here and there in the two days before that. It was probably more lack of food that made his head light, though. "I'm fine," Alex said, even as he realized how close he was to collapsing.

"Like hell you are," said his father. He pointed at the exit. "Get some rest. You can leave at dawn."

"But—"

"That's an order, Major."

Alex didn't dare disobey, especially when his father directed Lieutenant Colonel Murray to set a guard on him. But he wouldn't be able to sleep knowing there was the chance he'd only arrive at the Western Strong to find another grave—this time with Sage in it.

55

HUZAR SAT BY the campfire late into the night. There were only embers left now. The wineskin at his side had been empty for over an hour, and he was sobering up. Which meant he had a decision to make.

Brazapil Donala's treason was obvious. The only way he could know about the queen's agreements was if he had sent the assassins. Huzar's first thought was to expose him to the rest of the council, the minister of war in particular.

But then the day after the meeting, General Oshan had found Huzar to tell him he'd investigated Donala's claim and found over half of the Demoran soldiers had left in the last two days, though the remainder still outnumbered the Kimisar. The minister of war believed Donala correct that the ones who'd departed now surrounded them.

The general gritted his teeth. "I hate to admit it, but we'll need Donala's army. We're lucky he sent for it before that perimeter went up."

Huzar knew Oshan suspected the Demorans or Casmuni, but he saw too many clues it was Donala, the man who wanted to replace his queen as regent. "But Brazapil Donala could easily turn those troops on you, sir."

"I do not think so." Oshan shook his head. "He may threaten to overpower me with this army and take control here, but he will not harm me or his own countrymen. The council would never side with him after that."

"It is he who sent the assassins," hissed Huzar. "Those proposals he made were from the queen's own agreements with Ambassador Fowler at Bey Lissandra."

General Oshan silenced him with a look. "You forget yourself, Captain." He waited for Huzar to lower his head in apology. "Brazapil Donala is many things, and he has sources of information I do not, but he is not a traitor."

Something about Oshan's absolute belief in Donala's innocence made Huzar pause. What if Brazapil Donala was only trying to seize power before his claim to the regency—a legitimate one—was automatically conferred on General Oshan?

"It's all rather embarrassing," Oshan continued. "Our own queen going behind our back, and now you are telling me she made a list of concessions to our sworn enemies?" He narrowed his eyes at Huzar. "I hold you innocent, as you were only following her orders to take her there, but it's not a stretch to say her actions were treasonous. In that light, we are fortunate she's dead."

At the memory of that last sentence, Huzar tilted the wineskin over his mouth again, but only dregs fell on his tongue. He turned and spat. Donala and Oshan may have acted at odds in the presence of others, but deep down they were of the same mind. The brazapil was instigating a war while claiming loyalty to the crown, as he steadily drew power to himself, while the general considered Zoraya's actions treasonous and was glad she was dead. It was too dangerous for her to return now.

As the alcohol faded from his thoughts, Huzar couldn't dismiss the idea that perhaps this was something Zoraya had planned all along: to fake her death, leaving the decoy child to be controlled by Donala or Oshan while she escaped with Mesden.

If Kimisara's queen had turned her back on her nation, then Huzar, too, owed nothing to the brazapilla and generals who plotted against her, but where did that leave him? Huzar knew where he wanted to be, if Zoraya would have him.

That was where he would go.

But Donala's troops were coming. They would punch right through the Demoran line. It would take a few days, but General Quinn would regroup, and then . . .

Huzar closed his eyes. The face of every man who'd died under his command paraded through his memory. There were so many. Some he didn't even know their names. More good people, both civilians and soldiers, on both sides would die if he didn't warn the Demorans before he left.

The captain lurched to his feet. If he was going to commit treason, he needed more wine first.

Negotiations had begun for the day, so when Huzar told the Demoran sentries he needed to speak with General Quinn, he knew he'd have to wait several hours for his return.

At the Demoran perimeter he was stripped of all weapons and blindfolded, then led under heavy guard to the command tent. Though he'd half expected it, they didn't bind his hands, but apparently they didn't want him to know his way around or to let him see the condition and numbers of their soldiers.

He sat cross-legged on the ground, dozing occasionally and ignoring his growling stomach the rest of the time. He hoped General Quinn would be curious enough to deal with him at the break for midday meal.

Voices. He concentrated on listening.

"He speaks Demoran?"

"Yes, sir. Very well."

"Did he give a name?"

"Captain Malkim Huzar."

The question of whether Major Quinn had told his father anything about Huzar was answered when a few seconds later the blindfold was yanked away. "You're Captain Huzar?" the blurry figure said.

"I am." Huzar squinted up, eyes burning in the light. "May I have some water?" he rasped.

The man nodded to the bald officer beside him who stepped away and returned with a cup. Huzar drank eagerly. His tongue was sour from last night's drinking, though he'd been sober when he left the Kimisar camp. "Thank you," he said, handing it back.

His eyes had begun to focus again, and he looked up. The man before him could be none other than Major Quinn's father. Though his hair and beard were gray and his complexion much lighter, there was no mistaking the resemblance. The general raised an eyebrow. "I'm told we have a defector."

A nicer word than *traitor*. Huzar nodded.

"What do you have to offer me?"

Huzar licked his lips. "Information on what is happening on my side."

Except it wasn't his side anymore. The weight of his betrayal and the lingering effects of the wine suddenly made him feel like he would be sick. He bowed his head and drew a long and shaky breath.

"And why would you bring this to me?" asked General Quinn.

"Because you're in danger."

Quinn crouched down in front of Huzar and lifted his chin with one finger. His brown eyes had flecks of gray, like steel. "Why should I trust the word of a man who has no loyalty to his country?"

"I am loyal to My Queen," Huzar said.

"So we've heard." The general dropped his hand, and though Huzar felt his neck grow hot with embarrassment at what they knew about him, he continued to meet Quinn's gaze. The Demoran rose to his feet and glanced at the bald man beside him. "Is this truly Huzar?"

The second man studied Huzar with piercing eyes set over a nose as sharp as a hawk's beak. Then he nodded. "I'm sure of it." He smiled a little ironically. "Also, that ear is pretty hard to hide."

Huzar shifted, his legs and backside protesting from staying in one position for so long. "Will you believe what I tell you?" he asked.

Next to the general, a staff officer was setting up a folding table to take notes. Quinn's mouth quirked to the side in a half smile. "My son trusted you, and while he's impulsive in most things, he is much less so when the safety of the ambassador is concerned. He left this morning—you missed him by a few hours."

The staff officer dipped his quill in ink, ready to record Huzar's every word.

Quinn locked eyes with Huzar. "I will trust you. For now."

"Good," Huzar said. "Because an attack is coming."

"You think we've not been expecting that?" the general asked. "We've been ready for days."

"No," Huzar said. "You aren't ready for this."

56

SAGE COULD HAVE pushed their group to reach her uncle's home by late on the third day, but she worried at finding little welcome when it was too late to go anywhere else. Instead they set up camp outside the small town of Garland Hill, next to the Tegann Road. Clare, Lani, Zoraya, and Mesden were able to stay at the inn once Casseck was satisfied the place could be guarded and the streets adequately patrolled.

When they were settled, Sage went straight to Darnessa's house, opting to ring the bell out front rather than knock on the back door. If she thought she could surprise the matchmaker, she was wrong. Darnessa opened the door before the bell finished its backswing, and stood with one hand on her hip. Her graying hair was drawn into the high, tight knot that to Sage had always meant business, and gravity had pulled the matchmaker's large frame down a bit in the last two years, but her blue eyes were sharp and shrewd as ever. "I expect you never thought you'd come to my porch willingly," she said.

Sage grinned. "Yes, but did you?"

Mistress Rodelle laughed and swept Sage into a hug. Sage sank into the comfort of the matchmaker's heavy arms, inhaling the familiar rosewater scent of her hair and dress and . . . She lifted her head. "Do I smell spearmint tea?" she asked.

Darnessa arched a painted eyebrow. "You did tell me you were coming." She stepped back and indicated a spread of Sage's favorite cakes and biscuits laid out on the low table in the sitting room. "I'll even let you sit on the sofa."

The last time Sage had sat in this room—on an uncomfortable wooden chair—had been at her disastrous evaluation. In the months she apprenticed, Sage had avoided coming in here. It didn't look as scary now.

After a short lecture for not having told her anything about Princess Rose and the match Casmun and Demora were setting the stage for, Darnessa addressed the reason Sage had come. Her new apprentice, a fourteen-year-old from the orphanage whom Sage had tutored only a few years ago, was hard at work in the next room at that very moment, writing letters and recording the promises that had already come in.

When the high matchmaker showed her the troop rolls she expected to have drummed up, Sage's jaw dropped. Most families were only able to spare a half dozen men-at-arms from their estates, but the numbers added up.

"You also apparently forgot my niece married the baron at Galarick," Darnessa said. "I've already made arrangements for you to stay with them, and anyone providing soldiers has been directed to send them there. The castle isn't terribly strong, but it's better than camping here in the open."

"And it's right on the intersection with the Span Road," agreed Sage. "We'll have a straight line to Arrowhead." She hugged the older woman, wondering how she ever could have been so ignorant about her before becoming her apprentice. "I can't thank you enough."

Darnessa brushed off Sage's gratitude. "I've spent over thirty years building alliances and preventing conflict. If these peace talks fail, Demora will survive, but we'll need generations to recover." She shook her head. "As it is, this will take at least two Concordium cycles to settle down again."

"Clare's sister, Sophia, will need a new husband, too," said Sage. "You ought to put an eye to finding the best candidate to serve as guardian of Tasmet until her daughter, Aurelia, comes of age. If you make a recommendation to the king, I'm sure he'll listen."

The matchmaker drew her eyebrows down as she frowned. "Sophia Holloway is quite capable of managing the province herself."

"Maybe at some point she was," said Sage. "But I've seen her myself,

266

and Clare would agree—the past years have broken her. She's terrified of her husband's allies, mostly for Aurelia's sake."

"I suppose that's understandable. The circumstances of the child's birth were quite traumatic, too."

Rewel D'Amiran had dragged his very pregnant wife out of bed in the middle of the night to flee from General Quinn's forces, only to abandon her after she gave birth to a useless girl. The coward had gotten what he deserved. Sage looked forward to telling Sophia she no longer had to fear his return. Or, rather, she would let Clare tell her.

Darnessa sighed, squinting at the ledger in front of her. "Improper matching damages more than the couple. Even love matches can be dangerous. They're often too hasty, for one thing." Here she gave Sage a pointed look.

Sage's stomach twisted, Alex's reluctance to marry her coming to mind. "Is that supposed to be a warning?"

"About you and Captain Quinn?"

"Major Quinn."

"You must give him my congratulations." Darnessa went back to the book. "I don't think either one of you would suit anyone else, if that's what you're worried about, but events at Tegann sealed your attachment much too quickly, as life-and-death matters tend to do. The army regulation that has forced the two of you to wait was a good thing. Both of you needed to grow a little yet."

Sage's face felt like it was on fire. The matchmaker might as well have called her a child. It was all the more insulting that Darnessa regularly arranged weddings for girls three years Sage's junior, and had matched Clare at fifteen.

Though Sage had said nothing, Darnessa glanced up with a smile. "I'm glad to see at least one of you has found your way."

A more pleasant warmth spread through Sage. The high matchmaker never complimented lightly, and if she'd ever made a mistake in her assessment of someone, Sage had yet to see it.

The question now was whether she and Alex had grown together, or if they were growing apart.

57

GENERAL QUINN MIGHT say he trusted Huzar, but not, apparently, enough to return his weapons to him. The captain felt agitated without them, and combined with his anxiety over the coming attack, Huzar thought he would burst from his skin. He paced the Demoran general's tent for hours under the watchful eye of two guards. There were more outside, he was sure. Huzar snorted. Where did they think he would go?

Somehow he'd expected to feel a sense of freedom once he'd passed the point of no return. Instead, he only wanted to drink and forget what he'd done.

The light increased as the hanging canvas door was lifted and General Quinn strode in, looking haggard. His recorder followed; then the man Huzar now knew as Colonel Traysden, the Demoran king's spymaster. Traysden was also the last Norsari commander, and he rubbed the stubble on his head as he met Huzar's eyes.

His warning had come too late.

Quinn walked around the wide table and sat, pinching the bridge of his nose with one hand and closing his eyes. The other two officers took chairs on either side, and the general waved to Huzar. "Have a seat, Captain."

Huzar obeyed, his mouth completely dry.

There was shouting and movement outside the tent. Men were gathering weapons, preparing to march, as many had this morning.

After a full minute, General Quinn lowered his hand and looked up. "Guards, dismissed," he said, and the pair disappeared, leaving only the four men at the table. He focused on Huzar for a dozen heartbeats before saying simply, "Two full companies are gone. Captured or killed."

He'd betrayed his people for nothing. "Spirit give them peace," Huzar whispered, drawing two fingers diagonally across his chest.

"And now we find ourselves at a disadvantage." The general's fist clenched where his own gesture had stopped over his heart. "In our own country."

Huzar swallowed with difficulty. "What will you do now?"

"Brazapil Donala and General Oshan have called for a temporary truce, thank the Spirit," said General Quinn. "I wonder if they realize how easily they could overrun us right now."

"You spread too much around the Kimisar camp," said Huzar. "That strategy also made you look guilty, which made Donala more willing to use force."

General Quinn scowled. "Yes, I realize that now." He glanced at Traysden. "We set them far enough out that you shouldn't have known you were surrounded."

It had been Huzar who had confirmed the existence of the picket line he'd crossed, but he'd be damned if he'd be made to feel that telling them had been wrong. "I imagine having called this truce, now they want to talk."

"Yes." The general studied him for a few seconds. "I want you there when we do."

Huzar jumped to his feet. "No! I need to be with my queen. Let me go to her."

General Quinn pursed his lips. "Do you know where she is?"

On a ship sailing up and down the Western Sea. But from the look in Quinn's eyes, Huzar suddenly knew that wasn't true. What had the Demorans done with her?

"She is safe," said Colonel Traysden before Huzar could ask. "And we intend to keep you safe as well. Sit down, Captain." When Huzar did not respond, Traysden added, "Please."

Huzar sat.

"I'll make a deal with you, Captain," said Quinn, leaning his forearms on the table. "If you attend this meeting today and give me your honest opinion of what is happening on your side, I'll tell you where your queen is and release you to find her and bring her back."

Huzar considered. Zoraya was probably with Ambassador Fowler. "Is that where Major Quinn went?"

The general affirmed with a single nod. "I don't intend to let Donala and the others know you are present—they'll demand you be apprehended as a traitor if they do. The guards we've posted inside the talks have always worn helmets, did you notice?"

Huzar glanced back and forth between the general and the spymaster. "The two of you have been in there."

"On occasion." Quinn tilted his head at Traysden. "The colonel was there the day of the candle."

The memory made Huzar shudder. Sage Fowler had screamed in a way that still curdled his blood to think about. He'd also picked up on something the general had said: *Donala and the others.* Quinn knew who was really in charge over there, and it wasn't General Oshan.

"Do I have your word that I am free to leave after this meeting?" Huzar asked.

Quinn nodded. "Satisfy me with your assessment, and you can be on your way first thing tomorrow morning."

"Tonight," said Huzar firmly.

The general tapped his fingers on the table, then nodded again and turned to the staff officer at his side. "Murray, get this man a uniform and a helmet. The meeting is in less than an hour."

It may have fit well, but the Demoran uniform was the most uncomfortable thing Huzar had ever worn. He would've preferred the all black of a cavalry officer, but instead he was dressed as a foot soldier, with an additional long over-tunic of vivid green and yellow. Beneath his helmet, sweat that had little to do with the heat trickled through his hair and down his neck as he watched Brazapil Donala, General Oshan, and few others take places across the table from Prince Robert, General Quinn, and the remaining council member. Colonel Traysden stood opposite Huzar at the tent opening to the Demorans' back, wearing the same clothing but looking much smaller than him.

Donala smirked. "I would thank you for coming, but I know you didn't have a choice."

"Explain yourself, Brazapil," said General Quinn. "Why have you attacked us?"

"We realized Demoran troops had moved to surround us," Donala replied, the smile gone. "We felt threatened."

Prince Robert sat forward. "They were soldiers in their own country who had done you no harm and intended none."

"And how were we supposed to know that?" snapped Nostin. "Especially in the face of what else has happened?"

The prince raised his eyebrows. "Do you refer to the incident which caused Ambassador Fowler to leave? Our actions had nothing to do with that."

"Do not pretend to be ignorant," said General Oshan coldly. As the minister of war spoke, Donala sat back in his chair, like he'd given him permission to talk. "We know she left only to lure our queen into secret negotiations in Bey Lissandra, where assassins waited for her. When you received word Queen Zoraya was killed, you moved to surround us."

Quinn did not respond right away, and Huzar wanted to tell him honesty—to a point—would be best here. "The queen regent initiated those talks," the general finally said. "But I will admit the last part is true. While we had nothing to do with her death, we expected you to blame us, and I acted to contain your reaction for the safety of my nation, which is my first responsibility."

Donala looked a little surprised, like he'd expected Quinn to deny everything. The general continued, "If you believed this of us, then why are you still here? Why haven't you simply used your new army to return to Kimisara? It's obvious you now can. If you return the Demoran soldiers you captured, I will not move to stop you."

General Oshan frowned, glancing at Donala, which told Huzar that the brazapil again had more information than he did. Donala raised his chin. "We have learned our beloved queen may still be alive," he said.

Next to Huzar, Colonel Traysden swore softly. General Oshan's eyes shot to the pair of them, though Huzar doubted he could have heard him clearly from that distance.

"*May* be?" said Prince Robert. "It sounds as if you doubt the accuracy of your source."

"The report is several days old," said Donala. Huzar saw a flicker of distress in his eyes. "If she is alive, we want her back immediately. Unharmed." Donala paused. "Or we will destroy you."

General Quinn shared a long look with Prince Robert, who nodded slightly, then turned to address Brazapil Donala. "She is alive," Robert admitted. "But it will take several days to bring her back to Arrowhead."

"Do not take us for fools," said Oshan sourly. His eyes kept drifting to Huzar over Quinn's shoulder. "We won't give you time to call for reinforcements."

"It is the distance which makes the delay necessary," the prince insisted. "We don't have wings."

"If she is truly alive, we will wait." Donala locked eyes with Robert. "In the meantime, we require assurance that you won't attack us."

The demand was obvious. Donala wanted a prisoner of his own. Prince Robert didn't hesitate. "I am prepared to serve in that capacity."

Judging from the way his whole body tensed, Colonel Traysden didn't like that idea at all. Nor did General Quinn. "Your Highness—"

"Not you," interrupted Donala. "Valuable as you are, My Prince, you're a soldier, and I'd prefer someone I don't have to tie up and post several guards on. But you will stay here in this camp." His eyes shifted to Quinn. "That also excludes you, General."

Huzar frowned in confusion. Who else was there to take?

"We want Aurelia D'Amiran," said Donala.

"The child?" gasped Prince Robert.

Donala smiled. "You can send her mother, too, if you like."

Huzar understood the logic. It was unlikely the Countess D'Amiran would consent to send her daughter alone, giving the Kimisar two captives.

"I think you overestimate her value to the crown," said Prince Robert. His tone was light, but Huzar was sure no one in the room believed him.

"Perhaps." Donala shrugged. "Yet, as Aurelia is the rightful heir to Tasmet, your king could have a noble rebellion on his hands if one of their own is abandoned. I also don't think I underestimate how far General Quinn will go to avoid spilling the blood of someone so innocent, nor how much the countess means to you personally, Your Highness."

Prince Robert looked slightly puzzled by the last statement. General Oshan was eyeing Huzar again, but after a pause to let his words sink in, Donala stood. "Those are our conditions," the brazapil said. "You will give Aurelia D'Amiran to us by sunset or none of you will see the dawn, not even her. Prince Robert will stay here, in camp, where we can see him every six hours."

Huzar grunted. They were effectively keeping the crown prince captive as well.

"Return our queen to us unharmed," Donala continued, "and we will return the D'Amiran child in the same condition."

"And the Demoran soldiers you have as prisoner?" demanded General Quinn.

"You may have the wounded and the dead," said Oshan abruptly, making Donala scowl. "The rest we will keep as an additional guarantee of your cooperation."

Quinn clenched his fist. "I want all of this in writing."

"Very well," said Donala, like it didn't matter. "When you bring Aurelia D'Amiran, we will have a contract ready." He turned to leave. Brazapil Nostin jumped up from his chair.

"One more thing," said General Oshan, rising to his feet. Donala stopped, annoyance on his face, but Oshan ignored it. "I noticed your spymaster joined us." He nodded to Traysden.

Everyone turned to look at the colonel, who removed his helmet. He smiled tightly. "Can an officer not take a turn on watch, General?" Traysden asked.

"Most admirable," Oshan agreed, his smile equally strained. "And who is your partner in duty today, Colonel?"

Huzar's blood turned to ice. Donala focused on him now, suspicion dawning in his eyes. General Quinn wore a look of anguish, and Prince Robert shook his head slightly, but Huzar knew it was too late.

Slowly, Huzar reached up and lifted the helm off his head. The change in light made the colors he now wore all the brighter. Blinding. Yet Huzar made himself face the men he'd betrayed.

Without a word, Brazapil Donala spun around and stomped outside, a stunned Nostin running after him.

Oshan waited a handful of seconds before speaking. "I expected so much more from you, Captain," he said. Then he turned and strode out.

And just like that, Huzar was a man without a country.

58

HUZAR WATCHED THE young woman at the end of the table, staying quiet and out of the way as the prince and the general laid out the situation for her. The minister of foreign affairs and several other officers contributed, describing how Donala's army had marched in and taken out a wide swath of the perimeter, cutting off the general from half the forces remaining. They showed her on the map where everyone was and illustrated how long it would take for Demoran soldiers to respond if the Kimisar turned on them here, even if a red blaze signal went out. Her face became paler and paler.

"In those few days, my lady, they could easily overrun us," said Quinn. The captain could see how painful it was for him to admit he'd mishandled the situation, though Huzar wasn't sure how else the general should've acted, given the situation.

"So you will give my child to our sworn enemy?" Tears dropped from her face and onto the girl now dozing in her lap.

Robert winced as he glanced at Huzar. "Now that they know we have their queen, this is a fair demand, Countess. We have every intention of returning her, but this is the only way we can prove that to them."

"And if you refuse, are they strong enough to take her by force?" she cried. "Would they do that?"

"Yes, Your Ladyship, they can," said General Quinn quietly. "And they will."

"Can we not simply flee?" the countess begged.

Quinn shook his head. "Doing that would provoke a fight, and we must do whatever we can to avoid more bloodshed. This is how wars begin, my lady." He glanced at the map. "And as you know, the land east and north of here is full of your late husband's allies—men who want control of your daughter even more. They would use her to unify and wield power. The Kimisar only wish to assure the safety of their queen."

"There would be no good that could come from the Kimisar harming your daughter," added Prince Robert. "They know my father would not let that go unanswered."

Huzar watched the countess rock in her chair, clutching her daughter and gazing blankly at the map in front of her. He wanted to assure her that the Demoran prince was correct, and that women and children especially were never harmed by his people in these situations, but he judged it better to remain silent.

After a minute, the general took a deep breath. "My lady," he said. "I will never force this on you, and I'll do everything in my power to protect your daughter. Every man here will fight to the death, if necessary."

"I will go," the countess said abruptly. "*We* will go, for I will not part with her."

Everyone at the table breathed a sigh of relief, but General Quinn wasn't ready to accept that just yet. "Are you sure?" he asked, his voice gentle. "This is my failure, and I will answer for it."

"I cannot let you die for us," she said dully. "I have also failed in coming here, believing it was the safest place for us to be. This is the consequence of my poor judgment."

The countess looked down at her daughter. "We women have always been pawns in this game," she whispered. Then she raised her chin, though it trembled. "But I will play my role, for even a pawn may bring victory in the end."

59

EARLY IN THE morning, Sage rose and saddled her horse, planning to visit Broadmoor Manor alone, but Clare, Lani, and Zoraya were already in the stables attached to the inn, dressed and ready to go. "You don't need to come," Sage protested. "I probably won't be very welcome."

Zoraya raised an eyebrow. "For an ambassador, you make a lot of people angry with you."

"*I* wish to meet the man who thought he could marry you off," said Lani, grinning.

Clare was silent, but she probably wanted to witness Sage's discomfort at returning home, though it certainly came nowhere near her own.

With a sigh, Sage led the way north. Casseck and the other Norsari and Casmuni stayed nearby as always, riding ahead and behind. Mesden rode with the captain this time, and Cass let him control the reins—or at least let him think he controlled them. Lani smiled as she watched them. "I think he will make a fine father someday, don't you?"

Sage bit her lip. Lani's attraction to Casseck had shown no signs of fading. Also, from the crimson blush spreading down the back of his neck, it was obvious Cass had heard Lani's comment.

As the manor house came into sight, Sage's apprehension peaked. Aunt Braelaura might be happy to see her, seeing as she'd continued to write, but Uncle William hadn't spoken to her since her disastrous interview with the matchmaker. When Darnessa had offered her the apprenticeship,

Sage had left his home without permission, and he'd made no effort to bring her back, unlike the time she'd run away at twelve.

Everything looked the same, down to the tree near the wall she'd always used to escape the manor for a few hours when she could no longer bear the cage. Two riders came trotting down the road toward them. One—a barrel-chested man—sat astride a stallion big enough to be a warhorse. The other—a short, plump figure—rode sidesaddle on a traveling pony. They approached together, and there was no mistaking who they were. Had Uncle William come to tell her off himself before she even reached the gate?

Casseck dropped back to ride beside Sage, and when they came within shouting distance, she pulled her white horse up short, holding her breath. Aunt Braelaura also stopped and jumped down without waiting for her husband to help, then ran toward Sage, her graying blond hair escaping the loose bun at her neck. "Oh, my dear!" she cried.

A thousand memories of kindness and care came flooding at Sage. Without thinking, she threw her leg over Snow's neck and practically fell into her aunt's outstretched arms.

Braelaura sobbed, clutching Sage and stroking her back. "I thought I might never see you again!" To Sage's surprise, she nearly wept herself as she buried her face in her aunt's neck. After a minute, Braelaura eased her hold and put her hands on Sage's cheeks, taking in every detail. "Look at your short hair," she scolded. "And you're sunburned and freckled as the end of summer."

Sage grinned and blinked back her tears. "I missed you, too." She became aware of Uncle William standing beside them. Braelaura released her and moved aside to allow Sage to face him. The belt around his thick waist was cinched a little tighter, his blackened hair a little thinner on top, and his face more lined, but his smile was unstrained, which was new to her, and when he lifted his arms tentatively, Sage stepped into them and hugged him back.

He embraced her and kissed the top of her head while Aunt Braelaura tsked and fussed around her, tugging Sage's tunic down to better cover her backside. "Oh, stop pestering her, Brae," Uncle William said to Sage with a wink.

Wiping her eyes before she turned around, Sage introduced everyone, though she suggested waiting until they were at the manor house before getting down from horses for formal presentations. William helped Braelaura remount, and they turned back to the estate. Sage rode next to her uncle, though she felt shy asking about what she'd written him for. Fortunately, he brought it up.

"I haven't heard back from too many yet," he said, referring to his friends. "So no promises, but I think we can gather about ninety men-at-arms in the next week. Mistress Rodelle suggested they go to Galarick, and I trusted her on that."

Sage gaped at him. When she was younger and chafing under his rules, she'd assumed half the wealthy lords he claimed to be on good terms with were hollow boasting. Father had always described her uncle as respected, but there was a difference between respect and friendship. "That's . . . amazing."

Uncle William shrugged. "I could probably count on twice as many if I could reach the duke, but Welborough went to the talks, as you know. Sent me a letter right off, telling me how you impressed him at dinner the first night." He chuckled. "His opinion only grew better during the talks, though I worried when he wrote what happened with the candle. It surprised me you would run away after that."

The compliments coming at her were dizzying. "I didn't run away."

"Apparently not." He cleared his throat. "But I did send a message his way, telling him what you were doing."

Sage grimaced. That might not have been such a good idea. She should've let her uncle know how secret this was all supposed to be, but she hadn't expected such a positive response. On calculating the distances, however, it didn't seem that bad. It would still be several days before the message reached the Cresceran duke at Arrowhead. And with whatever was going on down there now, General Quinn—and Alex—would appreciate an update about where she and Queen Zoraya were going, especially since things had changed and they hadn't stayed at the Western Strong.

Inside the manor house gates, Sage was swarmed by her cousins. Even Jonathan, who was only a week from turning fifteen, was happy to see her. The Casmuni sword she wore at her waist interested him particularly, and she promised him a few lessons. Aster cried, making Sage cry again, and she wouldn't leave Sage's side until Mesden shyly approached. The boy king hadn't had a playmate in months, and it was only minutes before they ran off, hand in hand, to climb apple trees in the orchard—the very trees Sage had taught her cousin to climb years ago.

Zoraya watched him go, a sad light in her blue eyes. "He so rarely gets to be a child," she murmured.

Sage's family convinced everyone to stay overnight as there was no rush to get to Galarick yet. Clare's mood lightened after a few stories of the scrapes Sage had gotten into over the years and how her tantrum during her interview with the matchmaker had become somewhat legendary. She wasn't cheered enough to share a room with Sage, however, opting to sleep with Lani instead. That left Sage to stay with the queen, and she couldn't convince her aunt and uncle not to give up their own bedchamber for the night, seeing as it was the best they had.

After a wonderful soak in the bathing closet attached to the room, Sage took a long time combing her hair and rubbing lotion into her scars, thinking about how right Darnessa had been about her. Only two years ago she *had* been a child, and spoiled brat, too. Her devastation at losing Father and their way of life had blinded her to the family she still had. That her aunt and uncle held no grudges had little to do with what she'd accomplished. They'd understood her better than she'd understood herself, and they loved her. It was as simple as that. Now that Sage had a stronger sense of the world, it was clear they'd only been trying to prepare her for the future in the best way they knew how. This was at least part of what Darnessa had meant when she'd said Sage had needed to grow. How, then, had Alex needed to change? Had she grown so much she'd left him behind?

Or was it Sage who had taken too long? Her behavior last year, her unwillingness to see how her presence at the Norsari camp affected him, had threatened his ability to make life-and-death decisions. Even now, marching toward Galarick, she'd shown complete disregard for his need to keep her safe.

No wonder he'd hesitated when Article Twenty-Nine had changed.

Unable to justify staying in the bathing room any longer, Sage crept to the door, hoping the queen was already asleep, but she heard two voices in the room. She peeked through the crack and saw Lani in a nightdress, sitting cross-legged on the bed next to the queen, who reclined.

"I think he is afraid to show interest in you," said Zoraya. "Women with power can have that effect."

Apparently the Casmuni princess had decided to seek romantic advice. Sage pressed her ear to the opening and closed her eyes, listening.

"Either that or he thinks I am ugly," said Lani. Sage imagined her pouting with her lower lip out.

"I'm not one you should cast your net toward for compliments, *Chessa*," said Zoraya wryly. Sage covered her mouth with her hand to keep from giggling. Lani knew very well she was beautiful, and she liked hearing it said too much for her own good. While the conversation was safe to walk in on, Sage stayed where she was. Zoraya could probably relate to Lani's problems better than she could.

"You are so far above him I think your captain does not allow himself to consider having affection for you," the queen said. "Either out of humbleness or to protect his own heart. Perhaps both."

"Then I am destined to fail?" Lani asked.

"Possibly," said Zoraya. "But those are the men most worth having." She paused. "You should consider also whether your interest is because he is something you cannot have."

Sage opened her eyes in surprise. That was exactly what she'd always been afraid to say.

"His performance in battle and his goodness to others is what attracts me," retorted Lani, then mumbled something that Sage couldn't hear but suspected was about his looks before sighing. "Is Saizsch ever going to finish bathing?"

"Oh, she is done," said the queen. "She's listening behind the door."

Sage jumped back, cheeks flaming. A few seconds later, Lani opened the door, scowling, and put her hands on her hips. "I came to tell you that

Captain Casseck would like to leave an hour after sunrise tomorrow. The troops on the road will be ready to move on when we reach them."

"Thank you." The heat spread to the tips of Sage's ears.

Lani turned and headed toward the door to the passage outside. "I'm sorry, Lani!" Sage called to her back. "I didn't want to interrupt. I think Cass is good for you, I just . . ."

The princess turned around and folded her arms across her chest. "You just what?"

Sage took a deep breath. "I don't know if you're good for him." There. She'd said it. "I'm his friend, too. I don't want you to break his heart."

Lani shook her head sadly, hurt in her eyes. "Saizsch, that is the last thing I want to do."

"I'll talk to him," Sage said. "If you want. I'll tell him how you feel."

Lani's eyes flicked to Zoraya. "I thank you, Saizsch, but no." She smiled a little. "I think I need to decide my intentions first."

Sage could only nod as the princess left.

"I have realized something," said the queen, pulling the coverlet back up from where Lani had wrinkled it and settling deeper into the cushions. She had to sleep propped up or the weight of her arm pressed on her healing shoulder.

"What is that?" Sage asked wearily. She didn't think she could take any more soul searching tonight.

"I am sleeping in the same bed as the person who killed my husband."

Ragat's death hadn't been something Sage intended, but she'd triggered the panic that caused the Kimisar king to be thrown from his horse. Intent aside, the comment tore at her. Who knew how many hundreds of other women's husbands she'd killed?

Zoraya calmly watched Sage turn down the lamp by the door and climb under the bedclothes next to her. "Are you afraid?" Sage asked, trying to keep her voice light, but she sounded tense to her own ears.

"I am always afraid," said Zoraya. "That is what being a mother and a queen means." She settled a little deeper into the cushions. "But here and now deep in Demora and inches from you, I am less so than I have been in years, which is ironic, no?"

There was only one candle left, making it difficult for Sage to see the queen's expression in the shadows. "I suppose it is," she replied.

When Zoraya said nothing more, Sage leaned away and blew out the candle next to the bed. For most of the night she lay awake, wondering what could make someone return to a life of fear, and if the queen was willingly doing so.

60

KNOWING REALITY WOULD settle back on their shoulders once they returned to the road, Sage lingered a little longer than Casseck wanted the next morning. Zoraya was the first to express impatience to leave, however, and they reached Garland Hill well before noon. Darnessa met Sage with an update on the responses she'd received the day before, but they didn't stop long before turning their company east.

The last time Sage had traveled this road, it was with the matchmaker and her selected brides for the Concordium, including Clare. Their first stop then had also been Galarick, where they'd met the ceremonial escort—Alex's group—assigned to take them to the capital. She wondered if Casseck felt strange coming back to where the mission that changed their lives forever had begun, or if it was only important to her . . . and Clare. Her friend rode in silence the whole day, doubtless remembering she'd met Luke Gramwell at Galarick, too. Sage wasn't sure how to reach her now that Clare was withdrawing as she had in the first few weeks after Luke died. It didn't feel like that was the root of the problem this time, though. If Lani had told her about last night, that was probably it. Now Zoraya was the only one left for Sage to alienate.

Casseck was friendlier again, after his initial annoyance with Sage's delay. When they met the men-at-arms already gathering outside Galarick, he quickly took charge, merging them into a single force with Clare's troops. Now that there was a military unit to run, he was in his element, doing so well that Sage thought it was a shame he'd stayed under Alex's command for this long. And if Sage wasn't mistaken, Cass was almost showing off. Not for her benefit, though. He never made a report to Sage and Clare if a certain princess wasn't also within hearing range.

It was late afternoon by the time Sage and the others made it into the castle itself. The baron and baroness fell all over themselves accommodating their guests. Unlike two years ago, all the women were offered individual bedchambers, but Lani linked arms with Clare and said they would share. Zoraya preferred to stay with Mesden, which left Sage in her own room. She hadn't slept alone since Jovan. Even in the ambassador's tent at Arrowhead, Clare had been only a few feet away.

The room was modest in size, but it echoed like a cavern as Sage dressed for bed and then sat by the fire late into the night. Every snap and pop from the hearth bounced off the stone walls, emphasizing how empty the room was. Sitting cross-legged on a sheepskin rug with a cup of tea was also a reminder of how Clare had reached out to her on the journey to the capital city two years ago, offering friendship Sage hadn't known how to accept.

Or keep, apparently.

Sage stood and yanked on the dressing gown and slippers given to her by their hosts and let herself out of the room. After some wandering, she found herself on the highest guard tower, gazing out over the smoke that hung low over the army camped below. Above, the half-moon struggled to shine through clouds growing thicker by the minute. According to Casseck, over three hundred troops were down there, and there would be more tomorrow. Then what?

Was she willing to use this army? To what end? To restore Zoraya to her place as regent? Secretive and scheming as she was, the queen was probably Demora's best chance at creating a lasting peace, but if her rule was unstable, maybe a Kimisar civil war was better sooner rather than later. Sage shook her head at the thought. She was as bad as Zoraya when it came to ruthless pragmatism.

Sage turned away from the view and padded back down the steps. She didn't remember Galarick well enough to know her way around in the dark, but somehow her feet found their way to the library. The fire was out for the night, and only meager light came from the open window. Outside, a mist of rain had begun to fall, making the room colder and more damp than it already was.

She sat at the table with her back to the hearth, like she had the night Alex had brought her dinner and they gave each other false names. Of course, they'd almost immediately gotten into an argument. Sage curled her toes inside her loose shoes and tugged the dressing gown tighter. The frilly nightshift underneath chafed her scarred arm. Like the robe and slippers, it had been given to her by the baroness. The woman had recognized Clare from the Concordium trip and fawned all over her, but Sage received only a blank stare. She wasn't surprised or insulted. Back then she'd wanted be invisible, as had Alex.

Yet they'd seen each other.

She smiled a little. The Mouse and the Starling, searching for crumbs, finding each other instead.

Spirit above, she needed him now. She needed to know what was going on at Arrowhead. It could be a battlefield for all she knew. By now Alex had to have learned that she'd gone to the Western Strong rather stayed on the ship. Going through Galarick was the fastest way to get there, so they should have crossed paths on the road. Why hadn't he come? Was he angry with her like everyone else? Was this what would break them, telling him she would always betray him, that she'd never consider him when all he wanted was for her to be safe?

She hadn't worn the rank of ambassador well. Trappings and honors were important, but Sage had let them go to her head. She'd not only refused to listen to her friends, the people she trusted more than any in the world, she'd completely disregarded them, relying on all of her nineteen years of experience. Not that her friends were that much older or wiser, but they at least acknowledged their dependence on one another. This mess now was entirely her doing.

As miserable as that thought was, at least it meant Sage had a chance of fixing things.

If she could figure out how.

61

EVERYONE AGREED TO meet Sage after breakfast, which was a start. She stood nervously at the table in the library, facing Clare and Lani sitting on the opposite side. Both wore dresses given to them by the lady of the castle, which Sage hoped was because they were tired of breeches and not because they were making some sort of statement by not dressing like her. Zoraya sat to her right, wearing Sage's clean spare clothing, but her posture was rigid, like she expected unpleasantness. At Sage's back, the hearth was now lit and burning merrily, though its heat was not what made her sweat.

"Thank you for coming," said Sage, trying not to fidget with her hands. "We have much to discuss."

"When are we leaving?" asked Clare, her voice flat.

"I don't know," said Sage. "That's why I wanted to talk." No one spoke for several seconds. "Look, I still think coming back to Demora was the right choice, but I was wrong not to involve you in that decision, and I'm asking for your help now. I need it more than ever."

Clare shrugged. "If you're asking if we'll go with you, the answer is yes."

Her friend's enthusiasm couldn't have filled a thimble. Sage bit her lip. "I appreciate that, but I don't want you to just follow me."

Lani rolled her eyes. "Follow you, march by your side. They are the same." She leaned back in her chair. "We will be there for your triumphant return."

"My . . . what?"

Clare waved a hand at the open window. "When you take this army back to Arrowhead to restore the queen." She crossed her arms. "But when it's over, I'm taking my two hundred troops to Jovan and giving them to Sophia. She'll want me to stay, too, so I likely will."

"That's an excellent idea," Sage said, though she hated the thought of losing Clare's companionship. Her friend blinked in confusion. Apparently she'd expected Sage to object. "But I need you to help me decide where to go first, if anywhere at all."

Lani and Clare glanced at each other. "You are not planning to march south?" the princess asked.

"Well . . . that was the idea." Sage faltered. "Now I'm not sure." She frowned, going back to what Lani had called her triumphant return. Was that the kind of thing they'd thought she wanted? "Did you think I was doing all this to be some kind of hero?"

Clare raised an eyebrow. "Did you think you weren't? Don't tell me you didn't envision riding into Arrowhead with an army to save everyone."

Sage shrank back, realizing how right her friend was. "Maybe a little," she admitted. Lani snorted, and Sage threw her hands up. "Fine! Maybe a lot." Her voice fell to a whisper. "I need to do something *right* this time."

"What have you done wrong that you feel this way?" asked Zoraya.

Sage's eyes were drawn to Clare, whose harsh expression softened after a few seconds. "Oh, no, Sage," she said, reaching across the table for her hand. "You did nothing wrong. Such things happen in battle. It wasn't your fault."

"Not just Luke." Sage pulled away before Clare could touch her. "I killed so many with the waterfire. I changed the whole world in a matter of minutes." She gestured to Zoraya. "I made you a queen, forced you to rule for your son, made you think you had to come begging Demora for peace or we would destroy you."

"I was a queen when you were learning to spell your name," Zoraya said dryly. "And Ragat's age made me expect his death before Mesden would be old enough to rule. How else do you think I was ready to beat

Brazapil Donala at his own game?" She smiled. "As for 'begging' for peace, I have more pride than that, and you know it."

"But I nearly got you killed in Bey Lissandra," said Sage.

Zoraya shrugged her good shoulder. "There were arrows for you, too. You merely ducked faster."

Everyone chuckled a little, even Sage. She turned back to Clare. "Then I dragged you to your father's home though you were terrified to face him, and you stood up to him for me. I thought we'd leave with nothing and you gave me an army."

"Well, the beginning of one," said Clare modestly. "You're doing the rest."

"That's not the point," Sage said. "You did that for me, and then *all* of you followed me, even when I treated you like baggage I was carrying on my own personal crusade."

Zoraya smiled ironically. "Some of us did not have a choice."

Sage choked a laugh, then took a deep breath to hold back tears as much as to prepare for her next words. "I'm sorry." Her voice cracked, and she cleared her throat. "I'm sorry for taking you for granted and making decisions without discussing them with any of you. I'll apologize to Cass later, too. But . . ." She paused to stay in control. "I need your help. Please?"

"Well, don't cry about it, Saizsch," said Lani. "We *want* to help."

Clare stood and walked around the table to embrace Sage. "It's I who should thank you and apologize," she whispered in her ear. "Because of you I was brave enough to face my father, and now I'm free of him. I can do whatever I wish with my life."

That did it, now Sage was weeping, but so was Clare. When they finished hugging, Sage grinned. "What is it you'll do with your life, then?"

"I don't know," Clare said with a laugh. "It's a little scary."

"This is all very touching," said Zoraya. "But now I think we should discuss our next move."

Sage wiped her face. "Yes, let's." She and Clare sat. "Our biggest problem," said Sage, "is that we don't know what's happening at Arrowhead."

"I disagree," said Zoraya. "Our biggest problem is that we have no goal beyond survival."

Sage frowned. "We wish to uncover who tried to kill you and why."

"Yes, but we have left that to Captain Huzar and Major Quinn," said the queen. "Here, now, we can do nothing toward that."

Clare frowned. "Is it possible no one knows the queen is still alive?"

"Yes." Sage turned to Zoraya. "And the one behind the assassination could easily be Demoran or Kimisar, would you agree?"

The queen nodded. "Whichever side they are on, one of their goals was to disrupt these talks and any chance of future peace."

"Our first goal should be information, yes?" said Lani. "Then we will know when and how best to return you and your son to the throne." She nodded at Zoraya.

"No," said the queen. "My priority is the safety of my son. If that means we can never return to Kimisara, so be it."

Everyone stared at her. "You would have him abdicate?" asked Sage.

Zoraya shook her head. "There is a child in his place who will grow to be whatever those over him mold him to be. Mesden does not matter as much as who is regent."

"It's supposed to be you," Sage insisted.

"And I am dead," said the queen. "Staying that way has certain appeal. It will certainly protect my son."

"You would abandon your duty to your country?" asked Lani, drawing her brows down. "Kimisara could descend into chaos."

"Kimisara has never cared for me except in what I could sacrifice for it," the queen snapped, her blue eyes hard and vicious.

Sage had half expected this since their conversation two days ago. "I won't force you to return," she said quietly. "But neither will I allow innocent people to die when you could stop it."

Zoraya looked down at her lap and sighed. "Nor would I. It is also possible that my return could make things worse. I ask only that we consider this option."

The other three women nodded. Lani said, "That is one possibility, then. What are some others?"

"We march south," said Clare.

"If we are going to plan for that, we will have to include Captain Casseck later," said Lani. "But we can start now."

Sage grinned and grabbed a sheet of parchment. Clare handed her a quill and ink.

62

THE FASTEST WAY to the Western Strong was north through Galarick and then west. Alex caught up the small Norsari detachment following the Duke of Crescera's caravan on the Span Road and questioned them about the nobleman's actions, but his lieutenant reported nothing suspicious. He updated the group on events and left them in place, continuing north until he overtook the duke himself. Welborough rode at the head of his two hundred troops, and Alex paused only long enough to speak briefly the man, who he held in contempt for abandoning the talks. When he mentioned the Countess Sophia had taken his place at the negotiation table, the duke merely nodded, saying she should've been there from the beginning. Then he asked Alex if he was heading to meet Ambassador Fowler at Galarick.

Alex pulled Surry back and faced Welborough. "What do you mean?" he demanded, not wanting to give away where she'd headed, in case the man was only fishing for information. "Why do you think she's at Galarick?"

Welborough dug into a courier's satchel on his saddle; then he passed a folded parchment to Alex, appearing glad to be of service. "I received a letter from her uncle yesterday."

Alex seized the page. It was dated only four days ago. The last paragraph was the most important.

I don't know what circumstances have brought her here, Your Grace, but my niece has asked for my help in gathering men-at-arms as she heads in my direction from the west. Knowing she would not make such a request unless her need was dire, I have done my best, assembling them at Galarick, as I believe it the best place strategically within reach. This letter may find you too late, but in any case I beg you to contribute to her cause when you can.

In your debt,
Lord William Broadmoor

"There's no mention of whom she travels with," said Welborough when Alex looked up again. "But I assume the Lady Clare and Princess Alaniah are with her."

And Queen Zoraya and the young king, but Alex didn't say that. What the hell was she doing? Why was she risking herself this way?

The answer came to him almost immediately: because she believed it was the right thing to do. She wasn't acting recklessly, though. Sage knew they needed protection, but she was preparing to bring Queen Zoraya back with force if necessary—no matter who was behind the assassination attempt. It would be a brilliant political maneuver if she could pull it off. Alex handed the letter back to the duke and thanked him.

"You're welcome to ride with us, Major," Welborough said. "Though with these wagons and all this mud I don't expect to make it until tomorrow."

"No, thank you, Your Grace," said Alex. "My men and I will push to get there by tonight. Thank you again for the news."

The duke nodded. "Give my regards to the ladies then. I look forward to seeing them, especially the Lady Clare."

Alex kicked his horse ahead, calling to the platoon behind him. Poor Surry was tired. The mare had faithfully traveled hundreds of miles back and forth over the last few weeks, and Alex hated to push her so hard now, but Sage was at the end of this road.

A Norsari patrol met them outside Galarick. Alex could see the castle on the hill in the distance, surrounded by a military encampment of hundreds. Corporal Maddox saluted him with a grin and assured him everyone was safe and well. "Cap'n Casseck will be very glad to see you, sir," he said.

Cass was probably more worried Alex would strangle him for letting Sage change what they'd planned. Maddox offered Alex his own horse, and Surry finally got her rest as Alex took the soldier's stallion and galloped the last mile at full speed, leaving the platoon he'd brought from Arrowhead to follow at a slower pace.

Someone must have recognized him, because by the time Alex was dismounting in the outer ward, Casseck came running down the steps from the wall. He approached with a salute and wary look on his face. Alex didn't bother returning the gesture; instead he embraced his friend, clapping him on the back. Cass was still cautious when Alex stepped away.

"Alex—" he began.

"Don't bother," Alex said, waving him off. "I never try to tell her to do anything anymore. You kept her safe; that's all that matters."

Casseck exhaled heavily and relaxed. "It's more complicated than that, though, as you probably noticed on your way in."

"I didn't realize her uncle was such an influential man," said Alex, glancing around. Where was she?

"It's not all from him," said Cass, tallying on his fingers. "The first two hundred she and Lady Clare pried from Baron Holloway, the next hundred or so came from Mistress Rodelle's connections, another few dozen from the matchmaker at the Western Strong calling in favors. The rest was Lord Broadmoor's friends. More are arriving hourly. We'll have nearly five hundred by tomorrow."

"More than that," said Alex, explaining how the Duke of Crescera was on his way with everything he'd had at Arrowhead. Welborough may have left under poor circumstances, but he was about to redeem himself. Alex craned his head around, scanning every face he could see. "The duke has large company at least."

"That makes around seven hundred, including the Norsari and Casmuni I had." Cass looked amused by Alex's fruitless searching. "That's a full battalion, though they aren't professionals."

"I brought a platoon, too," Alex said. "Nadira's got most of the rest of the

Norsari chasing Baron Underwood and other D'Amiran loyalists." Except for the lost escort group buried outside Jovan. Alex suddenly felt sick, remembering how close he'd come to losing Sage and how someone undoubtedly still wanted her dead. "Where is she, Cass?"

His friend grinned. "She's in the library, where else?"

It was almost too perfect. Alex was tempted to swing through the kitchens first and bring her a tray of food, like the night they'd met, but she'd probably consider that sentimental and silly. Besides, it was also a reminder of how he'd been hiding his identity and his true thoughts back then. He was done with that.

Though it had been almost two years, Alex still remembered all the stairs and passages he needed to take to get to the library. He walked in without knocking, and found her sitting at a table with her back to the hearth, as she had that night, though the light for writing had to be much better by the window. Perhaps she was just as sentimental as he was.

Sage looked up, and her sunburned cheeks lit with a joy so fierce it made his heart skip. She dropped her quill and jumped up to face him, guilt and apprehension quickly replacing the happiness. "Alex—"

He silenced whatever apology she was about to make with a kiss. She didn't relax, though, and Alex wouldn't break away until she did. Eventually she put her arms around his neck and melted against him, but he held on a few seconds longer. Then he released her slowly and pressed his forehead to hers.

"Alex," she said, voice trembling. "I'm sorry."

"Don't be," he told her. "You're safe. That's all that matters."

He kissed her again, shortening it a bit this time, knowing how badly he needed to bathe.

"We're doing this together from now on, though, all right?" Alex said.

She nodded, sniffing. "Together."

Alex glanced down at what she'd been writing, which appeared to be a letter. "What's that?"

"An update for you. We feel secure here, but we have no idea what's happened at Arrowhead and whether it's safe to bring the queen back yet." She laughed a little. "Clare and Zoraya want more information, but Lani is in favor of marching down there tomorrow."

At the thought of the Casmuni princess, Alex's heart fell, thinking of the men she didn't know she'd lost. And sweet Spirit, none of them knew about Sophia fleeing to General Quinn yet. "Then we'd better bring them all here," he told her. "I have bad news."

63

WHEN QUEEN ZORAYA, Princess Lani, Lady Clare, and Cass joined them in the library, Alex told them first how Countess Sophia arrived with Ash Carter. He explained she'd known nothing about the decoy escort group, which led Alex to the grisly discovery.

Lani sat down heavily, her face pale. "All of them?" she whispered. "No one survived?"

"No one, Palachessa."

"Not even Feshamay and Mara were spared?" Her hand on the table closed into a fist.

Alex's throat clenched, remembering two of Lani's maids had been among the group. "We didn't uncover more than a few of the bodies," he said, shaking his head. "It's possible they were instead taken by whoever did this, but it would have been difficult not to poison them with the group."

"Was it D'Amiran loyalists who did this?" asked Sage. "Baron Underwood?"

"Perhaps, but there was no trail to follow, and the baron left Arrowhead." Alex described how at last word, Captain Nadira had Underwood and some of his allies pinned down at his minor fortress two days to the east.

Sage laid a hand over Lani's clenched fist. "We will find who did this, Lani," she said. "And we'll make them pay."

"And what of my sister?" asked Clare. "She's in danger wherever she goes. What is General Quinn doing to protect her now?"

"The Kimisar demanded she attend the peace talks, and so she did, to keep the process going," Alex said. "But I promise her safety is one of my father's priorities."

Clare scowled. "Saying 'one of' his priorities does not inspire confidence. From the sound of it, the general doesn't tell her very much. I know from experience how frustrating that is."

Sage cringed, though Clare didn't look at her.

Queen Zoraya sat forward. Alex thought she was recovering pretty well, considering how rough her conditions had been for healing. "Why do the talks continue?" she asked. "I thought for certain when Captain Huzar arrived with the news they would blame Demora."

"We're not sure Huzar ever arrived, or what he told them when he did," said Alex. "The Kimisar have acted as if they don't know, though Brazapil Donala started putting forth proposals very much like the ones you agreed to at Bey Lissandra." He hesitated. "Captain Huzar said your personal papers were stolen. The plotter may have delivered those to Donala, or . . . Huzar himself did."

"Not possible," snapped Zoraya. "He is loyal."

Alex wouldn't argue with her. "Then something must have kept him from delivering the news," he said slowly.

The queen blanched, grasping the implication that her bodyguard was likely dead. On her right, Clare moved half a step closer until their shoulders touched.

Sage also looked stricken. "Then Brazapil Donala is likely the one who sent the assassins," she said.

"If so, he has allies within Demora," said Casseck. "How else could he have a reach as far as Jovan?"

Queen Zoraya, who was still pale after Alex's last statement, cleared her throat. "I must return. My presence will solve things one way or another."

The women exchanged sad glances. Alex would have to ask Sage about that later. He nodded. "My orders are to bring you back to Arrowhead, but I'm glad to see you wish to do so, Your Majesty."

"We might as well wait for Duke Welborough to get here tomorrow, though," said Cass. "We can add his forces to ours and then march south as strong as possible."

"The sooner the better," said Clare.

Sage frowned. "Why did the duke leave in the first place?"

Alex shrugged. "I guess he gave up on the process once he heard Zoraya was dead. He was there voluntarily, representing Cresceran interests. Father couldn't force him to stay."

"And his absence is the reason Sophia is now forced to sit at the negotiation table with plotters and assassins," said Clare bitterly. "He'd better contribute."

That only made Sage's frown deepen, but it was Lani who spoke, standing. "In the meantime, we must honor the dead this night. They have gone far too long without prayers." She nodded to Alex. "Maizshur, if you will provide a list of your names, I will include them in the ceremony."

Alex said he would, and the princess left, Queen Zoraya following, saying she wished to assist. Clare remained where she stood numbly, and Sage put a hand on her shoulder.

"We'll end this, Clare," Sage whispered. "I promise. We'll take Sophia away with this army if we have to."

Clare nodded absently and turned to follow Lani, mumbling that she would also help. Sage sighed. "Just when things got better, they got worse again."

"I guess I'll go back into organizing this hodgepodge force into a single unit," Cass said, also heading for the door. "You should get some rest, Alex. You're going to need it."

Alex nodded in acknowledgment, and Sage began gathering parchment and ink to help him record the names for Princess Lani and write an update for General Quinn. She wore riding clothes, and her sandy hair was pulled into a plain horsetail at the back of her neck. After weeks of travel, her face and neck were now heavily sprinkled with honey-colored freckles. On the outside, she little resembled the Concordium bride he thought he'd met here two years ago, but when she glanced back at him, there were still the features that had struck him most that night—her open, genuine smile and the light of intelligence in her gray eyes, made brighter by a spark of humor.

He'd thought of her every day since.

Alex watched her preparations silently. Casseck's suggestion had been his friend saying that he had everything in hand for now, but he was looking forward to turning the reins over tomorrow. While Alex fully intended to get some rest before tonight, it was for an entirely different reason.

64

SAGE WORE A dress loaned by the baroness as she sat between Clare and Alex in the chapel, holding hands with each as Lani went through Casmuni funeral rites, calling the name of each of the dead three times and leading a series of prayers for the Spirit to accept their souls. Her voice was strong, though it faltered when she named her two maids. Sage shed tears for them and the princess determined to hold her own back. She thought of Feshamay, who had hated the cold so much she cried almost daily until she experienced her first snowfall, and Mara, who would sneak away with the Norsari sergeant Porter whenever they thought no one was looking. Lani had confided weeks ago that she fully expected Mara to ask to stay, which she would allow with her blessing. Sage hoped Mara was at least buried close to her beloved.

When Sage murmured that sentiment, Clare nodded in agreement, tears streaming down her cheeks, but Alex only closed his eyes and lowered his head, shuddering.

It was nearly midnight when Lani finished, as the princess had given full ceremony to all the Demorans as well, of which there were just as many. Alex made no move to stand when Sage did. Thinking she understood, Sage hugged Clare and Lani as they left, then sat back down beside him and took his hand again.

Alex was silent as the chapel emptied and the priest went about extinguishing candles. When only the perpetual lamp on the altar remained, they were left alone. Sage leaned her face into his shoulder, burying her nose in the brown leather jacket, breathing him in.

"It wasn't your fault," she whispered. "No one could have expected something like this, not even from the D'Amirans."

Alex shook his head. "I know better than anyone what our enemies are capable of."

Duke D'Amiran had cut Alex's nine-year-old brother's throat right in front of him. Charlie had died in his arms less than a minute later.

"Morrow D'Amiran was an evil, desperate man," Sage insisted.

Alex took a deep breath. "We caught two of the assassins in Bey Lissandra," he said so quietly she had to lift her head to hear. "They had a list, Sage. You were on it. I could have lost you there just as easily."

Sage tipped his face up. "But you didn't," she said softly. "I'm here."

"Yes, you are." Alex stood abruptly, pulling her up with him. Sage led him out of the pew, still holding his hand, and headed for the doors, but Alex stopped in the aisle, wearing an expression she'd never seen before and couldn't define.

She took a step closer to him. "What's wrong?"

"Nothing," he said. "Everything."

"I know." Sage shook her head sadly. "The world is broken."

"That's not what I meant," Alex said. He pressed her hands to his chest, drawing her against him. "I meant . . . marry me, Sage. Here. Now."

It was the last thing she'd expected him to say. "Alex—"

"The world will always be broken, but I can fix one tiny corner of it," he said. "If I have you."

Sage realized what was in his eyes now, or rather, what was missing. There was no trace of doubt whatsoever. Any of her objections would have fallen apart in the face of that certainty. As it was, she couldn't think of a single reason to say no. "All right," she whispered.

Alex pulled her with him to the front of the chapel and left her by the altar while he fetched the priest, who was in the preparation room off to the side. Then he returned, brushing invisible dirt from his sleeves and straightening his jacket and sword belt. Sage glanced down at her own dress, realizing she wasn't even sure what color it was in the darkness. Feeling awkward, she reached up to smooth her hair, which she'd worn loose to her shoulders, but Alex caught her hand in his and held it like he never intended to let go again.

The priest came tripping out of the shadows, adjusting his robes around him, which he'd probably had half off when Alex found him. After Sage assured the man this was what she wanted, he turned and fumbled with his keys to reopen the cabinet with holy oils and other items of ceremony. The clattering of glass vials being moved around paused briefly as the priest pivoted back to toss several grains of incense in the lamp, creating tendrils of sweet smoke.

She glanced to Alex, who watched the priest squint and leaf through the chapel's book of records. Finding the correct page, he flipped the ledger around to face them, then appeared to realize there was no place to set it down except on the altar itself. To Sage that seemed rather appropriate, but the priest hesitated before laying the book on the marble slab and pointing to a blank line with a charcoal and oil pencil.

Alex bent over to write his and Sage's names where indicated, and she smiled a little, thinking of the matchmaker's ledger she had recorded his name in two years ago, in this very castle. She'd found the book at Darnessa's the night they worked together, blushing at the list of harsh and ugly adjectives she'd written below. *Arrogant. Distant. Proud. Secretive.* Sage had considered crossing them out but realized most people saw Alex that way. *He* saw himself that way. Rather than strike the phrases, she'd written her own name at the bottom of the page and added one more word of description.

Mine.

When Alex finished, the priest took the pencil and snapped the book closed, releasing a musty whirl of parchment dust, and shoved them back into the alcove. Then he turned to face them again, scratching his head. Sage imagined they were skipping everything but the essentials. Had her own parents' secret wedding been similar? "Place her hand on the altar," he directed Alex.

Cool marble pressed against her palm. A tingle traveled up her arm, and Sage wondered if it was nerves or something else, and if Alex felt the same thing.

Then Alex's eyes met hers, and he began to speak after the priest.

"I, Alexander Raymond Quinn, son of Pendleton and Castella of the House of Cambria, do swear by the name of the Spirit, which is too holy for human utterance, that I will love, honor, protect, and cherish you as my wife for the rest of my days. All that I have, I give to you. All that I am, I offer freely."

A tiny spark of panic went through Sage. Whenever she'd imagined this moment, she'd only ever thought of him as Alex, but the formal statement was a sudden reminder that he brought so much more to this union than she did. Even her name was the simplest kind. Sage's fingers shook as they reversed their hands, putting hers on top, but when she looked back up to Alex, her fear vanished. He only wanted her.

"I, Sage Fowler, daughter of Astelyn and Peter," she said, repeating after the priest. "Do swear by the name of the Spirit, which is too holy for human utterance, that I will love, o—" She broke off as Alex pinched her hand with his thumb and shook his head.

"Don't bother with obey," he whispered, eyes twinkling in the lamplight. "We both know you won't."

Sage giggled, and the priest frowned. She cleared her throat and straightened her face before continuing. "I will love, honor, and cherish you as my husband for the rest of my days. All that I have, I give to you. All that I am, I offer freely."

"Do you accept these promises you have received?" asked the priest, still looking displeased.

"I do accept," Sage and Alex said together. Holy oil from two different jars was rubbed into each of their palms, and then they pressed their hands together.

"As these oils now mixed can no longer be distinguished, neither shall you be, as long as you both draw breath." The priest stepped back and nodded. "You may kiss if you so wish."

"Oh, I do wish," Alex whispered before taking her mouth with his. His lips were eager, yet gentle and lingering, like he never wanted to forget this moment, and Sage melted against him, kissing back with all she had. She wasn't sure when the priest left, but everything was locked back up when they finally separated. Still clasping hands, they turned and walked down the aisle and out into the night. On the steps Alex kissed her again, this time with a hunger that made her light-headed.

"I have to take care of a few things before I can come up to your room," he said softly in her ear, his rough cheek dragging along her smooth one. "But I promise I won't be long."

Spirit above, through all of that, somehow she'd not even thought of what would come next.

65

SAGE MADE HER way back to her room in a daze.

She turned her right hand up to study it. The oil across her palm glimmered in the firelight. If it hadn't been for that, she might have thought she'd imagined everything, that the wanting she'd seen in his eyes hadn't merely been a reflection of her own, but she'd never seen him so sure of anything, to the point that her certainty had risen to meet his, finally unbound. Finally free.

Sage dropped her hand to stare at the four-poster bed and its coverlet embroidered with sparrows and lily flowers, thinking about what would happen tonight. Every other time they'd come close to . . . that, it had been unplanned. This was different, expected. And yet, nothing about them had been expected. She'd just taken her vows in a dark, empty chapel while wearing a borrowed—Sage glanced down—blue dress. If it had been up to her, they wouldn't have bothered with even that formality, but it had been important to him.

After some deliberation, she decided to wait for him by the hearth. Sage left her shoes next to the sheepskin rug, then sank to her knees and swung the kettle closer to the flames. Making tea seemed like the thing to do, though she wasn't sure she really wanted any.

By the time she heard the door open and close, and the bolt slide into place, Sage had organized and composed her thoughts. She didn't react as Alex came to the edge of the almost-white rug. He set what sounded like a saddlebag and sword belt on the floor and began unbuckling his jacket.

"Would you like something to drink?" she asked. The tea had been ready for several minutes, and she was on her second cup. It was a calming brew of mint, elderflowers, and hawthorn berries, but so far it hadn't done her much good.

"Yes, please." The jacket landed softly on the bag, and he hesitated, then eased his boots off before stepping onto the soft rug. Alex knelt, then sat beside her as Sage focused on adding honey to his cup. The scent of evergreen came with him, causing her to glance over. He'd shaved. Over-quickly, too, as she could see he'd missed a couple spots, but it made her smile a little. She offered him the tea and met his eyes for a brief second. The naked surety was still there. "Thank you," he said.

They sipped and watched the fire, or at least Sage did. She only saw him from the corner of her eye, his linen undershirt stark against the black of his hair and the golden-brown skin of his hands and neck. Neither spoke. Likely he knew she wanted to talk and was waiting.

"What changed?" she asked finally, setting her cup down.

He took a few moments before answering, though she was positive he'd known the question was coming. "It was foolish after Tegann, after Charlie," he said, his voice heavy with pain. "Even after Black Glass I somehow still believed I could protect you. Maybe because I couldn't comprehend that anyone could truly ever *want* to harm you."

Alex stared, unfocused, at the shifting flames, the half-empty cup cradled in his palm. "I was only lying to myself. The truth was too hard to face."

It had taken the deaths he couldn't have foreseen to show him how easily he could lose her. Without thinking, she reached for his free hand. Her touch made him look down, and he traced his forefinger over the scars on her wrist.

"I realized I'd been pushing you into the future at the expense of our time now," he whispered. "All my life I've sacrificed or delayed what I've wanted because there was something higher I was aiming for. Putting you off felt necessary precisely *because* you were so important, *because* there was nothing I've ever wanted more. Then there was guilt, too, at the idea of having something so good when things were so bad for others."

Without a word, Sage took his cup and set it aside before climbing into his lap. "Then what?" she asked.

Alex took a deep breath. "Then I saw all those lives left unfinished. I've seen death before, but this was different. What they were doing—where they were—wasn't supposed to be dangerous. I kept imagining what they would've done with their last days if they'd known. I started wondering . . ." He turned eyes bright with anguish to meet hers. "What if now is all we have? All we'll ever have?"

Sage took his smooth cheeks in her hands. "That's why we have to live," she said, running her thumb over a trio of stray whiskers. "We have to live for everyone who can't. For everyone who's died to give us these moments."

He gazed up at her. "I love you, Sage," Alex whispered. "That's the only thing that ever should have mattered. I'm sorry I took so long to see that."

She couldn't think how to tell him he was more than forgiven. Instead of words, Sage let her lips on his and her hands in his hair speak for her, and when she finished saying it that way, the right words finally came.

"I love you, Alexander Quinn," she said softly, closing her eyes and feeling a tear slide down her cheek and onto his. "Of everything I've said and done, that is truth."

In response he held her tight to him with one arm and kissed her with a yearning she felt to her core. His other hand followed the curves of her body wherever they took him, until she stopped it where she wanted his attention, on the laces of her bodice. The invitation was all he needed. Alex tugged them loose while she pulled his shirt free of his breeches and over his head. Layer by layer, clothing came away and was tossed aside, mouths and fingers caressing and exploring. Sage found every scar he bore and memorized it, taking each for her own, and he did the same, somehow making the ravaged limbs—and her—feel beautiful. There was no room for thoughts or fears or anything outside their tiny circle of warmth and light, and they reveled in each other and the driving need to be closer until there was nothing left but skin on skin and the soft rug against her back. Alex abruptly pushed away, gasping, and held himself over her, asking if she wanted to move to the bed, but Sage only shook her head and laughed, saying it was too late for that. He smiled and agreed and let her draw him down to her again, a moan escaping his lips as she arched up to meet him. Then his mouth was on hers again and she tasted the salt of his sweat and the sweetness of his tongue and felt his heartbeat echoing in her own chest. Or maybe that was her heartbeat.

She didn't think there was a difference anymore.

And this time when she looked into Alex's eyes, Sage saw only firelight and passion and her own face reflected in their depths. No secrets. No walls. Only him.

Only her.

Only them.

Afterward they moved to the bed.

Sage brushed the stray whiskers at the corner of his mouth, smiling lazily. "You always miss this spot," she said, then leaned up to kiss it.

"My mind was on something else," Alex replied. He dragged his own finger down her stomach and lower, and she shivered. "You realize, though," he said, "we'll have to have a regular wedding for everyone else. Mother will kill me if we don't."

Sage chuckled. "She might anyway."

"There's no way she could considering when I was born. They had to backdate the official marriage documents by two months. At least we're already legal."

Her eyes widened. That meant Alex was born seven months after the wedding, rather than nine. "I knew it was a hushed matter, but you never told me it was *that* scandalous."

"I actually didn't know until a couple years ago, but the last thing you needed was encouragement." Alex lowered his head and nuzzled her collarbone, the first place he'd kissed her. "It was hard enough to resist you as it was, even without knowing how good it would be."

"And now that you know, are you still glad you waited?"

"Absolutely." His dark eyes were serious as he raised his head, but there was already a heat building in them. "Because now there's no possibility on this earth of my ever being able to resist you again."

Sage arched an eyebrow. "Even right now?"

Alex pulled her against him. "Even right now."

Outside, the world was full of assassins, bitter politics, and the threat of war, but here, in this one place, for one night, everything was perfect.

66

IT WAS MADDENING to stand next to her all day, acting as if nothing had changed. Alex found himself reaching for her at every opportunity, tucking hair behind her ear, putting his hand at the small of her back, brushing his fingers across her hips and rear. Sage was just as bad, leaning up to whisper promises in his ear and finding any excuse to touch him. It was a wonder he got anything done.

Duke Welborough arrived at Galarick around noon, adding his company to what Sage had gathered. Now over six hundred strong, Sage's army was enough to help defeat the Kimisar force that backed up their delegation, should Brazapil Donala resist Zoraya's return. From the watchtower, Alex observed the newly assembled platoons drilling under the leadership of the Norsari. Nearby, the Cresceran duke walked with Lady Clare, proudly showing her his ranks. He'd readily joined their cause, showing a fickleness which annoyed Sage. "He was quick to leave Arrowhead," she muttered. "It makes me wonder if he might suddenly decide our cause isn't worth getting involved with, either."

"Your uncle trusts him," said Alex.

Sage shrugged. Lord Broadmoor's unquestioning support had surprised her. Yesterday evening she and Alex had spent much time sharing details of the last couple of weeks, and she had a lot of guilt over how she'd acted in the past. "I don't know how he forgave my behavior so quickly," she'd said with a sigh.

"It's been a couple years," he'd reminded her. "And you're a national hero now."

That had earned a scowl, but he enjoyed vexing her with that as she'd teased him with the same idea last year. It also gave him an excuse to immediately make her smile again.

"Maybe Welborough is trying to butter Clare up," Sage said, frowning at the pair from the distance. The duke walked with a swagger and kept his hand on the sword belted at his waist. "Apparently he sent her father a letter saying how pretty he thought she was. Baron Holloway took that as an invitation to offer Clare in marriage."

Alex glanced at her in alarm. Welborough hadn't mentioned anything like that. "How did the duke respond?"

"Well . . ." Sage tilted her head to the side. "I'm not actually sure the proposal was made, just that Clare's father assumed he would accept."

Pesta lundamyetsk. Alex murmured it under his breath, and Sage turned to him. "Did you say something?"

Last night he'd described the note found on the assassin in Bey Lissandra, but that part hadn't been important at the time. "Do you know what *pesta lundamyetsk* means?" he asked.

"Sounds Kimisar." Sage paused, concentrating. "But an older dialect. 'Your life hangs on this one,' or something similar."

Alex nodded. "It's a phrase used by Kimisar assassins to designate targets who are not to be harmed at any cost. At least that's what Huzar said." He clenched his jaw. Where was the captain? Why hadn't he returned to the Kimisar camp?

"*Dolofan* were at Bey Lissandra?" Sage paled. She'd met two up close in Casmun and had seen how ruthless they were.

"Huzar insisted it couldn't have been them," said Alex. "Crossbows and killing from a distance isn't their style. Nor is failure. The last one wouldn't have run away like he did. Or she," he added, remembering one body had been female. "But whoever sent them specifically said they didn't want Clare harmed."

Sage grunted. "If Donala's not the one behind this, then someone wants to make us *think* it's Kimisara, or they have a flair for the dramatic." She stared out over the colorful ranks of Duke Welborough's troops, bright flags flapping in the breeze. "Or both."

Alex wasn't ready to begin slinging accusations. "Yes, but does the Duke of Crescera gain enough from your death or the queen's? Or Count D'Amiran?"

"Getting Rewel out of the way frees Sophia to marry his son," said Sage. "Baron Holloway said that *had* been discussed."

"All right, that sounds bad," Alex admitted. "But he knows Sophia is there, at Arrowhead. He left before she arrived, but the news had caught up to him. You'd think he'd want to swoop back and be her protector."

"Yet he's also one of the few Demorans with enough power and reach to have killed the escort." Sage suddenly gasped. "Alex, what if that was done to make Clare's sister feel vulnerable enough to run to your father? You said yourself if the Norsari had been there, she would've been secure."

Alex frowned. "I could see wanting her to *be* vulnerable, but who could have predicted she would flee?"

"Maybe that's why Welborough left—because she was coming, and he didn't want to appear to know anything about it." She grabbed Alex's arm, gray eyes wide. "Sweet Spirit, it was his courier!"

"What courier?"

"Clare sent word to Sophia at Jovan that the escort would be arriving. The duke offered to have one of his couriers take the message. You said the countess didn't even know they were coming. He never arrived."

Alex finished the thought for her. "And would have made Welborough one of the few people who not only knew about the escort, he could have learned where you and Clare and the others really went."

Sage looked out over the field again. Exercises were breaking up and some of the troops were forming lines at their mess tents for the evening meal. "Alex, Duke Welborough makes up almost a quarter of our force."

"More than that, really," said Alex. "When you consider how inexperienced most of the others are." He tapped his lip. "Maybe we can break some of his units up into the others." Of course, that could be disastrous if Welborough's soldiers were aware of some alternative agenda and smart enough to act on it.

"Someone's coming." Sage pointed down the Span Road at an approaching rider. "Look, he's carrying a courier flag."

Alex squinted at the figure, who was flanked by several Norsari, escorting him in. In the longer shadows of the end of the day, it was difficult to distinguish the man's features, but it was impossible to mistake the familiar posture.

Huzar.

67

SOMETHING NAGGED AT Sage as they ran down from Galarick's outer wall to meet Huzar, but whenever the idea seemed to form, it took wing like a butterfly in her head. It didn't help that all day just the sight of Alex had set her off of her thoughts. Every time he moved, she found herself envisioning the way his body was shifting beneath his clothes, remembering every inch of the solid muscles and how last night everything about him had been devoted to her. She'd spent half the afternoon calculating the time remaining until they could be alone again.

But, dammit, she was missing something important.

"What exactly was on the list again?" Sage asked Alex. It had to do with that. The butterfly almost landed whenever she thought of it.

His mouth tightened as it always did when he spoke of the parchment Huzar had found on a dead assassin. "The queen's name, and Rewel D'Amiran's. Then your name. At the bottom were the letters *PL* and Lady Clare Holloway."

And *PL* stood for *pesta lundamyetsk*, which meant Clare was not to be harmed. Not only that, the phrase implied if she *was* harmed, the assassins would die. Lani's name was also absent, which was puzzling.

It wasn't until Huzar came into view again that she realized who else was missing. Why hadn't Huzar been on the list? So he could bring back the news? And if so, why didn't the perpetrator immediately take advantage of it?

"He's carrying a Demoran crossbow," murmured Alex. "How did he get that?"

The Kimisar captain stopped in front of Sage and Alex, and she saw the top half of his left ear was completely gone, though the wound had mostly healed. "It is good to see you are well, Sage Fowler," he said. "And you, Major."

Huzar was armed to the teeth, though the crossbow was neither loaded nor pulled back. "Where have you been, Captain?" Alex demanded.

"The story is long, but your father the general is the one who sent me," Huzar answered as he dismounted. Every Demoran around him raised weapons, but the captain ignored it and turned to face Alex. "But before I speak of this, I must first see My Queen."

Alex gritted his teeth, and Sage suspected he was thinking how, under similar circumstances, his own first demand would be to see her. He gestured at Huzar's waist. "Weapons off."

Without a word, Huzar uncinched his sword belt and let it fall to the ground. Two daggers followed, and he held out his arms. Alex only stared at him until Huzar smiled a little and slid a third blade from his left sleeve. After that, Alex stepped forward and punched him lightly but solidly in the chest. Huzar winced, then opened his jacket and dropped a pack of slender knives, files, and lock picks on the pile at his feet. The crossbow, quiver, and a light battle-ax remained on the saddle.

"Where is she?" Huzar asked, his tone indicating he had tolerated this, but he was now at the end of his patience.

"I am here," said a voice behind Sage, and she moved aside before Huzar could run her over.

The captain fell to his knees in front of his queen, and—to Sage's surprise—Zoraya stepped closer. Huzar threw his arms around her and buried his face in her middle with what sounded like a sob. Everyone averted their gaze as the queen held his head against her with her good hand and whispered to him in their own language. Sage could only distinguish a few Kimisar words.

. . . done well . . . grateful . . . not forget . . . worthy . . .

Zoraya lifted his chin to meet his eyes, and in a flash Sage saw Huzar's love for his queen was indeed not completely one-sided. Then the moment was gone. Huzar stood, towering over the queen by nearly a foot, not a trace of tears on his face. Zoraya pivoted to their audience and nodded solemnly, as though she'd graciously allowed them to witness their reunion. There was optimism in her posture, too, for the first time since the arrow had struck her shoulder.

"All right, Huzar," Alex growled. "Where the hell have you been?"

"I have done exactly as planned," replied the captain. "But nothing happened as we expected." He nodded to Zoraya. "Now they know My Queen lives, and they know she is with you."

With those words, the spark of hope in Zoraya's eyes died.

Everyone crowded around the table in the library, giving Sage an excuse to stand close to Alex. Outside, the sun threw horizontal rays into the room, the setting colors making the bookshelves glow like they were aflame.

And the world, it seemed, was on fire.

Before Alex would believe anything Huzar told them, he demanded proof that the captain had truly been sent by General Quinn. The Kimisar produced a note from his jacket. Sage didn't know the general's handwriting enough to tell if it was his, but there was only one sentence. *I expect I've lost my wager by now.*

Whatever that meant, Alex accepted the message as genuine, and told the captain to report what had happened since he'd left. When Huzar got to the part about General Quinn having no choice but to surrender the Countess Sophia and her daughter as hostages to the Kimisar as guarantee he would return their queen, Clare sobbed into Sage's shoulder.

"Sophia and Aurelia have been there for days now!" she cried. "We won't get there for many days still!"

Lani wanted to know whether Brazapil Donala or General Oshan could have deceived Huzar from the moment he arrived, knowing the truth but letting him lie to see what actions he would then take.

"It's possible," Huzar admitted. "Especially seeing as they only acted once I was gone."

And Donala had more information. He'd been pushing agreements exactly like the queen's in the talks, telling Oshan he was doing as Zoraya had wished. "Until the general told me he considered her actions were treasonous and they were fortunate she had died," said Huzar. "In light of this, it then appeared Donala's actions were designed to get Oshan to reveal himself."

"But Donala had an army prepared to come north," said Sage. "That implies he was ready and waiting to seize power. You said he sent a force to guard the decoy king."

Huzar looked to Alex. "Perhaps he was ready for this, but to not expect me to believe that had the talks been held in Kimisara, Demora would not have been ready to march in swiftly, should something have gone wrong."

Alex conceded the point. "I guess we underestimated what Donala could bring to bear on his own, though."

"They will not harm your sister," Zoraya told Clare. "But the only way to end this is for me to return immediately."

"We can leave tonight," Clare sobbed. "Armies march in the dark in times of great need."

"Even the Norsari would have a hard time getting on the road before all the light was gone today, my lady," said Alex gently. "We also won't have any reasonable moonlight until well after midnight. That's too much for even professional soldiers to handle—which these men are not. We'll leave at first light, after a full night's rest."

Clare's eyes narrowed. "Yes," she spat, shrugging Sage's arm off. "A full night's *rest* is what you want."

Somehow Clare knew about them, but she was wrong if she believed that influenced Alex's decision. Sage couldn't argue or explain here and now, in front of everyone, and in her current state, Clare wasn't likely to listen.

Zoraya placed a hand over her heart. "Give me this army, Lady Clare," she said. "And I will return your sister to you using whatever force is necessary."

"You're awfully free in spending Demoran lives, Your Majesty," said Alex, raising an eyebrow.

"I am willing to shed my own blood if required," the queen replied coolly.

Sage heard the sincerity in Zoraya's voice, though others may not have detected it. "If we're going to break camp at dawn, there are preparations to make now," she said. "There's no point in deciding our final strategy in this room tonight, especially as things will undoubtedly change before we get to Arrowhead. We know we're leaving. That will do for now."

Everyone nodded wearily, and the group began to break up. Lani led Clare from the room, murmuring reassurances in her ear, and Casseck followed, gesturing for Huzar to come with him. "You can bunk with me, Captain," he said.

Zoraya lingered, plainly wanting to speak with Sage alone. Alex kissed Sage's temple and whispered that he'd be back in an hour or so, after passing word to the company commanders out in the camp.

"But . . ." In all the focus on Huzar's news, they'd forgotten Duke Welborough. "What about what we discussed earlier?" Sage asked.

Alex exhaled heavily. "Keep your friends up your sleeve, but your enemies in your breast pocket, I guess. We'll watch him closely. It's better than leaving him at our backs."

Once he was gone, Zoraya faced Sage across the table. "I need to know right now why you are willing to fight to put me back on the throne," the queen said.

"You're the rightful regent," said Sage simply. "And with your willingness to seek peace, Demora has a vested interest in keeping you in power. Your son also deserves to have his mother by his side, as no one will serve him better." When Zoraya did not respond, Sage asked, "Is there something you think would change that?"

The queen turned away and strolled along the wall of shelves, idly brushing her fingers over the spines of books. "What makes Demora sure that Mesden is the king they want in Kimisara?" she asked. "He's only a child. Is it that you want our nation weak for the next few years?"

Zoraya was deflecting from her true question, so Sage stayed neutral. "The end of a dynasty always brings war and instability, more so than a child king. Kimisara would be weaker if he were deposed." She hesitated, then decided to prod the conversation in the direction she wanted. "The brazapilla may squabble for power, but the people will instinctively support King Ragat's son. Your council ignores that at their peril."

"So you say, yet you know something which could change all that and have me executed." She looked over her shoulder at Sage.

The queen did remember telling her.

Zoraya turned away again. "You are an interesting person, Sage Fowler. You haven't used this information against me, and it does not appear to have lessened your opinion."

Sage was flattered that the queen cared what she thought. "You did what was necessary for your country."

"And if I say my first concern was not Kimisara's survival but my own?"

"Is it now?"

Zoraya shook her head. "No, it is Mesden's life which matters most."

"You're lucky to love someone so much," said Sage.

The queen snorted. "Love only complicates things." Her tone wasn't as hard as she tried to make it.

"I agree," Sage said. She counted several breaths before asking, "Did you love Mesden's father?"

"No. I could not afford to." Zoraya gazed out the window at the twilight, her words becoming measurably softer. "But he was strong and kind. I hid who I was from him."

"Where is he now?"

"Dead."

"I'm sorry."

"It was I who sent him to his death." Zoraya ground her teeth for a few seconds. "He was a soldier. There was a mission we knew none would return from. I made sure he was with it. He knew nothing."

"He didn't know he would die, or that you carried his child?"

"Neither." The queen turned to face her fully. "How do you think of me now, Sage Fowler?"

In truth, Sage was horrified by Zoraya's admission, but she obviously regretted much of what she'd done—or at least regretted that she'd had to do it. Each step the queen had taken probably hadn't seemed possible until she'd been faced with the choice, and Sage honestly wasn't sure how she would have acted in Zoraya's place. Rather than say any of that, however, Sage hoped to make the queen understand such things were no longer necessary. "Does Captain Huzar know all this?"

"Malkim knows everything," Zoraya said. A smile played across her lips as she said his name.

"And he loves you still."

The queen narrowed her eyes. "You have yet to answer my question."

"I think you are the rightful regent, and your son should sit on Kimisara's throne," Sage said. "That you're willing to sacrifice yourself if necessary to return Clare's sister makes you my friend."

"Friend." Zoraya smiled ironically. "As I've seen how you treat your friends, should I be worried?"

"No more than I at being yours, I'm sure," said Sage, arching an eyebrow.

The queen's face became serious in the blink of an eye. "I am not sure when we crossed this line," she said. "But I think our friendship may be the only thing that can save our countries from destroying themselves and each other now."

68

SAGE RODE BESIDE Clare most of the first day, though her friend was tense and silent. The one thing she did ask was where Mesden was. After glancing around to make sure no one was listening, Sage explained that the queen had asked Lord and Lady Broadmoor to take care of him. "It's not safe to bring him into what could be a battle, especially if he's the most valuable piece for either side. Huzar is with him."

The bodyguard had objected to his queen's order, but was forced to concede when she pointed out his known treason would make him—and likely her—a target. Staying close to Zoraya could make things worse for her, at least at first.

"So he will be retrieved when Her Majesty is restored to power?" asked Clare.

"Once Zoraya thinks it's safe, yes."

Clare's mouth tightened with Sage's casual use of the queen's name. "And what if we fail?"

"Then he'll stay with them," was all Sage would say. As would Huzar. Zoraya had made him swear it.

Sage's aunt had said if it became necessary, she would raise "Victor" as if he were another bastard child of her husband like Aster, who was close to Mesden's age. Uncle William had flushed a little but not challenged the idea.

"You needn't endure that kind of embarrassment again," Sage had told her privately later. "Say he is a cousin's child or something."

Aunt Braelaura shook her head. "You know, William could easily have left Aster at an orphanage the way his father did with all his illegitimate brood, but no," she said sternly. "He took responsibility for his actions, and . . ." Braelaura pressed her lips together. "You should know it was not entirely his fault."

Such a statement was unbelievable to Sage. "How can that be?"

"Christopher's birth was difficult, and we knew there would be no more babies. William didn't care, but I felt like a failure." Her aunt sighed as she tucked a stray lock of her dull blond hair behind an ear. "For months I was too miserable to even get out of bed, and I hated my poor baby because of what he'd done to me."

"That's still no excuse."

Braelaura shook her head. "I drove William away. Deliberately. Wouldn't share his bed. For years. I told him . . ." She took a deep breath. "I told him to find someone else. And he did. Once. Aster is my mistake as much as his." Then she smiled, her gray eyes brimming with tears. "But a darling, wonderful mistake."

Sage had come to live with them only a few weeks after Aster. Looking back, she realized she'd witnessed the slow and painful recovery between her aunt and uncle, but had misinterpreted most of it. Everything she'd grown up believing was much more complicated than outward appearances. "Why are you telling me all this?" she asked.

"Because you'll be married soon," said Braelaura, and Sage was grateful for the dim light so her aunt couldn't see her blush. "And you need to know that it won't always be easy. In difficult times, you must always turn to each other, never away." She squeezed Sage's hands. "Take it from me."

Sage thought of the conversation as she caught sight of Alex over the heads of a hundred soldiers between them. They hadn't had an easy road up to this point, but it wasn't a good idea to think their difficulties were over simply because they'd written their names in a book and made vows. Frankly, her aunt's advice would have been good to know a few times in the past year, though Sage wasn't sure she would've listened, stubborn as she was. Alex met her eyes and winked, and she smiled back. At least they already had some experience in how to work through their problems. And they knew it was worth it.

Heavy clouds began to gather that evening, causing Alex and Casseck to call an early halt, which Clare didn't like. The smaller tents required extra preparations to keep provisions and people a little drier when the rain hit, however. Sage was to share with Clare, but she fully intended to make a discreet visit to Alex's tent once the camp was quiet and her friend was asleep. The first drops of rain were falling when she crawled into their tiny tent.

Clare sat cross-legged on her bedroll scowling. "Why aren't you with *him*, seeing as you're married now?" she asked, acid dripping from her words.

Before Sage could reply, Clare lashed out again. "I'm your best friend, and you didn't want me there for it," she said. "You didn't even have the decency to tell me about it later."

"We didn't tell anyone," Sage insisted. "It's just . . . not the time for it really."

"No, it's not." Clare's eyes burned with anger. "We march at the head of an army to free my sister, who is a prisoner of your *friend* Zoraya, yet the only thing you can think about is yourself."

"There is *nothing* wrong with embracing happiness when you have the chance," Sage hissed back. "I would think of all my *friends*, you would understand that."

Sage immediately regretted her harsh words. At the same time, she was tired of the way everyone tiptoed around Clare's grief. And Sophia's situation was dire, but they were already doing everything they could to help her. "I choose to live," Sage whispered. "While I can."

Clare turned her back on Sage and lay down, pulling the blanket over her shoulder. "Go, then," she said to the canvas wall. "Live without me."

"Clare—"

"Just go. I won't tell anyone."

Sage shoved her way out of the tent, leaving her things behind, and ran. There was nothing wrong with keeping this one thing for herself.

"Hey there," said Alex as she crawled into his tent. The steady beat of rain made it difficult to hear him. He sat up and reached for her. "You're earlier than I expected. What's wrong?"

"Nothing." Sage wiped her face, grateful the wetness could be attributed to rain. "I'm here to stay, though."

"All right." Alex didn't sound like he quite believed everything was fine. He kissed her as she lay down next to him. "We can just sleep if you're tired."

Sage turned to snuggle into his chest and tilted her face up to kiss his neck, which was deliciously scruffy again. "No, I'm not tired. Yet."

She didn't need anyone's permission to be happy.

69

SAGE, CLARE, LANI, and Zoraya huddled together under a cramped tent, both for warmth and due to the small space. Outside, the sleet continued as it had for the past six hours. Their army had stopped sixty miles north of Arrowhead that afternoon, where the hills to the west ended. From here on, the land on either side of the road was a flat plain. While that would mean no one could approach without being seen, it also meant there was no direction they themselves could flee without being observed. Alex intended to move in the morning, but this was the best place to wait for an update from General Quinn.

Lani sipped hot broth from a mug. "In my country, rain is warm and children play in it," she muttered.

No one responded to the complaint. The princess had been testy since Huzar had told them Brazapil Donala suspected Casmuni involvement in the assassination and that even General Quinn had briefly considered it. Though no one believed that now—except perhaps Donala—it had hurt her deeply, especially with the loss of her soldiers and Mara and Feshamay. Her only comfort was that Casseck had been furious at the accusation on her behalf.

"I wonder if Sophia thinks her country has abandoned her," Clare whispered. Everyone glanced up in surprise. Clare had been withdrawn since leaving Galarick, saying barely a dozen words to Sage since their argument on that first night. Sage had wanted to smooth things over the next morning, but Clare was already dressed and gone when she returned.

She was afraid to try now, not wanting to be rejected in a way that would make things even worse.

The queen went back to her mug. "In some ways she would be better off if Demora did forget her."

"What's that supposed to mean?" asked Sage, frowning.

"Merely that she has been used for the purposes of others almost her whole life," answered Zoraya. "Starting with her marriage. Now Demorans have traded her and her daughter for temporary peace. When they are returned, the fight to possess them will only continue within your borders."

"No respectable matchmaker would've set up that marriage," Sage insisted. "It was her father who sold her off for his gain. We'll never let that happen again." She hadn't said that to please Clare, but her friend looked up, hope sparking in her brown eyes.

Zoraya met Sage's gaze calmly. "Those things happen in my country, too. It is something I wish to use my power to change."

"Maybe you need matchmakers," said Clare.

The queen smiled into her cup. "Maybe."

"Ladies?" Alex called from outside. "May I enter?"

"Yes," Sage answered.

He ducked inside and stayed hunched over, as the tent wasn't high enough for even Clare to stand straight. "We have a visitor for Her Majesty," he said.

The queen looked as puzzled as Sage felt. "Bring him in, then," Zoraya said.

Alex opened the tent flap and hauled a soaked and bedraggled man inside. Sage noted the "visitor's" hands were tied behind his back. Upon seeing Zoraya, he fell to his knees. "My Queen!" he cried in Kimisar. "I thought the news was too good to be possible!"

"General Oshan," said Zoraya. "I'm glad to see you." Her tone indicated otherwise.

He lifted his head, and Sage recognized him now. Water dripped off his balding head and onto the rug the women sat on. "My life is yours," he said. "I swear my loyalty to you and your son, the king."

Zoraya ignored the oath. "How did you find me?" she asked.

The minister of war sat up awkwardly. "I have spies among Brazapil Donala's servants," he said. "They told me."

"And your first instinct was to flee?" The queen did not look pleased.

"To warn you." Oshan shook his head. "I didn't wish to believe it, but I've concluded Donala was behind the attempt on your life. He was too ready to take control, and now he moves to undermine your return." The Kimisar general appealed to Alex. "Show her what I gave you."

Alex pulled several torn pages from his jacket and offered them to Zoraya. Sage leaned over her shoulder to look. "My personal notes on our meeting in Bey Lissandra," Zoraya whispered.

"My man recovered them from Donala's possession," explained Oshan. "The brazapil could only have gotten them from the assassins. He uses the contents now in negotiation with the Demorans, saying he is only following your wishes, even as it angers the other ministers and brazapilla and turns them against you, while he maintains an appearance of loyalty."

Given that Sage had witnessed Donala use Brazapil Nostin in that fashion, it felt very plausible.

"And what do you think of these offers I have made the Demorans," asked Zoraya. "Do you think them treasonous?"

Huzar had said that was the word Oshan himself had used.

The general hunched his shoulders. "I did at first, My Queen," he admitted, eyes on the ground. "Reading your efforts myself changed that. I may not agree with all of them, but you are regent. The power to make these offers is yours, not mine."

He lowered his head in obeisance, and Zoraya began to extend her hand, but Clare spoke up. "Wait! What has happened to the Countess D'Amiran and her daughter in Kimisar custody?"

After a nod from Zoraya, Oshan answered her. "Brazapil Donala treats them well, more like guests than hostages, but . . ." His eyes darted to the queen. "I do not believe he intends to return them to Demora."

"We shall see how his intentions stand in the face of mine," Zoraya told Clare. She brought her hand up again.

Oshan leaned forward to kiss her bare knuckles. "My life is yours," he said again.

"For which I am grateful," the queen said formally, settling her hand on his bowed head. "I shall not waste it."

Sage thought the phrases a little gruesome, but so were most Demoran oaths. Zoraya nodded to Alex and spoke in Demoran. "Please see that this man is fed and given dry clothes."

Alex dipped his head. "Right away." As the general's hands were bound, Alex helped him up before handing him off to the Norsari outside, then squatted next to Sage and the queen. "I urge caution, Your Majesty," he said quietly.

Zoraya held out her cup for more broth. "I did not survive the last twelve years by trusting blindly," she said.

"You do not believe him?" asked Lani, filling the queen's mug.

"I never accept as fact that which is too convenient," replied the queen. "The general comes to warn of a plot against me, yet he commands my army. Why leave it to Donala's control if he fears the brazapil's intentions?"

Alex nodded. "Do you want him sent to the Demoran camp, Your Majesty?"

"No." Zoraya shook her head. "I will keep him close, not because I trust him, but because I do not. You may change his ropes to iron shackles, though."

He smiled a little. "Consider it done."

"One thing is clear, however," the queen added. "A fight becomes ever more likely. I wish all of you to know that were it not for Lady Clare's sister, I would not want a single life risked in my name."

"Speaking of untrustworthy allies," said Sage to Alex. "Has there been anything from Duke Welborough?"

They'd all been watching him discreetly. When Sage had told the others of her suspicions, that had been the one time Clare had spoken more than a few words—and she'd even known the meaning of *pesta lundamyetsk*. "Stories of the *dolofan* were the only history anyone could get my brother Edmund to study," she'd explained. "He was obsessed with them, the way children love pirates and bandits."

Alex shook his head. "The duke hasn't put a toe out of line, and there have been no unusual communications, though he did offer to take Lady Clare under his personal protection."

Sage made a disgusted face. "What did you say?"

"I acted insulted by his implication the Norsari couldn't handle the job."

She nodded, feeling the tension rising among them again. They were almost to Arrowhead. If the duke was going to act, it would be soon.

70

WHILE THE FREEZING rain made everyone miserable through the night, it made their progress easier the next morning. What normally would have been slush was frozen solid. The sun warmed their path a few hours later, but by then the mud had given way to rockier ground.

Their apprehension increased with every mile, and the women became snappish as a result. Sage realized her aunt's advice should also apply to the four of them, and she made efforts to show support and concern for her friends, discovering that often just talking relieved a great deal of anxiety. They discussed scenarios of what could await them at Arrowhead, ranging from realistic to wildly improbable, and it not only passed the time, it made their fears seem smaller and more manageable. Twice they even laughed.

Clare smiled directly at her only once, but it was enough.

Some twenty miles north of Arrowhead they stopped again, and Ash Carter met them. As he'd been privy to everything that had happened, the lieutenant was able to give them much more information than previous messengers. He joined them around a campfire, and Sage first asked for everything he could tell them about Sophia, knowing that Clare wouldn't be able to concentrate until that was discussed.

"The general meets with both her and her daughter twice daily," Ash assured Clare, holding her hands and looking directly into her eyes. "She is well, my lady, though under considerable stress, but Aurelia is the picture of health. The Kimisar have a number of women in the camp, and they've been doting on her. Your niece doesn't realize she's a prisoner of any kind."

Clare relaxed a little, and he released her hands before continuing, "Otherwise, Countess Sophia has begun to understand their language enough for her to report a few things they've said in her presence, which has been helpful. Apparently General Oshan has disappeared, stealing valuable documents."

"He is here," said Zoraya. "And those documents were my own taken from Bey Lissandra. Brazapil Donala had them."

"Which makes Donala look guilty of sending the assassins," said Sage.

Ash frowned. "That's not what the countess said. She told us evidence was mounting against General Oshan, and one of the ministers—not Donala—suggested arresting him, but not in time."

That explained why the minister of war had left his army—he was about to lose it anyway. The question was whether he was truly warning them of Donala's treason, or trying to frame him. Sage grimaced. Every time the waters seemed to be clearing, they became muddied again. No one was obviously innocent or guilty, including Duke Welborough, who continued to act benign and helpful.

"Will Sophia be at this meeting tomorrow?" asked Clare. "Will they return her?"

"That's my main piece of news," said Ash. "The Kimisar have demanded to receive their queen in an open field, where everyone on their side can see her."

"Bad idea," said Alex. "She's too vulnerable that way."

"Your father agreed to it," Ash said with a shrug. "There have been so many rumors that he thinks it's better to let as many people see her as possible. He has the the Countess's squad of elite archers from Jovan at his disposal, and that gives him additional confidence." The lieutenant ran a calloused hand through his coal-black hair. "As for the countess, Donala says he doesn't believe that Queen Zoraya travels of her own free will and he won't bring your sister forth until his queen is safe and she's given him a full account of her treatment." He nodded to Zoraya. "As Her Majesty has sworn her intentions to return Sophia D'Amiran unharmed, General Quinn has accepted those terms."

"That assumes my return will be welcome," said Zoraya. "From what General Oshan has told us, Donala is the only one who doesn't consider my agreements with the ambassador as treasonous. I may be placed under arrest."

Ash blinked at her. "And knowing this possibility, you still intend to return?"

The queen's face was impassive, but Sage had learned to recognize her emotional tells. Her arm was still in a sling, and she brought her right hand up to twist the fingers of her left hand where she used to wear the ring that served as her royal seal. "There is no chance of Lady Clare's sister being freed if I do not."

Sage spoke up, thinking of one of the potential situations they had discussed that afternoon. "We know our intentions are honorable," she said. "Therefore it's not wrong to plan our own recovery of the countess."

"The Norsari are perfect for that," said Alex.

"I have a better idea," said Sage. "How many women are in the Kimisar camp, Lieutenant?"

"About thirty with the initial delegation," replied Ash. "Likely more since Donala brought his army up."

Alex was already frowning, but Sage ignored it. "Perfect. The Kimisar will make a show of all their ranks, especially if the Demorans do, but the women will almost certainly be left in the camp. With those numbers and many recent additions, one or two extras won't be noticed. Two of us can slip in, find Sophia, and sneak her out while everyone's attention is focused on Her Majesty."

"I like this idea," said Lani quickly.

"There's too much potential for something to go wrong," protested Alex.

"So we'll have a Norsari group ready to charge in as necessary," said Sage. "You know as well as I that they'd have to take out a sentry or two just to get inside the perimeter, which is risky in broad daylight."

"But if they have to 'charge in' and rescue you, they will do it with little to no stealth, which defeats their purpose," said Alex.

Sage didn't mind arguing with him. He would consider every contingency, which was useful. "I understand that," she said. "Will you concede that a woman walking through the camp carrying, say, an armload of firewood, isn't likely to be noticed and challenged?"

Alex flared his nostrils. "Yes. Will you concede that it may end up being more than you can handle?"

"Yes," she said calmly. "But Queen Zoraya is risking her life for Sophia, and she doesn't even know her." He stared at her, as though he suspected her willingness to risk herself had other roots.

"I'm not agreeing yet, but we'll discuss the details later." He turned to Ash. "Tell us how this meeting is supposed to go."

Ash squatted and laid sticks in a rectangle on the dirt in front of him. "The neutral ground in the middle will be used. Kimisar will line up on the west, Demorans on the east." He drew a line representing the Span Road. "Three hours after sunrise, you march in from the north and bring Her Majesty forward to meet in the middle, where the negotiation tent used to be, so everyone can see."

"Why that late in the morning?" asked Sage.

"The Kimisar want the sun high enough that we don't have it right at our backs," explained Ash. "It would make them unable to see us clearly."

Ah. Sage should have realized that, given how such light angles had almost allowed Kimisar to surprise the Casmuni and Demorans at the Battle of Black Glass. She still knew little about basic military tactics.

While Alex, Ash, Casseck, and Zoraya discussed how the queen would ride in, Sage debated who she should take with her in retrieving Sophia. Lani was the better swordswoman and was less likely to let emotion distract her, but Clare would never forgive Sage for leaving her behind. The Casmuni princess might be better at Zoraya's side, and keeping Clare away from Duke Welborough was also desirable.

"All right, Sage," said Alex, interrupting her thoughts. He drew her aside. "I will agree to let you do this on the following conditions: first, that you don't go in alone, and you never stray from your partner."

"Agreed," said Sage.

"Second, that should we deem it too risky, you will let the Norsari handle this."

"Agreed, on the condition that you aren't a part of it."

"What?" Alex nearly shouted. "You can't expect me to stay away!"

Sage shook her head. "If you're there, you won't be objective, and you know it." Alex clenched his jaw, a growl echoing from his throat. "Put Ash Carter or Cass in charge of the Norsari," she said. "I promise to abide by their decision. It's better for you to be seen at this meeting anyway—your presence will imply that I'm there as well."

Alex closed his eyes. "Sage . . ."

"Which makes better tactical sense, Major?" she asked. "For you to be in charge of a battalion-sized unit marching into what could easily become a battle, with an eye out for the one who might be a traitor, or to lead a dozen men on a side mission?" She lowered her voice. "Haven't I proved several times over that I can handle myself in dangerous situations?"

He muttered something she couldn't hear before opening his eyes. "Fine. Who's going with you?"

In the end, there was really only one choice.

71

SAGE AND CLARE left with a Norsari squad at sunset to be in place before dawn. Ash Carter knew the area well from his reconnaissance days, so Alex had chosen him to lead the group. Getting there took four hours of riding, and then another three of walking with only a sliver of moonlight to see by. Then they crouched behind a ridge, huddled under the cloaks they'd hastily adjusted to serve as over-skirts, watching the Kimisar camp come to life. Sage fingered the pommel of her curved Casmuni sword, wrapped in leather strips to cover the golden shine. The hilt of Alex's knife pressed reassuringly into her ribs. Clare carried two daggers—her own and the one with Sage's initials.

"There are several women down there," Clare whispered. Skirted figures slipped between the rows of tents, carrying buckets of water and bundles of kindling.

Sage pointed to the large tent near the center, flying a flag with Donala's blue-and-green family crest. "That's where Sophia is most likely being held."

Clare nodded her agreement. The next hour dragged by, and two of them took turns dozing until the soldiers below began to form into ranks.

Something had been bothering Sage while her friend slept. "Clare," she whispered. "You and Sophia both learned to speak Kimisar, right?" Clare nodded. "Then why would Sophia act like she doesn't understand it?"

Her friend rolled her eyes. "So they would talk freely around her."

"Yes, but why did she tell General Quinn she doesn't speak the language?" Sage asked.

Clare blinked. "She told him that?"

"Ash said she did. Or rather, he said she'd begun to understand some of the things said in her presence."

Clare bit her lip. "Maybe he misunderstood."

Sage frowned. It had sounded pretty straightforward.

"Perhaps she's rusty," said Clare with a shrug. "Or she was never as good as our tutor told Father. Master Walton was a bit in love with her." She grimaced. "Everyone was, actually. You should've seen the stack of love letters she kept."

"Jealous?"

"She was jealous of anyone else getting attention, yes."

Sage lapsed into silence; that wasn't what she'd meant. Clare had said many times how different Sophia had become, so it was quite possible Sage was being paranoid. And people often did change with circumstances—she'd seen it in Lady Jacqueline, who, before the Concordium, had been simpering and vicious. When Sage had bumped into her in Tennegol last year, however, Jacqueline was quite gracious, maybe because the pressure to marry well was gone. In Sophia's life, however, stress and misery had only ever compounded. Small wonder she clung tightly to Aurelia, the one good thing in her life.

Sage gripped the hilt of her sword. This would end today. Sophia and her daughter would never live in fear again.

One by one, the platoons marched out, heading for the cleared space between the two camps. The open area was barer than ever, now that the tent had come down. A large rectangular patch of dead grass lay in the center. Far to the other side, the Demoran army assembled.

For a split second, Sage thought she saw Alex's dark head next to General Quinn, but it must be Prince Robert. She stole a glance at Clare, wondering if her friend was truly unaware of the extra attention Robert gave her.

Alex's battalion was still out of sight, waiting for their signal to march.

She wished she could wait long enough to see him, but Ash Carter was creeping toward them now, moving silently across the rocky slope. "There's a place a bit from here where women are walking into the woods to relieve themselves," he whispered. "I think that's your best chance of getting into the camp."

He led them back the way he'd come and pointed out the nearest sentry. The man barely glanced at the women who passed him. Sage looked to Clare, who nodded, and they adjusted their skirts one last time. The *harish* Sage carried had to be angled to nestle against her left leg, and the hilt tucked under her vest. It wasn't very comfortable, but she wouldn't leave it behind. A small bundle of sticks carried against her hip served to hide any suspicious lumps, and Clare also helped by walking on that side.

They headed for the area Ash had seen women had been going back and forth from all morning. "I hope that guard hasn't been paying attention to how many have gone out," Sage muttered.

"We have your back, Sage," Ash told her. "If he twitches, we'll take him down. Same if we need to help you get out. You concentrate on what you need to do."

Just then a blast of trumpets from the cleared area sounded, and the sentry craned his neck in that direction. Sage took a deep breath. It was now or never.

Heads hooded and eyes focused on the ground, Sage and Clare strode past the guard and into the sea of tents.

72

SAGE WOULD BE fine, Alex reminded himself. She was smart and skilled and had a dozen Norsari watching her back. His main concern was Clare. Just as he would drop everything to get to Sage if she were in trouble, Sage would protect her friend at all costs.

The other thing that weighed on him was something Ash had taken him and Sage aside to discuss.

"Colonel Traysden doesn't want anyone extra to know this," he said. "But we've got a leak. Someone from our side has been feeding information to the Kimisar, probably Donala."

"What kind of information?" Alex asked.

"The most sensitive." Ash shook his head. "Things we only discussed in private meetings, like that Queen Zoraya was alive. Not even your father's guards were present."

Alex racked his brain, trying to picture the conversations he'd been a part of. There was one common element that was always present, always silent. Always recording. "Lieutenant Colonel Murray," he said.

Sage had frowned. "Your father's personal aide?" Alex nodded.

"I'm glad I wasn't the only one who thought of him," said Ash. "I brought it up to Traysden and your father, but neither would listen."

"Even I can hardly believe it," said Alex. "Murray's been with Father longer than I can remember."

"We are often most blind to that which is right under our nose," said Sage. "I don't know him very well, but it's too much of a coincidence."

Alex shook his head. "Between watching Donala, Oshan, and Welborough, and protecting the queen, I don't have any more spare eyes."

"I've already got Rob keeping watch," Ash had said. "I just wanted you to be aware, too."

Now Alex sat astride Surry, next to Queen Zoraya, who rode Sage's white stallion, Snow. On her other side was Princess Lani, wearing a dress and cloak she'd been given by the baroness at Galarick, which forced her to ride sidesaddle. When Alex had asked her about it, she'd opened her cloak to show him she'd cut the dress to allow a Casmuni *harish* to nestle in the fabric.

"They will see I am in a skirt, and they will not suspect I am also armed," she said.

Alex couldn't argue with that.

Behind them stood their gathered army. Ragtag as it was in actuality, it held formation as well as a professional army battalion. Alex would rather not have to prove them, though.

Cass came riding up from the direction of the field. He saluted before making his report. "Everyone is moving to their places around the center. The general wants your force to wait until both sides are assembled, then come in from the north at his signal."

"Very well."

Alex turned around to pass word and saw something that made his blood chill.

Duke Welborough had ridden up, ahead of his company, and was talking to General Oshan, who was shackled to his horse. Shit. He should have warned the guards not to allow the duke to talk to the Kimisar prisoner.

The sound of trumpets echoed from the south, the long notes bouncing off the rocky landscape and overlapping as they traveled.

It was time to go. Delaying could be disastrous.

"Cass, go stick to our duke like a burr." It was all he had time to do. Alex bellowed for the battalion to step off and kicked his horse into a walk.

The last half mile to the crossroad was the longest of his life. As soon as the Demoran side came into view, he searched for his father and Colonel Murray, finding them front and center, ready to cross the field and the dead rectangle of grass. Prince Robert was with them as well, and behind them stood a line of ten Jovan soldiers who'd come with Countess Sophia. They wore their cloaks with the right side folded back over their shoulders, exposing both the crossbows they carried in the crooks of their arms and the silver arrow pins that declared their marksmanship. Alex felt much more secure with them there.

At their backs, rank upon rank of Demoran soldiers stood at attention. Kimisar assembled across the field, mirroring them. General Quinn had called as many as he could, forcing the other side to bring the same amount, leaving the camp behind them less guarded.

Alex called a halt at the edge of the field, and a silence descended as over one thousand boots behind him stopped. Brazapil Donala strode forward and Robert went to meet him. Alex tensed and tried to quell his stomach at Rob's vulnerability.

"We have word that Zoraya, Queen Regent of Kimisara, is in your possession," Donala said, his voice ringing across the open area, loud enough for half of both armies to hear. "We demand her return."

"That is not truth," said Rob clearly, causing a murmur through the Kimisar lines. "She comes of her own accord." The prince raised his arm and gestured for Alex and the others to approach. As Donala had come alone, Alex didn't dare bring anyone else besides Lani.

Exposed.

They rode forward a few steps to separate themselves from the force behind them, then dismounted, Alex assisting the queen and then Lani. Zoraya led the way, head high. She stopped several feet from the nobleman. As her blue eyes met Donala's, the brazapil fell to his knees.

"My Queen," he whispered, lowering his head to the ground.

Behind him, spears and shields were dropped and line after line knelt in their ranks. In the back, a small crowd of women gaped before sinking to their knees. Alex scanned the area frantically. This had to be a trick. Rob and Lani exchanged nervous glances. Even Zoraya looked startled.

Donala raised his head, tears in his eyes. "My Queen, I have done everything in my power to preserve your rule. The king is safe, and the traitor Oshan has fled, but we will have him soon." The brazapil crawled forward and pressed his forehead against her feet. "My life is yours."

The queen backed up a step. "Because I have an army at my back?" Zoraya asked him. "*Now* I am your queen?"

Donala sat back, his brow wrinkled in confusion. "You have always been my queen." He turned a little, throwing out his arm to indicate the ranks behind him. "*This* is your army. I give it to you."

Either the brazapil was putting on a hell of a show, or he was being completely honest. Everyone held their breath, waiting for the queen's next words.

And in the silence, Alex heard the faint sound of Sage screaming.

73

MOST WOMEN WERE heading toward the edge of camp, wanting to see what was happening on the field. Sage and Clare added their firewood to a small stack, then picked up a pair of abandoned buckets of water and headed toward Donala's tent. Clare's face was white with tension beneath her hood as they approached the two guards outside, but the men waved them in. As they passed, one smacked Clare's rear end, making her jump into the tent with a squeak. The man laughed and let the canvas door drop. Clare turned back and made an obscene gesture with her free hand.

"Spirit above, Clare," whispered Sage, pulling her deeper into the tent. "Who taught you that kind of behavior?"

Clare grinned. "Who do you think?"

They pushed their hoods back and peered around the gloomy space, letting their eyes adjust. Soft light came from a half-partitioned area near the back, and Clare headed straight for it while Sage loosened her makeshift skirt to free her *harish*. When she came around the curtain, Clare gasped and dropped her bucket, spilling water on the rug. "Sophia!"

The Countess D'Amiran looked up from where she sat, sorting through a stack of parchments under a branch of candles. Her young daughter sat at her feet, playing with wooden blocks. Recognizing Clare, Sophia jumped to her feet and ran to her sister, arms outstretched. The pair embraced for several seconds. "What are you doing here?" they both whispered at the same time.

"Reading through Donala's papers," Sophia answered, waving her hand at the table covered with documents. "They do not know I speak Kimisar."

Sage frowned. General Quinn could have used that information. It occurred to her Sophia might have withheld her understanding because he hadn't kept her fully informed, but that wasn't just spiteful, it was dangerous.

"I'm here to rescue you," said Clare. She gestured to Sage. "*We're* here to rescue you."

The countess's expression hardened. "Forgive me if I do not appreciate the one who has put my sister in so much danger."

Sage raised an eyebrow. "Clare insisted on coming along. She's pretty handy with a knife, you know."

"I meant in taking her to Bey Lissandra," Sophia spat. "Why could you not have just let her continue on to Jovan with the escort?"

"They all ended up dead, as you might recall," said Sage, drawing her brows down. "I find it odd you wish she'd been with them."

Sophia slashed her hand through the air like she was sweeping a chessboard clean. "I knew there were roving bandits in the area. If she had been with the escort, I would have sent my forces out to meet her for additional protection, but you had dragged her along on your foolish quest."

"I wanted to go with her," said Clare, shaking her head. "Don't blame Sage."

"You said she *needed* you," retorted Sophia. "I am your sister, Clare. In every letter, I begged you to come back to me, and when you finally had the chance, you chose *her*."

Rather feel than triumph at the countess's words, an icicle of dread lanced through Sage's middle. Duke Welborough's courier had been sent ahead to Jovan, but Sophia had fled to Arrowhead claiming she knew nothing about where Clare had gone, or that the escort group existed at all, because the courier had never arrived.

Or had he?

Sage's hands drifted to the weapons at her waist. "It must have burned you up knowing she chose to go to Bey Lissandra rather than Jovan," she said, putting a taunting edge to her tone.

"Jealousy is beneath me," Sophia snapped. "I was worried sick about her every step of the way here."

"Except you didn't know anything about the escort, so who told you where Clare went?" asked Sage.

"I did," said Clare. "In my letter. She deserved to know."

"But she never got that message, remember?" Sage's right hand gripped the hilt of her sword.

"Lieutenant Carter told me where you went," said Sophia dismissively.

"No, he didn't," said Sage. "He didn't know anything about it until he arrived."

"What difference does it make who told me?" Sophia threw her hands up in the air.

Clare's eyes darted back and forth. "Sage, what are you saying?"

Intelligent. Ambitious. Bold.

The matchmaker had seen it in Sophia years ago.

"I'm saying there was one outside person who knew we were going to Bey Lissandra." Sage drew her sword, and the countess stumbled back, gripping the edge of the table. "One who then had enough time to send assassins."

Clare moved to shield her sister with her body. "Sage! Are you out of your mind?"

"What was the poison you used on the escort, *Your Grace*?" Sage hissed.

"Why in the name of the Spirit would she have done that?" cried Clare.

Sage raised her blade to point it at Sophia. "Because with those Norsari and Casmuni at Jovan, your sister couldn't have claimed she was in danger. She wouldn't have had an excuse to flee to General Quinn."

It hadn't been Lieutenant Colonel Murray or anyone else as Ash had feared.

Sage kept her voice low as she advanced a step. "She wanted the count dead because she hated him, and she wanted Queen Zoraya dead to end the possibility of peace. They were necessary, but I was extra, so you could never choose me over her again."

Pesta lundamyetsk. A phrase that Sophia had grown up knowing but in use implicated a dozen other culprits.

"Sophia would *never* conspire with Kimisara! Why would she?" insisted Clare, but behind her, a fierce gleam sparked in the countess's eyes.

"Not conspiring," said Sage. "Informing. The Kimisar never learned Zoraya was alive until she did. *She* was the one giving Donala information." Sage shook her head. "But she was just using him and everyone else to get what she wanted. So she could end up right here, as a hostage Kimisara would never give back after the death of their queen. She played us all for fools."

Sophia's mouth twisted into an ugly smile. "You make it sound more difficult than it was."

Clare's jaw dropped as she turned to face her sister. "Oh, Sophia, no!"

"Be quiet, Clare." Sophia never took her eyes off Sage. "Our own father treated us as tools for bringing him more wealth. My daughter faces a lifetime of being fought over and used for the advantage of others. Aurelia and I are nothing but packhorses to Demora, carrying titles and power we can never wield ourselves for the king and his council to bestow on whomever they want to have it."

"That doesn't justify treason," said Sage. "Nor murder." Clare still stood between them, keeping Sage from moving closer. "How did you get Donala to go along with this?"

"Same as everyone else, by acting helpless. It is easy when that is what everyone expects." Sophia gestured to the table behind her. "The damn fool is still too loyal to his queen to leave. Otherwise I would be in Kimisara by now."

She'd given Brazapil Donala Zoraya's notes, thinking it would cause him to leave, but instead he'd tried to implement them, because that's what his queen had wanted. Sage thought he probably didn't know who had sent them to him. It was safer for Sophia to appear she didn't know anything or she risked being questioned more. "How does Baron Underwood fit into all this?"

"Like a sheepdog," said Sophia disdainfully. "Once I told him I would consider Aurelia for his son in a few years, he went wherever I told him, and he enjoyed causing trouble for General Quinn. Demora can keep him."

"What about General Oshan?" Sage took a step to the left, trying to get around Clare, who was rooted to the spot. "Did you send him to kill the queen when you failed the first time?"

Sophia snorted. "No, but he will take the fall when she dies today. Donala already half believed he was behind it. I did not even have to plant evidence."

Zoraya was in danger right now, but there was nothing Sage could do. "What happens after you get to Kimisara?"

"Donala becomes regent, and I become his wife."

"The brazapil is already married," said Sage, though she had no idea if that was truth.

The countess slid a sheet of parchment from the pile behind her and held it up. "Not for much longer, according to this."

Sophia dropped the page, and Clare reached for it as it fell. Sage's eyes reflexively followed the movement, and in that split second, with Clare bending down and out of the way, the countess hurled the branch of candles over her sister's back and at Sage.

74

IT WAS MUFFLED and distant, but it was her. Sage was screaming.

Before Alex could react, Brazapil Donala launched himself at Zoraya, knocking her to the ground as arrows sliced over them. Robert fell to his knees, clutching his arm. Alex sprinted for his cousin with his sword drawn, and a crossbow bolt hit the blade, shattering and throwing splinters at his face. None hit his eyes, but blood quickly poured into them from a gash in his forehead.

The shots were coming from the Demoran side.

The deadly whistle of arrows filled the air, followed by the unmistakable sound of them hitting flesh. Casseck came flying at them on his horse. He leaned down to scoop Lani up, but the princess already had her sword out and waved him off as she stood over Zoraya, one foot on Donala's back.

"I'm all right," the prince said, clutching his right shoulder as dark blood leaked through his fingers. "It just grazed me."

The arrows stopped as abruptly as they'd begun. Alex wiped blood from his eyes and looked back at the Demoran ranks. The Jovan archers had been pulled down and subdued by the soldiers behind them. Robert staggered to his feet. "Give me my sword, will you?"

It took Alex a second to understand his cousin couldn't draw his weapon with the only arm he could use. He wrenched the sword from the scabbard and offered it to him. Robert gripped the hilt with his bloody left hand, leaving the wound in his right arm to bleed freely. Cass had dismounted and kicked Donala aside, standing back-to-back with Princess Lani, ready to defend Zoraya. The brazapil's pants and shirt were soaked with blood, but Alex couldn't see where he'd been hit. A line of soldiers on horseback led by Duke Welborough came rushing at them, and for a moment, horror overwhelmed Alex at the sudden impossible odds he and Rob faced. Then he set his feet and raised his sword to challenge the duke when the man waved his arms and shouted for those behind him to form a perimeter. As the box of men assembled around the arrow-studded ground, weapons pointing outward, Welborough paused to salute him, and Alex realized the duke had come to defend them. He saluted back, relieved, but now Kimisar were charging across the field at their fallen queen.

Sweet Spirit, what a mess.

The wall of soldiers between them and the approaching Kimisar solidified, and more were coming from both General Quinn's army and Sage's battalion. Within the box surrounding them, it was almost quiet for a moment, but it wouldn't last long.

"I heard her," Rob said to Alex. "I heard Sage right before this started." He tilted his head toward the Kimisar camp. "Go."

Alex didn't need to be told twice. He grabbed Casseck's loose horse, threw himself up on the stallion's back, and kicked the beast into a run.

75

THREE TINY FLAMES.

That's all it was. One even snuffed out in midair, leaving only two.

But it was enough.

Sage dropped her sword and screamed like she was on fire, because in her mind she was. Searing-hot wax hit her neck and scent of burned hair was in her nose as she covered her face with her arms and curled into a ball. Her left leg and arm felt like they were melting and she thrashed, swatting at phantom flames on her clothes.

The sting of a slap hit Sage's cheek, knocking her to the ground and ending her hallucination. She was lying facedown on a carpet, trying to remember where she was, when a hand gripped her hair and hauled her to her feet. Two Kimisar guards stood in front of her. The dagger at her waist—*Alex's knife*, she thought in a daze—was yanked from its sheath and pressed against her neck.

"This does not concern you," a voice in her ear snarled in Kimisar. "Go back to your post."

Both men lowered their weapons and backed away until they were outside the canvas flap. "Funny how easy some men are to bribe," said Sophia now in Demoran. The countess jerked Sage around to face Clare, who knelt on the ground, looking around wildly. Aurelia stumbled to her feet and threw herself at her mother, wailing. Sage felt the little girl clutching both her and Sophia's legs, but she couldn't move her head with the blade at her throat.

"Hush, darling," Sophia soothed. "Stand behind me." The tiny arms moved away from Sage as the child obeyed.

Clare stood to face her sister, eyes wide in horror. "What are you doing?"

"It was strychnine," Sophia whispered in Sage's ear. "I brought them a barrel of wine myself and offered a toast. They did not dare refuse." Tears rolled out of Sage's eyes and into her hair as she thought of Mara and Feshamay. "I did not stick around for the messy part, though."

"What are you saying to her?" demanded Clare, taking a step forward. "Let her go!"

There was distant shouting outside and the clashing of weapons. "It sounds like the queen has really been assassinated this time," said Sophia. "Which means you have a choice to make, Clare."

"What choice?" Clare shook her head in confusion, tears welling in her eyes.

"Donala will be regent now, and he will return to Kimisara with me as a guarantee that the Demorans won't attack. But I am not coming back. It is the only way to keep Aurelia safe."

"King Raymond will keep her safe!" cried Clare. "He promised me!"

Sophia shook her head. Sage wanted to break free, but the knife was so tight against her that she had to stand on her tiptoes to keep it from cutting her, and it still scraped her hard enough to draw blood. One move and she was dead.

"I am done with Demora," spat Sophia. "I was supposed to marry Prince Robert, did you know that? Mistress Gerraty had me down for his match. I was going to be queen one day."

"Actually," gasped Sage. "She picked Clare for that. I've seen her notes."

"Liar!"

"None of that matters, Sophia," Clare pleaded. "Neither of us got what we wanted."

"I will now," Sophia said. "Come with me. I will marry Donala and rule with him. You can stay with us."

"You'll betray your family, your country, for a *regency*?" Sage couldn't understand why she was taunting the woman with a knife to her throat, except that she hated Sophia, and she wanted her to know it before she died. "You're more pathetic than I thought."

"Not another word, you common wretch!" The knife had definitely broken skin. Sage felt blood trickle down under her shirt. "And it will not be like that," Sophia told Clare. "I will raise Aurelia alongside the boy king. I will be his new mother. And who has more power than the mother of a king?"

"I'll come with you, Sophia," said Clare quietly. "But only if you let Sage go."

Sophia shook her head. "NO. I cannot have you running to Demora the minute my back is turned. You are coming along, you just have to choose whether it is in a carriage or in chains."

Sage had seen how Prince Robert looked at Clare but never said anything because her friend wasn't ready for the possibility yet, not while she still mourned Luke Gramwell. Somehow Sophia had learned of his attraction, too, and she'd never chance Clare having what she believed should have been hers.

The knife across Sage's neck moved a fraction of an inch sideways, and more blood dripped over her collarbone.

"No!" Clare cried. She stretched one arm out to Sage, but stopped short of touching her. "I'll go! I'll go! I'll do anything you want!"

"Then pull out your knife and prove it."

"How?" gasped Clare.

"Use it on Sage here," said Sophia, jerking her by her hair again. "Show me you mean it. Choose me this last time."

Sage took three shallow, painful breaths before Clare whispered, "And if I won't?"

"I will do it for you, nice and slow," said Sophia. Her voice was cold as ice. "Then I will call the guards back in for you."

Sage closed her eyes. She couldn't even swallow without cutting her neck more. Sophia was going to kill her one way or another. Maybe she should just relax her body and save Clare from the decision.

"Do not even think about it, you little bitch," Sophia hissed in her ear, and Sage tensed and opened her eyes again. "If she does not do it herself, it is the dungeon for her."

To make sure Clare could never return to Demora.

There was fighting close, right outside, but even with the rhythmic crashing of metal, Sage clearly heard the whisper of a dagger being drawn in front of her. Her own. The one she'd loaned Clare so she'd have two. Alex's knife at her throat and her own in her gut. At least she'd die among friends.

"Sage," said Clare. "Look at me."

Sophia eased enough for Sage to lower her head. Tears streamed freely down Clare's cheeks. The dagger in her hand twitched. "I'm sorry," she whispered.

"Me, too," said Sage.

"Turn away, darling," Sophia told Aurelia. "Close your eyes."

The fight outside ended with a grunt and the sound of a body hitting the ground. Clare suddenly lunged forward, and Sage gasped as a lash of pain went through her left side. Her legs gave out, and Sophia released her. Sage fell to her knees, clutching the handle of the knife as Clare let go. Warm blood leaked through her clothes and over her fingers.

Sage heard the smile in Sophia's voice. "Well done, Clare."

76

ALEX TORE THROUGH the Kimisar camp, hearing the sounds of battle behind him. Women screamed and scattered as he charged through any soldier who challenged him. Outside the tent flying Donala's family crest stood two guards with their weapons drawn. Alex threw a dagger from his belt into the neck of the nearest man as he passed. Then he swung around and dismounted to face the second, who fought for a full minute. As the man lay on the ground, breathing his last, Alex paused only long enough to retrieve his knife from the first dead guard before running inside. At the far end of the open space, Lady Clare and the Countess Sophia stood facing each other, with Sage on her knees between them, clutching her middle.

Before Alex could figure out what had happened, Clare punched her sister dead in the face.

Sophia D'Amiran's head snapped back, her body following, and a black-and-gold-handled dagger fell from her hand. She landed flat on her back, dazed. The child who'd been at her feet clutched her skirts, wailing.

"I'm sorry, Sage!" Clare knelt in front of her, sobbing. "I'm sorry! Don't move! Stay still!"

Alex reached Sage's side to see another black-and-gold hilt sticking out of her stomach. "I'm all right," mumbled Sage thickly. "I think."

It was so absurd Alex took several seconds to understand. "*She stabbed you?*"

"I had to do it!" Clare cried. "I heard you outside and if I didn't Sophia would have cut her throat as soon as you came in!" Sage's neck was pink and red with abrasions and bleeding from a shallow cut.

Sophia began to sit up, coughing on the blood dripping from her nose. Clare scrambled around Alex to reach the knife the countess had dropped, then swung it up, hitting her sister across the temple with the hilt. Sophia dropped back like a stone. Clare let go of the dagger and sat on her heels, a faint, hysterical giggle escaping her lips.

Sage turned her head to look. "I'da done that, 'cept I got a knife in me." She sounded drunk. The side of her jacket was wet with blood, but not as much as Alex would have expected from a gut wound.

"Hold her upright," he told Clare, unfastening Sage's sword belt so he could pull her clothing back. The dagger lifted away with the vest, revealing a clean cut at her waist. Alex raised her shirt and probed the wound, prodding it open to see how deep it went.

Only into the muscle. Praise the Spirit. But she could still bleed to death.

He yanked the knife from her jacket and pressed her clothes back against the wound. "I'll get help," said Clare, jumping to her feet. "Lieutenant Carter and the others are probably already coming for us."

"Be careful," Alex told her, but Clare only nodded as she picked up Sage's sword and then ran out. Alex held Sage with his arm around her back, putting pressure on her side with his hand. "Stay with me, Sage."

"Don't blame Clare," Sage mumbled, her words slurring. "I knew she'd aim to the side. She always hesitates right before. Gives herself away." Her head lolled back as she struggled not to pass out. "And Sophia was going to kill me if she didn't. Had to be real."

"But why?"

"She was behind everything." Sage whispered, pausing for a deeper breath. "The assassins, killing Lieutenant Hatfield's escort group, passing information to Donala—though I don't think he knew it came from her. But she did it all." She looked over her shoulder again. "That poor baby."

Aurelia D'Amiran was hiccuping next to her mother, confused and terrified, several strands of hair stuck to her tear-streaked cheeks. Alex didn't dare let go of Sage to reach out to the child.

"She wanted power, but she also wanted to protect Aurelia," said Sage, tears leaking from her eyes. "And she knew she'd never have control over her own destiny in Demora."

Sage's head was turned, giving Alex a full view of the cut on her neck. The shallow wound had clotted and the bleeding stopped, but the countess could have so easily pressed a little harder and ended Sage's life in a matter of seconds. "I don't care," he said. "What she's done is unforgivable."

"I didn't say it was forgivable." Sage sagged against him but managed to stay conscious. "Just . . . tragic."

IT WAS ALEX who carried Sage back to the Demoran side of camp and held her as the surgeon stitched the crescent wound closed, but Clare also never left her side. Her friend hovered silently, tears making messy trails through the dirt and blood on her cheeks. Sage wanted to say something reassuring, but it was difficult enough to hold still through the sutures. She refused any kind of pain relief, though Alex had offered, and afterward Sage fell right asleep.

He was gone when she woke a few hours later, but Clare sat by her cot, hands in her lap, gazing blankly at Sage's feet. She still wore the same clothes from that morning, which were stained with Sage's blood, and her face was unwashed.

"You need a bath," Sage said thickly. Her tongue was so dry she had to peel it from the roof of her mouth.

Clare's head jerked to face her. "You're awake." She started to reach for Sage's hand but then drew back. "How do you feel?"

"Thirsty," answered Sage. "And the inside of my head is fuzzy."

"You lost a lot of blood." Clare poured water from a canteen into a cup, but her hands were shaking so badly she spilled almost half.

Sage pushed up on her right elbow, and Clare nearly panicked. "You have to stay down!"

"I can't drink anything flat on my back," Sage protested. "And it only hurts a little."

At least compared to before.

Clare pressed the cup to her lips. As Sage sipped obediently, she noticed Clare was focusing on her own hands. When she finished drinking, Clare took the cup away, again refusing to meet her eyes. "More?"

"No, thank you," said Sage.

"Major Quinn said you need to drink a lot of water."

"I'm fine for now, but I could use a pillow to help me sit up a little."

Clare immediately shoved a cushion Sage recognized from the ambassador's tent under her shoulders. Then she fussed around, trying to make sure it was just right, never looking directly at Sage's face. "How is that?" she said at last.

"Wonderful," Sage said, sinking back and smiling for Clare's benefit, but Clare had pulled her hands into her lap and was staring at the bruises on her right knuckles. For a half minute she twisted her fingers, mouth trembling.

"I'm sorry," Clare abruptly sobbed. "Sage, I'm so sorry!"

"I'm fine, Clare. Really."

Clare let her tears fall freely. "She wanted me to kill you! I almost did!"

Sage shook her head. "You didn't have a choice."

"The worst part is that Sophia thought I *would* choose her." Clare rubbed her face with her soiled sleeve.

"Did you ever consider siding with her?"

"Not for a second!" Clare cried.

"If it makes you feel better, I never thought you would."

Clare gaped at her, disbelief in her bloodshot eyes. "Even after everything I said over the past weeks? After how I acted over you and Major Quinn?"

"Well, I deserved most of that." Sage shifted a little and sighed. "I haven't been very considerate lately."

"You were just trying to take care of me," Clare said, wiping her eyes again. "Like you always have."

"Sometimes," Sage admitted. "But really most of it was being unable to accept that you don't need me anymore."

"I do need you, Sage."

Sage grinned crookedly. "All right, you need a friend, not whatever I was doing before. I'd say I was acting more like an older sister, but that may not be the best comparison, considering."

That made Clare laugh a little before sighing. "Sister or not, you never would've tried to make me choose between you and anyone else." She shook her head. "I still can't believe she did that. Or actually, I can, and that's why it hurts so much."

"I'm sorry you were put in that position," said Sage, reaching for her friend's hand.

"I stabbed you, and you're apologizing."

"It was better than the alternative; you saved my life. Nice aim, by the way."

Clare clasped Sage's fingers but didn't manage a smile this time. "What will happen to Sophia now?" she whispered.

Sage squeezed back. "There'll be a trial, but there's probably enough evidence that you won't have to testify if you don't want to."

Clare's eyes were dry as she nodded. "And Aurelia?"

"Will need a new guardian. I think it should be you."

"I agree," said a third voice. Sage and Clare looked up to see Prince Robert standing over them, his nearly black hair hanging over his forehead. He was pale—from blood loss, if the bandage on his upper arm was any indication—yet color flooded into his cheeks when Clare met his eyes. She began to rise, but he gestured for her to stay seated. "I was planning to suggest that to Father, assuming that's what you wish, Lady Clare."

Clare bit her lip and blushed a little. "It is, Your Highness. I thank you."

"You're more than welcome." Robert dragged a stool to Sage's left side and sat. "I told Alex I'd check on you. He's out there cleaning up the mess, since Cass is out of commission. His leg caught an arrow aimed at Queen Zoraya."

"Is he all right?" Sage asked, worried.

"He'll be fine," the prince assured her. "He'll just limp for a while. How are you?"

"Tired," she answered.

"I can stay with you if Lady Clare wants to rest."

Clare flushed deeper and stood, picking at her bloodstained sleeve. "I don't need rest, but as you're so kind, I'll take a few minutes to clean up a bit." She curtsied and left.

The prince watched her go, a soft smile on his face. "How is she holding up?" he asked Sage when they were alone.

"As well as can be expected."

Robert nodded as he turned back to face Sage, his eyes serious. "I want to do Sophia's trial at Jovan, and as soon as possible so the Kimisar can participate."

Sage nodded. "And then?"

"The punishment for treason is death." The prince shook his head sadly. "And Princess Lani especially has the right to demand it. Queen Zoraya, too. Sophia's execution may be the only thing that allows this fragile peace to hold."

"Isn't the king needed for that sentence?"

"I've sent for him." Robert sighed and ran a hand through his hair. "Sophia fooled us all," he said. "Manipulated me—and the general—into giving her information, which she then used to manipulate Donala. Wept like you wouldn't believe when the Kimisar demanded Aurelia, then soldiered up and agreed to go." He shook his head again. "We all thought she was quite the heroine, but it was her plan all along."

Sage grimaced. "She'd been traded and exploited and abused by her own father and then her husband and his family. She didn't trust that that would ever change."

The prince raised his eyebrows. "Are you pleading for mercy after what she's done?"

"No, no. The dead deserve justice." She sighed. "And some of it *was* about ambition and power, though maybe she craved it because she had so little. I meant that it didn't have to happen that way. We—Demora, the laws that allow women to be traded like pawns—we created her. Unless you can honestly say Sophia's fears were completely baseless."

Robert thought for a minute. "I see your point. How do you propose we fix it?"

"I don't know," Sage admitted. "But the nobility must lead the way and commit to correcting what's wrong in Demora. The whole of three nations will be watching."

"Starting here in Tasmet." The prince's mouth curled up in a smile. "I'll speak to Father about what you say."

A trickle of wetness from her side made Sage aware she'd been sitting up a little, straining her wound, and she relaxed against the cushion. "Thank you."

"Yeah, don't do that again." Robert dabbed the blood with a towel. "Alex'll kill me. Speaking of . . ." He glanced up. "When's the wedding?"

Sage felt her face grow hot. "Um . . ."

The prince winked. "I mean the official one." He lifted the towel to peek, looking relieved that the bleeding appeared to have just been that bit, and that had stopped. "We should do it at Jovan, don't you think? So there's something good to counter the trial? Everyone will be there anyway."

"Except Alex's mother." Sage frowned as Robert gave her a too-innocent smile. "You already sent for her, didn't you?"

"Actually, Uncle Penn did," Robert said, referring to General Quinn.

"Did you tell Lani about this?"

Now he looked guilty. "I may have mentioned it."

"Then it's probably half planned already." Sage rolled her eyes.

Clare returned then, much refreshed, though still pale and weary, and took her seat again by Sage. The three of them chatted for a while, and after another drink of water Sage acted as though she was sleepy and pretended to doze off.

After all, she wasn't the one Prince Robert was sticking around to talk to.

78

ON THE THIRD day, Sage was moved back to the ambassador's tent and the much more comfortable bed. Alex came by to tell her he was leaving and probably wouldn't see her again until Jovan.

"I'm sorry," he whispered, holding her hand to his rough cheek. "We have to find the rest of Underwood's people before the trial can start. They were in on the assassination, though Sophia used them as much as she used everyone else."

"Don't apologize," she told him, then smiled. "But do hurry, please."

He returned the smile and added a wink. "You'll be recovered enough by then to properly celebrate."

"You mean the wedding?" Then she had to explain what Robert had set in motion.

"I'll be sorry to miss all that planning," Alex said.

"Liar."

He grinned and leaned in for a good-bye kiss. "Don't let Lani get too carried away."

Clare continued to keep her company, while Lani spent most of her time fussing over Casseck. The arrow wound in his leg was serious enough that he had to stay behind when Alex left. "Better than in the butt," said Lani.

Apparently Donala was hit there, in addition to a grazing wound across his upper back. The brazapil had seen the archers taking aim from among the Demoran ranks when he'd turned back toward the queen, and then saved her life by knocking her over. In the confusion that followed, soldiers on both sides were wounded until General Quinn managed to calm things down. When questioned, the Jovan guards who'd started the shooting admitted to also being the ones who had killed the escort group, all acting under Sophia's direction.

Zoraya visited, too, saying she'd agreed to stay for the trial. "I'll never get this sling off," she muttered, shifting her cloak over her re-broken collarbone as she sat on the couch next to Sage's.

"How are Brazapil Donala and General Oshan getting along?" Sage asked.

The queen chuckled. "For the first days they fell all over each other apologizing for believing the other had plotted my death, but they do not hold grudges. They are friends now."

"And Huzar?"

"Pardoned for his treason, of course. He is bringing Mesden back from your family's estate," she replied. "The brazapilla have sent for the decoy king to please me." Her sapphire eyes sparkled. "I look forward to their reaction when I reveal how I fooled them all."

"I would pay to see that," said Sage with a grin. "What will Huzar do then?" The queen didn't answer. "You deserve some happiness," Sage pressed. "Both of you do."

Zoraya gazed down at her lap. "That kind of happiness is weakness. My son is the only weakness I can afford." Her hand shook, and she clenched it into a fist. "Malkim already knows too many of my secrets."

"He will never betray you."

The queen glanced up, eyes narrowed. "I do not plan to send him on any hopeless missions, if that's what you're thinking." Sage held her tongue. "But I cannot keep him near me. He knows Demora. I will make him my personal courier."

"And spy." Sage relaxed a little.

Zoraya arched an eyebrow. "Observer."

Sage couldn't laugh, it would hurt too much. "Where do we go from here?"

"I've asked your prince for a year of truce, and he agreed. Both our countries need to sort some matters within." Zoraya put her hand over Sage's. "Talks will resume next summer, with our agreements from Bey Lissandra as a starting point. Will you come?"

"Honestly?" Sage sighed. "I'd rather my life was much less exciting than it has been for the past few years."

Zoraya smiled—a real smile, not the wry this-is-painful-in-an-amusing-way grimace Sage was used to. "So I will see you there?"

"Of course."

As quickly as Sophia's trial was assembled, it still took several weeks for the necessary people—notably the king—to arrive. Sage insisted on riding to Jovan when the time came. As she had written out her entire testimony, her presence wasn't strictly necessary, but she wanted to be there to support Clare, who had decided to testify. The king and queen both came, bringing Rose, who would leave for Casmun with Lani when everything was over. Over the weeks leading up to the trial, the Norsari sent a steady stream of captured D'Amiran loyalists to Jovan, many of them more than willing to spill information when they realized how the countess had deceived and used them to further her own goals.

The trial was public but fair, and also swift, as Sophia denied nothing. She acted above the proceedings, providing few answers, though most were not needed thanks to the confessions of others. When the determination of guilt was formally announced, the king ordered the verdict and sentencing recorded so to be carried to all corners of the nation. Sophia stood in the center of Jovan Fortress's main hall, wearing a plain brown dress, her thin wrists in shackles and her ankles chained together. Her hair, face, and hands were clean and well groomed, however, and she still carried herself like a noblewoman.

"Do you have anything to say before your punishment is declared?" King Raymond asked.

"My words are only for my daughter," Sophia said, chin high.

The king didn't look pleased by that, but he allowed Clare to bring Aurelia forth so Sophia could speak to her. Sage fidgeted where she stood as the countess knelt and whispered in the child's ear for several minutes. Aurelia was barely two—surely too young to remember this—but Sage herself had vague memories of her own mother. It was the emotions of the moment she was likely to retain, and those would be traumatic.

When she was finished, Sophia stood and leaned around Clare to address the king. "What will be done with her?"

"Your sister has been granted guardianship."

Sophia stood straight again, staring blankly ahead. "I have no sister," she said flatly.

Clare picked up Aurelia, who cried out and reached for her mother. "Neither do I," she replied, turning and walking back to stand by Sage.

The king waited for everyone's attention before speaking again. "Countess Sophia D'Amiran, you are judged guilty of conspiracy, treason, and murder. You have done much damage to our nation, which, in itself, is reprehensible. Worse, your actions have harmed other countries. It is easier to forgive—though not forget—wrongs that have been done to ourselves, but it is much more difficult when done to our friends."

Sage smiled a little at the truth of that. She didn't care much about the thin scar on her neck, but she could never forgive what Sophia had done to Feshamay, Mara, and the other Casmuni, let alone Clare and the Norsari.

King Raymond stood. "Therefore, as a gesture of peace and in begging our neighbors' forgiveness for what has been done to them on our soil, your fate will not be my decision." He extended his arm to the two women who sat at a right angle to him and Queen Orianna on the dais. The Casmuni princess and Kimisar queen stood as one and came forward. Both wore black dresses, as they had every day of the trial, though Zoraya's was heavily embellished with silver threaded designs.

The king bowed his head. "Queen Zoraya, Princess Alaniah," he said formally before taking a step back. "The sentencing is yours."

Zoraya pivoted and Lani stepped around until they were between Sophia and the king, facing the countess. The queen spoke first, her face regal and impassive. "It is our decision," she said loudly and clearly, "that you shall be imprisoned for the rest of your days."

Sophia snorted in contempt. "You do not even have the courage to execute me," she said.

Lani ignored Sophia's words. "Though you shall be well treated," the princess said, "you shall neither see the sun nor feel the rain again, like those whose lives you have taken." She paused. "And you will only know how many days have passed by the number of times you have written the names of the dead."

Sage had gotten the idea of making Sophia write the names every day while watching Alex struggle to list them so he could write letters to their families. That he couldn't name every man under his command without help—or at least recall who he had sent where—tore at him.

Sophia sneered at the princess. "I will live long enough to fill a hundred books with those pages."

Lani only smiled, though it didn't reach her green eyes.

"We hope you do," said Zoraya.

At that, Sophia's proud expression faltered.

79

THOUGH EVERYONE WAS relieved the trial was over, there was little sense of celebration. Queen Zoraya left almost immediately, hugging Sage with her good arm and apologizing for not staying long enough to attend her wedding, which had been put off somewhat indefinitely because Alex had yet to return. His family had arrived with the king and queen, and at the solemn banquet that night, Jade Quinn, who was to go with Rose to Casmun, grumbled that she would miss the wedding, too, until Lani assured her she would remain an extra year if that's what it took. Sage's family also intended to stay, which embarrassed her because it had to be uncomfortable. Space was so tight at the fortress that Aunt Braelaura, Uncle William, and Sage's four cousins actually had to sleep all in one room.

Her mood lightened, however, when a serving girl slipped in to deliver a letter. Recognizing the handwriting, Sage opened it right then and was able to tell everyone Alex would return in two weeks. Her cheeks warmed as she continued reading. Alex missed her very much, and he was eager to see her again. He was also rather . . . explicit.

"*Sestu Sperta!*" Lani exclaimed, peering over her shoulder. "That man knows how to make a heart beat faster."

Sage flushed and yanked the page away. "That is private!"

"I'll say it is." The princess winked and went back to her food.

Sage shoved the letter into the pocket of her dress. "You really need to learn some boundaries, Palachessa."

The king stood from his place at the head of the table, motioning for everyone to stay seated as he did. "It is unfortunate, then," he said, gesturing to the queen beside him, "that Her Majesty and I will not be able to stay for the wedding. We've been away from Tennegol for two months now, and the journey home requires another two weeks."

Sage's face fell, but inwardly she was somewhat glad. She loved Their Majesties, but when you were a commoner, having royalty at your wedding was a little overwhelming. Plus there would be much more room at Jovan once their retinue was gone.

Raymond lifted his wine goblet to her. "But we offer our blessing, and look forward to seeing you and Major Quinn—and your future family—often in the years to come." Sage blushed as everyone joined the toast.

He set the cup down and rubbed his hands together. "That also means we will take care of other business tonight as well." The king raised his right arm to the side and a steward rushed to place a sheathed sword in his hand. "Lord and Lady Broadmoor, will you please come forward."

Sage's aunt and uncle fumbled with their napkins and chairs, wearing identical looks of shock. Lord Broadmoor had presented himself at court in Tennegol many years ago, swearing fealty as all nobles did within a year of inheriting their titles, but he hadn't been foolish enough to think the king remembered him. Until now, Uncle William had stayed in the background, avoiding notice. He and Aunt Braelaura approached His Majesty arm in arm, and the king stepped back from his place and turned to the side so they could kneel before him.

King Raymond spoke loud enough for all to hear. "Events of the past few months have left gaping wounds in our nation, but I have been glad to also find the places where loyalty and duty are strongest. When your support was called for, you provided it without hesitation or reservation, and I wish to reward that." The king paused to draw the sword. "I therefore confer on you the ranks of baron and baroness and grant you the castle and lands formerly held by Nestor Underwood, confident in the knowledge that you will fulfill your noble duties to the crown as he did not."

With that, King Raymond put the point of the sword on the floor in front of him, holding it upright, and Uncle William extended a shaking hand to carefully grasp the blade and recited the oath of fealty. When he finished, Aunt Braelaura did the same. Sage had tears in her eyes when she led the table in a round of applause as the pair stood and accepted the resheathed sword. The new Baron Broadmoor appeared ready to faint as the king clapped him on the shoulder, and as the noise died down they returned to their seats.

"The Duchy of Tasmet is vacant," His Majesty continued casually, edging around his chair to sit again, "But when my candidate has accepted the title, you will then swear your additional allegiance to them." He lowered himself down and picked up his wine goblet again, turning clear hazel eyes on Sage.

"Whomever that may be."

Sage paced the length of the suite she shared with Clare, uncomfortably aware of how large the room was. Lani watched from a chair by the fireplace next to Clare, who cradled and rocked Aurelia in her arms, gently kissing her forehead and cheeks every few minutes. The little girl had cried herself to sleep, and the hair around her face curled fiercely with the dampness from her tears.

The princess smirked as she studied her flawless nails. "When will you start listing the reasons why you do not deserve this title, Saizsch?" she asked. "I am ready to argue."

"Not funny," Sage snapped.

Clare's soft brown eyes followed Sage as she crossed in front of the fireplace for the eighth time. "May Aurelia and I stay with you?"

Sage stopped short and looked at her friend. "Clare, you are *always* welcome to live with me. You know that."

"It's still polite to ask."

A knock sounded on the door, and Lani jumped up. "I will answer!"

Sage stayed in place, wringing her hands as the page announced that her presence had been requested by Their Majesties. Then the boy leaned around, saying, "Lady Clare is also invited."

Clare glanced down at her niece, hesitating, but Lani was already halfway back from the door, holding her arms out. "Give her to *Shasa* Lani."

Aurelia was passed to the princess, and Clare joined Sage in walking down the passage. "That little girl is going to be spoiled by all her 'aunts,'" said Sage casually.

"None of that will make up for what she's lost."

The pair entered the royal quarters holding hands. Together they curtsied and greeted the king and queen, who sat in comfortable chairs arranged side by side like thrones. Prince Robert was to their right, leaning against the fireplace and wearing a silly grin. Sage couldn't think of anything to say, so she waited.

"I suppose you know why we called you here, Ambassador," King Raymond said as preamble. "The Tasmet province needs a ruler."

Clare squeezed her hand, and Sage took a deep breath and nodded.

"This duchy is important, strategically and diplomatically," he continued in a formal tone, much like the one he'd used when passing judgment that morning. "We need someone who is loyal to Demora, who is trusted by our neighbors, and who understands the needs of both commoners and nobles. That someone will also need to work closely with the army, in a relationship of mutual respect."

Sage bit the inside of her cheek and focused on a spot between the royal couple.

Queen Orianna now spoke. "We need someone who is honest and forthright, who will not hide difficult matters from us, who does not desire power for power's sake, and who understands the importance of marital alliances." Sage heard the smile that crept into her voice. "And last but not least, we desire to reward someone who has risked and sacrificed much for the sake of others."

King Raymond said, "Sage Fowler, you are all these."

The list was overwhelming, as was the conviction with which they spoke. Sage wiped one eye with the heel of her hand and sniffed. "And if I do not want this honor?"

"It will not be forced on you," said the king gently. "This is a position of great responsibility."

She couldn't protest that she was too young. The Duke of Mondelea was only thirteen, and if one wanted to be technical, the true heir to the province was only two years old and sleeping in "Shasa Lani's" arms a few rooms away. "What about Aurelia?" she asked.

"By law, a family that commits treason may be stripped of their titles and lands," answered the king. He shook his head sadly. "I have no wish to punish the child for the crimes of her parents, but I think it best to officially remove her from succession. She will probably be safer that way."

Sage glanced at Clare, who stared ahead blankly. "When do you need an answer?"

"You may have a few weeks to decide," the queen said. "And I expect you will want to discuss this with Major Quinn, as it will affect him, too."

"But Tasmet needs a duke or a duchess soon," added the king.

"What about my post as ambassador?"

Robert stood straight, tugging his rumpled tunic down. "That's why we asked Lady Clare to come," he said. "We wish her to now serve as ambassador to Casmun."

Clare blinked like she was waking up, focusing on the prince for a few seconds before looking back to the royal couple.

"There are two reasons, my dear," said Queen Orianna. "First, you are eminently qualified to perform such duties. And second . . ." She drifted off, biting her lower lip.

Clare finished the sentence for her. "It would take Aurelia far away."

"Things will settle down eventually," said Robert quickly. "But this way, she can grow up free of anyone's expectations or manipulations. People might even forget who she is. It's only temporary. If you want."

Queen Orianna's blue-green eyes slid to her stepson, and a smile tugged at the corner of her mouth. Her glance then went to Sage, who felt herself mirroring the expression. The king didn't appear to notice the silent exchange.

"I will accept," said Clare. She released Sage's hand and sank into a low curtsy. "I thank Your Majesties for their generosity and consideration."

Sage also curtsied. "And I will give Your Majesties my answer after I discuss it with . . . my husband." It was the first time she'd ever called Alex that. The king and queen both nodded, perhaps not realizing what Sage had just admitted, but she supposed it didn't matter anyway.

The queen stood and embraced Sage. "We are leaving tomorrow morning, but the royal decree is written, and Robert may enact it in our absence." As this was good-bye, she stepped back, extending her hands, and Sage reflexively clasped her fingers. Orianna smiled at her one last time. "We sincerely hope you choose to accept."

80

IT WAS LUCKY for the D'Amiran loyalists that Alex was only responsible for their capture and arrest. If he'd had any part in their sentencing, they would've received little mercy for keeping him from Sage for so long. As the gray stone towers of the Jovan Fortress came into view, Alex had an odd sense of coming home, though he'd only ever been here in passing. Home was wherever Sage was, he supposed.

General Quinn met him at the outer gate of the fortress, frowning at the Norsari riding in behind Alex. "Did you bring the whole battalion?" he asked, shaking his head.

Alex grinned. "Yes, but I did tell them it was voluntary." He looked around. "Where is she?" Before the general could answer, Alex said, "Let me guess: the library."

His father nodded, strangely sober. "She's doing some research."

"Where's everyone else?" Alex dismounted and tugged Surry around to face the general. The courtyard bustled with activity, but he saw no one he knew. "Aren't Mother and most of the girls here?"

His father waved a hand at the chapel at the far side of the ward. A garland of white flowers was draped across the front. "They're getting ready for the wedding."

"They want to do that tonight? Isn't that a little rushed?"

The general raised his eyebrows. "I suppose you could've done it a couple months ago." Without waiting for a response, his father took Surry's lead from Alex's hand. "Go, let her know you're here."

Alex nearly sprinted for the second gate and up the stone steps to the main castle within. Unlike Tegann, the fortress here was built more for comfort than withstanding siege, and the living areas were spread over a wide keep that wrapped around the inner ward. There was no royal flag flying from the top, meaning the king and queen had returned to the capital already. Alex had also missed Sophia D'Amiran's trial, but he couldn't say he was sorry for that. His emotions had been mixed when he heard Princess Lani and Queen Zoraya had spared her life.

Not knowing his way around, Alex had to ask directions from passing servants twice. He burst into the library without knocking, hoping to the Spirit she was alone.

Sage raised her head from where she sat at a table with several open books and maps. Her face was pale and her expression weary, but only for a second. Then her eyes lit up and her smile was as wide as his own. Alex never broke stride, and she leapt straight from her chair and into his arms.

Her lips were soft and warm and eager as they met his. He pulled her close, wanting—*needing*—to feel her again. "I'm sorry," he gasped between kisses. "I'm sorry I took so long to get here."

"It doesn't matter." Sage shook her head, looking like she was about to cry. "You're here now."

She wore riding clothes rather than a dress, enabling him to scoop her up against him and set her on the table behind her. Sage tugged at his jacket, loosening it. With one hand he undid the buckles and clasps, too, then shed the jacket without caring where it fell and reached for her again. Books and scrolls tumbled to the floor as he pressed her back and down, working the laces of her vest open. Somewhere in his mind, Alex knew this wasn't the time or place for what was happening, but he didn't care. He only knew he didn't want this moment to end.

"Ahem."

They both froze for several heartbeats, then turned to look at the doorway, which was wide open. Princess Lani stood there, arms crossed. Casseck loomed behind her. "They really are the worst," Lani said to Cass.

Alex stood straight, pulling Sage up with him. Her face was scarlet with embarrassment. "You should knock," she told Lani.

"You should close the door."

"Oops," said Alex as he nuzzled Sage's hair. "Sorry about that." She responded by kissing his neck, and he leaned down to find her mouth again.

Lani charged into the room, waving her hands. "No, no!" she cried. "You cannot do this!" She reached them and pushed Alex away, then grabbed Sage's arm and heaved her off the table. "Clare says you should not see the bridle before the wedding!"

Sage glanced back at Alex apologetically as the princess clucked her tongue and dragged her past Casseck and out the door. After a few steps, Sage stopped resisting and went with her friend. "The word is *bride*, Lani."

81

SAGE DIDN'T REMEMBER much of the preparations. The whole afternoon she swung like a pendulum between elation that her life with Alex was finally beginning and apprehension at what that life would entail. After spending the last few days studying what would be expected of her as duchess and what kind of powers she would have, she still had no idea whether to accept the title.

As the dress Lani had made for her was put over her head, Sage was struck with a vision of all the good she could do for the country and for the people of Tasmet. Jovan would be her home—there was no way in hell she would live at Tegann, but she could still travel—she *should* travel—and see what Tasmet and other places had to offer. And she had the best Demoran relationship with Kimisar royalty in . . . well, ever.

Her aunt and Alex's mother and sisters fussed over her hair and face paint as Sage thought of everything Alex would have to give up. She'd not been able to find a single historical reference to a duke who'd held a military rank or job. Cambria, his family's estate in the Tenne Valley, would have to be managed by someone else, if not relinquished entirely—which was a lot to ask. The army and his home had been the only constants in Alex's life, and Sage couldn't bear the thought of taking either from him.

"Sage." A sharp fingernail tapped her chin. "Wake up."

Sage blinked and focused on eyes of liquid onyx. White teeth flashed against smooth mahogany skin as Castella Quinn smiled at her—just like

Alex, with one side of her mouth higher than the other. "You have to stop worrying," she scolded.

Alex's mother was one of the few who knew about the looming decision. The king had told General Quinn, who of course told his wife. "I can't help it," Sage said. "I'm afraid Alex will give up too much because of what he thinks *I* want."

Castella dabbed a rose color stick on Sage's lips. "Do you want this?"

"I don't know!"

Everyone around her froze, eyes wide in horror. Sage realized what they must think she meant. "We're not talking about the wedding," she said quickly.

"*Wohlen Sperta!*" Lani exclaimed, clutching her chest. "For a moment my heart stopped."

Sage glanced around. The light in the room had taken on a golden glow as evening approached; it was almost time to go. "Am I ready?" she asked. Her face felt remarkably lighter than it had the day she'd met the matchmaker.

Clare offered her a hand mirror. "What do you think?"

Sage braced herself before looking. To her surprise, the face staring back at her was little enhanced, and the colors were soft and natural.

Lani frowned. "I would have done more, but your aunt is right. You should be as you would wish." Then she smiled smugly. "Your hair is my doing."

Tipping the mirror up, Sage found her sun-streaked hair woven with tea roses and sage flowers, but otherwise little bound. Then she looked down, also seeing her dress for the first time. Green Casmuni satin dyed in a dusty sage color at the neckline gradually darkened as it went down, ending with a deep shade of pine at her feet. The high waist was fitted in Lani's favorite style, but the sleeves draped and widened down the arms as Sage now preferred. Other than the gold-threaded trim, there were no embellishments.

It was simple and elegant. Perfect. She loved it. Alex would, too.

Her eyes flooded with tears, and Aunt Braelaura was instantly dabbing her face before it could ruin her makeup. "I don't know how to thank all of you," Sage whispered.

"The look on Ah'lecks's face will be enough," said Lani.

Less than an hour later, the chapel was packed so tight Sage thought it would burst through the mortar. She bit her lip as she waited at the top of the steps outside, uncomfortable with the number of eyes watching her back. Clare and Lani stood on either side of her, helping her to block the doorway. A few steps lower were General and Lady Quinn, facing Sage's uncle and aunt, the newly titled baron and baroness, who still looked uneasy in their ceremonial sashes of rank. The wait felt like an eternity, though it was probably less than five minutes, as the sun barely lowered itself farther behind the outer walls in that time.

Everyone was quiet, allowing them to hear the party's approach before they saw it. Alex had chosen only Captain Casseck and Prince Robert to stand with him, but they all wore their uniforms with sword belts gleaming and sashes decorated with military honors, making every step ring with the sound of a dozen bits of metal colliding. The sun was shining directly in Alex's eyes, so it wasn't until he reached the bottom of the stairs that he was able to look up to her.

He almost missed the first step.

Alex recovered quickly and continued, moving fast enough that Casseck started taking the steps two at a time. Sage pressed her lips together to keep from grinning like a fool. She saw that Alex hadn't shaved, which meant her note asking him not to had found him in time. She rather liked the beard now, especially as he kept it short. Alex came even with her, one step down, and stopped. His dark brown eyes swept over her, and he swallowed nervously.

After several seconds of silence, General Quinn cleared his throat. Alex was supposed to ask her permission to enter the chapel, and Clare and Lani were meant to support Sage if she refused—though in Demoran tradition, doing so meant she couldn't leave until she'd taken vows either as another's wife or as a Sister of the Spirit. After another long moment, Sage glanced around. Casseck and Robert would be no help. They were both focused on the women on either side of her.

"Do you wish to come in?" Sage finally asked.

Alex blinked, realizing what he'd forgotten. "Yes, please," he said, flushing. "May I?"

Sage couldn't hold back her smile anymore as she extended her hands and he took them, letting her draw him up to her. Then he suddenly kissed her, which was definitely *not* part of the ritual, but she didn't care, nor did she care about the chuckles and exasperated sighs she heard around them. Alex slowly pulled away and raised her fingers to his mouth—as he was supposed to have done—and brushed a kiss across her knuckles, leaving a light smear of lip color that her lips had transferred to him. "Thank you," he whispered.

Walking up the aisle with him was much like the first time, as Sage was aware of no one else but him. Alex signed Jovan's book as he had at Galarick, adding the date and place of the first wedding next to their names, which made the priest frown in puzzlement. With much more pomp and ceremony than before, Alex placed her hand on the altar. All she could think about then was the first time she'd seen him, acting like a common soldier, bringing her dinner. Part of her ached for the simplicity and innocence of that hour, when neither of them knew how complicated their lives were about to become. But then Alex finished his vows and raised his eyes to meet hers, and again she saw there were no secrets veiled behind them as there had been that night.

Complicated lives or not, there was nothing better.

She almost stepped up to kiss him then, but remembered it was her turn to speak. She rushed through the vow so fast the priest wasn't ready when she reached the end, and he probably didn't notice the word she omitted again. The priest fumbled with the holy oils while they waited, then dabbed it on their palms and said the binding words as they pressed their hands together and finished with "You may now kiss."

But again he was a few seconds late.

With Alex by her side and so many people happy for them, Sage forgot her troubles through the feast and dancing that followed, all the way to the final toasts given by Alex's parents and her family at midnight. Then Alex led her from the great hall to the sounds of cheers and catcalls. "You'll have to show me the way," he whispered in her ear. "I have no idea where your room is."

"Our room."

Alex grinned. "Our room."

Every nerve in her body humming, Sage pulled Alex up stairs and down passages, stopping often for kisses and wandering hands. Her hair was a complete mess, and she suspected she left a trail of faded flowers behind her. At last they reached her door and after a long minute pressed against it, Sage opened the latch and dragged him in with her.

Alex kicked the door shut behind him, yanking his ceremonial sash off as he did, then stopped short as he saw the room, which was decorated enough for royalty. "Wow," he said. "They gave us the best, didn't they?"

Reality came crashing down. Robert had insisted on putting her here as soon as the royal family had left, probably to encourage her to accept the king's offer. Sage looked around at the enormous carved bed and the elaborate tapestries, which only made the room appear larger. The fireplace was twice the size of any other at Jovan, and half the wall facing west was windows of stained glass, so at sunset the room was painted like a rainbow. "Do you like it?" she asked.

"It's fancy," he said, still glancing around in awe. "I'd just as soon be with you in a tiny tent, with the sound of the rain, but . . ." He shrugged, grinning. "This'll do."

Exactly how she thought he'd feel.

Alex was coming toward her again, longing and heat in his eyes, when she held up her hands. "Wait. We need to talk."

He stopped, puzzled. "Is something wrong?"

"No." Sage wrung her hands. This probably wasn't the best time, but it was too late; she couldn't think of anything else. "Nothing's *wrong*."

Sage led Alex to a seat by the fire and let him pull her onto his lap. She held his left hand, tracing the oil in the creases of his palm as she told him about the king's offer. Then she continued, describing all she'd learned about the duties and responsibilities of a duchy, and how such a high title wasn't compatible with any military rank below general—or maybe colonel, but Alex was already so young in his rank it would be years before that promotion.

As she spoke, Sage realized how much she wanted this—not the title but the chance it would give her to fix the laws and traditions that had made Sophia into a monster. She *wanted* the work.

Alex leaned his head on her shoulder as she talked, rubbing her back with his right hand and asking occasional questions. When she finished, he was silent for a long time, then said, "Are you asking if I think you're capable?"

"Well, that's one of many questions."

He tilted his head up at her, dark eyes shining in the firelight. "I know you are. Next question."

"But . . . what about you? Can you—do you *want* to be a duke?"

Alex pursed his lips. "Is my name on the decree?"

"No, but if you're married to a duchess, doesn't that make you a duke?"

"Usually." His arms snaked around her. "But can't I just be your consort?"

"Will you be serious?" She swatted his chest.

"You can use me for pleasure purposes."

Sage rolled her eyes. "Spirit above, Alex." When he didn't say anything, she looked down on him. "What about Cambria?"

"Serena can have it." Alex named his eldest sister, who was barely two years younger than him. "I'm never there anyway."

She waited for him to say more, but he didn't. "You mean that?" she asked. "Consort?"

"Absolutely. As long as you'll have me." His smile was teasing, but his eyes were earnest. "And if you let me keep my job. I worked rather hard to get where I am."

"It—it won't bother you to be married to someone with a higher rank?"

Alex raised one black eyebrow, wrinkling the faded white scar on his forehead. "The idea never bothered you when our positions were reversed."

"Yes, but . . ." Sage gripped the lapel of his jacket, her thumb tracing the black oak leaf sewn into the collar. Shiny silver pins were impractical for an army unit whose chief attribute was stealth, but his rank wasn't something he ever felt the need to call attention to. In many ways, it was the least important thing to him. She smiled coyly. "Pleasure purposes, huh?"

He leaned up to kiss her neck where it met her jaw. "Lots and lots of pleasure."

"In that case, Consort, I order you to take me to bed."

"As Your Grace commands."

82

WITH THE WEDDING over and shortly followed by the ceremony installing Sage as Duchess of Tasmet, it was time for Lani to return home if she wanted a Casmuni delegation ready for the second talks next summer. "You won't come with them?" Sage asked, catching the phrasing Lani had used.

"That depends on something else," was all she would say.

Clare and Aurelia were to travel with Lani as far as Vinova, but the Casmuni princess kept finding reasons for delay. It wasn't until Alex received a report from Casseck, who'd taken a Norsari company to Tegann, that Sage realized why. When the captain finally returned a week later, Lani was suddenly eager to depart.

"You've waited three extra weeks so you could see Casseck, and you're leaving two days after he gets here?" Sage asked. "Are you going to tell him how you feel or not?"

"It is more complicated than that," retorted Lani, sticking out her tongue before turning serious. "Will you be there with me when I tell him?"

"If you want." Sage scratched the scar on her waist through her clothes. Alex had assured her the itching would eventually fade, but it hadn't yet. "That seems like a rather personal conversation, though."

Lani nodded. "Bring Ah'lecks and Clare, too."

That was how Sage, Alex, and Clare found themselves in the garden the next morning, watching Princess Lani offer Cass what she called a "choice of gifts."

"You don't need to give me anything, Palachessa," Casseck said, then caught the princess's glare. "Ah, Lani."

The two of them had become even closer as Cass recovered from his leg wound, but after Sage and Alex's wedding, he'd suddenly resumed his earlier formal manner with the princess. Lani had been crushed when he left for Tegann without saying good-bye, but Sage thought he was trying to make things easier for both of them. He probably hadn't expected her to still be at Jovan when he returned.

"I feel I must give you something," Lani said, her voice trembling slightly. "I have come to admire you as both a soldier and a man." She clasped a silk-wrapped object in her hands, but it was her maid Tishi who held up a finely made Casmuni sword. "And so I offer you this *harish*, that you may know, and others may see, my admiration."

"Admiration," repeated Cass blankly. Sage detected an underlying tension, like he was insulted—or hurt—and trying not to show it.

"Yes." Lani looked down, fumbling with what she held. "And as *Rosachessa* comes to Casmun to teach us the ways of royalty in Demora, I had hoped you might wish to teach us your ways of warfare." Her hands shook as she pulled away the silk. "But it is with no expectation that I offer you the position of captain of the guard in my brother's palace in Osthiza."

The sword Lani held out to Casseck was nearly identical to the one Tishi had, with one important difference—carved in bold, scrolling letters down the length of the curved blade was a name: *Alaniah*.

In Casmun, a gift with one's name or initials on it was a proposal of marriage.

Sage's jaw dropped open. "Does . . . does he know what that means?" she whispered to Alex. On her other side, Clare brought a hand to her mouth, her eyes wide.

Cass stared at the sword for several seconds, then raised his blue eyes to meet Lani's. The princess pressed her trembling lips together. Without a word, Casseck strode across the space between them and took her face in his hands and kissed her. The sword landed on the gravel, barely missing their toes, but neither noticed.

Apparently he did.

EPILOGUE

AS SOON AS the Jovan Pass was cleared enough for regular traffic early the next spring, letters began pouring though, including a few from Casmun. Several bundles arrived from the palace and Alex's family at Cambria, most to pass on to General Quinn, who camped farther to the west but visited frequently. Alex had based the Norsari out of Jovan, as the location was ideal for quick deployment to either side of the mountains. Captain Ben Nadira was now second-in-command, and Lieutenant Tanner had opted to retire from the army, though he'd accepted the post as Sage's personal guard captain.

Sage and Alex lounged by the fire in their room, dressed for bed, as they worked their way through the stacks of correspondence, saving the personal letters for last. "How is Cass settling in?" Sage asked.

"Sounds like he's doing well," Alex replied from behind his letter. "Sunburns a lot, though."

"Lani is disgustingly happy," said Sage, flipping her page over to read the back. "They're expecting a baby this fall, so she won't be coming to the talks." She made a face. "They didn't wait long, did they?"

"It's not a race, Sage," said Alex.

No, and she wasn't quite ready for that, especially with all the work and travel she had to do over the next couple of years. She folded the parchment and tossed it in the read pile. "Darit has switched back to being minister of finance," she said. "And Lani's taking his place as minister of war." The position traditionally belonged to the king's brother, and Banneth had none living. Why not his sister?

"Cass mentioned it. Good for her."

Now for Clare's letters. Sage sighed as she read, sensing her friend's loneliness, but also her joy at raising her niece. Aurelia was clever and affectionate and loved learning new things, which Clare said reminded her of Sage. After six months, the child had finally stopped asking for her mother.

"Everything all right?" Alex asked her.

Sage realized she'd been frowning. "As well as can be expected," she replied.

"Aurelia sounds like a handful," he said casually.

Sage lowered her page to look at him. "And how would you know that?"

"Rob's at Vinova." Alex raised his parchment to show her, though she couldn't read the prince's handwriting from that distance. "Official visit to make sure Clare has everything she needs and meet the Casmuni delegation when they arrive." He raised his eyebrows, but Sage avoided looking back. "He got there much earlier than he needed to. The Casmuni aren't expected for another month, and this is dated over two weeks ago."

The letter Sage was now reading had the same details about Robert's visit—and Clare sounded much happier.

"Clare's planning to be at the next Concordium," Sage said, grinning. "For the meeting with the king's council on marriage laws that will be held right after." Change was slow, especially with the evolving relationships with Casmun and Kimisara demanding attention, but His Majesty had been very open to the joint proposal Sage and Darnessa had made. The extra months were needed for a consensus within the matchmakers' guild to be reached on what suggestions ought to be put forth. "I probably won't see her until then."

Two more years. Sage sighed and set the letter aside.

"Done?" Alex asked.

Sage realized that letter had been the last of them. It had taken only an hour to catch up with five months, but at least with spring here, couriers would be more regular. "Done," she said.

He stood and stretched, then looked down on her with a smile. "Ready for bed?"

"Almost." In her eagerness to get to reading, she'd forgotten to treat her scars with oil for the evening, and sitting by the fire had made them itchy, so she couldn't neglect it now.

Alex watched as she found the bottle and lifted her nightdress to rub the lotion into her leg. "I can do that for you, Your Grace," he called from the bed.

"Next time," said Sage, replacing the bottle and climbing in beside him. "I've been thinking."

"When have you ever *not* been thinking?" Alex buried his face in her neck, letting one hand roam lower.

Actually, when he did things like that, it was very difficult to think. She shifted away. "What happens to Aurelia if Robert marries Clare?"

Alex sat up on his elbow and frowned. "Aren't you getting ahead of yourself?"

"Judging from the number of times she mentioned him in her last letter, I think not."

He sighed. "I honestly don't know, but I rarely worry about things that far above my rank and pay." Alex reached for her again. "I leave that to people like you."

She let him pull her close, still thoughtful. "She'd be a wonderful queen. And I think they'd be happy."

"Mmm," said Alex noncommittally. "What about you?" he whispered in her ear. "Are *you* happy?"

In truth, this title and its responsibilities had been even more overwhelming than Sage had anticipated. There were grain shortages and squabbling lords and generations of mistrust to overcome, not to mention her own nightmares, though they were less frequent, but none of that changed her answer. She turned toward Alex and found his mouth with her own. "Disgustingly so."

ACKNOWLEDGMENTS

As always, Dear Reader, I owe you the first thanks because you chose to live in my world for a few hours not once, but three times now. I am truly honored. The art, fanfiction, bookmarks, and candles dedicated to this series that many of you have taken the time to make have blown me away. To those who have written me to say that three books about Demora aren't enough, there is no greater compliment. We'll see what the future holds.

I will never tire of the *Deo Gratias* owed to the One above, who guides and strengthens me, plus Frankie and Dymphna who worked overtime on my behalf in round three, and the four Thomases, on whom I depend pretty much daily in other aspects of life.

And then there is my Superagent, Valerie Noble, who guides me through the stress and confusion that is the publishing world, ready to make me feel better or address my (usually blown out of proportion) concerns, and who also takes hour-plus-long phone calls wherein I try to explain entire plots and figure out where things are going wrong. I couldn't do any of this without you, Val!

My editor, Nicole Otto, who worked so hard with me to get this book in great shape, was also ready for phone calls full of confused babbling, and that I discovered was my first champion at Imprint: I hope I've made you proud. My only question is whether real authors take the same amount of coaching to get things right. (Don't answer that.) Thanks also to Erin Stein for taking a chance on me, and then taking two more before I was fully proven. Rhoda Belleza, your presence is missed, but I know you've gone on to bigger and better things. I will never forget your patience and guidance in these first years of publishing.

Thank you, Brittany Pearlman and Ashley Woodfolk (and team), for all the publicity and marketing work you've done, and for keeping me in the loop. Natalie C. Sousa and Jessia Chung, who outdid themselves on the covers for this series—you wouldn't believe the number of people I've heard from saying they first picked up my books for their beauty. Jessica White, I'd promise someday to get the proper use of *that* and *which* correct, but it would be a lie. Thank you for saving me from those and other embarrassing mistakes. My plot shines thanks to content editors, but copy editors bring the word glitter.

There are always parts I don't have the chops to address without help, so a million thanks to Joshua Gabriel Lontoc and Nikkia Parker for helping me scope problematic phrases and issues. Any remaining mistakes are my own.

To Kim, Amy, Ron, and Dan, who read my drafts, sometimes multiple times, to either stroke my ego or give tough love, and then help sell my books to their friends and family: never underestimate how important you are in this process. I owe you all multiple adult beverages of your choice. There are always too many friends and family to name that don't get to read until the final product, but your enthusiasm and love (and glowing reviews) are also the fuel that keeps me going. And gratitude once again to Dr. Kate and her medical knowledge on stab and burn wounds and the healing process.

Hampton Roads Writers and The Muse Writers Center, especially Lauran and Rick and Sherrie and Nancy and Susan and Michael and everyone else: I miss you guys so, so much. I was willing to come back to Norfolk solely for you, but it wasn't in the cards this time. Maybe someday.

A special thanks to Bob and Carol for their support—whether it be babysitting or reading—and enthusiasm for their "daughter." Also thanks for raising some great sons (third time's the charm).

Mom and Dad, I thanked you at the beginning, but I have to thank you here, too, because you are always everywhere I need you to be. Sorry you didn't get a dedication until the third book, but I think this is the best one (so far).

There are five human beings who owe their existence to me (and another guy, who's pretty cool), and it's been bittersweet watching them grow, especially my oldest pair. Writing a book is nothing compared to seeing these two young men take their first steps into the wide world. I love you nuggets—and nuggets you will always be to me, I don't care how tall you are now. As for the rest of you scurvy brats, let's go have an adventure!

Michael, I'd follow you to the ends of the earth. My bags are packed. Let's go. Sarang-hae.